Life Against The Current

By
E.O. Smith

Distributed by: Ingram Spark

Amazon.com

ISBN: 978-1-7374898-1-8

Edited by: Phiona Watkins - U.K.

Cover Design: Eddie - Designed Conviction – designedconviction.com

Publishing Assistant: Marsell Morris - marsellmorris@aol.com

Published by: Blowboi Entertainment

Printed in the U.S.A

1 2 3 4 5 6 7 8 9 10

Epigraph

Your best stories will come from overcoming your greatest struggles.
E.O. Smith

Dedication

This book is dedicated to everyone that has suffered from addiction. Always remember, that temporary happiness is not worth long-term pain.

E.O. Smith

Chapter 1

Sara stared across the darkened motel room at Andy, the man she loved with all of her heart, sleeping peacefully in the room's worn and stained bed. She could not help but laugh at herself for only noticing the room's sad condition after going twenty-four hours without using heroin. When she was high, she had only two concerns about motel rooms: that they were cheap in cost and safe for her to get high in, a place where she could safely enjoy her opium dreams without fear of being interrupted by the police. But now that she was going without using heroin, and was unable to sleep because of it, she could not help but study the many stains and scars as they shimmered and danced in the sickening green glow of the motel's neon vacancy sign. A sick green light that had no trouble seeping into the room through gaps in the window blinds no matter how tightly they were closed.

Without Sara making a conscious decision to do so, her mind drifted back to playing a game. Trying to guess what had caused each glimmering stain, a game that she had been playing most of the night while trying to forget her desperate need for a shot of dope. In the far corner, she could easily see where someone had thrown an used condom at the wall. It had stuck there as its contents had spilled out, racing down the wall and leaving trails behind, trails that under this type of light looked like tiny green rivers. Just across the table from her was a large shadow on the wall, the remains of a large bloodstain spreading out over the wall in the same pattern that a water balloon would make when thrown. Only a short distance above this stain was a dent that Sara was certain was a bullet hole, it had been as poorly repaired, as poorly filled in, as the blood splatter that had been cleaned off the wall.

The motel owners had not even cared enough to repaint the room.

Sara could not help but wonder about every other room that she had gotten high in and the many hidden secrets they held too — how many beds had she slept in where someone had died, been raped, or was so trapped in a cloud of depression that putting a bullet through their own head became an option? Sara could not help but shiver each time she looked over at the room's other chairs that sat only inches away from her directly below both the bloodstain and its cause, the bullet hole. The idea that someone had sat in that very chair and took their own life shook her to her core. Had it not been for Sara wanting to watch Andy sleeping as she fought her body's growing pain from opiate withdrawal, she was sure that she would have chosen that chair instead of this one.

The dead man's chair offered a view of the room's only window with its busy sidewalk outside. Through a gap in the dusty blinds she could watch the people outside as they went about finding drugs to get high on, turning tricks to earn money to get high, and all of the many other pointless motions of lives being lived with only one purpose to get high.

"It's all pointless!" Sara whispered to her unborn child as her hands instinctively moved down to rest on her small, but growing mothers paunch. The only outward sign that Sara was pregnant. Looking once again at the stained wall, she wondered if the person whose death had created that odd work of art had found peace in death, or was the stain on the wall the only thing gained out of that poor soul's lost life and a well-placed bullet? Does the stain artist have a tombstone? Would Andy or Sara have a tombstone to mark their passing? If she gave in and aborted their child, as Andy wanted her to do, would the child have a tombstone, even one as faint as a poorly washed bloodstain on the wall of a cheap motel?

Sara's body began to shiver once again as she wondered exactly what they did with the aborted fetuses. Did they call them children, or did they have some cute way of referring to this waste product that did not remind people that it was a human or at least the makings of a human? She could search for the answer to that question on the computer, but to do so she would have to wade through far too many political and religious opinions about abortion along with an equal amount of hateful rhetoric about abortion. Andy had told her not to think of it as a child, or as a baby at all, but while some pieces of Sara's upbringing were easy for her to forget, others were almost impossible to vanquish from her heart, and her child's fate was one of those that would not go away.

Her parents had raised her to believe that abortion existed for medical reasons or in cases of rape. Her family believed in responsible people using protection. To emphasize this, they stressed the fact that it was a child, a living being, that should be aborted only as an act of mercy for the child or the mother and not because of a foolish night of sex. She had been taught that yes, she had control over her mind and body, but that control did not begin after she became pregnant, but when she decided to lie with a man. She had been taught that abortion was not a safety net to be used to save her from responsibilities that she accepted the moment she chose to have unprotected sex.

Yet what her parents failed to teach her was what she should do or could do in the event that Sara's drug addiction, her own foolishness, led to her getting pregnant with a baby that, as Andy said, was already "Fucked up from the neck up!" Already an addict. Yes, Sara's heart and mind were free to abort her child to save it from a lifetime of being subjected to becoming addicted, or of being born somehow damaged, by her drug use. Her parents had simply not told her what was morally the right thing to do in the event that Sara's own self-hate was the reason for her to have medical concerns for the health of her unborn child. So now Sara felt lost and very alone.

The motel room sick green tint was starting to bother Sara. She tried to push her chair back deeper into the darkness of the corner, but the green neon light was like the truth, it was always there, reminding her that the world was nothing like she wanted it to be. For her, this cheap motel room was a cocoon, a safe place to curl up and float in the warmth of her high, but for the maker of the bloodstain that painted the other wall, the room must have been a torture chamber, a place of despair.

Tonight, for Sara's own child, it was going to be either the room where its life begun or the room where its death sentence was decided. Sara hated her parents for not being clearer in their moral views on abortion. She wished that they had taught her what to do when your own bad acts were the cause of your child's pain and medical risk. If she chose to have her child and it was damaged by her addiction, she would hate herself even more than she did now, or worse by then Andy would be long gone from her life. Sara did not try to fool herself, Andy loved her, Andy needed her, but Andy wanted her to be a certain way. She could never be what he wanted her to be while raising a child. Especially not if she were saddled with a disabled child. Andy needed her to be free to hustle. It cost money, a lot of money, to get high every day, money that a special needs child would not allow. It would be so much easier to blame the failings of society for the decision that she was being forced to make tonight, Sara thought as she remembered her father's opinions on abortion.

Sara's dad accepted the abortion issue as it was, but he swore that the money, in the room of political donations, had destroyed the courts' plans and goals in the case that allowed legal abortion. 'Roe vs. Wade' as Sara remembered father calling it. He was also sure that the courts used a woman's right to privacy only as a legal starting point for legal abortion, and that they hoped that someone would then ask the courts to rule on the medical age that a girl changed into a women. Not the age that she was wise enough to give her consent to have sex, but a standard age that her biological needs commanded her right to privacy. Her father swore that once that age was legally set in stone, girls could get birth control without their parents' consent, thus ending almost all nonmedical abortions, forcing girls to become responsible for their own bodies.

Sara was certain this was true because of all the girls in her high school who had gotten pregnant that she knew, not one of them had planned to do so, and all would have gladly asked for birth control if that choice did not involve their parents. Sara's father had explained it to her, saying that people will pay to win any fight no matter how stupid it is. As stupid as Sara knew she would be for thinking this, she began to daydream about placing the blame over her child's fate on political donations instead of her own foolishness. She laughed at how insane it was for her to be so desperate to find someone or something to blame for an abortion that she was sure she wouldn't end up having if Andy would simply share in the responsibility, take his part in the blame instead of laying all fault at Sara's feet.

Prostitution and expensive drug addiction are major pieces of the same puzzle. There are no women or men, selling their bodies for marijuana. It's just too cheap and the high last too long. Now on the other hand heroin, methamphetamine, cocaine, and prescription drugs are so expensive that prostitution is the only way to stay high. Sara remembered how hard it was to stay high before she had given in to Andy's arguments and started turning tricks to help them earn money. Before that day they seldom had the money for a motel room, a good high, some food, and a morning shot of dope to start the next day with. They would flop where they could, sleeping in places where others like them were living. They were never alone to have the luxury to lie down and enjoy their high in peace. Never able to make love in private, but above all never able to feel truly safe.

In the past Andy had a few good days hustling addicted housewives and upper-class white kids. They were able to stay high, fed, and bathed within the comforts of their own motel room. Their own cocoon of dreams and love. As we all know, some dreams end quickly. Soon they were back to couch surfing with meth heads, and crack monsters. Basically, anyone else too poor to get high and take care of themselves at the same time.

Andy had started pointing out the merits of Sara selling her body early in their relationship. It wasn't too long after she had quit attending college, ruined her credit cards, bounced checks, and lost her car after the insurance lapsed due to her not having the money to pay for it. The loss of her car still stung. Had she made the conscious decision to sell it the proceeds would have kept them high for weeks. Instead, one ill-fated day the police would pull her over. This encounter would result in the car being impounded until she could show proof of insurance and pay the release fees. That was something that Sara knew they could never do while maintaining their addictions.

Soon after, Andy convinced her to allow an old man to watch them engage in sexual intercourse. He paid them well, even bought them a nice meal, rented the motel room, and provided a few shots of dope to the couple. It wasn't long before the old man wanted to see more of Sara's actions and less of Andy's. In one sense Sara enjoyed the old man's attention. It felt good to be the center of attention after being nearly invisible all of her childhood. In school, she always said or did things that made her feel stupid, ugly, and less desired than the other girls. In front of the old man, she felt like a star and would do things to Andy that the other girls at school would never dream of doing to the boys who would run past Sara on their way to get a kiss from her sisters or pretty classmates.

But the old man did not seek them out every day as their growing need of heroin did. Moreover, he wanted to pay Andy to allow him to watch Sara having sex with a man other than Andy. Sara assumed that Andy would get mad at the old man for even suggesting something like that. Andy had been her first and only lover. The idea of being with anyone besides Andy was almost stomach turning to her.

"Sara, we make love, it's not the same as having sex. Hell, every time you have sex with me while the old man is watching, you begin to get into it and put on a show for him," Andy said with a laugh that shocked Sara. She had no idea that Andy knew that she secretly enjoyed performing for the old man.

"It's all cool," Andy said, "we've all got our freaky side and sometimes it's nice to see you give in to your freaky side and enjoy that part of yourself. Besides, it's not what you or I do with our bodies that matters, it's why we do it that counts — this old freak wants to pay you five hundred dollars to get down with some guy other than me. It's five hundred dollars Sara, it's not making love."

So, she gave into Andy's wishes, but soon she was sleeping with men for far less than five hundred dollars. It took time to set up online ads in each new town they moved to, and being an escort was only a small part of the prostitution trade. Andy pointed out that sometimes it seemed like every woman in town was online claiming to be an escort and it drove the prices down.

This lead to Andy taking Sara to a truck stop, where she learned quickly that there is a vast difference between making love and having sex. Just like sleeping with men for money and turning a trick are completely different. All the while, her need for heroin was growing, and the price for her sexual favors was lowering until they both leveled off at twenty dollars. Now Sara could count the daily price of their addiction in men serviced. They would often laugh and joke about the number of weenies it would take to get them high today if Andy failed to come up with money or dope on his own.

Moving from town to town did not help Sara to find the type of men who would pay her a high price for sex. Real pimps saw Sara as a potential money earner for themselves and they were not above setting Andy up to go to jail in order to get to Sara. Andy explained that truck stop security guards needed to bust pimps or hoes every now and then. Andy wasn't a real pimp so he didn't have the money to tip the guards to keep them on his side. Sara's looks were beginning to be obscured by her addiction, and Andy could easily be sacrificed to the police in place of a real pimp.

Jail was not apart of Andy's life plan, so they often moved on to a new town as quickly as they had arrived in the previous one. The constant travel was fun, learning the many ways to ask for a glass of Coke or Mountain Dew. Depending on where you were in the United States, it could be called a soda, a soda pop, or just plain pop. The waitresses were quick to correct you if you said it wrong or placed too much emphasis on the wrong vowel sound. They would laugh at the many different slang languages and terms used in the world of vice and then marvel at the terms that seemed universal.

Sleeping on beaches was Sara's favorite though. Hearing the waves as they gently rolled up the sands. Lying in Andy's arms, waiting on tomorrow to tell them how they were to go about earning the money to stay high for that day. Sara took pride in the fact that Andy would try to get the cash together some other way before he would send her off to work the streets or parking lots, and that he was always near watching to make sure that no one hurt her. Ever since returning to Nashville, Sara's hometown, he had refused to allow her to work Trinity Boulevard or Old Hickory Road. He did not want to embarrass her by ending up in a car with someone she had known in her life before addiction. Andy did send her on a few escort calls, but these were before Sara's world fell apart and she found out that she was pregnant.

Chapter 2

Morals and upbringing play a large part in all of our life choices. Sara's morals and upbringing caused her to refuse to allow any other man to touch her beside Andy as long as she was pregnant. She knew that she would have to stop using any and all drugs for the sake of her child's future. It was fun to be a rebel, to be everything that her family would dislike. To pretend to be a porn star in an old man's fantasy, to travel the world with the man she loved all the while claiming to be Bonnie and Clyde. At the same time parenthood meant that it was time to grow up and face their child's needs.

Sara still hated the shy girl that she saw in the mirror. The fool who could not hold a conversation unless she was high. The girl whose arms instantly wrapped around her body if someone looked her in the eyes. That girl, with all of her faults, was still there inside of her. All of the drugs and prostitution had not made up for her lack of self-confidence, or self-worth. Sara's child did not deserve to be punished because of that. In fact the child might just be something Sara could hold on to. Something that she valued more than she hated herself, but Andy simply did not see it that way. He was adamant that the child was not his. That it was ruined and should be aborted.

It was an easy argument for Sara to accept — abortion would mean that they could carry on with their life as it was. But it was Andy's refusal to believe that she was carrying his child that caused Sara to cling so tightly to the hope the child offered her. The baby's DNA would prove to Andy that she'd been faithful to him by the rules as Andy had explained them to her. She had been faithful in using a condom with every other man she had been with; only

Andy's seed had run free inside of her body. For Sara, it was proof that the act of making love was far removed from the act of sex or turning tricks to support them.

The early light of morning was starting to overpower the green of the motel's neon sign. Sara could hear cars and trucks beginning their day on the street in front of their motel as the city tried to slowly awaken. But dawn offered no comforts or rewards; it was easy to sit in a dark room and debate the question of their child's life with a sleeping man, Sara knew that she could not argue with Andy other than silently in her mind. Andy knew her too well; he could make her bloom like a flower or wilt and retreat within herself. That was something she had always done when confronted by conflict or any potential failure.

She began to wonder again if the creator of the bloodstained wall art had found peace in their death or not, as her death over the child's parentage would prove to Andy that she loved him. It would save her from deciding her child's fate, as well as it would save her the embarrassment that she faced when she went home to her family. She knew that she would have to do that if she choose to keep the child and to remain clean of drugs as a parent should. Death was an option, Sara thought, but she knew that it was something that she could ever find the courage to do herself. It was then that Sara accepted that she could not save her child from a fate that she was not strong enough to change: heroin, Andy, the sure loss of Andy, and returning home a pregnant heroin addict, without a father for her child. These were each insurmountable obstacles on their own, and monstrous when combined. "Andy will be happy," Sara mumbled in self-defeat, as she heard a child begin to cry.

In almost every motel that they had stayed in during their travels, there was an addicted mother and her child. The day always began with the pleading cries of a hungry, wet child. At times, it reminded Sara of a long lost call to prayer as the sun climbed in the dawn sky, but Sara knew that this was not a call to kneel before God, thankful for a new day. No, this was the child of an addict who had not learned to avoid her instinct to rise with the sun. Sara knew that soon she would hear the child's mother screaming for the child to be quiet and those screams would end only after the child had been beaten into silence again. Each terrible smack caused Sara to flinch in pain as the child's cries turned to sobs of pain muffled by a bottle being pushed into the child's mouth.

The room exploded in orange light and went dark again before the sound of Andy's cigarette lighter striking and lighting could reach her ears, shocking Sara to be caught off guard, lost in her own thoughts as she had been.

"That's going to be you, and that thing you call a baby," Andy said as he laughed. Trust me, if you have that tricks baby, you'll beat it everyday to get even with it for making me leave you, Sara. You know that kid isn't mine, you're a whore, a hooker, and there's no way you know for sure who the father is!" Andy said those hurtful words to convince her to abort their child. His words left her unable to speak as her arms instinctively began to wrap around her body. Her hands clenched into tight balls and her eyes looked for safety on the floor at her feet. She was broken, completely unable to tell Andy that she agreed with him, that she would get an abortion, that she wanted to take a shot of dope, and that Andy did not need to be mean to her anymore, that he could love her again.

"Hell you went a whole day without a shot of dope, but trust me that isn't shit. Wait till later today, you'll beg me for a shot." Andy said as he tossed his dope kit on the bed beside him and began to ready his morning shot. "You need to let them vacuum that trick's baby out of you. I knew that you were a whore by the way you acted when that old man would watch you. You can't tell me that's my kid — a whore is a whore. I knew that you agreed to fuck truckers way too fast. Sara, you didn't even argue about only earning twenty dollars a trick."

Andy laughed again as he made the sound of a vacuum roaring while moving his hand back and forth as if sweeping the floor. "Fuck it, Sara, I don't need to argue about it anymore. Watch me take a shot, whore, you'll get on your knees and beg to get high as long as it's been since you used any dope. Andy said as he pulled their dope spoon out and poured two papers of heroin into it before tossing two papers of dope to Sara. "You'll need them soon Sara, trust me."

Sara's eyes began to focus only on Andy's syringe. A needle for a dope fiend is like a Crucifix to a Catholic Nun: the addict can't help but to pray when they see a syringe, and for Sara it was even worse. She had met Andy only a few days before taking her first shot of heroin. She had seen the ugly marks on his arms the first night they met at a campus party. Andy was there to help his friend's band set up to play.

Sara had fooled herself into believing that she had left at home the shy girl she had been while growing up. Her whole childhood, Sara swore that it was somehow her sisters' fault that she always embarrassed herself in front of boys. She was sure that now while away at college, she would be able to be herself, the real Sara, and not the shy ugly girl that she saw herself as when she fumbled over her words in front of boys. But she had been wrong. Within moments of arriving at her first college party, she found herself staring down at the floor, unable to speak, wanting to run away, but frozen in place.

Andy rescued her — he saw her fear and lovingly took her hands as he unwrapped her arms from around her body. He lead her away from the center of the room to a quiet corner. He softly assured her that she was going to be alright, and that as high as everyone was, no one had noticed her standing as she had been. This had been Andy's first act of love. The gallant way that he had acted to save her upon seeing her standing there, frozen with fear, only to then reach out and save her. He didn't ask her if she needed help, nor if she was alright. He simply took command of the situation, rescuing her like the prince in a fairy tale would save a peasant girl from a dragon.

They spoke all night, actually, Andy spoke as they huddled together in the corner of a busy room, yet very much alone, as if in a bubble. Andy was honest about his heroin use. He told her about it at the beginning of that first night as a way of allowing Sara to decide if his drug use was something that she could accept or not. She loved his honesty. He told her that he did not wish to start their friendship by lying to her. In Sara's eyes that meant that he respected her, something Sara had never felt before.

In the days after the party, she began buying him shots of heroin. If she didn't Andy did not have the time to spend with her. The doctors had known that Andy's mother had been addicted to opiates at the time of her pregnancy. It was there in the computer records, and it popped up anytime Andy's name went into a medical database. Andy had even told the doctors that he couldn't use any type of opiates because of this. They really didn't care and still gave Andy opiates after a car crash that he'd been in. Now Andy was an addict, forced to roam the streets each day searching for new ways to feed his habit.

In high school, Sara had learned about an American opiate epidemic that had occurred at the turn of the last century. During this time several powerful opiate pain medications were allowed to be prescribed to almost anyone for any type of pain from a hangnail to a brain tumor. This opiate epidemic spurred a new economic class in America. The nation had long ago learned that by labeling people mentally or physically disabled, they could remove these same people from the unemployment records. This caused it to appear that there were more jobs than people seeking or needing work, thus, it appeared to be a more robust economy than it really was. Yet the addicted class became a far better tool for balancing the unemployment rates. First, they labelled addiction as a medical issue, allowing the treatment of addiction to be paid for by the government, and creating jobs in addiction treatment. Secondly, they removed the criminal aspects and punishments for using drugs. That led to a steady death rate for addicts.

Prisons and jails had been a backstop in addiction. You would slam into this backstop, go to jail and dry out. When your addiction became out of control, by going to jail the addict would not die from an ever increasing use of heroin. Some addicts would seek help in recovery programs for addiction after jail. Others would use again and return to jail many times. Once the prospect of going to jail was removed, the government started new programs. One of these programs paid for the cremation of the remains of addicts and another which paid for addicts to receive free abortions. There was never a program that promoted the idea of free birth control while in recovery or while still using. Without jails there to stop the addicts when their addiction made them reckless, addicts died within months of becoming addicted and not in the years it had taken with jail and prison standing in the way.

Death due to addiction was killing off working-age, physically fit people, and was, therefore, very effective at lowering the unemployment rates. As the years went by, presidents and other leaders would try new things. One of these measures included the re-institution of prison and jail time for repeated long-term addicts. Those like Andy who had been in and out of every kind of treatment program that they offered, and were too smart to chase the dragon of heroin until it killed them.

Sara knew that if he was caught again, he would be sent to prison for years for an addiction that government doctors had saddled him with, and Sara saw this as unfair. The creation of the addicted class of Americans was too profitable. It employed far too many people to be changed without a civil war, and heroin addiction, as Sara soon found out, does not lend itself to the notion of a civil war — hell addicts can't keep a job so there was no way of rallying a group of addicts for any cause other than getting high. Andy had told her about a book called 'Brave New World', that was written many years ago. Its author, a man named Huxley, a drug user himself, created a fictional world where a class of people were addicted to pills provided by the government powers. These people worked and benefited the world around them. Whereas the only contribution the addicted class of today made to society was first become addicted and then to die quickly after an attempt at recovery. Thus, allowing government money to flow first through rehabilitation and treatment programs. Then out through the towns these centers were located in, eventually reaching the undertakers' hands.

Society had realized that it was too expensive to feed and house families who did not have a work ethic along with their children, like welfare, free school lunches, and prisons did. So everyone closed their eyes to the truth about America's addiction problem. The government had found a way to turn lemons into lemonade. If it cost a few families with good work ethics and morals a son or daughter every now and then, so be it. No one was forcing people to use drugs, everyone had a choice. America's other option, a military draft, the forced enlistment into the military, only worked if there was a long-term war to fight. Wars cost far too much money in military funerals versus cheap addiction cremations. Not even to mention the price of treating wounded soldiers after a war. America had decided that Andy did not matter, and Sara had decided that she did not matter without Andy.

Chapter 3

Andy laid out his shot kit as if the things contained inside were, sacred, and to Sara, they were. Her love of the sacred needle was abutted to the joy she felt as she gave her body to Andy the first time. She had been a virgin, never having been high, nor touched by a man before. First, Andy had her snort a small line of heroin. This instantly made her sick causing her to vomit into a trash can that sat beside her bed in her college dorm room. They were alone and would be the whole night as Sara's roommate did not understand Andy, and she would not make any attempt to like him. She also didn't understand Sara's growing need to be with him.

Shortly after being sick, a warmth raced through Sara. It felt good, she felt lighter, with no conscious fear of the world around her or of people's views of her. Only after he had helped Sara to clean herself up did Andy allow her to feel the loving bite of the syringe. "You won't get sick this time, I promise," Andy had said as he convinced her to lay on the bed naked before him. He then heated a spoonful of water and dope until the room smelled of the sweet musky smell of warm heroin. Then he gently tied a shoestring around her extended arm. The pressure from the tie forcing her veins to rise to meet Andy's needle exactly like Sara would soon rise her pelvis begging Andy to enter her just as the needle had done. Both offered a small sharp pain that would become enjoyable shortly after the pain of penetration.

"Watch," Andy had told her as she bit her her lower lip and watched the needle easily slide into her arm. Then she saw her blood spin up into the syringe, proving that heaven was very near. She watched as the blood rose grew, bloomed, and died as Andy depressed the plunger of the syringe. This caused the bed, the room's floor and the world around Sara to drop from beneath her as she fell into a mist of heroin bliss. Only then did Andy undress, exposing himself for Sara as she had exposed her body and love to Andy. He then prepared his own shot of heaven, giving equal concern to its blessing as he had to her shot just moments before.

Sara realized that she was daydreaming when she saw Andy smile at her from across the room while tying his arm off and making his veins ready to receive the needle. Andy knew that Sara could not turn away. She could not stop herself from staring at anyone preparing to take a shot of heroin in front of her. Andy had seamlessly melded the act of injecting heroin with the act of making love. By the virtue of this association and the fact that before Andy, before heroin, and before making love, Sara had been terribly alone even when surrounded by people.

Andy saw the blood rose, grow, and bloom in his morning shot just as Sara could see it from across the room. He smiled at her as heaven entered his veins, his heart, his world, as he softly mumbled "I love you." He then pulled the needle from his arm, allowing a tear of blood to form just like Sara's blood had formed on the bed beneath her when he entered her the first time they'd made love. Andy was right, sex was an act as much as it was a meshing of their souls in a way that only true lovers could understand.

Andy's smile softened as his eyes glazed over and he allowed himself to fall into the bliss of his true love's gentle touch, then he nodded off. Sara stood up from her chair, easily forgetting the bloodstained wall, the crying baby's suffering under the abusive hands of his addicted mother, her family's opinions about abortion, and the future of the child she grew in her womb. Sara simply could not live without Andy's love. She told herself this as she stepped to the bed to ready her own shot and to join Andy in heaven. Andy was probably right, she told herself: the child was not his and he was most certainly right in saying that no matter who the real father was, the child was conceived by a mother addicted to opiates. Abortion was her only option. She could not saddle their child with the monster that she had faced every day since she decided to leave college and follow Andy.

As she began to ready her shot, the room exploded with the sound of someone forcefully knocking on the cheap motel door. The sound both shocked and stunned Sara at the same time. Only bad news knocked on the anonymous doors of drug motels. Sara knew not to make a noise. She instinctively knew to grab all of Andy's dope kit so that she would be in her possession if the police decided to enter the room. Sara had been raised in a world where it was rude to ignore someone knocking at your door. She had grown up believing that the police were not her enemies, but instead they were her friends. So, she looked at Andy, passed out. The bloody tear on his arm was the only visible sign of his recent drug use. Sara felt safe in giving in to her parents' teachings and opening the door for whoever was so intent on getting her attention. She approached the door complete shot kit in her hand ready to turn in to the police to protect Andy from the prison cell he would face if caught in possession it.

"Who is it?" Sara asked, opening the door at the same time. A postman stood there staring at her, smiling at the syringes, spoons, lighter, and shoestring in her hand with a look of pure amusement in his eyes. Sara was sure his facial expression came as much from her caring enough to open the door and greet him as from the drug paraphernalia in her hand.

"Sara Anne Austin?" the smiling postman asked. "I have a package for Sara Anne Austin," he stated as Sara saw the return address and, like a child at Christmas, snatched the package from the man's hand at the same time saying, "Yes sir, I'm Sara Austin." The postman simply rolled his eyes and laughed before giving Sara a look that told her he would like to come back to turn a trick with her someday as he turned to walk away.

Sara quickly shut the door of the room and became lost in the smell of the small package. Just knowing that it had been mailed to her from her home on Dogwood Mountain brought tears to her eyes and she could not help but look at the name of her great aunt Page Anne Austin, written in the shaky hand of an aging woman who Sara remembered cleaning the graves on Cemetery Ridge as she spoke to the many people buried there. Sometimes Sara would see Aunt Page at church on Sundays, but the old woman seemed to had given up on the world of the living to spend her time with her memories instead of with her living family.

Seeing the old woman's shaky handwriting reminded Sara of early mornings waiting for the school bus, hearing the other kids trying to interrupt Aunt Page's conversations with people that only she could see or hear. Aunt Page could cuss like a sailor and would do so if interrupted by the children. Sara had been sure that Aunt Page enjoyed her morning interactions with her many nieces and nephews living on Dogwood Mountain because she would grin a cute little grin and begin to talk louder the closer she came to the playful children, as if she craved their attention.

Smiling at the memory of her aunt cussing in the early morning sun, Sara sat down and opened the package that the crazy old woman had cared enough to send. Inside of the package was a handwritten notebook, and a letter addressed to her. Sara laid one hand on her mother's paunch, looked over at Andy as he floated in and out of his dreams. She then opened the letter to face her mounting fears of what it would say and why it had been sent to Sara here at an address that Aunt Page simply could not know.

Chapter 4

"Dear Sara, Girl, you always were an odd one!" Aunt Page's letter began. This caused Sara's heart to sting in pain — the idea of an odd if not crazy old woman calling Sara odd was all the proof she needed to know that she would never return to her home and family.

"But you were always my favorite of all of the babies born on Dogwood Mountain," the letter continued. "I could see that you were hurting and very lonely, but what could I say that you would want to hear? How could I help you to see yourself as a beautiful person and worth the sacrifice I made when I decided to never love anyone or to have a family of my own. I thought that if I refused to have children, the mental illnesses and drug addictions that haunted both of my parents would die with me and not be passed on to your generation. But Sara, you taught me that Bobby, my father, was right and that by hiding our family story, I was sentencing you to a life of addiction and all that comes along with the lifestyle of an addict. Sara, you may believe that you are living life that no one in your family will understand, but you are wrong. The child that you're carrying deserves a chance to live and grow up as you did, here in the safety of your family, not in the type of hell that I grew up in.

"Yes, Sara we know that you're pregnant. When you went to the hospital seeking pain medications, the blood test showed that you are carrying a child, a child that I sacrificed my life for. Most mail, as you know, first stops at the tombstone shop where I sort it before delivering it to the home that it belongs to, but where does a letter addressed to you belong? You went off in search of peace in a way of life that is honestly a family tradition getting high and selling yourself with the hopes of being loved by a man. You may think his love will give you a sense of self-worth, but you are wrong girl. You are worth more than you can ever understand; you are a mother, and you owe it to your child to come home to us. If you won't do that, then at the very least read the book that I have included with this letter. This is your home girl, you have done nothing that you should be embarrassed over yet! But if you harm that baby, because I failed to teach you about the life you are living, then my time alone upon this mountain was pointless. Please read our story, and please come home. We love you, no matter what you have allowed yourself to do. Love Aunt Page. P.S. I am only a phone call away girl. I love you and the baby growing in your womb."

"Any money come in that box, Sara?" Andy asked from the bathroom where he'd managed to get up and go without Sara noticing as she concentrated on her aunt's puzzling letter. Who else had been a drug addict in Sara's family? What exactly did Page mean about giving up her life for her family's children?

"No Andy, no money, just a letter, and a book — see Andy," Sara said as she tried to show him the gift she'd received from home.

"Next time you call home crying, remember you're a whore and an addict, and that you don't know who the daddy really is of that thing growing inside you. Also, face it you ain't going to make it the rest of the day without getting high Sara. Ask for money next time, and stop fooling yourself — you almost took a shot this morning!" Andy said as he walked to the door to leave.

"There are a couple of papers of dope, it's good. When you stop trying to fool yourself, use it to get right and come to the park to help me hustle up enough money to get by on today. It's about time to hit the highway again. I don't like people mailing stuff here that ain't got money in it — next thing you know, your mommy and daddy will be stopping by to read your little dope fiend baby bedtime stories!" Andy stated as he walked out of their room, slamming the door behind him.

Fighting back the urge to cry or run after Andy and assure him of her love, Sara rubbed her stomach and said: "I guess it's just us honey." Although in her heart Sara knew that going back home was not something she could bring herself to do, no matter what crazy Aunt Page said. Sara sat there in thought, before opening the book that her aunt sent and forcing herself to read.

I have struggled with my heart over a promise I made more than sixty years ago. It seemed to be such an easy task; writing down your family's story. So, at the age of twelve, I made foolish promise to write down and share Bobby and Momma's story. Bobby, the man I call my father, believed that families doom themselves to repeated failure generation after generation because they bury the truth about who they really were in life.

"Page, girl" I can hear my daddy saying, his voice smooth with southern charm and tempered with the manipulative tone of drunken preacher, "people just can't wait to have lies carved deep into their tombstones. Just go and take a walk through any cemetery in the world and you won't find even one stone that says Asshole, Pervert, Liar, Creep, Drug Addict, Whore, or anything like that. When I die, girl, I want you to carve the word asshole somewhere on my stone. Then every few years or so, when the new people at the church get all upset over my resting place having a cuss word on it, why, you just hand them our story, girl. Then maybe, just maybe, we can make something good grow out of all the hell our lives have been."

People joke about death, it's just how we are. Although I knew that Bobby meant every word he spoke to me that day. I never understood just how hard it would be for me to keep my promise. How hard the task of placing words on paper would become the farther away from my childish innocence I grew. As you age and mature, you tend to get overly concerned with the type of person the folks up the road believe you to be — no one wants to sit next to a drug-addicted whore or a stone-cold killer at church on Sunday morning; oh, people will say that everything is forgiven. Just get down on your knees and accept the Lord in your heart and God will forgive your sins, but I never found myself sitting next to anyone named God in church. No, church is full of people, and people tend to avoid what they fear. I ain't got much family, never did, so I don't like being avoided — it's nice to be invited to folks' weddings, baby showers, and Christmas parties, it's nice to be respected.

So, keeping my word, allowing folks to learn from my family's shame, was just not something that I could see any reason to do — after all, I lived through it, hadn't I suffered enough? Do you think Jesus is up there in heaven talking about how his father was so insecure that he forced boys to chop off their foreskin, and even allowed his own son to be crucified? No one would want to sit next to Jesus after a while. I can hear the angels crying: "We know, Jesus, we know, they beat you, put you on a cross, we know, now ain't you got anything else to talk about? You didn't meet any pretty girls or do anything cool? You act like you're the only person to have a crazy father.

Bobby just never considered or even contemplated the fact that I would refuse to live any type of normal life after he and Momma left us. I believe that Bobby was afraid that I would have children of my own and that those babies would suffer from the same mental pains and failing as their grandparents had, but I thought different. I had once watched a man kill all but one pup from a litter of dogs because they showed no interest in hunting. "I'm raising hunting dogs, not cute little petting dogs," I heard the man say as he picked the animal to keep and those that were to die. I knew that if my family's unsociable traits were passed on to my children, I could not strengthen our bloodline by culling the weak. I decided to just never have children, to let the past, along with Bobby's fears and my foolish promise, die with me.

As time has passed it seems that all I have left is my television, and all they show anymore are programs about one grave-robbing archaeologists or another; maybe it's God trying to tell me something. Lil Dee says that I hate archaeologists on TV shows because they remind me that I'm really afraid of what I would learn about myself if I took the time to write down our story. Lil Dee went to school more than I did, so she always has some smart-ass

31

school taught idea about things. She even said that some fool back in Greek times said that an un-contemplated life is a life not lived. Meaning, I guess, that I was not living any type of life, but that's not why I hate archaeologists. No, I hate them because they lie — no one can look at some bones and broken pottery and understand who those people were. But if you put a pudgy man in a shirt and shorts covered in pockets. Give him one of them funny hats, some homely looking coed girls and a couple of them nice boys who like other boys, a few shovels, a handful of gullible smiling natives and a bag of snacks. That fool will get on my television set and swear on a stack of Bibles that them poor folks he just dug up ate each other like kids eat candy!

Momma's old car rests just outside the window behind the television set, exactly where Bobby told us to park the car on our first night on Dogwood Mountain. We loved that car. A big 1972 Oldsmobile Delta 88, a land yacht. A car so big it seemed to float down the highway. That car was old when it was gifted to Momma. Today it appears almost ancient covered in milkweeds, honeysuckle vines and wildflowers, with an oak tree that has to be more than fifty years old itself growing up through it, anchoring the old car in place. Proving that her highway adventures are long in the past.

That car has set there for as long as I have avoided keeping my promise to Bobby. Sometimes I see the sun's joy flash off of a piece of the old car's chrome and I have to wonder just what some fat grave-robbing archaeologist would think of our car. Would he know just by looking at those rusted remains that the car had once been our home? Could he glean from its chrome emblems that the old car was the only thing of value that my momma ever owned?

"No" is the answer to those questions and to others like them because life is not the teeth marks we leave on our neighbors' bones, rusted chunks of steel, nor dull chrome automotive emblems. Life is emotions and emotions are ephemeral. Ephemeral things decay, rot, turn into dust, leaving behind no signs for idiot archaeologists to read. A shard of pottery is just a piece of a broken dish. Unless you were there to eat food from that dish with the family that owned it, you can never know or understand their hearts. Archaeologists are simply guessing, farting into the wind, wasting my time, reminding me of my failures.

I remember how angry I was when I first saw that an oak tree was growing inside of Momma's car. People have a way of turning an ordinary object into something that is sacred and with that car being all that I had left of my life with Momma, I viewed it as almost holy. I can understand how an archaeologist in a thousand years might believe that old car was some type of altar that the people buried here on Dogwood Mountain danced naked around as we sacrificed virgins all the while begging for rain.

My first thought was to run over and snatch that stupid tree out of Momma's car, and to clean and polish it the same way that we would do when Momma was still here. But the reality of the suffering that the poor tree would face trying to grow and make our car its home made me smile in an evil way. I just knew that stupid tree was destined to try to live. Destined to beg to live, only to die just like Momma had, broken and twisted. Each year, the rains would give the tree just enough water to live and grow, but the car's windows and roof would not allow the limbs of the tree to find the sun's love.

I took joy in watching that tree sprout new limbs that grew deformed like the arms of a monster. Certainly not the kind of tree limb that a good father would hang a swing from so that he could enjoy gently swinging his daughter as he watched her grow. "Just die you stupid tree!" I would find myself whispering. "That car failed us, stupid tree. Momma could not start a new life within that car's embrace and you won't either. Your ugly limbs are as deformed as my soul. Die, and I will chop you into firewood, burn you, turn you into ashes."

Yet the petty prayers of an old barren woman are seldom rewarded; God seems to enjoy ignoring us. And so, with each year, that tree grew larger stronger, twisting into large powerful knots of strong oakwood until one year the car's windows exploded, as fresh green limbs sprouted out of old rusty holes in the roof and doors. Today, the tree grows straight up towards heaven, dressed in wildflowers, vines and butterflies. I suppose it has become an altar in some ways, as I find myself praying, thankful that the tree did not die and leave me alone like Momma did.

Chapter 5

My name is Page Anne Austin. I was born in Kermit, West Virginia. Momma was not very book smart, and I have paid for how she spelled my name for as long as I can remember. Like a painting that hangs crooked on a wall, it bugs some people until they cannot help but explain to me how it is wrong to spell my name the same way that you spell the word page in a book. "That's not how you spell the name Paige!" A know-it-all will say as if they feel superior to me because they know how to spell. My momma was fifteen years old when my daddy and the spring carnival came to town. She was just sixteen years old and very much alone when I was born, so I can forgive her for misspelling my name — after all, my name, that old car and my memories are the only gifts Momma ever gave me. So, it is fitting, sorta special, that she spelled it in a unique way.

Momma was like most girls in West Virginia. She grew up with the idea that the world was better anywhere else but here at home. Some girls think only of the romance that a new town will be. That makes them easy prey for liars and conmen — carnival men, truck drivers, preachers and pimps who fill the heads of lonely girls with visions of a better life just across a state line. For some girls, it was TV shows or movies that made them willing to trade their young bodies for a ride to a better life. For others the need to escape poverty made the lies these no-account Romeos spoke palatable. For some girls, anything was better than being touched by a male family member, molested by a stepfather or uncle while their mother pretended not to notice. Momma had not told me why she gave in to my father's lies and traded her body and love for the promise of a new life somewhere else, but she took that gamble and lost. My daddy swore that he would return for her just as soon as he could afford to do so, but of course he never did.

My earliest memories are of Momma dressing me in our best clothes and us walking around every carnival midway that she could take us to. Momma seemed to take pride in showing my father that he had not hurt her, nor tricked her, but her pride was false. Had we ever found the man, she would surely have allowed him to trick her again. Each carnival search would begin with pride and end with Momma drunk in the arms of any man who would have her.

I remember Lil Dee's father more than she does. I am six years older than my little sister, and I loved her dearly; she represented us becoming a normal family, with a mother and a father. Having both parents would make me a safe child to play with, to go to church with, things like that. Women are not stupid — as long as Momma was single, alone and without a steady man of her own, she was a threat to these women's homes. She might take the others woman's man, so I was not a safe little girl for their daughters to play with. But Lil Dee's daddy would make us whole, normal, as he could tame Momma's easy nature with men.

Although I have never had a man myself, I grew up watching Momma hunt for love, going from man to man, so I can understand the fear an easy woman can inspire in other women, and why the girls at school were taught to avoid me. But my understanding of things does not mean that it did not hurt my heart, being avoided as if I were a dog or I had lice.

The day that Lil Dee was born was the best day of my life! Her father took the time to call the school so I would know the exact time when Lil Dee was born, which made me feel as though I was part of her birth. The school's principal even announced it over the school's public address system so everyone could hear that I was a normal girl; he said that my father called, and my new sister and mother were doing well. The moniker stepfather was not used; step is one of those words that mean one thing to adults and nearly the opposite to children. Mothers often use the word step to not saddle their new man with the full weight of being a parent to a child that is not his creation, as if creation is completed with the planting of a seed. Whereas it seems to me that creation includes watering and pruning the plant too. At the same time, mothers use the word step as a way of letting the man know that she is the boss when it comes to her child. But kids hear the word step as if it were a question and not a fact. When you're a child the intention of the word step, its meaning, seems to change with the wind, leaving you wondering just what you are worth to either of your parents.

That night Lil Dee's father chose to surprise me by taking me to a fall carnival. People are funny that way, ritualistic is what an archaeologist would call it, but to Lil Dee's father, it just made sense to take me to the carnival and allow me to enjoy myself with my new father; it was his way of assuring me that I mattered to him as much as his own blood daughter. But it was the worst night of my life. He knew about Momma and the carnival, everyone in town knew about it, yet he had no way to know my heart. There were no bones or pottery shards to be found to point my fears out to him. Momma had taught me that my father would recognize me at first sight. She swore that I was the spitting image of the man. It was this knowledge that caused my fear and ruined the night with my new father. Each step we took, each face I saw, brought me closer to losing the normal family that I desperately wanted and that Lil Dee's birth offered.

I was praying for my father not to see me, not to recognize me as his daughter. I was sure that if he saw me, he would start a fight with Dee's father. "She's my baby girl" they would both scream as they clashed like wild bulls for the right to be my father. Had this been my only fear, I could have found the words to explain my heart to Dee's father. In the years since that night I have dreamed many times about how Lil Dees father would gently put my fears at ease. He would swear that I was his baby girl and we would joke playfully as we rode every ride that the carnival had to offer, but God seems to enjoy watching our hearts shutter as our eyes filled with water, frustrated, unable to find the words we need to explain our soul. God certainly enjoyed my pain and fears that night because, as afraid as I was that Lil Dee's father would meet and fight my father.

I was equally afraid that they would meet and not fight for the right to be my daddy. Worse still, that they would laugh at me, laugh about how easy it was to get Momma to do things for them in bed at night. How easy it was to manipulate Momma's fear of being alone, to use it against her. Men like to brag, I had heard many men speak of Momma in this way, but these men were not going to be my father, so their words were dull and painless; yet tonight, these men were to be my father and the thought of them speaking of Momma in an evil way cut deeply into my heart. So, I suffered in numb silence all night, only to go home unable to sleep, afraid that I had ruined our new normal family. Fear is very much like rust — it just slowly eats you. In the end though, Momma needed no one's help in ruining our normal family.

Men had always come and gone from Momma's bed and my life. I know that for Momma, having a man meant having a home, so when Momma became a prostitute, selling herself for money, I was neither stunned nor shocked. I knew without any words of explanation which men Momma honestly liked and wanted compared to those who she gave herself to as means of paying the rent. Children are free to think without the guilt that comes from the world's social ideas of right or wrong; that's why a black child is just another child in your baby's eyes until you point out why they are different. So when a child see its mother trade herself, stay with a man that she does not really like, and then she becomes a true prostitute, the child sees no difference in her actions.

We love to pretend that children are too innocent to understand what we adults do, but it's the child's innocence that allows them to see us without judgment in their tender eyes: Mommy gets high, Mommy stays with a man she does not like so that we have a place to live, Mommy needed some money so she spent time alone with a man — these are just events to a child because all Mommies are perfect in the child's eye and do no wrong.

When Momma honestly cared for a man, she was a storm of contradictions. When she became pregnant with Lil Dee, all she did was plan for the day that Dee would be born; there was a focus in my mother — she had to get her nest built, and this time she had Lil Dee's father there to help her. Even my life was focused on how Momma having another child would make us a family. Yet after Lil Dee was born, Momma's old insecurities, her fears, seemed to steal her focus away, and all hell would break loose over the smallest things. In the end, Momma needed no one's help in the task of ruining our new family.

Chapter 6

The world has a way of trying to protect the unprotected. Crazy women learn early in life that if they call the police and say that their man has hit them, then the man goes to jail; he is guilty until he proves to everyone that he is not, and even then, we laugh, rolling our eyes wondering how he convinced the woman not to come to court. Every few years, the local police get tired of women abusing the system. They often stop arresting men or responding to calls, that's when a true monster hurts. Then all hell breaks loose as the police rush to arrest men even when they know that the woman is lying and that he may or may not be guilty. Don't get me wrong, there are truly rotten men out there hurting the women in their lives, but these girls seldom get to call the police.

Momma used the police and the jail as if she owned them. She would call the police and then start a fight with Lil Dee's daddy, screaming louder when the poor police officer pulled up. "I saw you look at that girl at the red light! Is she who you're fucking now? Lord knows it ain't me!" Momma would yell, as they would drag Lil Dee's daddy off to jail, only to then scrape up enough money to pay his bail bondsman the very next morning. By the time Lil Dee was potty trained, her daddy couldn't take it anymore. He swore that he loved us girls, his girls, as he called us, that it was Momma and the way that she was that he was leaving, not us. Yet I could see in his eyes that once he walked out the door, we would never see him again. That was the day that I learnt that carnivals were not the culprit in Momma's failing ways.

Momma seemed to understand her fault in our family being torn apart this time; she never once said a bad word about the man. Had she tried to treat him in a respectful way just a little sooner,

I would not be old and alone writing to you now. But, 'would-a', 'should-a' and could-a' don't matter in the end do they? What mattered was that we were alone again with only Momma to guide us through the storms that her soul brewed up. These storms were epic, as Momma now not only distrusted men, but she seemed to hate herself for the way that she would abuse men who were good to her.

As I look back on memories from the safety of nearly seventy years. I can see that Momma believed all men to be rotten, just trying to get her to do things for them in the bedroom. Things that she would gladly give to a man for true love. But Momma didn't understand true love, so nice guys seemed like conmen, reminding her of my daddy.

Her storms would rage, from punishing herself for needing someone to love her, to hating men for tricking her with their kindness. All the while, our need of a home would pressure her to make silent deals, trading her body for a roof for her children to live under.

Thunderstorms seldom rage for weeks. They seem to blow through town ripping up a trailer park, then the sun comes out for a little while as the next thunderhead builds just over the horizon. That's a pretty good description of our life after Lil Dee's daddy escaped; one terrible storm, then sunshine; just keep an eye on the skyline and you could see the rage building. Boiling grey into purple clouds seething with pent-up anger, energy soon to explode. Yet these storms were gentle in comparison to the storm that opiate addiction is. No more would we enjoy sunny days as Momma's self-hate, fear, and disgust built into a storm out past the horizon. No, OxyContin brought a kind of storm that just never stops.

From as early as I can remember, I heard women whispering about Momma when were near; about the girl Christy who they had known and played with in school and the sad woman she was now. 'It' was always mentioned as if 'It' was a school class that Momma took, read the books and was changed by. But this 'It' was not enlightenment. This 'It' that these women spoke in whispers of was said to have killed the sweet child, their friend Christy, and like Jesus, after he rolled that big stone away, 'It' replaced her with someone that her friends knew but could not recognize. These women, some genuinely old friends, others just gossips, happy to hear of another's pain, never took me to the side and explained this terrible 'It' to me. So, knowing that my daddy had abandoned Momma to have me alone, I often felt sure that I was the monster who had killed these women's gentle childhood friend. That I was the cause of Momma's pain, as with every storm, every new low we sunk to, 'It' was again blamed.

I remember preparing a meal after a church service one Sunday not long after Momma and Bobby left us, and the other women included me in their chatter. They were telling memories of their mothers. Things they taught them, like how to fry chicken, or how one woman's mother used store-bought cake mix and lied for years that it was a secret recipe. This made all the women laugh as if they all understood raising a family can cause a mother to take short cuts sometimes. So, I spoke up and told them about how, after Lil Dee's father left, Momma would go into small stores and picks fights with the store clerk, cussing up a storm. All while Lil Dee and I would stuff our coats with food, tampons, and other things we needed. Then we would run away, all three of us laughing as we ate our free dinner.

"The Three Musketeers, us against the world," Momma would say as Dee and split the candy bars in half. Each of us had stolen different types so we could share them. In my mind, these were some of my dearest memories of life with Momma. Us against the world, as we made our way through an unending storm. But the other church women did not laugh with me that day and I saw that 'It' had not died with Momma. These women, my friends, all had the same look on their faces that Momma's childhood friends wore when they spoke of the death of their girlhood friend, Christy.

OxyContin was pure poison; it was destroying West Virginia and most of the United States, but history books are as bad as archaeologists, lying, making up stories just to sound smart. Never once considering the culture of the people they're making up those stories about. The fact is the people of my home state are very moral, yet also rebellious at the same time. We all claim family ties that go back to America's first rebellion: the Whiskey Tax uprising. It was a small thing really, but can you claim to be from a neighborhood that forced George Washington to come talk to you? No? Then be quiet!

Well, this started a culture of doing what you have to do to care for your family no matter what the government says — as long as you can go to church on Sunday and look Jesus in the eye, then it's not a sin. This culture would be reinforced many times when jobs were scarce and grandparents had to make moonshine to feed their babies, or when coal miners had to go on strike and grandpas made good clean safe liquor. Not rotgut, the bathtub gin that made folks go blind.

People believed that doctors did not give out heroin or poisons, so just like grandpa's corn mash, OxyContin must be safe to take, and sell people thought. It was this sad belief that led to people trying Oxycodone. People who would have screamed as they kicked you out their house if you had offered them heroin — remember, you can take pills from a doctor and Jesus won't mind come Sunday morning, but heroin is a sinner's drug they say, although for the life of me I cannot find heroin mentioned anywhere in the Bible.

By the time we realized that Momma was addicted to OxyContin she had been taking it for nearly a year. Addiction is never a problem until you run out of pills, and Momma ran out. Men who normally saw no harm in giving Momma a pill or two were now trying to sell them. Everyone wanted them, and the thousands of old people who had prescriptions for Oxy were happy to sell them — it was a family tradition, Grandpa sold moonshine, didn't he?

Suddenly a night in bed with Momma was not even worth one small pill, and Momma was a very pretty woman who men swore was a wildcat in bed. I saw fear rip through Momma when she realized that she was sick, hurting, and angry when she was not high; it was this fear that led to Momma making deals with the same store owners we had stolen food from. She would spend time with them in a backroom, or she would go to the houses of old men who had prescriptions to earn pills or money.

I remember painfully that there was no more laughter, no more Three Musketeers, as Momma tried to hide the truth of her actions from us girls. We spent more than a year staying in cheap motels or at friends' houses as Momma sold herself to feed her addiction and us; all the while, she was still searching for a man, a home, a dream. I hated this time in our lives as Momma was never happy, never laughing, and some of the men seemed to take pride in knowing that Lil Dee and I were sitting outside of the room door that they were using our mother in. They would get louder and louder as Momma would say: "Please, my girls can hear you!"

We could not live this way for long. Momma could not continue to juggle her growing addiction, prostitution, and the embarrassment that comes with it, while caring for her children in a meaningful way. Her actions were well known to the gossips and busybodies in town. They believed that they would have to answer to Jesus if they did not intervene, or save her from herself. 'It' would have to be faced — they had allowed this child killer to rule my mother's life long enough. So calls were made to the police and children's service's; moral codes would be kept, Momma's whoring would not stain their angel wings, nor dent their halos.

The police kicked in our motel room door at exactly six o'clock on a cold Sunday morning. Guns in hand, red laser dots dancing on the bodies of two children and a drug-addicted whore, evil masks covering their faces — all done in a spirit of community service and the love of Jesus. I do not like the 'Bacon Boys' as Bobby called them. The police use fear to make people talk to them, to get you to tell on other people; they don't arrest you, they attack you in the most fearful way that they can. Even children are roughly treated until a room is deemed safe and clear of guns.

Momma knew nothing more about drug deals in town than the Bacon Boys already knew. She never owned more than two pills at any one time, but they didn't care. Fear was their goal and fear is what they gave us, as Momma screamed for me to watch my sister. Her words forced me to struggle to get free from under the weight of an officer and hold my crying sister, who was snatched out of my arms as soon as I reached her. Momma was whisked off to jail, Lil Dee was taken somewhere, and I was hauled off to a foster home. No goodbyes, no explanations, just masked men, guns, tears, screaming, and fear.

Today I have to think that the officers thought that children's service's would explain things to us girls over cookies and ice cream; and that children's service's must have thought that the people who ran the foster home would explain things to me. But there was never any ice cream and cookies, nor any meaningful explanation. I went from living on the streets with Momma to bedtimes, school tests, and church three times a week as my foster family made sure that Jesus gave them a gold star beside their name for saving yet another lost child from Satan's evil grasp. Although I had clean and nice clothes to wear, good food to eat, and nice people caring for me, the days without family were unbearable. Children do not know that their parents' lifestyle is wrong, it is simply 'Life' to the child; and the skill set, the mental manipulation that a child molester uses to gain control of a kidnapped child, is the same skill set that a foster family must use to gain the trust of a foster child. I must sound completely crazy to you right now, yet what I am writing is true.

When a child molester steals child, it is a violent act. No matter if they have tricked the child into their van or snatched the child by force — at some point, violence will be used to instill fear and to assert their authority over the child. Adults fear rape and think about why a creep has just stolen them, but children only think about how to get back to their family, to the life they know and the people they love. There is little difference between a child molester and a police officer in the mind of a child who has been separated from their family and known way of life — kidnapped or rescued, good intentions or pervert reasoning's, the child's only known world has been destroyed.

I spent just over ninety days crying, worrying about Momma and about my being the 'It' in her life, the 'It' that once again had ruined her life. When would Momma decide that I was too much trouble? If she did forgive me and came back to pick me up, would she be mad that I had lost my sister? Would she allow me to help her find Lil Dee? And would Lil Dee ever trust me to protect her again? I would try to go to sleep at night with these evil fears and the overpowering guilt poisoning my dreams, ruining my hope.

I stumbled through each day, broken and dying a little more with each passing second. This is why I am sure that child molesters and foster parents use the same tools on their wards, because, had anyone offered me love, an explanation, and the promised return of my sister or my mother, I would have done any of the things for them that Momma did to earn pill money. When you take a child from their only known world, that child will cling to any offer of hope and do anything to please you — foster parent, Bacon Boy, drug dealer or pervert. Home and the people you love are irresistible, no matter who is offering them to you.

She appeared at the back yard gate of my foster parents' home. I was sitting in an old car tire that my foster family had hanging from a tree as a swing, daydreaming about how I would escape as soon as I heard my foster parents say where Lil Dee was living. My daydreams were vivid, like movies: I would fight to steal my sister back so that Momma would not abandon me, the terrible 'It' who had ruined her life and killed the innocent child that her school friends had loved. So, seeing a silent smiling woman standing at the gate, with a halo of the sun glowing around her, emphasizing her beauty, I could only gasp and softly cry the word Momma. As my heart recognized the angel before me and I ran to her without the fear or guilt that had haunted my soul since I was stolen from her. Momma is such a meaningful name — like the name God, it is unexplainable. Momma's gentle touch felt like heaven to me as she held me, crying deeply herself, mumbling her words, trying to explain how sorry she was to have lost me and how happy she was to have found me again. Love needs no explanation, both of

46

our words from that day are lost, gone, leaving no pottery shards or chrome emblems to prove that they were ever said at all; no archaeologist will ever understand the joy I felt the day that God gave Momma back to me.

I was so happy, so relieved, that I forgot to blame my mother. Us humans have a way of allowing ourselves to be fooled by our desires. I suppose that is what I allowed my heart to do — to trick me into forgetting that life is hard and that my mother had been killed by a monster politely spoken of as 'It'. Fooling myself, allowing my heart to dream, is the only way that I can explain my lack of memory from that day so long ago. Oh, I remember packing my things and leaving the foster home, but I cannot remember any of the conversations I'm sure Momma had with my foster parents, nor their goodbyes.

Somehow, as if by magic, I found myself on a Greyhound bus sitting beside a woman I had prayed to meet my entire life. Momma was not Christy the whore, or Christy the sly and untrusting woman who had taught me to steal food and tampons. No, this woman wore none of the mask that my Momma had so easily worn. This Christy seemed to glow: she was at peace, happy, and ready to face life sober.

"I can't date for a year!" Momma said in joy. "No men until I'm ready, and I won't be ready until you girls and our lives are right. I'm sorry Page," Momma said as she pulled me in to her side. The bus's gentle roar as it raced north towards my baby sister seemed to ease Momma's soul and I asked her: "For what Momma? What are you sorry for?" I was foolishly unsure of what my mother had done that she felt the need to apologize for. "Page, some bad things happened in my life. I'm still not sure of how to explain them to myself or to you, but I haven't been a good mother to you girls. At rehab, they got us to look into our hearts. I'm still learning honey," Momma said as she hugged me even tighter, "but I'm going to change, I promise!" I wish that I had doubted her, as an adult would have done, but no child doubts their parents, it's just not natural.

Momma spoke of our case plan. First, we had to go to

47

Huntington, West Virginia and get my sister from her foster home. As long as Momma turned in a clean urine sample by noon tomorrow, we would receive an apartment, some money to start our new lives with, and Momma would be enrolled in school.

"We have to go to Narcotics Anonymous meetings everyday for some time to come, but I enjoy those meetings Page," Momma said. "They help me to figure out some things, things that I have been hiding from."

I wanted to ask her about 'It', to prove to her that I was smart and that I understood more than she thought I did. But resting my head on her chest, hearing her heartbeat as the bus swayed its way down the highway, had left me feeling at peace, and unable to measure her words by the nasty world that I knew.

Chapter 7

Bus stations are odd places, always full of both hope and despair in almost equal proportion. You can look in one direction and see a person full of joy as they start a new adventure in life, but turn your head and there will always be a desperate fool praying to get away from lives that they have ruined. If you learn anything from reading about my life, from exploring my shames and secrets, please let it be this: no person has ever ruined, destroyed, or messed up just one life.

We tend to need people don't we? And just what effect do you think self-destruction, drug addiction, rape, suicide, child abuse, and self-hate have on those we love? Thinking back to that day so long ago, I wonder who the people at the Greyhound bus station in Huntington, West Virginia, at first sight, thought that Momma and I were as we walked from the bus, full of joy, at peace, and happy that the Three Musketeers would soon be together again.

Like sharks swimming around a boat, the addicted and the sleazy people of the world who are comfortable in their filth and addiction float around the edges of bus stations praying to taste blood mixing in water. "Oh, maybe the young man who just got off the bus needs a friend?" "Oh yes, that young girl over there is too innocent to be alone in the big city." "Look at the pretty woman with her daughter, surely she wants to get high?" These ideas, and other thoughts like them, are all things that the pimps, whores, and drug dealers said to themselves as Momma and I walked across the bus station's parking lot.

That's because they saw my mother for the addict that she was and were quickly offering her the drugs and friendship that they knew she wanted and needed. One man even laughed at Momma when she turned down his offer to help find us some pills as if he could see weakness in her. I wanted to punch him, kick him, and ask him how did he know that my mother got high? What made him think that she might want drugs?

Why couldn't we be two church-going women? Normal, clean folks like the others who had ridden the bus to Huntington? Sharks taste blood in the water, that makes sense. In the years since that day I have asked myself many times, while reliving our mistakes, hoping for a better outcome, and dreaming of a better ending to our story. Just what it was that Momma did to draw the attention of the drug dealers and the pimps as we searched for a taxicab. I am still not sure of the answers, but they knew that Momma was a drug user and that we would soon be back, seeking their help.

We rode without speaking in a cab to the address children's services had given Momma of where Lil Dee was living. Both of our hearts racing faster the closer we came to Lil Dee and being a whole, complete family again. For three months, I had dreamed of finding the hidden safe house, or the old dark prison that they held my baby sister in, and like a spy in a movie or a lone soldier who was now forced to do wrong to make the world right, being forced to break the law in order to rescue my sister, no matter the cost.

We humans are silly — we measure right and wrong, good or bad, by our emotional needs at the time. Movies had influenced my dreams, so I was a warrior, killing those who got in my way with the snap of their neck or a kick to their groin; I was a master thief bypassing alarms and computer codes with ease. Funny, there are no movies showing us the right way to rescue a mother and sister from 'It' or from the unsteady moral values of an opiate addict. You see, our morals shift when we want to get high, or spend this month's rent money at the bar.

This is one reason why opiate addiction is so hard to overcome — like a devil, it takes control of your heart and emotions leaving you willing to do absolutely anything to feel opium's warm embrace again. Anything to bask in the glow of our false God, like a lizard resting on a rock enjoying the sun. The problem is that the lizard has no choice but to warm its body in the sun. For us humans, after a few heavenly tastes of opiates, the addicted or mentally broken become just like the lizard, very much unable to live without our false God and the warmth he offers.

I'm sorry, there I go again trying to avoid a painful part of this story by speaking like a smart person or one of those love-struck co-ed girls swooning over a fat archaeologist who has not showered for days, working at some faraway jungle dig site. Watching him point out teeth marks on the leg bone of what was surely a person who died like I am certain to do, alone, and not at all very tasty. Just another life wasted, unlived, aged meat too tough to enjoy.

I ran from the cab before it came to a complete stop in front of Lil Dee's foster home and raced up the steps of a grand front porch. The type that wraps the home in its protection, complete with a large swing to enjoy your evenings on as honeybees play in the flowers coloring the rows of green plants surrounding everything. Lil Dee stood only a thin sheet of glass away from me. Her pudgy baby hands open wide, her palms gently banging out a rhythm of joy on the window as, an angel, she sang out "Sissy, Sissy, Sissy," over and over again.

Her one simple word spoke volumes as her eyes said, "I love you, I miss you, I need you," all things that I both wanted to hear her say and that I needed to say to her myself. That one joyful word, Sissy — it is no wonder people believe in magic, because only magic can explain how one tiny word can mean so much when said at the right time, in the right tone, and by the right person. Melting inside, all I could do was stand there smiling, fighting to remember to breathe as I basked in the beauty of my little sister's joy. I heard a stair squeak behind me, and I saw that Lil Dee's body seemed to shutter. Her hands slowing as recognition of the clean angelic woman on the stairs behind me dawned in her heart.

She gasped out an almost inaudible word, "Momma," her tone so full of love, need and joy that I began to silently cry along with her. The woman, the mother who we both wanted, and needed was there, standing in the shade of that grand front porch, ready to face the world and to be our mother, ready to make our world right. In that moment, the memories of perverted men's moans vanished, along with the knowledge of the price of an Oxycodone, and the bulky feel of a stolen box of tampons hidden under my coat. At that moment, we were more than the Three Musketeers — we were humans, we were normal.

As I have said before, God is a complete and total asshole, a straight dick who has to enjoy this game of right and wrong he forces us to play. If he ever gives me the chance, I will speak to him about it when we meet; the worst that he can do is send me to hell, and after that day on that grand front porch, hell will be no worse than riding a cheap carnival ride as you search the crowds for the face of your absent father; hell will be a joke after watching your mother wipe gravel and dirt from her knees after kneeling to service a man for the price of a pain pill. Hell? I have been there too often to count.

Time seemed to freeze, to a slow crawl, as Momma grabbed me, screaming at the same time to "get off their porch, get to the street Page, now!" I couldn't think and had no time to ask why as Momma pulled me off of the porch, dragging me to the streets edge and the freedom that it represented to her. Only then did I see the police car racing towards us, its large motor roaring like a lion. A sound that every drug addict or street person understands without explanation, a sound that means someone is going to jail.

To street people, the sound of a siren means that rescue or protection is on the way. But the throated revs of a police car's roaring motor means that the Bacon Boy driving that car is pissed off or so insecure that he needs the car's powerful roar to announce that he is the boss, the man with the gun, and your God at that moment in time. To this day, I still hate Bacon Boys. Police officers are fine, generally they are good people doing a needed job, just feeding their families; but Bacon Boys are worthless, insecure pricks who abuse the trust they receive with their badges. And on that day in front of Lil Dee's foster home, listening to her cries of joy become screams of pain and confusion, I knew that this officer was an asshole before he bothered to taze me with his stun gun as he yelled for me to stop resisting arrest.

The early summer sun had warmed the asphalt street. I remember lying there face down, confused yet, at the same time, enjoying the warmth of the pavement, as it contrasted with the gritty roughness of the street. To this day, the smell of sun-warmed asphalt reminds me of the silent, peaceful, cocoon I found myself awakening in after being shot by the policeman's stun gun. God, I suppose, had allowed me to enjoy a moment of peace before the noise, fear, and confusion caused by that same stun gun rushed back into my mind, heart and ears. Somehow, Momma was now lying on the ground beside me, her hands cuffed behind her back, a venomous sound in her voice that I had never heard before.

"She's a baby! Get your fat ass off my daughter! If you hurt her again, I swear that I'll hunt you down and kill you!" Momma kept repeating as the officer, realizing that he had attacked a child, seemed to question his own actions. I could feel his weight changing with the tone of his voice as he replied to my mother's threats.

"She's old enough to be a drug addict. You two were trying to escape!" the policeman said as his weight pressed steadily against my upper back, forcing the asphalt, tar, sand, and dirt to sting my face.

"We have papers to pick up my daughter! In my pocket!" I heard Momma say as she began to tell the fat policeman that she knew his type and that him beating up a little girl would not make his little dick grow any bigger. There was pure anger and hate dripping from her words. I saw between the tires of the police car that another police cruiser was driving towards us, with its lights flashing. They looked so odd with my face pressed firmly on the ground.

The screams of its siren mixed with my mother's words of hate, my sister's muffled cries from within the house, and the confused voice of the policeman who was holding me down. His weight on me would lessen as his mind screamed at him that I was a child, and then just as quickly he would bear down on my back with his full weight as he screamed out an excuse, or a lie, that he hoped would save him from the hateful actions he now found himself committed to performing. Actions that I would later learn had been spawned in his heart by equal parts. The love of God and hatred of God's imperfect creations, drug addicts. It's funny, isn't it? The twisted things good men and women can do in the name of God.

"Tom, get your big ass off of that little girl! Just what in the hell have you done?" the new officer asked as I felt the man's weight removed from my body.

"They were trying to escape!" the officer named Tom stuttered as my mother, sensing the confusion and fault in officer Tom's voice, began to scream over Tom's voice that he had stunned me and tackled her for no reason.

"Shit! For Christ's sake, Tom!" I heard the new officer say. "You know I gotta report this, you know we gotta take this baby to the hospital to be checked out after getting shocked. Now tell me what happened, damn it!"

Tom started to laugh, a knowing pride returning to his voice. "I caught them trying to steal the other little girl, breaking that restraining order and trying to escape when I got here, plus assault and resisting arrest! So, I stunned the young one there, and slammed the other one. They ain't taking that sweet little girl and turning her into a dope whore like these two here are!" officer Tom said with conviction and pride in his voice. Momma screamed that we were not breaking any restraining order and that we were standing in the street and not on their property when Tom pulled up and attacked us.

The new officer turned out to be Tom's sergeant and not much of a fan of Tom either. I heard contempt, joy, and amusement in the police sergeant's voice as he ordered Tom to take the handcuffs off of my mother and help her to her feet. Officer Tom tried to complain but was silenced by the sergeant.

"Tom, one of these days that church and preacher of yours is gonna get you killed or fired from your job. I can only hope you get fired and then killed so the city won't have to pay out any money to your mother in death benefits," the sergeant said as Momma picked me up in her arms. Only then did I realize that I had wet my pants after being shocked. I was still dazed, but I could tell from my mother's actions that she was starting to play meek and in need for the sergeant as there was no anger or venom in her words.

I have already told you about me watching TV shows about archaeological stuff; sometimes though, I watch shows about animals. One time I saw a show about those funny looking lizards whose eyes can twist and move in different directions at the same time, and they can change the color of their skin to match almost anything; chameleons are what they're called. Most people fool themselves into believing those cute little lizards are nice gentle things who change their skin color to keep from being eaten by birds and other things. I suppose as slow as they do seem to walk, that is partly true. But the last part of their name is lion because they are ruthless hunters who change colors in the blink of an eye in order to catch their prey, and when it came to men, Mommy was pure chameleon.

In the space of just a few minutes, I had watched Mommy change from the clean fresh mother that we had always prayed for her to be, to the smart, knowing streetwise woman who instantly knew that something was wrong and to get off of that front porch before the police got here. Then into a nasty sounding woman who was swearing to kill a policeman. Now she seemed helpless, as if she needed the police sergeant's protection. Many times, since that day, I have wondered why she chose to play up to the police sergeant. In hindsight, I see that we owned the police that day for what they had done to me. No, we would not get rich or anything, but we could have forced them to return Lil Dee to us. Mommy could have called the county rehabilitation center and saved her plan, her chance to go to school, her hope of becoming more in life. More than a part-time whore, more than a grownup little girl trying to raise two little girls herself in a swirling storm of addiction, the need to be loved by a man, and crippling self-hate, all while running from her heart's monsters. But she chose to act helpless, exactly what the sergeant's ego would respond to.

He gently wrapped me in a blanket he retrieved from his car as Momma began to purr like a kitten. Not once did she act like the street whore that she most certainly was instead her actions and demeanor were soft, feline, and sexy, yet also questioning and helpless. I instantly knew what she had planned for the police sergeant, and to this day I regret the pride I took in my mother's pandering to his ego, as his coworker acted as if we were nothing, trash to be swept up and thrown away. But on that day, I only wanted my sister back. I had seen my mother service men for pills, food, money, a place to sleep. I knew she liked the sergeant no more than she liked officer Tom. Perhaps it was the sounds coming from within the pretty house that drove her choices — Lil Dee's happy cries had moved from breathless joy to a child's unreasoning anger, and now into the deep sobbing moans of a brokenhearted babe.

On that day, to retrieve my sister, for the three of us to be together again, I would have given my own body in trade to the police sergeant had he asked me to. I would have even held my mother down as he enjoyed her if that was what it would take to follow my mother's lead and gain his friendship. We all have shames, hidden sins that haunt us more than our other moral crimes when we remember our past, and this is a sin that today I almost hate myself over. But, on that day so long ago, I only wanted my family whole again, no matter the cost.

The police sergeant read my mothers actions as her needing him and he jumped to her defense, screaming for Tom to shut his mouth, and that Tom should pray that my mother did not choose to press charges. "In fact, I hope she does press charges, Tom, so I can arrest you and be done with you and all the trouble your strict church going morals cause me! Now get out of here, Tom before I forget that you're a brother police officer!" the sergeant said as he shook his head and began to explain to my mother how officer Tom would arrest people for doing things that violated his personal moral codes, and how these arrest would always force Tom's fellow officers to have to lie for him in court in order to make the arrest stick and not get Tom in trouble for lying.

Momma seemed to hang on the sergeant's every word as he drove us to a small but clean motel, one without open drug use going on in its parking lot. The sergeant even provided us with city vouchers to stay at the motel for free for a few days until we could go to court and retrieve Lil Dee. After he had assured us that he would return after work to take Momma shopping for clean clothes and things that we would need. When it was clear that Momma was receptive of his offered friendship, he explained to us the extensive nature of the restraining order that had been granted against my mother and myself in order to protect Lil Dee from us. It was drafted with the goal of overwhelming us, forcing us to jump through so many hoops that we would give up and return to Kermit without putting up a fight for the custody of Lil Dee.

Momma seemed to shudder as the sergeant told her that Lil Dee's foster family not only wanted to keep and adopt my sister, but that they felt it was ordained by God. The couple had been trying for years to have a child of their own, but God had other plans for them the preacher had told everyone the same Sunday morning that we were rescued by the police and children's services. He had claimed that a person needed to submit to God's plans and to stop asking God to grant their own wishes, but instead to tell God that they would accept his plan and goal for their life. Only then would God reward them, only then would God complete their hearts.

By the evening church service of that same Sunday, God had brought Lil Dee to Huntington, to be loved and raised by her foster parents and protected by the church. That was why officer Tom was so set on arresting us — he had even helped to draft the restraining order against not only my mother but against me. I was just ten years old, but TV had convinced the world that a ten-year-old was more capable of being a drug addict and that my mother was more than willing to sell me to support our habits. With just words written on paper, twisted just a small amount, I went from a protective older sister who stayed out of school to watch her little sister, to a willing drug user who her sister must be protected from.

Today, I understand how people form odd or funny misconceptions about people and cultures that they do not understand. Like I have said before, if an archaeologist on the TV says that the people whose graves he is robbing prayed to frogs and sacrificed their children on an alter shaped like Mickey Mouse's head, then people would believe him. So I understand that narrow minded strict church going people could believe that my mother would allow me to use drugs or would sell me to men.

We always try to accent our pains and traumas in life as we tell our story — a broken leg might in time be broken in three places, when just one break is all there was: we lie a little. I can almost forgive those good folks today as I think back, but almost is not quite the same as actually doing something. I was simply subjected to far too much humiliation caused by the twisted beliefs and misguided ideas of those good folks to ever forgive them for how they caused us to be treated, and for stealing Momma's chance to stay clean of drugs, to go to school, to try to learn to be more than the broken soul that she was.

Chapter 8

Being mentally focused is a powerful thing, and Momma was focused solely on using the police sergeant to retrieve Lil Dee without us having to wait to go to court. So focused that she failed to see the 'Forest' because all of the trees in the way! Had she forced the police to take me to the hospital or taken me there herself after the sergeant returned to work that day, we would have gotten the police to go before the judge in Lil Dee's case to explain that the restraining order was based on lies made up by officer Tom. But my mother stuck to what she knew would work, her tried and true method of sex performed by an experienced yet helpless woman. Like the fighter whose only tool for success is his body and who can't stop fighting even after he knows that his next fight will kill him, Momma had only one tool in her 'Life's Toolbox' — her body. It was understandable — it was honestly the only thing men wanted from her, and the fear that her easy sexual ways created in other women was her only trophy.

We were both ordered to give two urine samples per day and to provide proof that we were going to Narcotics Anonymous meetings once per day. One of these per day would be easy to accomplish, and would still leave time to go to work to earn money to feed yourself, but to perform all three everyday and earn money at a normal job would be impossible. They wanted Momma to return to selling drugs, or prostitution, so that she would relapse or go to jail. Then we would fail, and be unable to seek custody of Lil Dee. But Momma did not seem fazed by the daunting task before us.

I sat outside of our room that first night and listened as the sergeant vowed to help us, shortly after hearing his breathless pleas of joy and pleasure. Today, my memories of that night, listening to things that most mothers hide from their children, makes me sick, and disgusted with the evil child that I was, but that is because I'm now old and I have spent my life pretending as if I had no idea what the sounds of sex were. But I knew them well, they sounded no different than a mechanic working on a car, or a carpenter building a house. I suppose that what really makes me sick is that I do not know the sounds of making love, surely there is a difference? Surely one is more meaningful than the other? Or are my dreams and ideas all poisoned by the knowledge that a woman's body can be misused?

Daily urine testing was, in those days, the only way for addicts on probation, parole, pre-court bail bonds or under a judge's orders like Momma and I were to prove that they weren't using drugs. The problem was that no one had ever budgeted in the money it would cost to do this properly. Opiates, Oxys, and meth were all going to be temporary problems, so the county's methodology in urine testing was approached as temporary. A male and female jailer processed urines from 6:00am to 8:00am and 6:00pm to 8:00pm seven days a week in the booking and release section of the county jail. We had to sign in, then we were handed a small plastic jar and told to write our code number on it — we were always warned that trading bottles of urine would result in a failed test for both parties involved. Then we were told to step behind a curtain, remove our clothing, get in line, naked, holding nothing but our bottles, as we slowly moved forward to where we would stand facing the jailer as we squatted over a toilet and peed into our bottle.

These were methods that worked well in prison to process hundreds of urine samples at once, but convicts had lost their rights to privacy and could be stripped naked and searched at any time. Several women were known to complain about how humiliating it was to stand naked in a line or how evil it was to use the bathroom this way, in full view of everyone in the jail. One of these women was a large, very loud woman named Mickey, and she became my hero on that first morning as Momma and I suffered the embarrassment of trying to pee into a bottle in front of so many people. Mickey was smart enough to see that I needed help. The other women were as mad at Momma for having me even attempt to honor the judge's request as they were mad at the jailer for not giving me a more private place, or treating me like the child that I was.

"She's only a baby! She ain't even got no hair down there!" were some of the things shouted at the jailer, whose only reply was that she had not given me the drugs that I must have been using to be ordered to be here with "the rest of your bitches." I heard Mickey laugh as she said, "This bitch will stomp a mud hole in your fat ass!" as she stared at the jailer as if hoping that she would say something in response. What is so funny today is remembering that there were at least forty naked women, some with beer bellies, most out of shape, others thin and worn by drug use, while others showed that they had money. They were fed, clean and smelled of nice soaps, and all of them were acting as if this was normal.

"You gotta say 'Fuck 'em,' honey! Look at the cop and say 'You wanna look at my pussy? Well, get you an eyeful bitch!' It will help your bladder relax to let you pee honey. Think about this fat worthless pig having to play with your pee every day, disrespectful ain't it? Giving someone your pee? Well, this cop asked for this job, so she's asking to be disrespected," Mickey said as the girls around her started to join in, and suddenly I saw the police guard as an enemy and Mickey and the women in line as my friends, my tribe, and my bladder relaxed as everyone cheered "Pee!" and we all laughed.

Mickey was not the bull dyke she appeared to be, dressed in men's clothing with her hair spiked short. Even though she kept one or two girls around her, I was to learn that she was not a lesbian. Mickey would become a true friend over the next few weeks.

As Momma worked at a day job cleaning motel rooms to pay our rent, we fought to make it to our daily substance abuse meetings, urine tests, and to meet the always increasing needs of the police sergeant.

Mickey hated the police, so I began to act as if I hated them also although, at my age, I was not old enough to understand hate.

Even after being mistreated by the police as I had been, my attitude towards them simply mirrored the attitude of my favorite adult at that time. People tend to forget that children mimic the world around them and they have no understanding of hate, or the more complex learned behaviors of humans. Hate is a very complex feeling, the only feeling left in a heart after all the other emotions have run out, been misused or lost; then and only then can you honestly hate.

Mickey was loud and aggressive, and she did not take shit off anyone. She was also quick to stick her nose into anyone's business if she thought they were being abused or taken advantage of. In my eyes, she was a superhero, complete with a cape. But Mickey also did her best to teach me that her hard, tough image was as false as my mother's nightly moans of pleasure under the hands of her police sergeant. Today I know that Mickey used anger as a shield and that she was trying to teach me to be myself and not try and become another Mickey — why else would she have spoken so honestly about herself to me, a child?

Her father had abused her for years until Mickey found out that dressing and acting like a boy seemed to push him away. It was hard for me to believe that a real father would violate the love and fatherly bonds of his own daughter. It made no sense to me then, nor today. A hooker, after all, is a twenty-dollar solution to any man's needs, so to rape your own child, a man's need has to be more than sexual. At that time, I saw real fathers as saviors; I blamed Momma's pain on our not having my real father to guide and protect us. Mickey swore that after her father's abuse she did not care for men or women, but public opinion about her life left her with only women to love, and we all need love, we all need a hand to hold on to. Mickey and I would laugh as we sang an old song that said just that: "It don't need to be no strong hand, it don't need to be no rich hand, we all just need a hand to hold on to!" She seemed to need to explain to me that she was neither straight nor a lesbian, but instead someone who found safety in being the Mickey that I knew and loved. Maybe she needed me to love her, and not the big hard Mickey she pretended to be?

I learned to work the night shift at the front desk of our motel. The owners, an older black couple, taught me to say, "Yes Sir" and "No Sir," to talk politely, and that using manners is not a sign of weakness, nor of being less than the person that you were speaking to, but a sign of strength, pride and self-confidence. Mickey was beginning to rub off on me — my tone and actions were imitating Mickey more and more each day. I was told that it was fine to protect myself by pretending that I was Mickey twice a day as I stood naked, being stared at, peeing into a bottle. But that when I was dealing with the public, signing guest into the motel, I needed to be myself, and to use my manners no matter who I was talking to. Mickey seemed to understand what these kinds of people were trying to teach me, so she even tried to use her manners more when she was around them with me, to cuss less, and to act professionally. They all seemed concerned that I learned something good from each of them, and it was nice to be cared about by so many people.

Mickey began to hate the police sergeant, as each night if I was not working at the motel's front desk I would walk over to her apartment while Momma was entertaining 'The Lil Dick Piggie' as Mickey liked to call the police sergeant. It did not take long for her to also begin to be angry with my mother. She would argue that my mother knew that he had no intention of helping us prove to the judge that they should give Lil Dee back to us and that my mother was as weak and as needy as Mickey's own worthless mother had been as she turned a blind eye to the abuse that Mickey was forced to endure.

Mickey said that Momma had been a doormat for so long that she was incapable of ever being anything more than a doormat for men. Her words were hard for me to hear sometimes. Mickey could see this in my eyes and would apologize, only to then go and talk to Momma about how men would always use her heart's desires against her. But Mickey being Mickey, always having a couple of girlfriends nearby who she seemed to be pimping out even though she seemed to like them. This made Momma afraid that Mickey was trying to use her, just like the men that Mickey was so upset with her about. Today I am sure that Mickey did not want my mother in that way. I am also sure that, had Mickey's life been different, she would have had a man and children of her own. I think she and Momma were just different sides of the same dice that God had rolled letting fate pick the masks that Mickey, Momma and I would wear to protect our souls. Today I also know that there is a high price to pay when you only know how to live from behind the safety of a mask.

Within a year of meeting us, Mickey would complete her probation and daily urine tests, and then, free of the watchful eye of the police, she would overdose on opiates one night. Her girlfriends, all scared of going to jail themselves, would leave her in an alley besides a dumpster without ever trying to get her help, like garbage, trash, as if Mickey had never mattered to us at all, just another pointless life, a broken soul, and something that no archaeologist will ever understand. Yes, I know that at times in our past, humans were cannibals, but those folks' needed food. We, us, humans tend to eat only our tribe men's souls and not their flesh.

Chapter 9

Summer was coming to an end at the same time that our day in court was nearing. Mickey had been right — Momma's time with the police sergeant had not helped us at all, and soon I would need to be enrolled in school either up here in Huntington, or back home in Kermit. Failure to do so would only prove to that my mother was not fit to raise Lil Dee, nor me. Yet even knowing the importance, I was afraid of being sent back to school. I honestly did not fit in with girls my own age, and the boys seemed to believe their parents' gossip about sex and drugs and didn't want to be my friend. They instead wanted to play house, doctor, and other games that I am sure boys and girls have played and enjoyed for an eternity, but that I had no interest.

To this day it amazes me how my mother's lifestyle could not only affect others people's views of me, but also my view of them and the world around us. It would take years of embarrassing social missteps before I would learn that normal children and most adults do not know how to melt down a time release OxyContin so that the wax coating does not clog up the needle of your syringe; or that it's better to bounce a bad check than to forge a credit card receipt — one is a crime, and the other is a civil matter; or that men find out that they have a sexually transmitted disease far faster than a woman often will.

I would soon be eleven years old and I knew how to pop the ignition of a car to steal it, even if I had never done so myself. Drug houses, bars, and Mickey's apartment were not places where adults changed their conversations because little children were near. I was made to feel welcome by these broken adults; it was a feeling that the normal children in school were unable to offer. Yet I was still very much a child and it was this, my child's naive honesty, that would save us when we finally made it to court.

Our life, in spite of everything, was more normal than at any time since Lil Dee's father had left us. Momma worked hard to stay clean of all drugs, she was focused on proving that she loved her children and could raise them. This focus caused the motel owners to treat us like family, and Mickey to guard us. I also have to believe that Momma held on to the police sergeant even after he proved to be unwilling to champion our cause to the judge in our custody hearing because he gave her strength to stay clean, and not give in to the voices of doubt that I now understand had been plaguing her for years. Also, I'm sure that he would use her relapsing on drugs against her — men who know that they were wrong to blackmail a woman into going to bed with them will always use the woman's faults against her when they fail to uphold their end of the trade.

We were to meet Mickey and the motel's owners in the courtroom the morning of the hearing. The courthouse was full of people who all seemed to know who Momma and I were, constantly judging us with their eyes. Momma left me at a kiosk where they sold donuts and coffee as she went in search of our courtroom and hopefully Mickey and the support a friend would offer us. I felt very much alone as I seemed a curiosity to so many strangers.

I was standing at the donuts shop counter with enough money to buy a box of donuts like a normal patron. I had planned to buy a whole box of donuts to eat with Lil Dee after the court hearing, but what if we were not allowed to see her or to take her home? Should I buy a whole box? Should I save my money for Momma if we were told to go away and to leave Lil Dee here in Huntington? Confused, afraid, and embarrassed after being looked at as if I were a freak in a sideshow, I began to cry. I wanted the people to stop looking at me. I wanted my sister back, I wanted to go home to Kermit, and at the same time to stay here with Mickey and the motel owners. But above all, I wanted Momma to stay as she was now — clean, safe, a mother and not an addict sleeping with men for pills.

A tall kind man who had been standing behind me in line bent down and asked me in a caring voice what was wrong? I broke down completely and told him everything that had happened to me over the last few months. How I believed that all the people staring at me were from a church and were there to see that God's plan was carried out, and that the worst thing was that I didn't want to waste our money on a box of donuts that I might not ever share with my sister who I had allowed to be taken away from Momma. The kind man ordered me a milk and himself a coffee and told me to be strong, as no one really knows God's plan, but above all to buy a whole box of donuts as he was certain that I would get to share them with Lil Dee soon, the same way we had always shared candy bars and sweets our whole life. I remember laughing with the man when he said this because I knew that for him to know about us sharing our candy bars, I had to have told him about it and how special it was to both Lil Dee and me.

"Give her a dozen assorted donuts Bill," the man said with a smile and he nodded his head towards Momma who was concerned when she saw me crying and being cared for by a strange man. And then he was gone as I began to tell my mother of his kindness towards me after I had begun to cry.

We were to make our way to the courtroom without Mickey. She and three of her girls would sit at the back of the courtroom to show us support. Mickey was afraid that if they sat too close to us her lifestyle and reputation would harm us. So the only friends we had near us were the owners of the motel; just as Mickey had said, Momma's police sergeant was nowhere to be found. I felt small and near tears again as I sat there holding a box of donuts under the blazing stares of so many strangers. People who I was now sure were from the church and here to support Lil Dee's foster parents.

A courtroom officers called for everyone to stand as the judge walked into the courtroom. And I could not help it — I began to softly cry again, only this time my tears were tears of joy. I could not help but smile at the judge as he smiled down at me, and I was certain that I would soon be sharing donuts wit my sister. "It's him, Momma, it's him," I whispered to my mother, "the man who helped me earlier!"

He grinned at me as if we were old friends and then his facial expression changed to one of anger as he called out, "Willy, where are you? Preacher Will, get down here in front of this bench right now. Bailiffs, handcuff this lowlife." The courtroom exploded with noise as the judge beat his gavel on the bench, screaming for everyone to be quiet or they could go to jail right along with Preacher Will. I heard Mickey yell, "Lock him up, your honor!" Lock him up, damn it!" as I saw that our friends, the motel owners were doing their best not to laugh at Mickey.

Only after the judge had stood up, yelling over everyone in the room, did he regain control and begin to explain his reason for having Preacher Will handcuffed.

"As most of you know, I grew with Preacher Will, only back in those days, when we were kids, Preacher Will was known as Fat Willy, and God didn't send him any messages. No, in those days, Fat Willy was too busy selling the out-of-date adult magazines he got from his dad's drugstore to try to talk to God. But that was alright, because Willy would start telling the other boys just how special this month's issue of Playboy was, or how much trouble he would get into if his father caught him selling those type of magazines when by law, he was suppose to turn them in at the post office to be burned. Hell, Fat Willy swore that he could be sent to prison for years if he was ever found out. Willy had all of us believing that it was against the law to sell dirty magazines after the month that they were issued had passed," the judge said with a grin as he pointed his gavel at a blushing Preacher Will.

"I guess that I shouldn't be mad at Willy. After all, if it had not been for his adult magazine scam, I might never have become an attorney, nor the judge that I thought that I was until earlier this morning when I met this beautiful little girl right here," my friend the judge said as he winked at me.

"Well, it turns out that Willy tricked me again! I suppose that I should explain a little more and tell y'all more about this fat sleazy clown y'all call a man of God. You see, with all the boys believing that Willy could go to jail over those stupid magazines, he could charge us four and five times the cover price of the magazine — we were, after all, the only twelve-year-old boys in the state, if not the whole United States, who could get their hands on brand new Playboy magazines. Well, this didn't make much sense to me after I saw Willy's dad hand him a stack of out-of-date Playboys. So I searched every law book that I could find. I learned that there are state court law books and federal court law books, as well as why they are different. I found out that Willy was lying about having to burn the old magazines, and about jail — in fact, the unsold magazines were just to be thrown away. Boy, did I feel stupid!" The judge laughed at his memory as even Preacher Will smiled and laughed.

"It was funny, really, ole Willy made a lot of money that year off his foolish friends, but no harm was done really. That was a kid's stunt. What you have done to this child here, her mother, these good foster parents, that other sweet baby, the congregation of your church, and this court — that is almost evil, Willy plain evil. I believed your claims, your lies," the judge said with shame in his voice.

"Miss," the judge said as he looked at Momma, "court judges are suppose to read up on and verify the facts in the case put before them, but there is almost no time to do so anymore. This is West Virginia, and he opiate crisis is killing us — this week alone, ninety percent of the cases I will handle are directly connected to OxyContin. So when Willy's sister Gina came over and told me that you needed to be kept away from your youngest child, I blindly believed that you were addicted, as well as this young lady here with you. I was led to believe that she was far older and that you two were poison together. I'm sorry — I never once looked into your file. I didn't know that you had completed an inpatient stay of three months in a rehabilitation center. I was also led to believe that my young friend here," he said as he pointed at me, "I was led to believe that she was addicted and that was why your youngest daughter was transferred up here to Huntington, to be kept safely away from the two of you."

The judge began to turn red and shake as he said, "Willy, I trusted you. I had a ten year old baby girl urine tested twice a day for six weeks. Willy, this was wrong! Do these people know that your sister-in-law works at children's services in Kermit? I have heard the story of how God told you to convince these folks to open their hearts and let God's will be done. How you stepped up and prayed before the whole church on Sunday morning, and low and behold by evening service God had given them a sweet little girl. Do these folks know that you were aware on the Friday before that Sunday that the police planned to arrest the child's mother?

The whole thing was a setup Willy, and the worst part of it is not that I was made a fool of, nor that I will report my own foolish actions to the state's bar, and appoint this woman an attorney so that she can seek justice for the pain we caused this child. No Willy, those things are small in comparison to the fact that God gave you and your church three young lives to save, but you just tossed two of them away. Why didn't you come in here and tell me that you wanted to save both of the little ones? Or all three of them? "Hell, I would have helped save all of them.

"That would have been a good reason to lie, had you lied to save both children I could understand, but instead you painted this child as a villain," the judge said as he pointed to me. "Hell, most of the people here today only came down to court to see her, to see this so-called devil who abused her beautiful baby sister, the same child who these good foster parents thought God was gifting to them. We should all be ashamed of ourselves," the judge said as he motioned for the bailiff to remove the handcuffs of off Preacher Will. Then, with a smile, he said, "Willy, you fat liar, get your collection plate out and get a nice sized chunk of money out of these foolish sheep of yours, or you're going to jail for contempt of court and making racist threats."

"Now Joey, you're not still mad about the girly magazines, are you? And I ain't made no racist threats, nor said nothing racist all week, that's just not fair! Preacher Will said in his defense as he looked to see if his flock was willing to donate money to save him.

"Willy, if you don't come up with a nice amount of money real soon, fair or not, you can explain to the good African American brothers over at the jail how you would never say mean or evil things about them or their mommas," the judge said and we all began to laugh. "Now bailiffs, get this little angel here to her sister so they can eat their donuts. And again Miss, I am sorry that I didn't take the time to investigate before I separated you from your daughter. And please, I want you to make a claim against myself, the court system, and this fat liar here for the harm we have caused you."

"I will take some time and consider it your honor," Momma said as Lil Dee walked proudly into the courtroom holding a bailiff's hand, happy and unaware of the hell that we had gone through everyday without her. She simply smiled as she sat down beside me and opened the box of donuts, laughed and began to talk about the toys that they had bought for her and how much fun we would have playing with them, as if we had only been apart for a few moments, and not the lifetime that it had felt like to me.

Momma was trying to be polite to Lil Dee's foster mother. The woman had quickly raced over to us in an attempt to seem much as of a victim of the preacher's plans as we were, but Mickey would have none of it.

"Bitch, if you don't get your Bible thumping ass away from them, I will smack you into next week and then eat that pussy in ways your chubby husband ain't never thought of!" Mickey said as the motel owners both laughed and said "Mickey!" But Mickey was right to try to force the church people away from us as their sole objective was to convince us to stay here in Huntington where they could help us.

"Y'all folks weren't trying to help them pay their motel bill!" my friend and boss from the motel said. "Why y'all want to help them now?" he asked. "That little girl there is the same little baby y'all was calling a monster and a whore earlier before court, when y'all thought everyone in the courtroom was on your side. Y'all wasn't their friends then and you ain't gonna be now. Now Mickey, get your girls and let's all go home!" the motel owner said as he grinned at his wife and pointed out that one of Mickey's girls was trying to turn a trick with one of the men from the church. "Come on y'all, time to go. These are the type of folks that will laugh in your face and stab you in the back.

We made our way to the courtroom door and I saw that Preacher Will had not only handed Momma a large wad of money, but he also seemed to have noticed her in the way that all horny men notice a women with an easy reputation. It's a look that says: "I will enjoy this whore," and not the look of a man who is asking, "Will she allow me to enjoy her?"; as if it is a foregone conclusion that he could have my mother by simply asking or telling her that he wanted her. I could tell from the way that my mother was clinging to Lil Dee that we would be leaving Huntington without any of Lil Dee's new clothes or toys, just as soon as we could get away from the crowd of people who had looked down on us as they hoped to steal my sister this morning and who were now acting as if they loved and cared for us. To this day I believe that had they approached Momma in gentle way, she would have stayed in Huntington and I would have been there to get Mickey the medical help she would soon be denied. But Momma was scared — these people were snakes and we would not be around them ever again.

Mickey told me to never say goodbye. We were at the bus station ready to escape Huntington and return to Kermit. "There just are no goodbyes in life," Mickey said. "Only sad ones, and bad ones. We were family, so no need for stupid words," she said as she hugged Momma, Lil Dee, and I, and then she was gone. Off to make sure that the men looking at her girls knew that those girls were not alone.

Today, as I remember her, I wonder if Mickey prayed that a man would attempt to hurt one of her girls as Mickey's own father had hurt her, so that she could do to that man the violent things that someone should have done to her father. But I also see that she was afraid of her violent desires. No, today I know that Mickey's loud

72

voice and actions were false warnings meant to protect her from finding out if she could allow herself to give in and become the person her mask told the world that she was, all the while the little girl whose father had destroyed her found peace in OxyContin and opiates. It's sad really. Did her girls see the face of a broken child that Mickey honestly was when they dumped her in the alley? Did Mickey at least die in peace, as a little girl who felt the need to befriend me? It is so strange to think about her today. It makes me hope that there really is something after this life, and if so, I hope to see Mickey hanging out waiting for me. After all, she did say that there are no goodbyes.

Momma managed to stay off of the pills and booze for less than three days after we arrived back home in Kermit. We had more than enough money to get a nice apartment and to continue to live much like we had been living in Huntington, but Momma wasn't the same women in Kermit that she was up north. Her attempts to get help from her rehabilitation and social service counselor were done in a half-hearted way. That is easy for me to see after all this time, yet standing in Kermit besides Momma, with Lil Dee safe in our arms, we were the Three Musketeers once again and I never doubted Momma.

For the sake of being honest, I have to admit that Momma never really tried to get the help promised to her for completing a ninety day inpatient stay at the county rehabilitation center. No, she asked just one time for the promised help. She tried just twice to explain our position and then she accepted that she had broken her oath to return from Huntington, West Virginia within twenty-four hours and turn in a clean urine sample. Momma never called the judge for help, nor the preacher whose family worked here at children's service's and were more than aware of our situation. We had the proof to overcome any and all objections to our honest right to continue in the program, but Momma wanted to fail. This was Kermit, she had her babies back with her, but much like the mask that Mickey wore when she was in public, Momma only felt comfortable, safe, being the person 'It' had left behind when the little girl her friends once faithfully loved had died.

Addicts say old habits are hard to break, but that's a lie. It is just incredibly hard to feel safe living a life free of your old ways and ideas. For Momma, her time in rehabilitation and the time we spent in Huntington mirrored the time she had spent acting normal as we planned our new life with Lil Dee's father — it was now time to fail, time for her self-destruction, time to enjoy being the girl 'It' left behind, time once again to be the woman I called Momma. And I was not much different than her, how could I be? This was the only life that I knew, she was my mother, and Kermit was our home.

Addicts always have a plan. It's funny really to sit in a drug house and hear the ideas that addicts come up with to scam the system and to stay high. I have known alcoholics who swore to have back problems and then stay on prescribed drugs, but would claim years of being clean and sober. I was soon to learn that it's better to pretend to want help from the government than it is to be told by them that you need it. Soon Momma would be checking into the county rehabilitation center to detox from crack cocaine. A drug that lets go of your mind and desires after a few hours without using it, and that leaves your body in just days. Because of this, people would get high enough on cocaine to give a urine sample that would show cocaine use as well as opiates; cocaine would be your claimed reason for coming in to get help. The opiates were then viewed as a secondary drug, a drug of opportunity, taken only to ease the addicts desires for cocaine. Once admitted into the rehabilitation center for cocaine use, the addict saw every type of doctor known to man — the government was paying the bill, so doctors gladly lined up to do intake physicals that led to further treatments.

Momma was suddenly receiving prescriptions for OxyContin, as well as for antidepressants. When these ran out, she would leave us with one of her friends from the rehabilitation center, or her new boyfriend. She would return to rehab claiming cocaine addiction to the rehab counselors. She would stay for one week and, complain to the medical doctors that her back hurt her, who would gladly increase the number of pain medicines she received monthly. In the early days of the opiate crisis, this was a common practice accepted by the same doctors who created and fed the beast of addiction. OxyContin was made for long-term opiate use, even though any long-term opiate use is called addiction. This is something that we've known for millions of years, but if the government is paying the bill, you will always find a more than willing expert to claim a need of this treatment.

Momma had simply found a way to enjoy herself that was far less wear on her knees. For Lil Dee and me, having the rehabilitation center in our lives, and its demonic sister children's services, meant we were soon going to school. Every time Momma left the rehabilitation center, she would receive emergency food stamps, some cash, her prescribed medications, along with an apartment placement, so like good children we played the game, following Momma's lead. Lil Dee would get to enjoy free daycare and I would get to pretend to be Mickey in a new classroom, or one that I had been in before. Girls became cunts, whores and bitches and boys became little dick assholes' that I would rather smack around than fuck.

It felt good to scare the snobs, the girls who had always laughed at me. The girls who were lucky enough to know both their father and their mother. But, just as Mickey's actions had gotten her known as a dyke, mine were beginning to cause me troubles too. I remember that Mickey had told me about finding out that she had become a dyke, without much choice, so I was quick to tell the girls who asked me that I wasn't a lesbian. But nor did I like boys either. Rather, it was fun to scare the assholes who looked down on me or the boys whose fathers had paid for time with my mother, it felt good to tell them off. They may have had a normal life, in a normal world, but I could scare them. I was not powerless, I had value, I had found a mask — it would not become the mask that would define my life, but it was a mask that would protect me from my embarrassment at school, just as it had protected me from the embarrassment of being naked, peeing into a bottle in front of so many staring eyes.

Not long after Lil Dee began kindergarten classes, Momma left us with her new boyfriend to return to rehab again. The man had a nice house and was a nice person most of the time, but after Momma left for rehab he changed. He began to say things about how some "stiff dick" could fix my problems, or that after a "good fuck" I would never think about pussy anymore. I told him that I didn't like girls, and he said, "I KNOW!" in a tone that scared me more than anything I had felt before. Being a girl, I understood how it felt to have a man look at your body in admiration, but this man's tone said that he had done far more than admire my body. He had done things to me in his mind, and now he was telling me, not that he wanted me, but that he would have me, like it or not. I couldn't trust him, nor his thoughts about me; he scared me. And then one night he was high on crack cocaine, acting extremely paranoid, while staring out of the living room window and mumbling my name.

I took Lil Dee and ran away to one of Momma's girlfriends who would often take Momma out to Ruby's truck stop to take care of the truckers when we needed money. When I told her what had happened, all Momma's girlfriend said was for me to get used to it, and that as far as men go, Momma's boyfriend was a pretty safe place to get broken in. "Just the way things are honey," the women said with a laugh, as she patted my hand like a concerned aunt or older sister.

I remembered that I had once watched an older prostitute sitting at a table smoking crack, getting high as she taught a younger woman how to put a condom on a banana using her mouth and tongue, so that if the guy did not like to wear condoms, the girl could still be safe. The old whore's tone was the same as Momma's friend that night, and for the first time in my life I realized that there was such a thing as tomorrow. I had never thought about tomorrow, a year from now, or ten years from now. I cannot say that the woman's words inspired me to do so, because they didn't.

My only thought at that time was that when Momma got out of rehab, she would someday find the right man and we would be a normal family.

The idea that life was more than just today had started to invade my childish desire to remain naive and innocent, but I refused to face it. We would suffer a surprisingly high price for my failure to fully embrace the fact that my childhood was over, or worse that I had never had a childhood at all. But it's the high price we pay for our foolishness that makes us the person who we truly are deep inside of our hearts, hidden away where no one can see.

My mother was not happy with her now ex old man, nor was she pleased with the advice her girlfriend had given me. The women had laughed as she told my mother about the look on my face when she told me to go back to the guy's place and to let him break me in. As normal, Momma didn't get mad, but the woman's words and the reality of our life struck Momma's heart. To this day, I have never forgotten Momma standing up and telling me to get Lil Dee before handing her friend all of the freshly refilled prescriptions for pain medicine. "Here Kelly, you can have these, I'm done!" Momma said, and then we walked out of the door and into my first tomorrow.

Chapter 10

All of the many twelve-step programs like Alcoholics Anonymous are completely interchangeable with their sister groups, as all additions, aside from opiate and alcohol addictions, are very much alike. With both alcohol and opiates, there is the added chemical and physical piece to the addiction puzzle that makes staying clean extremely hard because as well as the many emotional reasons that we seek to destroy ourselves, even after we know that we are helpless and facing our death, there is that chemical reason, a physical monster that the other addictions do not have. Even addiction to cocaine lacks this beast of burden.

So for alcoholics and narcotics users, A.A. and N.A. meetings are the same — if you miss an A.A. meeting, you can go to an upcoming N.A. meeting and feel at home, surrounded by people who understand that your body is as addicted as your mind. It is not uncommon to find people who have both addictions or just one of the pair, but who feel safe at a Homegroup that by name represents treatment of the opposite addiction. Where it would be hard for a gambling addict to fit in at an over-eaters meeting, alcoholics and drug addicts are right at home in mixed company. We gain strength from the ties we make by being honest in the rooms, as we like to call them. It's the people in your Homegroup, and the honesty you bring with you, that matter, and not the chemical you get high on.

By the same token, there are people who pick a Homegroup because they feel that a particular group will not hold them to the daunting task of recovery, but those people seldom stay long — death and jail due to relapse tend to weed out those people who wish to hide from themselves. Death is an equal part of recovery, it hangs out waiting for you to get weak or for your mind to tell you that you have not gotten high in so long that this high will feel like your first time, heavenly. And then, not wishing to waste a chance to feel that good again, you fail to realize that your body is clean of drugs, or that opiates are poison, so you take a little too much and you die, simple as that. Death might cause one person to stay sober, but it normally becomes an excuse for others to relapse.

We were not strangers to the many rooms of A.A and N.A. as part of Momma's scamming the rehabilitation system was having to go to meetings. After all, the scam was based on the fact that she was trying to stay clean and sober, but just couldn't do so for any length of time. Relapse is an accepted part of recovery, so why not take advantage of its acceptance? Momma would always have Lil Dee or myself volunteer to help run the meeting we were attending. We would pick up coffee cups, empty ashtrays, make coffee, set up chairs, but above all we would stamp the many attendance slips brought into every meeting, day or night. These attendance slips were the only way to prove to your judge or probation officer that you were going to A.A . or N.A. meetings as the court had ordered. We would always put extra attendance slips into the pile and then stamp them so that Momma could sell them to people who had missed that meeting, people who would go to jail if they did not buy one from her. Us being little girls helped the people in the rooms to trust us.

There is an ugly fact that no one in recovery is without deep regret: we cannot help but regret the way that we mistreated the children in our own family, the ones we let down in order to get high. Even I regretted teaching Lil Dee to steal things with me, though I know that it was not really my fault. It was the same type of guilt that caused the people running the meetings to automatically assume that Lil Dee and I were not a part of the problem but victims of it, so it shocked me when Momma told us not to volunteer to stamp the attendance slips anymore. We were homeless, and very poor, yet Momma was done getting high, so we lived without money, staying all day and night in this meeting room or in that meeting room if no one had offered to let us sleep at their house for the night. I have to stress the overnight part of this, as addicts cannot live together for the first few years of recovery, as they tend to help each other relapse. Recovery has to become a daily part of your life in order for it to work, so instead of trying to forget about getting high, you talk about it every day, and it takes time to get strong.

After about a month of living like this, two old-timers, Mr. Bear and his wife Ms. Linda, started to show concern for us. They would bring us food, clean clothes, and have us sit with them through a meeting. They could see by Momma's actions that she was serious about staying off of drugs this time, so they offered her a job at a small diner that they owned over on the Kentucky side of Kermit. I always loved the fact that Kermit sat in West Virginia and Kentucky — as a child it seemed almost exotic. We silly humans really are easy to please when we're young, aren't we?

Her job came with an apartment that was right above the restaurant. "After all, it would be easier to feed y'all there rather than to constantly be bringing food and clothes to the meeting rooms!" Mr. Bear playfully said. Also, if a woman wanted to relapse, a meeting room was the perfect place to find whatever she needed to do so: "Horny men are always searching for someone to scratch their itch!" Ms. Linda said with a laugh, pointing out that Momma could be broke, not a penny to her name and still relapse with ease.

Momma's desire to get well was all that she had to protect herself and us with, so the Bears decided to adopt us, to reward Momma's hard work with love before relapse found its way into her heart, and death left Lil Dee and me alone, homeless, with only the monsters of addiction and bad family traditions to turn to. I will forever remember our time living and loving the Bears. They were some of the best days in our lives, and it is these simple pieces of my life that I worry that some lying archaeologist will misunderstand when he digs up my grave and displays my naked bones for all the world to see. I don't mind that the fool will swear on a stack of Bibles that I was a cannibal. Hell, I may just have folks bury me with a necklace made of teeth or a cannibal's cookbook just to mess with my grave robbers a little, you know, have a little fun.

But what scares me the most is that the Bears' gift of love to us will be forgotten, lost. Plates and bottles leave traces behind for history to find, but love, and the acts of kindness that are a part of that love, simply vanish once no one is here to remember them. Oh, we can look at the foundation of a grand palace said to be built by one human to show his love for another — surely it was built out of love we tell ourselves as we daydream about being loved that much, but how do we know that large grand palace was not built out of hate, or a need to stay as far away from each other as possible? Can you imagine Mark Antony laughing wholeheartedly at an archaeologists after hearing the claims that he had loved Cleopatra so much that he conquered the world for her?

"I didn't give up Rome and get into all of those fights because I loved Cleopatra, you idiot. I did all of that stuff so I would not have to go home and be around her. She was moody, always telling me that we were meant to die together and playing with them snakes. That bitch was stone-cold crazy — nuttier than a king-sized Baby Ruth candy bar!" Antony would laugh and say as the archaeologists, dreaming of the book contract and job promotion he would receive after landing an interview with Antony's ghost, would instantly start writing lies about what the great man had told him, because the truth must always be romantic, sort of dreamy, or no one will want to hear about it. Our life with the Bears was not romantic, but it is the one place in time that I wish that I could return to and relive again, only this time without Momma relapsing.

We had to go to school, and to daily A.A. meetings, and we all worked at the Bears' restaurant. Yes, it was a family job, not a real one, but Mr. Bear said that he was getting old and that we should know all of jobs there were in our family business or we might try to milk a bull once he passed on and not milk the cows. We would all laugh at him for saying something so silly and he would explain that this was not funny at all because if you don't know what you're doing, first, the bull will get mad and knock the barn down.

Second, the poor milk cows, having gone un-milked, will swell up and die, causing you twice the trouble. "So work hard and learn how to be responsible," Mr. Bear would firmly say. And Lil Dee, now five years old and bright as a button, would say in a serious tone: "Now, Mr. Bear, cows have big boobies and bull cows got a ding-a-ling! Everybody knows that!" We would all laugh along with her and you could see in Mr. Bear's eyes that he was trying to think of a way to explain things to Lil Dee that did not involve the obvious boobies or ding-a-lings as the cows did.

"Got yourself outsmarted by a five-year-old!" Ms. Linda would laugh and say, ensuring that Mr. Bear and Lil Dee were locked in a loving competition of words from that moment on.

Mr. Bear was no stranger to fighting. When most men are nicknamed Bear, it is due to their size, and not to their fearless nature. Yet Mr. Bear was not only large as a mountain, he was also fearless. But he was also gentle as a lamb, tender and sensitive to a fault, and he hated himself for having two completely opposite natures. It was as if life or God had conspired to make a man such as him, only to then sit back and watch him whirlwind out of control as the two halves of the Bear's soul fought for control of his one heart, always leaving a trail of pain and destruction behind after every fight.

In the twelve-step program rooms, you are taught to share your life story, to talk openly about anything. A person would think that these conversations would turn into a weenie measuring contest, with each person trying to outdo the other; but in the rooms, death, either your own or that of the person you are talking with, will be the price of playing such a foolish game. This is not a could be, nor a maybe, it's a fact. Each time you relapse on drugs or alcohol, the more your body will resist your next attempt to get sober and to stay clean. The longer you stay out getting high, the more chances death has to find you.

So in the rooms, talking and sharing are sacred parts of the program. You do not need to respond to what a person says. Most of the time it is not a response that they are seeking, but rather the understanding that they receive from putting their life into words. For most members, it is the first time that they have contemplated their own life. My daddy, Bobby, swore that every life story was pure gold, worth more than a person could imagine, but that story had to be shared with others, as you both contemplated its meaning. Only then would its value be felt, or its lessons learned.

So honesty in the rooms was the most important part of recovery and was treated as such. Lil Dee once told Mr. Bear that a man named Billy Joe was lying when he stood up and said that he had never smoked crack cocaine and that she and I had watched him smoking it and then laughed at how he looked like a chicken afterwards, walking back and forth while staring at the floor. "He ain't really lying Dee", Mr. Bear had said. "The man just ain't ready to admit that sin yet. Now girl, you cannot jump up and correct him, but after the meeting you girls go over and apologize to him for saying that he acted like a chicken when you watched him get high. That will be enough to remind him that God sees everything."

Chapter 11

I know that I must have seen and also heard Mr. Bear give a lead before, but I had never paid any attention to him. Our goal and reason for being at those meetings at that time was to support Momma in her quest to stay high, so the stories we heard in the rooms meant little to me. You can't imagine my surprise when I finally listened to the big man's story.

"I am a coward, plain and simple," Mr. Bear would begin each time he told his story. "That's why my son is dead, that's why Ms. Linda has no grandchildren, that's why I wasted twenty years drinking and running away from myself, that's why I am standing up here telling you my story," he would say, as he softly pounded his large hand on the speaker's podium. "My troubles with drinking did not start because I stole my daddy's liquor and cigarettes when I was a boy. Some of y'all like to stand up here and say just that, blame a childish stunt, but I don't believe that stealing a little moonshine when we were kids is the real reason why any of us are in this room tonight.

No, I'm sure that there is a deeper reason for us allowing alcohol and drugs to pull us down into this pit that we all find ourselves trying to climb out of today. Y'all will have to decide what brought you to the rooms for yourself, but for me, it's because I am a stone cold coward!" Mr. Bear would say this in a voice that challenged anyone in the room to try and contradict him. His size, as well as his hard eyes and the anger in his voice, all stood in stark contrast to his claims of being a coward, and the effect was chilling.

"The big war was over when a little place called Korea got our President's attention and he called for his boys to stand up and go fight. Now y'all know West Virginia came about because of a war, and our support of our President in that war. Plus, I had seen how my uncles and the other hometown boys looked in their uniforms and medals after the big war. So there was no way in hell you were going to stop me from signing up and going over there to get me a uniform, medals, respect, and the false sense of masculinity that came with them." Mr. Bear would pause here each time he told his story as if he was searching his mind for the right words to explain a great mystery.

"Those things are all petty, trash, nothing at all really. Hell, that old polio cripple Toby Fields up there in Wheeling, why he has earned more respect and masculinity by raising fighting dogs to feed his family than I ever earned by fighting in a war," Mr. Bear would say, his right hand raised in the air pointing to the east, towards Wheeling, West Virginia, as if no one knew the way.

"Now I know that fighting dogs ain't looked upon as respectful anymore, and to be honest I never saw much good in it either, but that ain't the point here. The point is that fate or God gave old Toby a hard row to hoe, a mean life to try to live; it let polio twist his legs up bad, but old Toby didn't let it twist his heart. He found a way to grow and care for a family of his own, and to never miss a day of being there to love and care for them. Whereas you and me," Mr. Bear would pause as he looked sternly around the room, "we waste years of our lives and our families' lives twisting our souls up on rotgut liquor and no-account drugs. I suppose what I'm trying to say is the drugs and the whiskey ain't the problem. It's something inside of us that makes us broken, and for me it was my ego, myself image, pride, and the name Bear are what led me to an addict's sufferings, but only after I killed my son. I killed my own son!" Mr. Bear would say this in such a way that you could feel everyone in the room gasp no matter how many times they had heard his lead before.

"My addiction started on a cold winter night in North Korea. Our unit was set on the top of a small hill, a hill that we were to guard and hold on to no matter what. 'No Matter What!' sounds good in a movie, but in real life it's about the scariest thing a man can hear in a war. I had been in Korea long enough to know that as far north as we were, China would be sending troops over the border to help them Northern Koreans we were fighting. Not that they needed any help, don't ever be mistaken in that. Those boys were as tough as any man in any war there ever was, and they didn't need any help at all. Trust me when I say that." Mr. Bear would inhale deeply, his eyes seeming to look into his mind and not out at the room around him, only to then snap out of this fog as if he had never left us at all.

"I don't want to tell my story to y'all in such a way as to draw your attention to the fighting, the bleeding and the dying. I don't subscribe to the modern media's idea that every man who went off to war is mentally broken by what he sees over there. I think that every man who volunteers to go fight, well he knows the definition of the world war, so he is ready to see the horror of it; not that he likes it, but the shock is lessened by the expected experience of war.

How many of us knew a girl in school who could not wait to find a way out of the hills, and like a fool, she accepted a ride from a pimp out at Ruby's truck stop, knowing full well the price she would have to pay for that choice? How many times have we heard women stand at this very podium, early in their recovery, and try to tell us that they were a victim of the pimp. Yet later, after they had matured in their recovery, we would hear them admit that they had fully understood the price of the ride that they had accepted, or that they had thought that they could easily trick the pimp and run off, once safely away from these hills? We have all heard them tell us over and over that they could not find and keep their sobriety until they fully accepted responsibility for the part they played in their own downfall. Y'all have to see that honesty means looking into the mirror and being honest with yourself.

"Well, that's what I'm trying to do in my lead, I'm trying to show you how to be honest with yourselves because if you don't get honest, then you might get dry and stay clean for a while, but you won't ever have the sobriety we all crave so much. So, look into your hearts and dig out the root causes of your addiction. Sure, a doctor gave you the pills you got hooked on, but you were the one who decided you liked getting high on them, just like I decided that I liked being a hero after that night them boys came at us over that hill over there. You see, it got really bad for a while, and a lot of my men, my friends decided to run away. I don't blame them, everyone was screaming and dying, it was real bad.

So bad, in fact, that I was too scared to even try to run away with them. I just prayed, begged God really, I mean, I really begged God to save me as I tried to stay alive. And then a flare lit up the sky, and them Korean boys stopped fighting, grabbed their dead and wounded and then slipped back into the darkness from where they had come. Now the Koreans, they knew that I was scared that night. They would look at me as they picked up their fallen and just grin at me, as if they knew I was done, through with fighting. That I was a screaming uncle, a coward, and that I would not shoot them. They knew something that I never told my son, something more important than anything else that I could teach my boy: they knew that I was scared and very, very thankful that those Koreans decided to pull back and leave us that hill." Mr. Bear would look into Ms. Linda's eyes at this point in his story as if asking her permission to continue and to talk about their lost son.

"Now, I had no intention of claiming to be a hero, but the Army gave me some medals," Mr. Bear would say as he took his medals out of his shirt pocket and held them up for everyone to see, their ribbons torn, dirty and stained. They didn't look like they were either loved or wanted — almost every house in the hills has Army medals hanging from its walls in glass frames, protected as if those medals were extremely fragile, but Mr. Bear's looked as if they had been in the war themselves.

"I'm growing old, so there are few folks left running these hills who knew myself or Ms. Linda back in the days just after the war. But some of y'all are as old as we are and I'm sure you remember how I let this Silver Star define the man that I was," Mr. Bear would say as he picked up the tattered medal from the podium where he had placed it with the other, a Purple Heart. "Why, turns out that nobody around these parts had earned a Silver Star in the big war and lived to march in local parades, or to judge the farm animals at the county fair each summer. Boy, it sure is funny how just having this star would get me invited to join social clubs, or churches, as if by earning it I was somehow changed. That by having this medal I became more than the son of a coal miner, more than I really was. Maybe if I had honestly earned it, well then, I might have grown a set of angel wings, and when I took a shit, harps would play and it would smell like a flower shop!" Mr. Bear would always pause at this point in his story and laugh along with us at the idea of a shit smelling like a flower shop.

"I asked my commander, when he came to the hospital to hand me this Purple Heart, why he was putting my name forward to be awarded a Silver Star as all I had really done was stay put, like I had been ordered to, and sure I had fought, but no harder than anyone else. My commander then motioned for the reporters and photographers from the military newspapers to give him a moment alone with me. It was then that he explained to me how, during the war, no single army had enough men to send human waves of soldiers at a hill or base, but that the North Koreans and the Chinese had more than enough men to overwhelm almost any outpost we had. It was doing something mentally to then men because many were breaking down and running away from the constant nightly human wave attacks. My commander told me that my not running away was heroic and if other men saw me get highly awarded and read my story and others like it, it would help them get past their fear of being completely overwhelmed by the enemy. That more would stay at their guns, and the enemy would learn that it did not own the night.

"Then my commander took out a flask of whisky and we shared a drink. He told me that medals, all of them, are bullshit, that they're handed out to men less for what that man did or did not do, but more to inspire other men to act as we had. He said that he knew I had been scared that night and had stopped fighting because the enemy had been able to retrieve all their dead and wounded. 'Had your hillbilly ass still been fighting, we would have found you dead at your post and not whimpering like a puppy as we did,' he said. Then, after sharing another drink with me, he told me it was now my duty to be a hero, and to act like it, because that would save more lives than the truth ever would."

Mr. Bear's voice would get very low at this point in his story and I could feel the humiliation he felt over his actions in the tone of his voice. After so many years, it still weighed heavy on his heart. Even at my age, I knew that the boys in the hills around home saw military medals as holy, so for Mr. Bear to have been so scared that he stopped fighting, as well as to then lie about it, and to accept those unearned medals, was a sin as unforgivable as cussing out Jesus or your mother. By telling his story, Mr. Bear was taking away the unquestionable glory and honor of every medal that hung on the many walls of family homes in the region.

For many folks around here, those medals were a sad but fair trade for the life of a cousin, friend or neighbor. Now, after hearing Mr. Bear explain that medals were often handed out as a means of troop motivation, it was as if Mr. Bear had killed Jesus, slapped Santa Claus, beaten up the Easter Bunny, and robbed the Tooth Fairy all in one night. I could hear disbelief in the mumblings of some of the men in the room after Mr. Bear would finish his lead, as they tried to come to terms with some small piece of the big man's story. Some would say that their own family members had been there in Korea that night, on the same hill, with 'The Bear' as men called him, and that Mr. Bear was lying to make a point to everyone about how important it is to be willing to look deep into your own soul and to be willing to sacrifice even sacred objects or your own name if you wanted to find your sobriety. Other men would laugh and say that Mr. Bear was a typical big man, large, loud, and harmless, but few men ever voiced their opinions to 'The Bear' himself.

"Once I got home, everyone treated me as if I was somebody. I was given bank loans on my word of honor; we, Ms. Linda and

I, were asked our opinions on just about anything that had to do with anything in the county; hell, when the governor would come to visit, I was always asked to be there. I was somebody, I was important, and our son grew up believing just that. So when the Vietnam War started, our boy took off and went up to Wheeling. Him and a bunch of other local boys thought the country folks would be proud that, while in other parts of the country, men were rebelling against the draft, West Virginia's sons were carpooling all the way up to Wheeling to sign up to fight for their country as their daddies had done." Mr. Bear would be softly crying and mumbling things like "Those damn fools!" or "Stupid kids!" as he would say the names of the three-county sons that he felt in his heart had died in Vietnam because of his ego.

"I wasn't worried at first about us losing our son; he was an only child, so I was certain that he would never even get sent to Asia. But a hero's son would never accept that, so our boy signed the papers and volunteered to go to Vietnam. I could have sat the fool boy down his last night home before he was shipped out and told him the truth, a truth that I had conveniently forgotten. I could have told him of my fear and cowardice and the truth about this Silver Star. But my ego was in my way, so I could not see how a son will always try his hardest to do at least as well as his father has done, it's human nature, simple foolish human nature." Mr. Bear would falter every time at this point in his story and look to Ms. Linda's caring eyes for support. Mr. Bear's own eyes seemed to plead for her to tell him that he had shared enough for tonight, to come and sit beside her where she could hold him and heal his heart, but she would always softly say, "It's alright Bear, go on, say it. He forgives you; I forgive you," and somehow Mr. Bear would find the words to continue.

"They shipped our boy home in a metal box, gave us some medals, a tombstone, a flag that it is now legal to burn or spit on, and an insurance policy that I used in part to buy that big old 1972 Delta 88 that graces that parking lots of these rooms now." Mr. Bear would then pull out two pristine military medals, a Purple

Heart like his own and a Bronze Star; their clean, loved appearance stood out in stark contrast to the worn and tattered look of his own, and even Lil Dee understood the meaning this symbolized. "Mr. Bear don't like his own medals but he loves Lil Bear's," she would say, placing an emphasis on the name Lil Bear as if she was his namesake and not the child of a woman that a man like Lil Bear wouldn't be caught dead with.

"I would spend the next twenty years racing around, going from bar to bar, drug house to drug house, getting drunk and high, picking fights. Some nights, I just wanted to die, other nights I was fighting to prove to myself that I was not a coward and that my cowardice and lies had not gotten our son killed. But most of the time, I got drunk and drove that big fancy car as fast as I could because my son would always be there in the car beside me: I could see him, feel him, even smell him, and the faster I went, the louder the tires screamed on these mountain country roads, the longer my boy would stay beside me.

"For years, I struggled with the choice of killing myself or continuing on as I was. If I killed myself and my boy was not there on the other side, then I would never see him again. So once again, I chose the cowards' way out, and I decided to continue to get drunk and drive fast, only now I would explain my heart to my boy, I would beg his forgiveness. And then one night, as I was driving fast, drunk and crying, I heard our son call me a liar. He said that if I really felt as bad as I said I did over lying about being a hero, then why was I being so selfish and hurting his mother?

It was then that I began to understand that my boy had saved me all of those drunken nights because if I had killed myself, it would have hurt his mother even worse than his own death had, it would leave Ms. Linda completely alone. I also realized that my ego had selfishly kept me from being honest about my own heroics. I never stopped to humble myself when people praised my war record — in fact, I would often get upset if I felt that I had not been properly admired as a hero. Funny the things we do to keep up a false image of who we think that we are," Mr. Bear would laugh and say as he smiled with relief.

"Now don't get me wrong, we spent a couple of hard years trying to get me to dry out after that night our boy spoke to me, and I had work the Fourth Step about ten times before I understood what it meant by a 'searching and fearless moral inventory.' You would be shocked at how many good hillbillies are rotting in their graves because of those words. Hell, most folks rush right through that step — they might make a list of what they own, and other foolishness, like saying that they lie a lot or don't like this or that, but few are wise enough to dig into their hearts to find the really tough things.

It's the wording of step four: 'Make a searching and fearless moral inventory of ourselves'. These are words most of us seldom use in our day-to-day life, so we make an inventory of our possessions, trying not to lie about them, being honest. Step four is an early step in the program, so surely it means for them to count how many things they own, and that is true, but it also means for us to search our hearts for the good and the bad feelings that we own, for us to look at the parts of our souls that we don't like to talk about, or for others to know about.

Mr. Bear would smile every time at this point in his story and begin to laugh. Most of the people in the room who knew his story would laugh along with as he would look to a man who was at almost every meeting, asking for permission to include him in his lead. "Y'all know Gay Tom there!" Mr. Bear would say as he pointed to Tom. "Of course you know him, ain't a person in this room that ain't got help from Tom at one time or another. I always get a kick out of the new guys who the judge sends over for meetings, and how they mumble about Tom being gay; it must scare them some. But then they need a ride home, or some kind of help, and Tom steps up to help them. Before long, them same fools who was mumbling about Tom being a little light in the loafers are now his friend.

But what few people know is that Tom drank and drugged for years, he couldn't stay clean; he worked the steps and relapsed.

Then tragically his daddy died. I figured that I would need to take Tom some underwear and stuff down to the county jail soon, as most people will use any reason that they can as an excuse to relapse. But Tom walked into this room, stood up behind this podium, and told us that he was gay. He went on to say that we were to call him Gay Tom from now on, and that his daddy's death had freed him to live and to be happy. And Gay Tom just passed five years clean last month!"

Mr. Bear would pause and allow the weight of his words to sink in. "Y'all see — Tom could never stay clean as long as he was lying to himself and to the world around him about who he truly is inside, and that was Gay Tom. He had to get honest to stay clean. So don't cheat on step four, always remember that you will evolve and grow as you start to live a dry or clean life. There are going to be places in your heart that you may not be ready to open the door to just yet, it will take time. In my opinion, step four is not an action that you do and then it's complete, but instead it becomes a daily part of your life — you teach yourself to inventory the good and the bad events, emotions, and attitudes that you own everyday. Now you're conscious of how things affect your heart, soul and life, you begin to stock up on more of the good things in life, and less of the bad. You stop poisoning your soul by allowing your feelings to grow into hurtful monsters. Tom de-weaponized his being homosexual by telling everyone to call him Gay Tom. I suppose that I'm telling you that no one really completes step four. Once you learn how good it feels to be honest with yourself, you come out of your own closet, no matter what that closet may be. You find the happiness that drugs and booze promised but never really gave you."

Mr. Bear's grin was a warning that he was about to end his lead with his favorite catchphrase: "Honesty saves lives." As a group, those of us who knew Mr. Bear's lead would loudly follow Mr. Bear, saying "Honesty saves lives, so get honest!" and then we would all share a short laugh before closing the meeting with a prayer. It was not that we were laughing at Mr. Bear's words, but instead at how everyone had learned to speak together as one, as a family, like us calling Mr. Tom 'Gay Tom' or 'Mr. Gay Tom' — he was family. He enjoyed the laughs and odd looks his name got him from the new people in the rooms. We were not being mean, but instead relaxing and enjoying the family that being honest with yourself brings you.

September was coming to a close. Momma had just over ninety days clean, and Lil Dee and I were enjoying school. I didn't wear Mickey as my mask — both Dee and I were happy to be wearing the mask of good normal children whose grandparents loved then dearly. It is very easy for children to believe what their tiny hearts want them to believe, so Lil Dee and gladly accepted and played the role of loved grandchildren, as we pushed Momma in her role as the loved daughter. Today, I feel so stupid when I think back to that time in my life — Kermit was just too small for me to tell lies like that. We could never have been the Bears' grand babies, their son was dead long before Momma was born, plus the whole town knew that Momma was a drug addict and a whore. But this is an understanding, a knowledge, that comes from the heart of the lonely old woman that I am today and not the child I was, a child who enjoyed every day she shared with the Bears.

No day was better than the day that they gave Momma the Beast, that big old 1972 delta 88, the same one that rests in my yard today. The same one that I hope to drive up to heaven in and give God a piece of my mind once I leave this earth. Momma had proven herself trustworthy to the Bears, as well as us girls, by working hard to stay clean, working hard at her job, and working hard to be the type of mother that we had always wanted her to be, so the Bears rewarded her by giving her their old car. "It kept my Bear safe all those years girl, we know that it will keep you girls safe too," Ms. Linda softly said as she hugged my mother after Bear told her that the car was now ours.

From that day on, Momma did her best to make time for us to go racing around the countryside, laughing as she pushed down hard on the gas pedal, and screaming over the roar of the old car's motor, as the tires screamed back at her. We would shoot through curves, sliding from one side of the backseat to the other, laughing happily, only to race down the straight roadways, praying to find a belly tickler of a hill to go over so we could feel the joy of the ground dropping out from beneath us. On days that we didn't go driving, Momma would let me and Lil Dee wash and wax the old car and Mr. Bear would laugh at me when I would drive the big car in the parking lot of the restaurant with my head fighting to see over the steering wheel, singing my heart out, practicing the songs that I hoped to hear on the radio the next time Momma took us driving.

I will never forget the sound of Momma singing to the radio, then holding my hand with a look in her eyes that made up for all the bad things that we had seen, all the pain that we had felt, and all of the unknown hells we were sure to face with her in the future. When you're broken inside, you have a clock that beats deep within your heart. It tells you that you don't deserve to be happy; that your world will fall apart soon; and that nothing good ever came from love, as love is just an illusion, sweet words and jesters hidden by the foggy poison we call love. A poison so desirable that it will cause broken people, lonely souls, to race headfirst into destruction when they hear the clock bell tolling, telling them that life has been good for too long; telling them that they know that they are not normal; telling them that God is toying with them like a cat toy with a mouse; telling them to run before the pain begins. And in the case of addiction, that horrible bell's ringing tells them it's time to relapse.

Chapter 12

Momma meant to return to the other women in the rooms the love and care that they had shown to us when we had lived in the rooms. Her intentions were both good and honest, but all Momma owned was that car, and where would one addict drive another addict to so early in their recovery? There are so many reasons why opiate addicts continue to use at the start of their recovery — the key one being that the physical part of their addiction drives them to use just to stay well enough to go to a meeting, but that can't help but lead to them getting high. At first, Momma would turn down any offers of free drugs made by the women she drove to or from meetings — car rides that always had an extra stop at a store, or a dope house.

Momma knew that men would use her for her body, but she did not understand that she was now a woman with a car and that the other woman would cling to her friendship because of that car and her understanding of their need for drugs. Momma's car stopped her from having to service random men to get high, just as her car stopped the other women from having to service men for a ride to the dope house. Addicted women learn early that the price of their addiction will always be paid at some time or in some way with their bodies unless they own a car, and now Momma had her body as well as that damn car.

I could see in her eyes that she was high one afternoon as we raced around the hills in that car. "I needed it, Page!" Momma said as a means of apology to us for getting high again. "Just gonna get high every now and then, I promise," she said. But all three of us were addicts — we had followed Momma this far, so like a fool I did not scream liar, or tell the Bears on her. We were the Three

96

Musketeers weren't we? Three foolish ones, and it would not be long before we proved it once again to the world, at the cost of the Bears' love.

Thanksgiving was fast approaching. Lil Dee and I were looking forward to having a normal family dinner. We were doing our best to act as if we weren't extremely excited at the prospect of being with our loved ones, eating turkey, pie, and cranberry sauce. But Ms. Linda knew that we had never known a normal holiday. She began to teach us how to bake cookies and treats. Things that her mother and grandmothers had taught her how to cook, rather than the sweet treats that have grown stale and moldy, rotting in my heart, that I was used to. But like so many other lessons that I learned as a child, the good things, the loving things, will always be hidden in the shadows of Momma's addiction and the pain caused by 'It'.

Momma had been coming in late to meetings, even missing one or two. She always had another woman to blame, but excuses that were good enough to fool a normal person did not go far in a house full of addicts. Mr. Bear saw them for the lies that they were, and tried to gently pull Momma back from the cliff's ledge before she began to use drugs everyday again. But Momma didn't respond to anything handed to her gently — it was as if she was nearly blind and could only see an object after she had run into it or it had knocked her down.

At that time, I didn't have sixty years of reliving my memories, searching my soul for what I could have done differently, how I could have saved our family. Today, I would have the strength and the knowledge to tell the Bears how to deal with Momma: "Go at her hard! That stupid bitch has no understanding of love, you have to make her listen to you! Like a dog that pees on the carpet, you have to rub her nose into the wet spots as you scream 'No,' over and over before tossing her outside!" But I was just a stupid child who loved her mother to a fault.

Momma could not keep her eyes open or her head up as we began to set the dinner table for Thanksgiving. Mr. Bear and several other men from the other rooms were in the living room trying to watch the parade on TV. All of the women were scurrying around the kitchen, cooking and laughing with each other as Momma sat in a chair, nodding off, going in and out of that glorious dream world. I had rarely seen her this high, if ever at all, and I knew that she was not high on something she normally used.

Heroin at this time was still considered a bad drug, and could not find a market in the hills, but as with OxyContin, some asshole with a degree had made a new drug called Fentanyl which was put into a patch to be worn for three days at a time to treat pain. They called it transdermal pain treatment and, like Oxy, every retired person who claimed any pain at all was prescribed this new safe treatment — and it was, of course, paid for by the government. By the time Momma found out about Fentanyl patches, doctors were prescribing them to people for almost anything. People were beginning to die from misusing them — mixing them with other drugs, and cutting them open and eating part of the medicine and sharing the rest with their friends. I even heard one of Momma's friends tell another woman to get a patch then split it with her husband and his mother. Afterward take them to the bar and get them shitfaced drunk; that once her husband's mother went to sleep, she would die. The cops would call it heart failure, or an accidental death — either way it was an easy way to off the old woman and collect her insurance money. Funny thing about this story is that they all three died the same night from misadventure according to the police, and no one ever got the insurance money and no one was left to mourn their passing.

I hate both the government and the doctors for what they did to the hill country's people. This was not the first opiate epidemic in America, we had weathered many over the years, but those storms of addiction could not penetrate the hills of West Virginia, Kentucky, Tennessee, nor any of the mountain states. Country morals and fear of your grandmother, if not fear of God, kept people from using drugs like heroin in the hills. In order to become an addict, you had to move to the big city where the drugs were.

But with government approval of high powered drug treatment like OxyContin and Fentanyl patches, it meant that the government would pay the doctors for prescribing these types of treatments, as government approval equals money, period.

It's so simple to see, today, that had the government not been willing to pay the doctors, then these types of treatments would only have been prescribed in the extreme instances for which they were designed. But instead, they were used to treat anything and everything, robbing the hills and the rest of our nation of her people, thus only benefiting the doctors, pharmacies, funeral homes, and the political class — those on the inside who knew which pill was going to be approved, or in words, which pharmaceutical company to buy stock in. "Take your money out of coal, Bob, and place it in opiates — trust me, it's a sure bet, my fellow congressmen and I took a vote. It's for the best anyways, dead coal miners can't cry about losing their jobs, can they?"

I'm sorry, there I go avoiding the painful part of the story. But that doesn't mean that what I said isn't true — a lot of people made money off of the drugs that were handed out like candy and paid for through Medicaid, Medicare, and Welfare, at the cost of how many lives?

Mr. Bear tried to get Momma to sober up some, to drink some coffee, but she only stopped nodding off and became loud. This caused Mr. Bear to ask Gay Tom to help him get Momma upstairs to our apartment and into bed, which led to my mother saying some very nasty things. These things had been brewing in Momma's heart since the first day that the Bears had been kind to her. In Momma's world, no one was kind to you, or gave you anything nice, without wanting either sex, money, drugs or a ride in your car. And while she was high that day, she lost all of her discreetness and manners. Today, I believe that she was hurt by the idea that Mr. Bear was trying to get her up to her apartment to take advantage of her, and it was her pain that caused her to strike out in such an evil way.

"Why Bear, I knew you would sneak upstairs sooner or later for some pussy, but Gay Tom? Why you freaky old goat!"

Momma said with a slurred laugh. "Why don't you get that big black motherfucker Tony over there as well, he's been eye-fucking me since the day we met. Come on, let's all go upstairs and have us a good time. Asshole, I knew I couldn't trust you!" Momma screamed as Ms. Linda and the other women came in from the kitchen to assure Momma that Bear, Gay Tom and Tony meant her no harm. But Momma was broken inside, and broken people forget to be civil when they're drunk or high. They say what they want, and confront what they are afraid of. Momma attacked Ms. Linda with words as sharp as knives.

"No way, you old bitch. I'll let your old man fuck me for fun, but no way I'll ever let you take my babies, you old barren bitch. You had your chance at being a Momma, you ain't getting my girls!" Momma screamed as she looked at me and said, "Page, get your sister, now. They're trying to take her from us again!" Go to the car, now, we have to go, now, come on!"

This will forever be a point in my life when I know for a fact that our life would have been better had I not listened to Momma, had I stood there and refused to grab Lil Dee and run to the car. But Momma's voice was full of fear, and her fears where my fears, so we ran away with her. Today, I believe that the Bears let us drive away expecting Momma to calm down, sober up, and come home before it was time to eat. The things that Momma had screamed were mean, but they grew out of her fear — no one had ever loved us, the Bears understood this, so I'm sure that they felt it was best to let her go for now and to address her heart's fear with love, not anger, once she returned home. In fact, that day would have been a turning point in Momma's search for sobriety had she just returned home to them. But we left everything we owned in that apartment and never returned to the Bears' home or a meeting ever again. Like with Lil Dee's father, Momma knew that she was wrong that day, but as usual, her way of facing an issue of any type was to walk away from it, to move on — after all, she had her baby girls and that damn car!

That big beautiful car that today I worry no archaeologist will ever understand, that car, the single greatest gift anyone ever gave to Momma, was in this instance a tool of our coming destruction. I'm sure you think I'm crazy to love something that was instrumental in Momma's downfall, but a car is just steel, rubber, and gas, and in no way at fault for our life to come, but rather a simple witness. Before, when we had no car, Momma's options for starting over would have been to return to the rehabilitation center or to return to us sleeping in the rooms that would allow us to do so. But both of these would have led us back to the Bears and to Momma having to face the hurtful things she had said to them, as well as having to look into the hole in her heart that those feelings had come from — and my mother had no intention of ever facing her inner demons.

So instead she began to drive addicts to buy dope, or to Ruby's truck stop to turn tricks, or to the houses and motels of the men who found her and her girlfriends' escort ads on the internet. Our car became her lifeline, her friends needed her, for rides, and she needed them. Even though she spent most of the money she earned on gas and getting high, Lil Dee and I never once had to shoplift food to eat, nor did we ever do it for fun either. I sill take pride in the fact that no matter how low our life got, we never stole for the fun of it. I know that this is a stupid thing to take pride in, but I at least know that stealing is wrong.

I began to see him at night as Lil Dee and I waited for Momma outside of drug houses, or the homes of the men who called her to come over and entertain them. He would be standing in the shadows where the man made glow of the outside lights gave up its fight and allowed night's blackness to consume the world again. He would be dressed in green army clothes, like the men in the war movies that I had seen, and he would be watching us, protecting us. I know that he was the ghost of Mr. Bear's son and that we would be safe. That we were not alone, and that maybe, just maybe, Lil Bear, as we called him would go tell his parents how much Lil Dee and I missed them; after all, when we were with them, I could be a child and make childish plans for my tomorrows.

But out here in the world, surrounded by drugs, addicts and

whores, the only future that I had any chance at was to grow up and be like Momma. School was something I told myself that I could live without, but something that Lil Dee must not be denied, and I began to question my mother's need to eat every pill she earned. I wanted her to give me some to save and sell at a profit, instead of us having to race around the countryside every time someone asked her for a ride. No, I never said as much, never gave voice to these ideas, but my hints were certainly getting her attention.

Chapter 13

Sara's body had given way to the power of heroin withdrawal. She had only eaten a few stale crackers and drunk a mouthful of yesterday's Mountain Dew soda pop. Its sweetness tasted heavenly until her stomach screamed out a warning that forced her to race into the bathroom and put her face nearly into the water of the motel's toilet as she began to throw up a yellow-green vomit that seemed to be more bile than crackers or vomit. On her third wrenching stomach heave, her bowels let go and Sara found herself shitting out the same yellow-green bile that she was vomiting. Its smell, and the slimy feel of her own shit running down her legs, caused Sara to vomit even more. With each painful heave of her now cramping stomach, Sara shit more until she was dry heaving in pain.

"I can't do this," Sara said aloud to her child, as she found herself curling up in the cool clean bathtub, without concern for how nasty her body was, nor for the smells of the small room. "We can't do this, my child, Andy's right. Going completely cold turkey, without even one shot a day, has to be hurting you more than it is hurting me," Sara told her unborn child as she thought about the pain of her dry heaving. "I'll take one-paper shot. Your daddy left us two papers of dope, I'll shoot one now and then snort the other one later. Tomorrow we will only snort two papers," Sara said, convinced that this was the right bargain for her to make with her unborn child.

He seemed ten feet tall, standing at the threshold of the bathroom door between Sara and the drugs she desperately needed, with a look in his eyes that scared her even more than his still bleeding wounds, and his bloody, torn Army uniform. "You're not a killer, you're not a murderer, Sara, but if you get up and take that shot of dope, you will be! You know that you're going to have a child, a child who is a living part of you. A child who will die if you use any dope today. You're trying to use your own withdrawal pains as an excuse to give in to your own selfish desire to get high, you're not human enough to be honest with your own unborn child!

"You're being selfish, you're addicted because you hate yourself for being insecure, shy, and afraid, but those are things that are easy to overcome, if you want to. Yet you found a man who told you that the world at fault for how you see yourself. You chose to get high, and at times you have even been happy that your life was far different than the life that your parents hoped for you to live. A part of you even found joy in getting down on your knees or lying on your back as you gave your body to random men for money to take care of that maggot of a man you claim to love so much. Don't lie to yourself — every wrong, nasty, vile thing you allowed yourself to do, anything that was rebellious, or was something that you knew in your heart that not one of the girls you grew up with would do, you took pride in doing. At the same time, you knew that you were wrong to do so.

"Andy's habits gave you a sense of worth, a sense of need, but it is a hollow worth," the soldier said. "Would you allow some fat nasty truck driver to put his unwashed self into your mouth so you could feed your child? I would find honor in a woman doing that, as motherhood is a blessing," the ghostly soldier explained. "But no, a selfish bitch like you would not stoop that low to feed her child, but to get high, or to degrade yourself for the love of a man who hates you for being the very whore that you allowed yourself to become? Oh yeah, you would gratefully drop to your knees just to feel needed by him. Society has named you a victim of human trafficking, but few American born women are really victims — almost all of you chose to do what you did to yourselves and then you chose to play the victim because the victim is easier than being honest with yourself. Just as taking a shot of dope to ease your child's suffering is easier than being honest and taking that same shot of dope because you want to take it.

"Sara, men know that a woman's womb is the most sacred thing that there is on earth, that without that womb there would be no future, no tomorrow. That's why we become protective of our women. Just as God, the greater force, or whatever you call the power that gives us both life and a conscious, gave women the instinctive will to fight anything, monster or man, to protect both the mother and her child. The act of bringing a life into the world is so sacred that, like the nature of God, it cannot be explained with words. So any man who will send his woman out and allow other men to abuse her mind, body, or soul is a man who hates all women and enjoys seeing them hurt themselves. Yet you don't care do you, Sara?

If you use that dope today, you will be murdering your child, killing it to save Andy's fake love for you. For the rest of your life, you will see yourself as a child killer and that will be your reason for getting high. Your reason for loving men who are incapable of loving you in return. Your reason for lying down with the filth of the earth for money, almost hoping to be beaten or abused by them. Sara, no matter what lie you tell yourself, you know that your child deserves to live, all you have to do is read this!" Lil Bear's ghost said as he hit her with Page's notebook.

"Fuck me, "Sara said. "The ghost of my aunt's childhood hero is screaming at me, and throwing things!" She began to laugh at her illusion.

"You stinking cunt! I am not here to save you!" I failed your aunt, but I will not fail the child growing inside of you, bitch! You had a choice in deciding to get high, your baby cannot make any choices. Go ahead, laugh, get high, I can't stop you, but I will be waiting on you when you die girl, and you won't like me very much!" Lil Bear yelled as he faded into the mist.

"Oh God!" Sara cried as she jumped out of the bathtub and slammed the thin bathroom door, hoping that it could protect her from the truths of her twisted illusion, and evil things that her aunt's ghostly hero had said. His words were like stones in her heart.

"How could he understand the many twisted emotions that I have felt as I abused myself with men for money that I simply handed over to a waiting Andy? Sara's rational mind asked. "It's just your brain talking to you Sara, putting your fears and knowledge into words that you can understand. There are no such things as gods or ghosts, it's just your brain voicing the things about Andy that you have been too afraid to admit to yourself before today," Sara told herself as she began to once again read the words her dear aunt had cared enough to write. "There is no such thing as a ghost!" Sara mumbled to herself, and she was sure that she felt her unborn child laughing at her from deep within her womb.

I had known the man we all called Percodan all of my life and I believe that my mother had also known him most, if not all of her life too. Percodan was a funny outgoing person who you could not help but like him the first time that you met him, nor the second or even third time. Hell, most people never even realized that Percodan was an asshole, a vampire, and a creep. The type of person who was only nice to people so he could use them. The type of man who would be nice to young girls today so that in years to come they would trust him. His kindness was never true is what I'm trying to say. Percodan always had a reason or a goal in the way that he treated you and that's what hurts me the worst as I write, knowing that Percodan never really liked me.

I suppose that if some stupid archaeologist finds Percodan's grave to rob with his team of equally mentally retarded coed girls someday in the future, then they will for once have found the grave of a true cannibal; finally, after so many all expenses paid coed jungle slumber parties, they will have proof that humans never did stop eating each other. No, wait, I'm sorry, when we eat each other's souls, aid our friends in their self-abuse, it leaves no teeth marks on the bones left behind. Thus proving that archaeological expeditions have to be the biggest waste of money ever dreamed up by horny men as a way to get young girls out into the woods, scared, needing protection from the wild animals and the always smiling native tour guides.

Percodan, as his name should imply, was a long time functional drug addict. Oh, he went to jail — in fact, Danny Wilson got his famed name from the way that he had gone to prison once when he was younger. Percodan was the first in the line of Oxycodone pain pills to be widely abused. Most people never even realized that Oxycodone is the active active pain medicine in OxyContin — time released pure Oxycodone; Percodan is Oxycodone mixed with aspirin; while Percocet is Oxycodone mixed with Acetaminophen. It was these three demons that rode through the back hills of America, clearing the moral and religious barriers that had kept opiate addiction out of the rural areas of our nation. With no market for opiates, no one would ever risk going to prison for trying to sell heroin in the Hills, Oxy and the like changed that — Oxycodone was like one of the horseman of the Apocalypse, and Fentanyl and heroin were others.

It's hard for me to believe that these demons were not purposefully sent into the Hills. America was changing, moving away from the coal industry in those days; men were loosing jobs, which weren't being replaced. Unemployment was said to be the leading cause in the opiate epidemic that was killing so many. Seems to me that it was cheaper to let Fentanyl kill off unemployed coal miners than it was to retrain the workforce. Maybe Mr. Bear was right and that addiction needs a mental component to it as well as a chemical one — after all, Redneck's and Hillbillies, no matter their race, will run off to war when called without a thought, so opiate pain medications had to have been used in large quantities before the Oxy epidemic. Losing coal, being called stupid for your hillbilly morals, maybe these were the emotional monsters in the Oxy story.

But I'm old now, I tend to daydream when I don't take my dementia medicine on time. Yet, demented or not, I can see that opium in one form or another was always a problem after every major American financial downturn, or industrial shift. It sure is funny though. When I was about five years old, the older girls down the street convinced me to squat down and pee on an electric fence wire. They had told some boys that because girls didn't have a little pecker like boys, we couldn't get shocked the way boys did if we peed on the fence. Hell, they convinced me of this foolishness too!

So, of course, I proudly dropped my panties, squatted down and got the shock of my life when I started to pee! It was all just fun and amusement, kids being kids, no real harm. But I suppose the point that I'm trying to make is that I only had to piss on that electric wire one time to know not to do that again. Yet every time there is a new addiction epidemic, everybody acts as if they have never seen such a terrible thing before, even though our history books prove them to be liars. But what do I know about government or social history type things? I'm an old woman who takes dementia medicine, my mother was an addict, a whore. This makes anything I say out to be pointless dribble. Yet, just like old Percodan used to say: "If it walks like a duck and makes a quacking sound, it damn sure ain't no pussy cat! It has to be a duck!"

Danny Wilson got addicted to Percodan, so bad in fact that he found himself, gun in hand, robbing a pharmacy: "Give me all your Percodan!" Danny screamed at the pharmacist.

"We ain't got no Percodan, we're all out. But we got Percocet" and this or that other types of pain pills, the pharmacist screamed in reply.

And this according to Danny, started an argument that lasted until Danny walked out of the pharmacy into the waiting arms of the police without taking any pills or money. It was put in the newspaper that the pharmacist tried to give Danny every other pill that he had, but Danny Wilson only wanted Percodan! Once in prison, good natured Danny Wilson instantly became Percodan. A prison nickname that was just too true to forget.

Yet as funny as that story is, Percodan was like me — I only needed to piss on an electric fence one time, and he only needed to fail at armed robbery one time to decide that there had to be a better way to stay high for free than armed robbery, so Percodan became a drug broker. Now don't be confused, a drug broker is not the same thing that as a drug dealer, a broker is a man who knows where to find whatever you want and he robs both you and the drug dealer in the process — he uses you.

Our car was large and clean, the Bears had kept it in top condition, it had been treated as a shrine to their lost son, so Percodan saw it as safe means of sending Momma out each day with carloads of other addicts to doctors' appointments as far away as Columbus, Ohio and Knoxville, Tennessee. Momma would carry the money to pay for medical appointments and to get the prescriptions filled, as well as for gas and food. OxyContin sold for one dollar per milligram if you could only afford to buy one pill at a time, so there was more than enough money to allow Percodan to spilt the prescriptions with the addict who went to the doctor for him. Percodan wanted to get a group of friends who all worked together like Navy Seals or Green Berets. A trusted crew that would tell him if Momma stole from him, and Momma could tell on them also, each faithful only to Percodan.

Yet addiction does not lead itself to spending everyday trapped in a car traveling city to city to get pills that were not really even yours. So each fiend would go to a couple of doctors' appointments and then vanish until they were out of pills, only to magically reappear at Percodan's always open door. Percodan would then loan them pills at a price of two in return for the one he loaned them, until he could set up their next doctor's appointment. Often by the time they saw a doctor, they owed Percodan most of their cut of the pills. Momma being Momma, gentle at heart, always remembered times when people had given her pills and would try to help other friends out, only asking that they returned what she loaned them, not trying to make a profit. But after paying Percodan, the friends never seemed to have enough pills to return Momma's kindness, so she never really saved up much. Sure we had money and our needs were being met better than ever before, but somehow Percodan was the only one who ever seemed to profit. It's truly strange the things you see when you look back on your life from the distance that age provides and with an honest heart, why should we lie to ourselves? Momma had to have jacked off, spent a lot of money and pills in those good days, is all that I am trying to say, and for the life of me, I don't remember how she did it.

I am sure that Lil Dee and I missed the Bears, but children see excitement in new things, new friends, and new places. We tended to try to become the type of person that we needed to be in order to fit in with those around us — so when needed, Lil Dee and I could steal like professionals, or talk with manners of a queen as we checked guests into a motel; we could find humor in Mickey's nasty way of speaking, or we could be quiet little girls not burdening anyone as we stayed over with friends so Momma could play games with the rehabilitation system. We were slick little conmen scamming A.A. and N.A. meeting stamps when needed, and we were perfectly happy grand babies who honestly loved the Bears, but Percodan's house was an incredibly confusing place for us to live. I suppose because it was an incredibly confusing place on its own without us even being there.

Percodan had inherited his family's farm. The Hills tend to limit the size of farms in the Appalachian Mountains, so his place fit perfectly in the confines of life before big tractors, with its house and barn having been built in a time when homes were built by hand by your friends and neighbors. Somehow, everyone else had died off in Percodan's family leaving him to take pride in his family home, and he did. The walls of the house were all covered in framed pictures of those who had graced the land before Percodan and framed diplomas, mixed with the trinkets of family vacations to Florida.

There were also service ribbons and other things that hold value only to those still alive, still connected to them by memories and blood ties. All glorious trappings to the family that had earned them, but pointless trash after the last heir is buried and the farm is auctioned off. But Percodan would proudly tell anyone who asked about an item — exactly where it had come from and its place in his heart. His home seemed normal, it smelled of the millions of wonderful country meals cooked and enjoyed under its roof. The smell was sweet, it smelled of home, not bad or anything, and

Percodan's girlfriend Jessica kept everything clean, spotless, as if Danny just knew in his heart that his family was out there watching him, sure that his addiction would destroy generations of love, pain and the hard work a small family farm always is.

Jessica seemed mouse like, a trait that had attracted Percodan's attention. "Boys and men pass by my Jessica on their way to get fucked over and mistreated by some prettier sluts!" Whores like Page's Momma Christy will stab you in the back, call the police, and get you locked up. Then eat up all your dope, and not worry about it because she's pretty and knows how to use that pussy. My Jessica, she ain't that pretty but she would kill for me, die besides me, never steal a dime from me because I love her. Other men walked by her for years, never seeing her, "Percodan would say as he gently smacked Jessica's butt and laughed at how she would blush and say "Dan" in a private, personal tone that we reserve for lovers.

Lil Dee and I would help Jessica cook and clean as Percodan held court with the ever changing cast of addicts who came to buy drugs, use drugs, sell stolen things, hide from the police, and even beg Percodan for a free high. It was this that was so confusing to me because his house said 'home' the moment you stepped through the door — it smelled of freshly baked cookies and home cooking. It was a home that any preacher would feel comfortable stopping to visit or staying for a meal. But there, in the once formal dining room, sat Percodan in his big Lazyboy recliner with a bag of pills, a pistol, and a stack of money at the head of a table that would seat a large family. There was a painting of the Lord's last supper hanging perfectly centered between two windows, and the room's ageing small chandelier marked the center of a prized family gathering place. It cast its pale glow on to a large printed picture of Jesus. Its wooden frame's color failing to match the shade of the ageing china cabinet with its mix and match collection of china, each odd piece said to have once fed a king, or a villain at one time on its long path to Percodan's care.

It was in this room, under the watchful eyes of Jesus, that

Percodan would buy, sell, and trade drugs. He would sit in his recliner, timing Momma's pill runs, a bag of pills in one hand, a small pistol on the table before him, money left out as forgotten besides bags of syringes, lighters, spoons and colored shoelaces. The proof of foolish self-hate mixed easily with the memories of family life and the smell of freshly baked goods, with the smiling, happy, singing Jessica, happy to be loved and needed by a man like Percodan.

If you have never been an addict then you will never understand the vast difference between the two worlds. Drug houses were never well kept, they shouted out the words temporary, unloved, and not important; they were the backdrops of lives headed for destruction, nothing more. But Percodan's home still looked as it had when his grandmother had traded a spotted colored goat and two young hens for the hand painted picture of the last supper. A painting Percodan claimed a World War One soldier had sent home to his mother before he himself ate his last meal.

You have to understand that opiate addiction means death — you will die if you do not get clean and change your life, face your broken soul and learn to live without drugs. I know that Percodan understood this, he always said that death was why he refused to give out credit; "People are always dying not to pay their bills!" Yet he tried to act as if Lil Dee and I were children, to be taught to cook and say prayers before bedtime, as he and his friends raced headfirst into death's embrace, two vastly different points on fate's compass.

Christmas for addicts is a confused and busy time. For one thing, there are always stolen things to trade for drugs, families to pretend that you're sober for as you rush to sneak in a high before you take your children to meet Santa Claus, and for Percodan it meant speedballs. A black guy from Detroit had come to town to sell cocaine and got lost in the hills behind Percodan's barn. Black drug dealers would need a white girl to keep them warm while they were in town, Percodan claimed, so he and his nephew Orville acted out of civic pride and took the slick Detroit fool out to shoot guns in the woods. They then pushed his car down an old mine shaft, and set about using as much cocaine each day as they could. 'Can't have your Momma fooling around with a colored Page! No, we don't like no Negro lovers, no race trading bitches. Page, you can be a whore if you want girl, but if you ever fuck a stinking black guy don't you dare come around here no more!" Percodan would say as he made Lil Dee and me promise to never sleep with a black man. When I asked what they had done to the man from Detroit, they both laughed and said that they had sent him home and not to worry. They acted as they forgot that I had heard all of the jokes they made about just how stupid the man was to walk out in the woods with two white boys with guns.

Speedballs meant that Jessica was needed more as a nurse than as a cook. Jessica never got high herself. She had met and fallen in love with Percodan when he had brought one of his beagle coon dogs into the veterinarian where Jessica worked as a vet tech, as she referred to her job title with a sense of pride. Percodan had found out that if he let Jessica hook him up to an intravenous hospital line, he could inject shots of cocaine mixed with morphine or melted down Oxys all day without the need to try to find a vein every time he needed a fresh shot of dope. Speedballs took you as high as you could go on cocaine and then the floor would drop out from under your feet when the opiate took effect and you fell into a sweet pit of opium dreams only to soar up and out of the hole like an eagle: up and down, up and down again and again without leaving your chair Momma claimed.

Percodan's friends would line up for Jessica to hook them to an IV line. I had seen as many as ten men and women all seated at that big dining room table under the watchful eyes of Jesus. All getting high, laughing, telling lies and spending every penny they had saved for Christmas presents, their lives, or bills while getting high at Percodan's family table. It was then that I saw Percodan for the man that he truly was. He knew that once he had Jessica insert an IV line into a person's arm, they would not leave that table until they had spent everything they had, often resulting to them begging for credit for one last shot. Percodan swore that blacks used crack cocaine as a means of milking white men of their money, cars, and women, but to this day, I can't see no difference between what Percodan did to his friends and what crack dealers did to their own friends and fiends.

Christmas Eve found me praying that Santa would hurry up and get to Percodan's house. Maybe it was the time that we had spent with the Bears, or the fact that for weeks, Jessica had been trading pills or shots of dope to people to buy shoplifted, stolen presents for Lil Dee and me. I honestly got so caught in the spirit of Christmas that I forgot about the hollow feeling of having to go to church food pantries at the holiday times, or to save any gift that was good enough for Momma to trade for money. These were the normal ways of going through the holidays — everything was a hustle, a scam, a means of Momma getting high. But not that year. No, that year, I went to sleep happy and waiting on Momma to return from a doctors' run up in Charleston. Doctors were always less strict the last week of the year. Jingle bells I suppose.

Only Percodan, Jessica, Orville, Lil Dee and I were staying at the house that Christmas Eve. Momma was slowly driving home through a snowstorm, afraid of crashing her car or of drawing the attention of the police with the number of prescriptions each person in the car was carrying. Elvis sang "Blue Christmas' on the radio, followed by George Michael singing a song called 'Last Christmas'. I stared at the Christmas tree lights, thinking about how George Michael had died, and how Mickey had been taken away from us, along with a growing number of our hillbilly friends, some within hours of my last seeing them at Percodan's table.

Jessica swore that they had been fools for not just getting high with Percodan where she would have been able to save them using her nursing skills. These deaths were foolish and sad, but not as nearly as foolish as George Michael's. Years later, I found out that he was homosexual and that for a long time had felt it was best to try and hide it from the world in order to remain famous and keep selling records. I couldn't help but think about Gay Tom, and also that everyone knew that George Michael was light in the loafers, no one cared. But I had to wonder if living as he lived was not the emotional piece of his addiction that had kept him from getting sober.

Mr. Bear swore that step four would not work until you got honest with yourself about who you really were, what made you hurt inside of your soul. But like all of the other dead dope fiends in the world, no one thinks about singers once they're gone, or why they really died, not even when they listen to their music. We don't want to think about the sadness, or what we could learn from the sad parts of another person's life. No, we are all really just cannibals I guess, as each year we dig up that catchy Christmas song and happily nibble on the soul of a man who traded his happiness so that we could feel good as we sang along with him. No one ever realizing that George Michael gave us an even greater gift than his music. He gave us the lesson that he did not learn for himself from his own life before his last opiate dream.

Oh, I'm sorry, I told you that I tend to try and avoid the hard parts of my own story. The places where I failed Momma and Lil Dee, and this is one of those ugly hurtful places. Lil Dee stayed up to watch Percodan's beagle coon dog Lucy have her puppies, as I forced myself to go to sleep, praying that sleeping would bring Santa's gifts and the morning here just a little faster. Everything was right, perfect, so perfect that I forgot to say a prayer for the Bears before falling asleep. That night I dreamt that I was a normal girl, in a normal family, with a dining room full of odd pieces of mix and match china that family love had formed into a beautiful complete set that Jesus and his buddies watched over everyday. So what if Percodan had hurt a black guy, a black drug dealer who was preying on white girls' addictions? Or if the man's race was just the excuse Percodan told himself to justify killing the man and taking his two kilos of cocaine? Who cares? Percodan was my family and he would never let anyone hurt us, and Jessica had stacks of gifts for us. No one else loved Lil Dee and me enough to trade their dope to buy us presents for Christmas, not even Momma had ever done that.

'It' is a single life-altering event that at its kindest is no less than the evisceration of a child's soul. 'It' is that unseemly act of sex performed by horny men on children that we try to sweep under the rug as if it never happened. But it causes long enduring social problems that affect not only the child victims, but their children, family, friends, coworkers, churches, drug dealers and the world as a whole. Oh yes, I am a demented old bag of bones with a heart full of stony opinions about the world around me, but would you want the type of man who could rape a five year old baby as a world leader, with his finger on the nuclear button? Or worse, the victim of such monster, who hears a certain tone in the voice of an opposing nation's leader, and it reminds our leader of their own abuser.

Remember, our leader is a victim, and that victim now holds all of our fates in their hands. You see, the victims of child abuse and child rape belong to all of us, because what they do when they grow up affects all of us — from their personal views on raising their own children who go to school with everyone else's children, all the way up to starting wars that waste our young, and on up to the nuclear button. Go ahead and laugh at me if you want to, but you would never want me in position where I had to properly deal with any problems at all, trust me.

I learned early that dead people cannot hurt anyone anymore, because death is just that, dead! Like Bobby would say, "Some people you just gotta kill, ain't got no choice, they're broken and only gonna hurt more people, people who are weaker than they are. Hard to be a bully when you're six feet underground, arguing with God about the trip south you're about to be set on!" And he was right, so much spontaneous violence is caused by a vocal tone heard by a child abuse victim in a verbal confrontation. We don't hear your words, we hear the tone in your voice, and it warns us that you are about to hit us, or that you think we are weak and will not hit you. Then you get smacked upside the head and cannot understand why, and we cannot explain it to you. You were only trying to decide something trivial, but we heard the tone in your voice that reminded us of the past, and now trivial has turned into violence and you don't know why.

I was awakened the next morning not by the sounds of reindeer hooves clattering on the rooftop, nor by sounds of a fat man in a red suit wondering why there were people getting high in the dining room as Jessica ran from one to another checking on them with her eyes and hands, her cheeks twitching in ways that reminded us of a mouse. No, I was awakened by a wet, crying Lil Dee as she tried to burrow her body under my own for protection and Jessica begging me to wake up and to help her fix Lil Dee's broken body. I was too confused to understand what was going on. I wanted to get up and run into the living room to receive the gifts that I knew were waiting on us. At the same time, I knew that Lil Dee was bleeding from a place where no child should bleed from, and her left eye was growing black where she had been smacked and beaten.

Momma was screaming at Orville and Percodan, as Orville laughed and Percodan asked Momma just what she thought would happen if she left her daughters with drug addicts. My mother screamed the question, "Why not me, Orville?" To which Orville just laughed as he said, "No way, I might catch something with you Christy, everybody knows you got an ass like a doorknob, you'll let anybody take a turn, whore!" Percodan screamed for Orville to shut the fuck up before things got worse, and I felt a pride run through me at the sound of Percodan's voice and Jessica's assurances that Percodan would fix things. A part of me took joy in the idea that Orville would soon be out in the back of the barn, sleeping in the same hole as that Detroit dope boy who was always trying to fuck white girls.

But then, as I held my sister, I heard Percodan tell Momma that he had a good thing going and that he wasn't fucking it up over some pussy. He said that Lil Dee would be fine cause God had made pussy to be stretched out of shape and all. This too drew laughter from Orville as Jessica's eyes began to beg me for forgiveness; she had also been sure that Orville was a dead man over what he did to

Lil Dee. If he would do it to a child then he could do it to her also, and she was unsure now of Percodan's intentions, only knowing that she would remain faithful to him no matter what he chose to do. All Lil Dee would do was bury her face into my neck crying, "The puppies, the puppies, Sissy!" as I held her and began to cry along with her.

Soon Momma came into the room, grabbing our clothes and bedding as she told me to carry my sister to the car. I heard Percodan remind my mother that a deal was a deal: "No police! Christy!" I heard him say as Jessica tried to assure Momma that Lil Dee was not seriously hurt.

"There's more than enough room for y'all three out back, Christy! It's best you remember that! Now, don't y'all go pissing on your okra and lima beans!" Percodan said, meaning that Momma better keep her mouth shut and not ruin her own garden, as we rushed out the front door to our car and drove away.

Momma seemed lost in her own world as she drove every back rode she knew of, mumbling that she should not have fought to get Lil Dee back from her foster parents. She was crying and asking God why he had trusted her with Lil Dee when he had already placed her in a safe home. Soon though, she seemed to focus her thoughts as she told us that she had to turn herself into the rehabilitation center, that the speedballs she had been doing every night would mean that she would only need to stay a few days for using cocaine and not the six weeks they would ask her to stay for opiates. I was to watch Lil Dee, to keep her clean and to only drive the car to get gas because the roads were bad now, covered in snow like they were.

"No one ever checks the back parking lot of the rehabilitation center!" Momma said, telling us that we would be safe there until she got clean and could take Lil Dee to the police to have them get that son of bitch Orville for what he had done to her. "They will take you girls from me Page if we go there like I am today, honey," Momma softly said and we both began to cry, as much because of the pain Lil Dee had endured as from the fear of what the police would do to rip our family apart, instead of what they should do to help us. Today I understand that Momma's lifestyle had placed us in jeopardy with no way to seek help from the police. It was her fault, and not that the police were evil bullies. But back on that Christmas day I could only remember the sound of the police SWAT team as they broke into our room and stole my family away and I could not let that happen this time. Lil Dee was hurt, she needed me, and I honestly needed her. So there we were, the Three Musketeers once again with only each other to depend on.

Momma handed me five 20 milligram Oxys and told me to crush one pill per day and then divide it into eight piles. Then mix one pile at a time into some juice or something for Lil Dee to drink for the pain. She told me not to take any because with the car running to keep us warm, I might go to sleep and something bad could happen to us. "I'm not giving this to Dee to get her high, Page, but she has to be hurting," Momma explained as I told her that I never wanted to take any pills ever in my life. Then Momma opened the trunk of the car and stashed her prescriptions, handed me most of her money, hugged me, kissed Lil Dee's forehead and then she was gone, up the walkway and through the doors of the one place in the world we thought could save her from herself.

I gave Lil Dee some of the Oxy in her juice as Momma told me to do, and in time I could see her little body relax. She still refused to talk and kept her face buried in my neck or arms when I was not moving the car so that the wind would blow the exhaust away from us, a trick that we had learned when living in our car before moving in with Percodan. It was only after nightfall, when Lil Dee had managed to fall asleep, that the weight of the day's events began to settle on my heart. Maybe the darkness offered me a sense of being alone, unable to be seen, but I began to cry, angry at myself for not staying up with Lil Dee and Orville to watch the puppies being born. Why would Orville take my sister when I was old enough that Percodan has had to warn several of the younger men who came to do business that I was still just a little girl and just not worth snooping around trying to get to know "It's sure easy to end up back in the holler, but it's really hard to get out of one you know what I mean, son?" Percodan would say with a smile as he checked his gun and laughed.

It was things like this that hurt me as much as Lil Dee getting hurt. Jessica was my friend, and Percodan had acted protective like Mr. Bear had, I thought that we could trust him. What Orville did would get you run out of town if not killed over. But Percodan as good as held Lil Dee down for Orville when he took Orville's side and sent us away. Even as I write this, over sixty years past that hard day, I refuse to believe that Percodan protected Orville because Orville could tell on him about the man from Detroit; no, Percodan took Orville's side in the matter because Percodan was a coward and he needed Orville around to get up the nerve to act as he did. Funny how an old person can read the signs and understand that Percodan and Orville were cowards alone, but animals together. Maybe that black Detroit boy wasn't stupid after all. Maybe he could smell the yellow in the two of them and that's why he went into the woods with them. It was foolish of him, but being a fool is not the same as being stupid is it?

Chapter 14

At times, I swore Lil Bear's ghost was trying to tell me drive home to the Bears, but we were the Three Musketeers. I told Momma that I would do what she asked of me and wait in the parking lot, though I really wanted to go to the Bears and cry as I handed them Lil Dee to fix. But I couldn't abandon Momma — she was still pure, clean, without guilt in my eyes. But age has a way of sanding away the fairytale dreams of children and I would soon begin to feel age's abrasive effects and begin seeing Momma as she really was, and not the person I dreamed her to be.

We found a small cafe across the street from the rehabilitation center where we could go for breakfast and I could clean Lil Dee's wounds in private. Then I would let her eat as I hand washed her wet clothes. The smell of baby pee mixed with her blood and the odor of our car's old vinyl seats would make me want to be sick each time I turned the heater up high. It was not Lil Dee's fault I told her with a smile, but her eyes spoke the sad heartbreaking words of apology for making a mess and wetting on us as we slept again.

It did not take long for the cafe owners, a man and wife, to realize who we were and that we were living in our car. "You don't know that girl's mother, she's trouble!" I heard the woman say. "I don't care if she's King Kong," the man would say, "it ain't right to leave the babies like that." And then he would feed us. Once he took the car keys off of the table and motioned for me not to worry. "I can't sleep until I know that car's safe for y'all!" the man said as he walked across the street, only to return with our soiled blankets and clothes.

"I'll wash these. You, what's your name?" the man asked.

"Page, sir" I said. "Well leave the little one here and take some washing powder from the back and go clean your car. You gotta clean it everyday if you're gonna sleep in it. I don't like you staying there myself, but my wife says your momma is a mean one, so I can only do so much. But y'all babies are to come over here and stay everyday, use the washer and dryer, and eat as much as you want!" the man said as he looked at his his wife to see if she would countermand his orders. The sweet woman just looked down and said, "Y'all just don't understand!"

"I know ma'am, my momma can be trouble!" I said, and for the first time I began to see that our life was not as bad as it was because life was just bad, but instead, I saw that maybe Momma was some of the problem.

"What happened to the little one?" the man asked, concerned. "She fell in the snowstorm the other day," I quickly said before the truth overpowered my heart. I wanted desperately for Lil Bear to tell this parents to come to rescue us, or to break down and tell these good people what Orville had done and about Percodan, but I knew that if I did, the police would take both Momma and Lil Dee away from me. Dee was still cute, adoptable even, but I was too far gone and Mickey was dead so I could not stay with her until Momma did what she needed to do to get us back together again. And what if Momma decided that we were better off without her? Safer away from her as she had said on Christmas day? These were things that I could not risk.

Lil Bear knew my heart, he would bring his daddy to save us. I convinced myself, as my eyes told Lil Dee to agree with me, that she had fallen in the snow, nothing more, nothing less. We would survive like this for ten long days, each day becoming longer. I felt like I was dying, suffocating under the weight of Lil Dee's silence. Although she had begun to relax, to almost smile, or at least to acknowledge you when you spoke to her, talking with her eyes, she still had not said one word other than when she would scream in her sleep. Of all of the hells I endured in life, my not knowing how to help her through her pain was the most soul crushing of them all;

it took years for me to recover from it, if I ever really have.

I started to laugh when the restaurant owners would say thank God or things like that — there simply was no God, I told myself. Surely a God would have stopped Orville before he could hurt my sister — a lightning bolt, even just tripped him or something small like a stroke that would have left him shitting his pants and drooling all day. But nope! Nothing! Nada! Zip! A God would have smacked Lil Bear's ghost around for not bringing his parents to save us, but again, no luck.

There simply was no God I told myself. Then suddenly, a smiling Lil Dee said "Momma" and pointed to our best friend, our hero, who was walking towards us with a purpose filled stride. For a moment, I began to thank God, first for my sister's voice and second for returning our mother to us so that she could carry the weight of our life again. But I stopped myself from saying even one word of thanks to whatever narcissistic asshole who made this crappie ball of dust we live on, because I knew all of my mother's walks. The one she used when she was trying to catch a man's attention, the one she used to con doctors, the one she used when she meant to stay clean and sober. And I knew this one, the one that she was using to propel her body out of rehab — the one that said she would do anything for a pill.

She walked straight towards our car, my home, only to grab the car keys without even saying a word, opened the trunk and retrieved her drugs. Only after chewing up some pills did she think to ask how Lil Dee was or how I was. Then we drove out of the parking lot, past the restaurant where we had been allowed to stay in the warm safety of the good people who owned it, and I knew that there would be no police, no hospital. I knew that we would not seek help from the Bears or the rooms of A.A or N.A. We had simply wasted more than a week telling lies to good people. From that moment forward, I knew that I would need to protect Lil Dee because, unlike the nice man at the café, I knew my mother, and I knew that she was broken. Not chipped, or simply cracked, but broken. But at twelve years old, I had no idea how to help her and

I was doubting if I wanted to do so anyway.

Ruby's truck stop would become our new home within days of Momma's release from rehab. She offered us no excuses for not taking Lil Dee to the hospital or to the police, she simply stayed as high as she could until turning tricks at Ruby's was her only choice. Today I believe that she went there only to punished herself for allowing Lil Dee to be raped, but it brings me no peace. You see, I said that she wanted punishment for allowing Lil Dee to get hurt, but I did not say that Momma wanted to hurt herself, to be punished for the life that she forced us to live; the losses we had already felt and those we would soon endue; the foolish dreams we would pray for, like being normal kids, with a Santa Claus and presents. No, Momma was incapable of ever admitting that she was allowing drugs to destroy her life, as well as Lil Dee and my own. Orville had only been able to rape Lil Dee because Momma failed to get back in time to stop him because of a snowstorm and fear of the police, but not because her addiction caused her to place us in harm's way. Yes, I know that I seem to be splitting hairs, but it's all about being honest with yourself, but Momma could not be honest with herself ever while using drugs.

Ruby's truck stop was down in the valley where Kentucky fell into West Virginia. Not far from the Big Sandy River, but still a way north of Virginia. It had a reputation for being racist and not very friendly to blacks, but it was honestly not racist at all. It was just a place that did not allow pimping, and this automatically began the rumor that colored folks were not welcomed at Ruby's. You have to understand that pimps come to the hills hoe shopping, knowing that there are girls who want to get out of the woods or away from bad parents. Well, you don't hunt for grizzly bears in a shopping center, you hunt them in the woods, and you don't hunt young naive white girls at all, instead you slide down to the country and just wait — one will come to you sooner or later, dying to get a ride to the city. Carnival workers like my father knew this, and pimps did also. Maybe the girls automatically figured that the black guy with the slick car was not going to be staying long in small town, so he was safe to approach.

But whatever the real reason was, pimps were not allowed at Ruby's no matter their color, but no one explained this to the black pimps, who had grown up dependent on the race card as an excuse for any friction they faced as they pursued their American dream. No, neither Ruby's nor West Virginia was racist against blacks. Our state was founded by people who did not believe in slavery, and then the blacks joined the whites during the coal miner strikes, and moonshine wars, but some truths are lost, unless you look for them, and Ruby's was one of those.

Without pimps, the truck drivers could relax and take care of the woman they were partying with as opposed to clear cut business deal that would easily be negotiated by an angry, armed black pimp. Drugs were not sold out in the open, girls could not go from semi-truck to semi-truck without being asked to leave. Momma felt safe at Ruby's, and it became our new home.

Momma rarely sneaked back to the parking lot to turn tricks like a Lot Lizard as truck stop hookers were lovingly called by the truck drivers. We still had our car, and making drug runs was still popular, but not once did she drive out to Percodan's when asked to do so. Nor did she try to leave us at the restaurant inside of Ruby's so that she could drive someone to Percodan's either. I found love for her for this, although love was becoming hard for me to even look for in my heart or in the world around us. I was going sick of her smell, the smell of sex, sweaty men, and days without a shower; but I was really getting sick of her willingness to turn a trick to get high, yet not feed us, her daughters.

There were times when we were next to broke, but Momma was high and still had some pills left and a horny driver would ask her for a quickie, but Momma would not go off to the man's truck. It was embarrassing sitting in Ruby's restaurant trying to milk a cold order of toast for all the free coffee refills we could get before the waitress would ask us to leave. They knew who Momma was, that she would drop to her knees on a broken glass covered gravel parking lot for a pill in a heartbeat, yet she was in no hurry to do so to feed her babies. It was as if she was pretending that she was somehow above being a hooker, always daydreaming about putting the money together to start driving fiends doctor shopping for herself.

Today, I have the benefit of knowing her whole story and, as stupid as this will sound to you, Momma felt that she had risen above being a dope head who went to bed with guys for a good time or a free party. That's what most women tell themselves when they first realize that their body and companionship will get them high everyday for free: "I'm not a hooker! I don't turn tricks!" a woman will yell loudly when some guy offers money for a straight business deal — sex for money. The woman screams that she is not a prostitute until heroes join in to defend her, taking her side. Their words proving to her that she is still a good woman.

Momma had long ago sailed past this point in our Cinderella story, and accepted that she was a dope whore; she could then blame drugs for her nasty actions and still not admit that she was a prostitute. She was a victim of addiction not of her addiction. She could not personalize addiction by admitting that it was hers, that she owned it, because to do so would mean that since she owned her addiction then she owned everything that she did to feed and support her addiction — all of the pain it caused us, her children, and now the silence of her daughter, our little silent angel. But it was Percodan's grand plan that changed her mental view of herself — she was not a victim of addiction, nor a willing participant in her own self-destruction any longer. Now she could tell herself that she was a businesswoman, able to maintain her habit, not an addiction anymore, but a habit like coffee, or cigarettes, as she raised her children in the safety of her business partner's home. A man who was civic minded enough to keep Detroit boys away from girls like she had once been, girls like her daughters were soon to become.

Lil Dee saw him first as he raced up to the front window of Ruby's restaurant in a new Cadillac. He looked through the window at Momma, smiled, spun his tires in the gravel and raced to the back parking lot. Lil Dee seldom spoke, but her eye's said exactly what

I was thinking — that Momma would try her hardest to catch that guy's attention, and I instantly began to hate him. I prayed that he would drive away before I had to hear his lies about being someone important in some fantasy life or to have to hear Momma's fake moans of joy under the spell of his manly ways. The guy was an asshole, I told myself, a purebred rattlesnake, plain and simple. He would twist Momma around his finger without trying; hell, I was willing to bet that he could get her to sell herself to get them both high before the night was over. He was the type of asshole that Percodan should have been concerned about instead of the Detroit boys.

Bobby Austin was tall and thin. Momma, Lil Dee, and Bobby could have passed as family. All three looked like they were Native Americans with long dark hair, and this only made me hope that he would have a stutter when he spoke, or walk with a funny limp of some kinda, one leg twisted around funny, or have a tiny weenie that Momma would not be able to stop herself from laughing at. But he walked with the confidence of a man who even if he did have a tiny weenie, no one would dare laugh at it. No, I could see that Bobby Austin was a prick, and proud of it, and I hated him for it. "Rattlesnake!" I silently mouthed to Lil Dee, as he walked up to our table with a large duffle bag in his hand that he dropped to the floor at my feet as he sat down beside me, neither asking me if he could nor acknowledging me in any way. Asshole, I told myself as he told the waitress our breakfast order in a voice dripping with fake southern charm.

"Honey get this lady here y'all best steak breakfast, and bring these baby girls some of them pancakes y'all make that look like Mickey Mouse. Y'all girls like Mickey Mouse, don't you?" Bobby asked me as he acknowledged my being alive at the table besides him for the first time. "Nope, we don't like mice, rats, rattlesnakes or assholes like you either!" I said in my most hateful tone. Momma gasped and said "Page!" like she was auditioning for a part in an old southern movie, or that she was a lady and not the truck stop hooker that I knew that she was.

"Damn good thing I ain't none of those things!" Bobby said, causing Lil Dee to giggle and making me feel both happy that she was getting better and sad that she had betrayed me, she was a trader. I could see that she thought Bobby was far more than the cheap dope fiend clown that I was sure in my heart that he was. As the waitress bought our order, Bobby took a pack of cigarettes from his pocket and shook out several more 40-milligram Oxys than would be needed to get Momma and the whole truck stop high. Flashing, looking for my mother's price. She took two pills. I know that he saw her eat one and then hide the other inside of her ear. Stealing dope was dangerous, but Bobby just smiled at her. They had been chatting like long lost friends and I was trying to decide if I should throw up or tell Bobby to give me some money and finally force Momma to see that we could not continue to live as we were doing now.

We could not survive another weekend of her curling up in a motel room getting high with some guy who might buy us something to eat or be kind enough to let us shower in his motel room. The sight of his pills and the big wad of money he carried reminded me of the times when Lil Dee and I would go through Momma's boyfriends' pockets as they slept. With as many pills as this asshole was flashing, I was sure that both he and Momma would sleep deeply when they did pass out. So like my mother had found a way to blame our lifestyle on an addiction, I thought that I had a way to support her, to remain faithful to her, but to also begin to keep my promise to protect Lil Dee. If Momma wanted to pretend that guys were her boyfriend, then I could rob them as we had robbed her boyfriends in the past, I thought with an evil smile that made Lil Dee grin.

It was decided that we were to drive Bobby around town on some business he had to take care of and then down to Knoxville, Tennessee. Bobby claimed that his Cadillac had a busted fan belt or something. Good, I thought, because Momma will be in a hurry to get back home after I take his money out of his pocket. He won't be able to chase us down without his shinny Cadillac that I sure was stolen and not broken at all. So I began to act more interested in Bobby, the truck stop Romeo, aware that men are kind to women who seem to like them and wary of women who act as if they hate them.

"Now why do I feel like you just pickpocketed me, little lady?" Bobby said when I smiled, pretending to be interested in something that he had said. Bobby then caused both Momma and Lil Dee to giggle as he pretended to check his pockets as if I had stolen something.

"Page, my name's Page! I ain't your little lady, asshole! In fact, I hate you!" I said which caused Momma to act like I smacked the Pope!

"Oh, don't worry about her, ain't no sin to be honest, "Bobby said in my defense. "I most certainly am an asshole, trust me! I'll do my best to prove Lil Ms. Page right, that's a promise!" he said, and we all laughed along with our new friend.

I should have known by the number of pills Bobby flashed to get my mothers attention that any business he had in town was pill related and that would mean a trip to Percodan. Perccodan was like the sun — anything to do with a large number of pills would revolve around him. We were less than a mile from Ruby's but I knew that Momma would drive through hell backwards wearing a polka dot blindfold just to please Bobby. Lil Dee exploded into tears, crying, fighting to form the words to beg her mother to stop the car, wetting herself for the first time in weeks, and I began to hate Bobby this time for real because hating our mother would be simply pointless.

Bobby's voice became gentle and concerned as he sniffed the air, realizing that Lil Dee had peed herself, but he still reached over the front seat to pick my sister up. I instinctively smacked his hands away and then smacked his face, but Bobby did not stop, or get mad. He just gently picked Lil Dee up, whispering concerned words and trying to assure her that she would be alright.

"She peed herself, you'll get it on your shirt!" Momma shouted to warn Bobby.

"So fucking what!" Bobby said as Lil Dee laid her head on his shoulder, trying to burrow into his neck, making herself as small as possible.

"What happen to this baby, who hurt her?" Bobby asked in a tone that was devoid of all the southern charm he had used when we first met him, replaced by a tone that stressed the violent nature of the man who was now holding my sister.

Momma began to stutter, unsure of what to say, and I realized that not one of us had put the events of Christmas morning into words to be spoken between ourselves, and now there was a very upset man asking us to explain something simply unexplainable. "Orville raped her," Momma managed to say as Lil Dee mumbled puppies, and I blurted out everything I knew: how we stayed in the car at the rehab, how the people had fed us, how I prayed for Lil Bear to tell his parents to come save us. How Momma seemed broken completely now, and how I could not stand Lil Dee's silence anymore. That it was my fault, that Orville should have taken me and not my little sister.

"No Page, the motherfucker should not have taken anyone!" Bobby calmly said. "What about Percodan? Don't tell me that he just let Orville get away with it? Bobby asked.

"We've not been back there. I agreed to let Percodan deal with Orville. He's still around though, that's why I haven't gone back to driving for Percodan," Momma said and I knew then that she had tricked me into waiting, alone without her for those ten days. I knew then that she was waiting on Percodan to send Orville away or to be rid of him. That was why she could not make a decisive choice for what direction our lives should go in, and I felt violated, violated to the core of my being. My mother had planned to return to Percodan, after promising to never do so again, proving that we, her children, her friends, the other Musketeers, were not worthy of her honesty. Bobby stopped me before I could scream at her or revolt by asking me to get his black pistol out of his duffel bag that lay at my feet where he had placed it as we left Ruby's.

The duffel bag held several guns, large stacks of money,

many even larger bottles of pills and what would turn out to be a bulletproof vest. Today what amazes me most about Bobby's duffel bag was that not one of the things in it shocked me: I had seen everything in that bag or something like it before. I had helped Percodan bag up the Detroit boy's cocaine, even learned how to test its purity by using bleach and a small amount of cocaine, all while Orville made jokes and cleaned the guns that I am sure that he and Percodan had used to kill the man.

Seeing stacks of the money should have warned me, attracted my attention, caused me to plan a way to steal it, but something inside of me knew that Bobby was not pretending to care about Lil Dee, and that he was calm because he had no fear of Percodan. As I handed him the gun, I had no fear of doing so, even though he held my baby sister in his arms. He was softly rubbing her back with the same hand that he now held his pistol in, its barrel nearly touching her head. This should have inspired fear in me, but somehow, I just knew that Bobby would rather die than hurt us.

"Now shorty," Bobby said to Lil Dee, "if I go in here and deal with Orville and you don't see it for yourself, then you will always worry about him. So we gotta walk in here together. Orville's gotta know in his heart that he never should have hurt you, and you have to know that he regrets touching you. Trust me, honey, I'll make Orville and Percodan both pee their pants like the cowards they are if Percodan don't like me making Orville pay the bill he owes you," Bobby said, as Momma attempted to stop him, still hoping that Percodan would keep his word to deal with Orville himself so that she could return to her job of driving his friends around.

"I promised Percodan that I would let him deal with Orville," Momma mumbled.

"And you promised these babies to be their mother the day you gave birth to them. Now drive woman, take me to Percodan's house right now damn it, and fuck you and anyone else who doesn't like it!" Bobby said in the coldest voice that I had ever heard before and I prayed a prayer of thanks that my mother was a coward, knowing that she would do as she was told and not try to intervene again.

The dope game by nature is a lot of play acting. Hollywood makes shows that are no more honest than the archaeological TV shows — both are made up, full of lies. Good drug dealers are not violent, the goal is to sell drugs, not to go to jail for extended periods of time over guns and violence. Sure, lesser pretend drug dealers will try to act out a movie scene by killing a dope fiend or rival. Prison is full of those types, but true dope boys know that it is not worth going to prison for twenty years over an ounce of dope. You accept the loss, knowing that the person who stole it from you will rob an idiot sooner or later who will kill him.

But even real drug dealers pretend to be violent, hardcore, crazy, and they put on shows to make a point. As we followed Bobby into Percodan's house, I felt sure that Orville was going to have to pee his pants at gunpoint and maybe leave town for a while. I felt this way because no one would ruin their friendship with Percodan over a broken dope whore and her twisted children. But Percodan's face and voice told me that I was wrong when he saw Bobby walk into the dining room carrying Lil Dee, right behind Orville, and then smack Orville as hard as he could in the side of the head with his gun.

"Fuck me!" Percodan said, "Fuck me, God damn it, that bitch didn't need to bring you into this brother. Now calm down," Percodan said with fear in his voice.

Bobby looked around the dining room, shocked at what he saw. Besides Percodan and Orville, there were four other people hooked up to IV lines doing speedballs. Orville was now lying face down, knocked out, with his arms spread on the table in a way that caused the blood coming out of his head and ear that looked nearly torn off his head to puddle around his face.

"Exactly which bitch are you talking about Perk?" Bobby asked, as Lil Dee turned to face the man we had both called our friend.

"Now that ain't what I meant, Bobby," Percodan said as he pointed to my mother, and said, "That bitch, we had a deal, no police, no bullshit. Twenty Oxys, done over, I kept my end of the deal, bitch, and now you brought this retarded bastard here. Are you completely fucking insane or just stupid?"

"You said you would deal with Orville, Percodan," my mother said as her eyes searched the floor at her feet, as if she was afraid to look at him.

"Well hell, brother, Orville had it coming, he can't cry about it. Jessica, get my brother and his bitch here a line so we can all party like old times. I ain't mad at you Christy, in fact, we've missed y'all," Percodan said as Jessica began to act as if we were her long lost family and that people were always bleeding on her table.

There are points in life where everything can change, go off into a completely different direction, one that you're unsure of, one that you cannot turn back from. Fate is what some call it, or the hand of God maybe, it doesn't really matter. But this is a moment that changed my entire life — our life before this moment was over, the fate that we had been racing towards was going to be denied the company of our souls. Bobby could just sit down and get high. Jessica would try to fix Orville's head the best that she could. Percodan would give Orville some money and tell him to go away at least until Bobby left town again. Lil Dee and myself would have then gone off with Jessica in search of those promised Christmas presents, and our life would not have changed at all. Bobby had hurt Orville a little, scared Percodan, put on a show and would be considered a hero for it. But Bobby Austin was far from finished with teaching Orville and Percodan a lesson, and he was not done changing the direction of our lives.

Orville was awake but seriously confused; his nose was blowing bubbles in his blood when Bobby looked at Jessica and said, "We ain't' staying," as a way of stopping her from finding chairs for Momma and him to sit in. Jessica smiled at me as she pretended to be a nurse and attempted to turn Orville's face out of his own blood while she tended to his dangling ear and split head. Bobby asked the others in the room if they knew what Orville had done and, if so, how could they party or got high with him? I felt a power as I stood there besides Bobby, with my arms crossed over my chest like I was the biggest person in the room. Bobby was asking a question that needed to be asked as well as answered when Percodan tried to speak up but was silenced by a look from Bobby.

"What is it with you Bobby?" a man named Brad asked. "You ain't welcome hardly anywhere because you're always sticking your nose in shit that don't concern you. We ain't here for this bullshit, we're here to get high. Now Percodan said it's over, so sit down and get high. He paid her Momma what she asked for, and we both know them girls ain't going to be nothing but whores. You can't reset the clock and raise them all over again Bobby," Brad boldly stated. "I don't like what Orville did, and I ain't never liked you, so fuck off or get high, asshole!" Brad said as his friends mumbled their agreement. Percodan saw Bobby's smile and the tiny twinkling in his eyes and knew that they were all about to die. I saw Percodan slide a pistol from under his shirt.

"Is that a fact Brad?" he asked as he handed Lil Dee to my mother, nodded towards the door, turned back to Orville and, while laughing, blew the side of his head off, all the while staring at Brad and challenging him.

I saw Orville's head rip apart, his blood and brains splashing all over Jessica's face, who screamed as she tried to get away from Orville's twitching body, then he pushed me out the front door. I swear that it sounded as if God was speaking as one gunshot turned into an angry song of cries and explosions. Jessica flew out the house behind me as if tossed by a giant, her broken body crashing onto the porch, as Bobby, covered in blood, laughing like he had just heard the funniest joke ever told, stepped out of the house. He grabbed Jessica's lifeless body, shot her again and tossed her back into the house like a rag doll. Then he looked at my mother, shrugged his shoulders playfully and asked, "Now was that overkill? Damn it, Christy, I'm sorry, I'm always so damned socially awkward!" then he turned to me, motioning with his head towards the barn and said, "Gas! Now Page, get it!" Momma screamed, "What in the fuck are you doing Bobby?" as she reached out to stop me from running to get gas from the barn. "Burn it down!" Bobby said as he pulled his shirt off and began to wipe the blood from his face.

I can never honestly evaluate my feelings about the carefree, joking way that Bobby went about killing so many people I had once called friends. Nor can I evaluate my feelings about the price Orville paid for hurting Lil Dee because of how she reacted when Bobby said that he was going to burn Percodan's house down. "Not the puppies!" she screamed. The sweet sound of her voice stunned Momma as Lil Dee raced back into the house. This caused Bobby to drop his playful act screaming, "No Shorty, you don't need to see any of that! No!" Then he raced to follow her, with me in tow.

No matter if Bobby was right, wrong or insane, he gave my baby sister back to us and that fact alone will forever taint my opinion of the lessons taught that day. I don't remember getting sick or turning away from the bloody things I saw in the house as we chased Lil Dee, Jessica, my friend, was the only death that hurt me; she lay crumpled on the floor with her eyes open, her arms twisted and turned in an inhuman way. Orville had slipped from his chair and lay on the floor in a growing pool of blood, piss,and leaking IV fluids. Two of his friends died where they sat, one had turned in his chair to face Bobby and died there with a bullet hole just above his left eye; the other, the one who had remained quiet as Brad spoke, looked as if he had been so deep into an opiate nod that he never even knew that death had come for him. His head was bowed as if in prayer to a God that I knew did not care about Lil Dee and I was sure did not care about this fiend's prayers.

The third of Brad's friends lay across the table as if he had been trying to escape but Bobby's bullets had stopped him where he lay. Brad still sat in his chair, with the back of his head clearly gone, sprayed on to the wall beside him and splattered on the picture of Jesus. Percodan lay in his recliner, his face almost completely gone, breathing heavily, moaning Bobby's name, his eyes fixed on the painting of the last supper, its figures all dripping in Bobby's victim's blood. "They asked for it! Bobby said as he placed his hand on my shoulder to turn me away from the gore. "Sometimes humans don't learn from gentle actions or words, Page, and they leave you no choice but to kill them," Bobby said in calm, soothing voice.

"They're dead Bobby, they didn't learn nothing," I said as I noticed that a thick cloud of gun smoke seemed to hover around the family's chandelier, like a ghost dancing in its light.

"You got a point kid, but the other assholes around town will find out that Orville got what he asked for and the rest got killed for getting high with him. Trust me, that's a lesson that won't soon be forgotten!" Bobby said. "Now go find your sister." As I walked away, I could hear Bobby talking with Percodan who was now pleading for Bobby to help him, but I knew that his pleas were no use. I thought about making a joke, much like Percodan, Orville, and even Jessica had after they had killed the Detroit drug dealer, but I was not ready to be so cold.

Lil Dee was smiling, chattering as fast as she could, all of her words aimed at asking Bobby if she could keep the puppies.

"Puppies?" Bobby asked, a confused tone in his voice as he stared down at Lil Dee holding four small beagle pups as their mother Lucy began to lick Jessica's lifeless face on the floor beside my feet. "Are you fucking kidding me?" Bobby stuttered.

"They won't cost much money. Lucy don't eat a lot and she feeds the puppies. Me and Page can steal food for her to eat, it's easy. Please Bobby, please don't burn 'em up, please," Lil Dee pleaded as Momma walked into the house from the porch where I knew that she had hidden, afraid of what she would see if she stepped inside, but unwilling to stay outside alone any longer.

"Get them ugly mutts in the car! Damn it!" Bobby said with a laugh, causing Lil Dee to cheer as we raced past Momma on the way to the car. "Go on Christy, me and Percodan got business to tend to," Bobby said. I saw Momma step out of the house and off of the front porch into the light of the early evening sun. It was sinking to the west of us, causing the trees and the fence post to cast accusing shadows towards the house and us as if they knew what we had done. Momma's eyes were no longer blank, as they had been all the time that we were at Ruby's. Maybe Bobby Austin was

right and killing those assholes was the best thing for everyone —
it had given me the lost voice of my sister, four puppies, a momma
dog and what appeared to be my mother back to guide us through
tomorrow. It felt like a dream, mystical almost, until the sound of
Bobby's last gunshot screamed out goodbye to our friend Percodan.

"Come on, Page we gotta go!" Bobby said as he walked past
me heading towards the car. I noticed that his back was welted
with scars, and I could not help but feel concern for the pain that he
must have suffered when he received them. As I climbed into the
car behind him, I reached out and touched a scar that was up high
on his shoulder and asked, "What?" Meaning what was it? What
had caused it, and a million other questions that the word 'What'
represents when humans cannot manage to talk about things like a
scar left by obvious abuse.

"Lessons, Page, just lessons," was all that Bobby wanted to say
and we drove away, listening to the sounds of Lil Dee's sweet voice
playing with her puppies.

Chapter 15

The highway to Knoxville is littered with the failed dreams of people who thought that they could survive, make a better life outside of the hill country. Yet for all of the dreamers who failed in their attempt to find something more, there is an equal number of good people who made it, found their happiness in the larger world, carrying their country morals, ethics and pride with them. And there were even a few people like me who neither failed, nor even attempted to find any happiness, but instead, simply marked our time awaiting death. Fate had decided without asking permission that my life in West Virginia was over.

The killings at Percodan's house, despite being deserved, were wrong and the police would hunt Bobby down like a mad dog over them. Yet I could already tell by the look in my mother's eyes that she would follow Bobby Austin no matter where he went. When she had given herself to the police sergeant up in Huntington, she had done so praying that he would help us to get custody of Lil Dee, but he did nothing and, in the end, he was just one of many men who received the gift of my mother's body for lies. Yet this odd man had not asked for even a kiss in return for returning her daughter to her.

So that night, as we raced away from a world that I understood, heading into a world that I was honestly afraid of, I began to understand what Mickey had meant when she had said, "Woman are stupid! That's why I pimp them out, Page. Call me names even smack me around. A woman will give a man everything she has or allow him to abuse her body in the hope of him loving her simply because she allowed him to enter inside of her. You see Page, on the one hand, the bitch knows how sacred her womb is, but she cannot stop herself from trying to impress a man by doing more and nastier shit to her body, all just hoping to be loved. Stupid ass bitches never realize that pussy is cheap, it ain't special, it ain't unique, a man can get pussy for a smile, some dope, money or an unspoken promise of love from the next woman he meets.

"Yet a woman will give birth to a child who is born deeply in love with their mother, a child will know their mother's voice and heartbeat from across a crowded room; her child will feel her die from miles away because they formed in her womb, their tiny heartbeat for the first time in her womb, two drums beating out the rhythm of life instead of only one — it's sacred, magical shit, Page. Yet mothers will push that type of love aside as they beat, abuse, sell, and trade their children, or abandon them, just hoping to be loved by some man who sees her mistreat her own children. He knows it's wrong, even unnatural for a mother to act in that way towards her children, so he begins to hate her, even if he enjoys the abuse her children suffer for his sake. Hear me Page, as long as a woman is unable to love herself, unable to understand her own heart, then she is nothing more than a whore who no man will ever truly value or love: a whore either trading her body for lies or in exchange for money — it doesn't really matter what she is trading it for, like my own mother traded me to my father!" Mickey said, warning me about Momma.

I watched Momma drive while she tried to clean the blood from Bobby's face; Bobby was stuffing cigarette tobacco into a bullet hole in his leg to stop it from bleeding. I noticed that Momma's eyes were clear, focused, and alive, even though she was high. I had not seen them so alive since the day that she had walked away from drugs and into the Bears' hearts, but what would be the price of this joy? A simple ride to Knoxville? The misuse of her body while her daughters waited outside of a thin door listening? I asked myself this question knowing that, after what Bobby had done for us, my mother would be willing to pay any price he might ask just to be loved by him, even though he was, in reality, a monster, no better than Percodan, and that we were destined to fail again because she still had not learned to love or value herself.

Lil Dee finally noticed that Bobby had been shot by Percodan and she began to cry. "No, Mr. Bobby. No you can't leave us now. We just found you, please don't die."

I will never forget watching her dry tear-filled eyes on Lucy's small puppies, some of which thought that Lil Dee was howling and began to howl along with her. Those cute little puppy howls caused Lucy to howl like only a grown beagle can howl, a mother teaching her young by example. All of this caused Bobby to explode in laughter. Hearing his joy, Momma looked at Lil Dee in the rearview mirror and began to giggle and I could not help but laugh too. Bobby tried to explain to Momma that he had looked over the seat hoping to calm Lil Dee, but he saw that she was using a puppy like a handkerchief to dry her tears with and that the look on the puppy's face was one of anger — he was not howling along with my sister's sad crying, but instead because he was pissed off at her for wiping her tears on him and getting him wet.

"Poor dog thinks she might try to wipe her ass with him next!" Bobby managed to say, and we laughed even harder at the idea of a puppy being misused in that way.

"You're right, Page" Lil Dee said, anger clear her voice. "He's an asshole!" and we all began to laugh even more, as the stress and fear built up by the events of the day evaporated from our hearts. In time, I would come to enjoy many laughs with my family over odd things or at odd times that no normal family would laugh at nor understand. This is the point in our life where I know in my heart that we became a family because families all seem to have their own culture and languages, little things that only they understand.

Bobby laughed at Lil Dee and said, "That's right, purebred asshole girly girl! and don't you forget it! But I ain't gonna die tonight honey." Then he playfully made an ugly face at us as he pretended to die.

We were somewhere under a Kentucky night sky when the laughter stopped and the events of the day began to weigh on Bobby's strength. In one last attempt at being a playful jester, he took a bag of Oxys from his pocket, tossed some in his mouth, and grinned at Momma over the bitter taste as he chewed up enough pills for a weeks' worth of pain. This told me that Bobby was lying about being alright and that his leg was worse than he was letting on. He then playfully told Momma to open her mouth and he put a pill in her mouth, smiling as he said, "One for now, and these are for latter," before handing her the sandwich baggie of pills.

"You don't need to put any in your ears, Christy. Dope's cheap, a man can get as much dope as he wants for the price of a bullet if he lets his balls swing like God intended for a man to do. So, for as long as you're driving me around y'all girls won't be stealing and whoring. I'm a man, I won't allow it, and it is not open for debate. So if you're one of those crazy bitches who wants to turn tricks, or steal things to make daddy happy, then you need to let me out of this car right now, because I ain't your daddy. My dick won't get hard watching you mistreat yourself or the baby, so don't insult me by disrespecting yourself in that way for me, or by risking a confrontation with the police by shoplifting something stupid. Bobby said, moaning in pain as he pulled a large wad of money out of his pocket and gave it to Momma. "Spend it, as much as you want. I can get more money and drugs with a pistol in one night than you can by stealing or any other way in a year. I got a sister, and the idea of her trading herself to maggots for dope is not something that I like to think about. If it's wrong for my own sister or crazy ass mother to do, then it is wrong for any woman to do. So, get that through your head.

In prison, guys talk, they brag about their street girls, hookers, and friends, but ain't no man going to love or marry a hooker. They all say the same thing, that their street girl is cool, but she ain't wife material. Remember, if some ass clown tries to get you to go off with him to turn a trick, that I'm already dead and not above killing him too. So if that's the type of women you are, if your head's so fucked up that you think that turning a trick is a sign of love, then tell me now so you can go your way and I can go mine. I get it, you had to feed your habits, that's cool, you ain't my old lady anyway.

But I got plenty of pills, cash and bullets, so don't disrespect me by trying to prove you're a good whore." Bobby said. His tone was hard but truthful, and I saw that Momma was stunned by his honesty.

Lil Dee giggled at Bobby, who then turned towards us and said, "I mean it! No stealing dog food or anything else. We got money. Stealing is wrong — them men work hard to run those stores. Besides, if you steal something the cops will get called and then I gotta kill the store guy and the Bacon Boys, so don't fucking do it!" Bobby screamed.

His anger caused Lil Dee to slide over close to me searching for protection. This was something that she had only done on those cold nights when we were alone in the car after Christmas. I became angry at the memory of those evil nights, and I began to scream back at Bobby.

"Fuck you! You're as much of of a creep as them store owners who Momma used to fuck! You're all sick! I saw how they would look at me, like they were hoping for a chance to do things to me. Fuck you!" I screamed again as Momma tried to get me to calm down.

"No Momma, fuck you too! We had to watch out for you when them assholes would take you in the backroom, moaning as loud as they could, then staring at us touching their weenie every time we went back in the store. You got your pills out of it, but what did I ever get out of it?" I asked Momma as Lil Dee began to laugh at me.

"Sissy, we got to take as much candy as we wanted, don't you remember? It was fun!" she giggled as silence filled the car, leaving us with only the sounds of the tires on the road singing in tune with the big car's engine.

A drug addict's morality is as two-faced as that old fake Roman God, Janis. Lil Dee's honesty had shocked us all, forcing us to see the events of our past as we felt them not only in the moment that they happened, but as well as how we felt about them now. Bobby had been honest but mean in the way that he exposed his heart's needs to us, that is honestly what he had done. He was the type of man who understood that women have to do vile things in the pursuit of their addictions, but that he would be disrespectful if a woman friend of his sacrificed herself while he was there to care for her, showing us the dual faces of his morals.

Momma was no different, I could see that Bobby's words and tone had been insulting to her — he had laid her soul naked for all to see by telling her not to try and impress him in that way, as if she were a common hooker. And then my words about the store owners and asking her what I had gained from the degradation she heaped upon herself, forced her to see that no matter how she lied to herself, she had lived her life as if she was nothing more than a common street whore who valued dope above all else. But Lil Dee's honest heart and laughter showed me that I was either wrong for accepting what my mother was doing in those back rooms with those nasty men, by stealing candy, and joking as we timed them, or I was wrong now for being angry with my mother for allowing her addiction to make her willing to lower herself to that depth. I was no better than the men in prison who had no problems with a woman who was street or down for her man, but I disliked them for those same virtues. Seeing myself in the honest light of my sister's words, I began to understand why almost every addict I know of hides behind a mask. A mask worn to to protect their own hearts from seeing themselves as the world sees them.

Silence is the absolute worst way to apologize to someone you love. It hurts in an unexplainable way, but sometimes silence is all that you have to offer them. As we drove on that night, I did not have the words to tell Momma that I was sorry for saying the things that I said about our past choices, or that I now realized that it was not just her past choices, but instead our combined past choices that were eating at my soul, and that the way she abandoned us on Christmas day was poisoning my opinions of everything about her and our life together.

It's one thing to believe that you are a member of the Three Musketeers, but it hurts like hell to have to accept the fact that the Three Musketeers are fictional, make-believe, and that your mother's betrayal was very real and not easily excused. Sadly, I could not stop myself from leaning forward and hugging her over the seat. It was a false apology, but the only gift that I could bring myself to offer her with my heart still in turmoil. Today, when I look back on that hug, I know that I only touched her to relieve my own pain and guilt. I still wanted to hurt her for not loving us enough to give up drugs and to go to the police to get help for Lil Dee as she had promised.

"What about Bobby?" Lil Dee playfully asked as I leaned forward and hugged Momma.

"He's big enough to hug her himself!" I said, trying to return the laughter that our honesty had stolen from us.

"I think his balls might be swinging too much for him to hug anyone!" Dee said as she moaned, acting out the pain boys feel when they get hit in the groin, and we all erupted in laughter again.

"I'll try to keep them from swinging too much Lil Dee!" Bobby said between moans of pain and fits of laughter, as Momma wiped tears from her eyes with the back of her hand and I saw the way the car's headlights reflected on the small lane markers embedded in the highway and stupidly thought that they looked like large diamonds. Dorothy had Toto, a Cowardly Lion, the Tin Man, a Scarecrow, and the Yellow Brick Road to follow; we had five ugly beagles, each other and those diamond-like flashes of light in the center of the highway to chase down, one after the other, until we got to wherever it was that fate meant for us to be.

We stayed in a cheap motel in Knoxville, Tennessee, not because of the price or lack of money, but because cheap motels didn't care who you were. Bobby said that it was way too soon for the police to be after him over Percodan, but he had started this party long before meeting us and that in time they would find the Cadillac he had dumped at Ruby's and his blood at Percodan's and then all hell would break loose.

"I hate to act like I'm paranoid, Page, but we got a reason to be paranoid this time honey." Bobby said with a laugh, and

I remembered how Lil Dee and I would play with the paranoid crackheads who Momma would party with in motels rooms like the one we were in now. It was fun to make a noise and watch the guy freak out, but this was not a joking matter, so we did our best to let Bobby sleep in peace.

Bobby had chosen the bed closest to the door of the room. He put pistols under the pillows, on the floor, and on the nightstand under the light. Seeing this, along with our memories of Percodan's, we had no doubts about what he intended to do if the wrong person came to our door. Yet he slept as if he trusted us, never once waking up at the sound of the door opening when we went out to eat or to walk the dogs. Nor did he wake up scared at the sound of someone farting and pointing a gun at us like you always see guys doing in the bad movies. But we were small room trained. Jail cells and motel rooms have that in common — you learn early how to be respectful while others are asleep, and they learn that life goes on even though they are sleeping.

He made Momma sleep with us girls in the other bed, and she was not happy about it. Bobby had not hugged her, kissed her, nor done anything to prove to her that he wanted her, and I began to worry. Momma did not like to offer herself to a man for free and for that man to turn her down. For now, though, Bobby's claim of needing sleep, being hurt and wanting it to appear as if we were being held against our will was enough to ease Momma's temper. But if Bobby ignored her much longer, the nicest thing Momma would do is call him gay, cause a big scene and leave him somewhere, and at worst she would steal his money, drugs and guns, and sneak out of the motel room, leaving Bobby sleeping, snuggled up with the dogs as he seemed to enjoy doing and trying to figure out how the cops had found him. I could see it in her eyes that Momma was getting more and more pissed off every time Bobby accepted Lucy curling up to get warm besides him.

She finally decided to take us shopping for clothes and things that we needed using Bobby's cash, never checking the price of an item or asking Lil Dee to explain why the dogs needed two neck collars each. For the first time in years, she bought all three of us matching boots and tennis shoes — it was as if she wanted Bobby to get mad and complain about how much money she had spent, but Bobby seemed to enjoy seeing us happy and excited to have new things, complete with our own gym bags too.

I saw a plea in Momma's eyes as she gave him the new shirts, pants, socks and underwear that she had gotten for him. The fact that he seemed pleased with her choices made her happy. This was the second morning since the events at Percodan's. The radio and TV news could not help but to build stories from speculation, only causing Bobby to laugh until one news station reported that the deaths may have been related to claims of child molestation. After hearing this, Bobby decided that it was time to leave Knoxville. He began to split up his money and drugs, making a pile of each for Momma and himself.

Momma looked like she was going to cry as she pointed at the gifts Bobby intended to give her and in an emotional voice asked, "Why?"

"Why?" Bobby said with a laugh. "Because I put myself in the position I am in long before Ruby's. The cops are saying molestation — ain't nobody left alive but us here in this room who knows that's why they're all dead. That means either one of y'all called the police or they done figured out that y'all had something to do with it, and that can only mean Ruby's. Someone there told them at the very least you gave me a ride. Now seeing how the Bacon Boys ain't snacking on donuts out front of this motel trying to get me to come out without a fight, that means y'all ain't called them on me," Bobby said as he raised his hands, motioning for Momma to let him speak. "Molestation means that you're free of this, it's my fight. Y'all just hide the money and pills then go home and tell the cops that I did it on my own and forced you to drive me here. Then you're free to start a new life -- there's at least $80,000 dollars and about 20,000 Oxys, that's more than enough to get you set up. Bobby said as he looked at me as if seeking my help to convince Momma. But I was her daughter, and I may have recently come to the realization that the Three Musketeers were fiction, but that did not mean that I accepted it.

"If I didn't need to go see my own mother, I would go stash all this shit for you guys, "Bobby said as he motioned to the money and drugs. "Then tie y'all up and handle this shit on my terms with the cops. Just ain't never been one for running away from trouble!" Bobby stated with blank eyes, as if he was somewhere else and not here with us for a moment.

"Where's your mother?" Momma asked, and I saw her stand up a little straighter, stick her chin out and cross her arms. She had heard in Bobby's tone what I had also heard, and that was the sound of him being unsure, guessing, not the hard, cold commands that he had used to order her to drive him to Percodan's after he had realized that Lil Dee had been hurt or when he explained his feeling about Momma trying to turn tricks to impress him.

"Over on Dogwood Mountain, up northwest of Nashville where old Jesse James stayed back in the day," Bobby said as if everyone knew the story of Jesse James.

"Well, I guess we can take you there, seeing how we ain't never going back to Kermit again and you need a ride," Momma said with a cute smile on her face and a feline quality to her movements.

"Christy, this can only end one way — you know it and I know it," Bobby began to say, as Momma put her hands up to stop Bobby from speaking as he had done to her.

"We already voted Bobby and you lost, so shut up and accept it," Momma said as Lil Dee began to laugh and mimic Momma, crossing her arms and thrusting her chin out.

"Go south," Bobby said as we left the motel and headed for the highway. "I need antibiotics for this leg. It's too late for stitches but it might be worth asking. I got a feeling that tobacco was not the best thing to have stuffed into the hole because I couldn't wash it all out and now it's red and sore as hell!" This caused Momma to look at him with a question in her eyes.

"We have to assume that the cops will find out that we were here. We'll find a pain clinic down south near Chattanooga. I'll get a script from the doctor there and if he realizes who I am in a few days and calls the law, they'll think we're Florida bound or something," Bobby said as Lil Dee held her favorite puppy for him to see and Momma turned south on the highway, smiling happily to herself for not letting Bobby convince her to leave him to face the future on his own. Today, I know just how stupid it was for us to believe that we could somehow make more out of things than the horror show that it was sure to be. But just like Momma tricked herself into believing that she could manage her addiction over and over again, we needed Bobby so much that we gladly forgot that sooner or later, Bobby's face would be on every TV in America, and maybe ours as well.

"Look, Bobby! I named him Buttons — see, the spots on his tummy look like the buttons on one of those shirts Momma got for you at the store," Lil Dee said as Bobby looked over the seat at her and grinned at the way Button's fat stomach looked as if it were going to burst open.

"I think one of them ugly butt dogs should be called Bowser!" Bobby said as he started to howl like a dog, trying to get Lucy to join him.

"Bowser," Lil Dee said as she handed Bobby the smallest of Lucy's puppies. She smiled at me and said, "Now it's your turn to name one Page, you, and Momma, so everyone has their favorite," she said as she joined Bobby in his attempts to get all of the dogs to howl together. It reminded me of when we would sing along with Momma and the radio as we drove around the hills and countryside, going nowhere, happy just to be together.

Looking at the people driving along the highway with us, it dawned on me that they did not know who we were. There was no way for them to tell that Momma was an addict who sold herself just to get high, nor could a person in a passing car tell that the man with the long black hair riding in the passenger seat, playing with a beagle puppy, was just as much of an addict as my mother was. And if they could not see the stains left from a lifetime of living deep inside of the trashy lifestyle that is addiction, then they couldn't see me or Lil Dee as we truly were in our hearts. That meant that I could be anything that I wanted to be, and I began to practice changing my face to first appear as I felt a queen's face would look as she drove past a common person on the highway; soon I was pretending to be a teacher, Mickey, Bobby as he stood up to Percodan, Jessica, mouse-like and twitching, Ms. Linda and everyone that I had ever known.

It was far too easy to forget that Momma and Bobby were addicts, that they each had a pocket full of pills and another pocket full of money. Bobby had even given both Lil Dee and me money that we could spend as we wanted to, and money to keep us safe if something bad happened. Without Momma's normal need to find money for her next pill, I believed that Bobby and Momma were normal and not emotionally messed up.

People with mental issues, messed up heads and hearts, cannot live without storms. Their life is just not right if they are not dealing with some part of a storm. Had I realized this beforehand, I would have known that Bobby should never have gone into the little pain clinic we found just north of Chattanooga, after all, he was on the run from something bad when we met him, and he had more than enough dope to 'crawl in a hole and hide' as Percodan would say. But Bobby went out and poured gasoline on that fire without any concern over getting burned, so it was foolish to believe that he would act right in public. No, it wasn't foolish, but instead downright stupid!

Please remember that lots of addicts are mentally ill before they become addicted, but all addicts are mentally ill after becoming addicted. Traumas they went through in life that they never properly dealt with begin to roam free in their mind when they're high and dreaming; the walls that we build to imprison the hurtful parts of life seem to fall away when we are high, leaving us to face those old pains once again, reminding us of mental traumas, failed loves, guilts, anything that will make us question our strength to stay clean, force us to give up, to use again. It is most often a fight that is being waged in silence because the brain knows that if you

149

try to explain how you feel to someone else, they will convince you to stay clean or strong.

So, we fight a silent war, making it seem as if, for no reason at all, the recovering addict just relapsed, abandoned their loved ones, their self-worth one more time, adding even more reasons to feel guilty if they live long enough to return to recovery. Just like Momma could not bring herself to face the mean things she has said to Mr. Bear and Ms. Linda; they had only wanted her to return to the rehab center, just as she had finally decided to do on Christmas day, but her own guilt convinced her to leave us alone sleeping in a car for ten days when the Bears would have gladly let us come back home to them. Believe me, every aspect of this was weighted and measured by Momma's broken and mentally ill brain before she walked away from our car that day. The cost of facing the Bears was deemed too high of price to pay in exchange for the safety of her children. Little did I know that Bobby Austin was about to teach me a whole new aspect of mental illness: hate, pure hate.

Chapter 16

Momma drove up as close to the pain clinic's front door as she could. Bobby's leg had been stiff and hurting more. Both sides of the bullet wound were red and beginning to swell. Bobby said that there should be drainage as it was a deep wound that should have been stitched both inside of the holes and at their rims. He believed that the tobacco had caused the wound to swell and now, unable to drain, it was beginning to get infected.

I got out of the car to help him walk into the doctor's office. We had watched him lean over the seat and take a stack a money; put a small pistol like the one that Percodan had carried into his back pocket; and then stuff his big black pistol, the one he used at Percodan's, into the waist of his pants under his shirt as he fumbled to stuff extra magazines of bullets into other pockets. Lots of pills and lots of money equaled lots of guns in our minds, so to see Bobby arm himself as he had was not out of the ordinary in a world where few would actually use gun, but many carried them in the hope that having a gun would convince others to leave them alone. Yet, in this case giving Bobby a gun was like handing the Grim Reaper a chainsaw — stupid, just plain stupid.

"Go back to the car Page! Tell your mom I said for her to kick rocks! Beat it! Go on! Get lost!" Bobby said as he pushed me away. "Your mother cannot leave without you. Tell her to take the bag and go away, I don't need the headache of dealing with you bitches!" Bobby said and I could not help but begin to cry from the sting of his words. Earlier, as I daydreamed, pretending to be other people, each of their mask had two things in common — one was that we had become a family, second, that we had survived the storm caused by the killing of Percodan. So Bobby's words were like knives in my heart as I ran to find where Momma was parking the car.

"He doesn't want us!" I cried as Momma opened the door to get out the car. "He told me to go away, that you could have his bag, and that he didn't need the headache of a bunch of bitches!" I screamed as I cried in pain.

"Why that punk-ass, limp-dick motherfucker!" Momma said in anger as she slammed the car door and motioned for Lil Dee and me to follow her. I will never forget looking back at our car, our home, and seeing Lucy and her puppies looking back at me. My heart still stung, but part of me knew that Momma was mean when she was mad, and Bobby had really pissed her off.

The doctor's nurse was Barbie Doll pretty, not one bleached hair out of place, long nails and face perfectly painted to accent her natural beauty, and a figure that any man would like; even her gold jewelry matched her expensive tanning bed tan. Money had enhanced the woman's looks to the point that they would intimidate most women, but Momma was not impressed and firmly stated as we walked up to the front desk: "My husband just came in to see the doctor, which room is he in?" Then without waiting for an answer, she said: "Come on girls, your father's waiting on us." I could see that Lil Dee had Buttons in her arms and was sticking her tongue out at the pretty nurse as we walked past.

Bobby could not help but laugh as we walked in the room. "Damn! You got my dope and money, I ain't got nothing else," Bobby said as he tenderly hugged me, telling me that it had also hurt him to have been so mean to me and that we had to accept that this trip could not end well.

"No matter what, the hole I'm in is too deep to get out this time girls!" Bobby said. But desire is a monster, it can convince fools to pay thousands of dollars to climb up Mount Everest, up past the oxygen level. Now honestly, think about that, common sense says, 'No air and you're dead,' so it has to be desire that gets so many people pay so much money to die while climbing that stupid mountain, just as it was desire that blinded us to the train wreck that loving Bobby Austin was sure to be.

Bobby was leaning against the examination table, neither truly sitting nor completely standing, playfully holding Momma's hand in the first sign of romantic affection that I had witnessed. Lil Dee was mumbling something to Buttons as I looked at the doctor's desk, covered with family photographs, trinkets of love and the tokens of a successful and normal life, all camouflaging the doctor's true nature.

The doctor was short, chubby and balding, just like most of the TV archaeologists I'm forced to endure on TV. There must be something about money, and not needing to look good to find a mate anymore, that causes guys like the doctor to let themselves go, while still acting like they're God's gift to mankind. This doctor was so blatantly full of himself that he attempted to belittle Bobby as soon as he walked into the room by saying: "Your wife and daughters acted very disrespectful to my staff. They cannot be back here with you, nor will I treat you unless your wife apologizes for sticking her tongue out at my nurse."

Bobby began to look at Momma and giggle, finding it cute that she would have stuck her tongue out at the pretty nurse.

"This is not funny!" the pudgy doctor said pointing a finger and speaking loudly for the benefit of his nurse, who I was sure was standing outside of the office door. "You need me, I don't need you. You junkies are all the same, animals, and I won't put up with it!"

"I stuck my tongue out Bobby," Lil Dee said as she tried to keep Buttons from jumping down onto the floor from the examination table.

"This is a doctor's office — get these kids and that dog out of here right now!" the foolish doctor said as he reached out towards me as if meaning to push me out the door, all while yelling about animals not being allowed in the doctor's office.

I like to believe that Bobby was just too high to comprehend everything that the doctor was saying, but I am a daughter trying to paint a picture of her father in a positive light when the truth is Bobby heard every word the chubby doctor spoke, along with the tone he was speaking in, and then exploded in rage, striking the doctor to the floor with his open hand.

"Doctor, doctor, you're a fucking drug dealer like I am! Who the fuck do you think you are, asshole!" Bobby yelled as he beat the now begging doctor with anything that he could pick up from the desk. When a coffee mug broke, he grabbed a framed picture, a computer mouse, anything that he could reach, and beat the doctor with it until it broke into pieces, all the while screaming that the man was not a doctor at all but just another dope dealer.

Just like an addict's children cannot call he police to save themselves from things that go bump in the night, neither can prescription selling doctors. I had seen Bobby offer Jessica no mercy, yet I had no idea how evil Bobby was until he grabbed the doctor's nurse when she tried to stop him from savagely beating the doctor.

"You want some too bitch?" Bobby screamed as he wrapped his hand in her long hair and began to slam her face on the desk, looking completely evil as he explained to the doctor why he was only hitting her face on the desk and not her whole head. "Don't want her brain to swell doc, just want to smash this whore's whole face in, so she talks funny when the news interviews her, and she says that she doesn't understand why I caved her face in and left her cross-eyed and ugly!" Bobby laughed as Momma reached out to stop him and he tossed the broken nurse to the floor.

I was scared for Momma who could only manage to yell, "Enough, Bobby, enough," as Bobby looked around the room with a blank look in his eyes to see Lil Dee giggling at the pretty nurse's crumpled body lying in a puddle of her own blood, moaning much like Percodan had moaned just before his death. "Stop it shorty, this ain't funny!" Bobby said as the look of reality returned to his eyes.

"But Bobby, you say funny things when you're mad," Lil Dee grinned.

"Get them out of here," Bobby said to Momma as he pulled his black pistol from his waist and pointed it at the now pleading doctor.

"No Bobby! No, you gotta stop killing people! No Bobby! I screamed as Momma reached out and pushed the gun barrel away from the doctor. Only after grinning over at me did Bobby let go of the gun and begin to laugh.

"You know what doctor?" Bobby asked, if the doctor were a person of honor and not the slime covered greedy bastard that he was. 'You know what? They're right, neither you nor this bitch are worth the price of a bullet. Is this a picture of your fat ass wife doc?" Bobby asked as he bent down and smacked the man with the last unbroken framed picture in the room and I saw Lil Dee pick up one of the nurse's bloody teeth from the desk and smile.

"Yeah, as porky as she is, ain't no one can blame you for spending all your money on this whore over here," Bobby said, laughing, as he stepped on the nurse's outstretched hand and fingers, causing them to make popping sounds as she again moaned in pain.

"Playing possum! Not fair, whore!" Bobby exclaimed as he kicked the woman again to the delight of my sister. I could see in her eyes that she was enjoying what Bobby was doing as much as he was.

"What do you think this asshole was doing Christmas night Christy?" Bobby asked my mother who grabbed Lil Dee and said, "Come on Page, fuck this shit," as she pulled Lil Dee toward the hallway. I turned in time to see Bobby stab the doctor in the neck with a broken wooden picture frame, causing the man to gurgle on his own blood as Bobby smashed the back of the nurse's neck and head with his boot, repeatedly stomping her as he smiled, as if he were truly happy and in no pain from the bullet wound that had kept him from walking into the office on his own just moments before.

I wish that I could tell you that commonsense prevailed and my mother led us to the car and that we abandoned Bobby, but she had been the cause of most of her failed relationships and although Bobby would not commit to her as she hoped, she still decided not to abandon him the way she felt that men had abandon her over the years. Also it was easy to accept the events at Percodan's house because we were his victims in many more ways than the event surrounding Lil Dee and Christmas. When the hammer of fate falls on someone you know, or someone dies, we add up all of the good things that we remember about that person, the things we enjoyed with them, then we subtract all of the bad things that we remember about them; what you're left with is the amount of grieving you feel over their loss.

Let's face it, the cold way that Percodan had killed the black guy from Detroit was more than enough reason to laugh at Percodan's funeral, and tell some dark jokes — he was a snake and he got what he asked for! Bobby had acted in a mechanical way as he went about those killings, as if putting a sick animal to sleep for its own good. But this time, he had enjoyed himself, and Lil Dee was basking in the glow of her hero's joy. There was no way for me to begin an account ledger for Bobby's new victims in the pain clinic because at the time I was unsure how I felt about those people's deaths.

Today, I hate those types of doctors who first gave Oxys to anyone on Medicaid and Medicare — those prescriptions were paid for by the government, they sat unused in medicine cabinets throughout America, and it was this stockpile of unneeded drugs that fueled the opiate crisis. Then these same doctors who poisoned so many decided to open rehabilitation centers to once again milk the American people out of vast amounts of money. These are my opinions today, after a lifetime of learning, but on the day that Bobby, a man who had already accepted that his death was soon to arrive and simply did not give a fuck.

Momma's hand was shaking as she started the car. Bobby was laughing about the things that he had just done, and Lil Dee was smiling and giggling with him. I almost couldn't care less once we were safely back on the highway, I had the puppies to enjoy as I daydreamed about the future. Finally free from chasing Momma's addiction, I was starting to see that there was more to life than living at Ruby's truck stop. Bobby's leg had reopened, it was leaking fluids along with some blood, but all Bobby could talk about was how stupid he was to forget to get a prescription for antibiotics from the doctor before the man had died. I could see that Momma was struggling with what to say.

"Bobby, why did you do that? What's wrong with you? Do you see how the girls look at you?" Momma asked Bobby before she lost her strength to speak. We can't keep doing it, you can't keep doing it," she mumbled. Knowing her as I did, I knew that she would have been staring down at the floor around her feet if she had not been driving the car, headed for Nashville.

"We agreed to help you, to stand beside you. I should have stopped you from doing what you did at Percodan's. Maybe we could have found somewhere to hide, somehow built a new life like you keep telling me that I need to do. But you're crazy, and my girls really like you," Momma softly spoke, her words held more honesty and emotion in them than any I had heard her speak since she relapsed and ran away from the Bears' love.

"Please don't get mad or scream Bobby. We gotta talk this out. My girls, Bobby, please!" my mother begged, her voice so low that I almost did not hear hear.

"Jesus, Christy! You act like I'm an animal. My momma raised me right, I'm not gonna just start screaming at you and your girls like a madman. Real men don't need to scream at a woman, a real man can scream at full-grown men and back it up! Don't insult me by acting like you're scared to talk to me, Christy!" Bobby said in a flat tone, sounding shocked that Momma did not know him well enough to feel free to be honest with him.

I laughed at them, a long, loud laugh. "Fuck Bobby, you just beat that woman to death back there, smiling and laughing the whole time, and you're acting like Momma insulted you by being afraid to speak up, to tell you how she feels!" I boldly stated, shocking both my mother and Bobby.

"I did that shit back there for you girls. Guys like that live in nice houses that they bought with the money they make from getting people hooked on drugs, while you guys live in a car at a truck stop turning tricks. My life is over — I have to see my mom, and then I'm done. But until then, if I don't like something, I'm gonna to step to it and teach it a lesson! And that is fucking that!" Bobby said as he looked over at Lil Dee for support. "They can only kill me once — ain't that right shorty?" Bobby smiled as he asked Lil Dee.

"I thought you said that you weren't gonna die Bobby?" Lil Dee asked as she began to cry.

"That ain't what I meant, Lil Dee," Bobby said, shaking his head as if confused, and then he saw a sign saying Murfreesboro, pointed to it and told Momma to find a nice motel there for us to stay the night in. Then he looked over at Momma and said, "I get the point, Christy, I saw the way that Lil Dee was acting back there. I'm sorry, I just hate for people to act like money makes them the boss and us the slave. Add to that, I fucking hate to see what women do to get high on shit clowns like that doctor pass out. I just never thought about the girls watching," Bobby calmly said and I saw Momma relax, comfortable with herself for confronting Bobby.

"But Bobby, they're dead. No one knows why you killed them. There was no lesson in that except for how Lil Dee sees the world now," Momma told Bobby as she pulled into a motel parking lot to get us a room.

Shortly after we were settled in our room Momma went to the store to buy more stuff for Bobby's leg; I'm also sure that she wanted to be alone to sort her thoughts out. What Bobby had shown us was that he was simply crazy, and dangerous, although I had no fear of him. No, Bobby was like a sweet, retired fighting dog who would allow his master to beat him half to death and never try to bite him over the pain, but say the wrong thing around the dog and he would kill your neighbors' kids for you, all the while expecting praise and treat for doing so. Momma had best not play with Bobby as she had played with other men before — they were toys, Bobby was not, and there was no chance of us being a family if he hurt anyone else.

The evening sun was hanging low in the sky as Lil Dee and I ran and played with the puppies under the watchful eye of Bobby who, despite all that he had recently done and the fact that the police were sure looking for him by now, refused to close the motel room door as long as we were outside with the dogs. He wasn't watching us play like we had seen perverts and freaks stare at us before, but instead Bobby just laid on the bed listening to us enjoying life — there to protect us if needed, but not intending to interrupt us. I could not help but wonder if this is how it felt to be loved and cared for by a good father. I looked over to see Bobby light a cigarette and smile at the way Lucy would sniff the ground and her pups would then try to follow her. Maybe things would stay like this forever I thought as I ran over and tackled Lil Dee, rolling on the ground, happy to tickle her until she begged me to stop.

Later that night, as we got ready for bed, Lil Dee said, "Tomorrow, we meet Bobby's Momma, Page!" The sound of hope was thick in her voice. "I hope she likes us!" my smiling baby sisters said.

"Me too, Lil Dee, me too," I replied as we drifted off to sleep in Momma's arms, listening to Bobby snoring on the bed besides ours, comfortably sleeping surrounded by beagles, pistols, pills, and money.

Chapter 17

The big city of Nashville was little more than a dark spot slowly shrinking behind us in our rearview mirror, and Kentucky was beginning to quickly to fill the big car's front window, when Bobby told Momma to get off the main highway onto an old road that would take us west towards Missouri and the hills above the mighty Mississippi River. I could see a child-like joy in a man who I should have been deeply afraid of, but his joy was intoxicating, as true, real joy always should be. I know that if a normal person ever reads this, they will wonder why we trusted Bobby and were not afraid of him. Lil Dee and I had nothing to judge him by. We had been starving, sleeping in our car, and slowly beginning to see that our mother's addiction was the source of our sufferings, not Momma's choices.

We were like so many other people who believed the new medical mantra that addiction was to blame for her bad choices, and not that her bad choices might to be to blame for her addiction. So our life with Bobby was good; our days and nights were not consumed by helping Momma hunt for her next pill, as even just babysitting was helping my mother get high, and with Bobby, her addiction had stopped being a problem, so we never thought to doubt Momma's ability to make the right choices in life. You cannot be the Three Musketeers and doubt your fearless leader.

"Stop, over there!" Bobby excitedly said as he pointed to an emergency turnaround where cars would stop to allow semi-trucks to safely struggle up or down the steep mountain that the road was beginning to climb.

Bobby jumped out of the car before we had completely come to a stop, with Lil Dee and the dogs following closely behind him as he searched for the best spot to look over the top of the trees to the west.

"Y'all see where the trees turn into a straight line down there?" Bobby asked as he pointed down the mountainside. "That's the Mississippi River down there. On hot days, you can smell her from here, but them trees have always been too thick to see her. Now over there to the west," Bobby said as he pointed out above the treetops where the land turned to large flat farmland spotted with small patches of woods, "that over there is Missouri. My grandpa was half Blackfoot Indian and half redneck. He would take me hunting in those fields and woods and he would point over here, and say some prayers to his ancestors, as he swore this mountain was kinda sacred."

Then Bobby turned to point up towards the top of the mountain. That up there, up at the top where the woods just seem to end, that's Cemetery Ridge he looked as if he had seen something up there, but all I could see was the outline of trees shadowed by the land around them.

"Give me the keys, Christy, I'll drive!" Bobby said.

"What about your leg Bobby?" Momma asked. Bobby smiled playfully, tossed some pills in his mouth, grinned and gently took the keys from her outstretched hand. We climbed back in the car to begin the climb to what would become my home.

The town of Dogwood Mountain owes its name and survival to the cemetery that sits atop the mountain. The town, like the mountain, once had different names, those which have been lost to time, long ago forgotten. What is amazing is that Cemetery Ridge was built as a way to punish the residents of the neighboring little town that now shares the name. Funny how things turn out. The small town looks today just as it did that day when Bobby drove us home — its schools, stores, post office, and houses are as neatly painted and trimmed as they were that day so long ago when Bobby was greeted with the kind of waves and smiles people always reserve for a hometown boy who has returned for a visit. I began to pray that Bobby looked like his daddy and that his Momma would look more like me, then everyone in town would believe that I was Bobby's daughter as I'm sure that they would have no problem believing that Lil Dee was. Looking at both Bobby and Lil Dee made me hate my father and his light-haired carnival blood.

At the base of Cemetery Ridge sat an old farmhouse, built on a flat strip of land facing out and away from Cemetery Ridge towards the southwest and down the mountain to the Mississippi River. This always seemed odd to me as the house and its two workshops all had their backs built towards the cemetery, its church, and the hidden cabins that decorated the very top of Cemetery Ridge. Slightly odder still was that not one building or house on Cemetery Ridge had any windows facing towards the little town. Bobby said that the builder of the graveyard had once planned to have the main road to town, the one that we had just driven down, changed so that it bypassed the town, coming up by the base of Cemetery Ridge to the front of the large old house, thus forcing the people from the town to move away.

"The old man absolutely hated that little town Page," Bobby said as we pulled up at the back of the tombstone shop and parked beside an aged but still shiny black Cadillac hearse.

I will never forget stepping out of the car that first day and looking up Cemetery Ridge as it steeply rose up to the sky, each step covered in old tombstones and tall skinny dogwood trees. I was wondering why anyone would want to take the time to turn a mountain top into such a lovely place.

The man that I would come to know and love as Brother Carl stood tall and razor thin. His teeth had long ago been lost from his deeply wrinkled face, and his long grey hair was a contradiction to his playful, happy nature, a nature that in time would cause me to question if he was honestly that much older than Lil Dee. But a joy-filled soul has no age, does it?

"Karen, Karen, it's our Indian boy, I told you he would come home, I told you!" Brother Carl shouted back towards the house as he raced up to us, hugging Bobby, Momma, Lil Dee and me as if he had known us his whole life, instantly teaching me that angles smell like lye soap, homemade red sumac berry wine, country cooking, and granite dust.

"You done brought me some beautiful babies to spoil son!" a smiling Brother Carl said, Ms. Karen did not show her age as Carl did — from a distance, it was hard to tell that she had spent over seventy winters on Dogwood Mountain.

"I won't lie to you," Ms. Karen said, "I done had five phone calls from folks uptown telling me that you was finally on your way to see your mother's resting place, but I still don't believe that you're here. Now stop being selfish and give me a hug!" Ms. Karen said and then hugged Bobby as if she would die if she had to wait another second. I could see in Momma's eyes that she was shocked as I was to hear that we were here on Dogwood Mountain to see a dead woman, ending any chance of getting the woman to help us find a way of taming Bobby.

"Is them coon dogs boy?" Carl asked as he bent down to pet Lucy and scratch her ears. "I sure miss my old dogs, but Ms. Karen won't let me get no more after I shot my last one," a smiling Brother Carl stated, as if shooting your dog was a completely normal thing to do.

"You shoot one of my dogs and I'll get one of Bobby's guns and kill you, old man!" Lil Dee said as she stepped in between Brother Carl and Lucy with a look of pure evil in her eyes.

Momma could only gasp, as Bobby laughed and Ms. Karen reached over and pinched Lil Dee's arm and said, "Young ladies don't say things like that, nor do they go around killing old men, even if the old man deserves it! Now Carl ain't allowed to drink, go hunting, nor own any dogs anymore, so don't you worry about them pups being around him, young lady."

"Yes, Ms. Karen," Lil Dee said as she rubbed her arm where she had been pinched and looked to Bobby for support.

"Don't look at me to help you — my arm still hurts from being pinched by her when I said stupid things as a kid," Bobby said with a laugh as he rubbed his arm where Ms. Karen had pinched him as a child.

"From now on, I'm going to pinch you two times for every time I have to pinch one of the babies — it's your fault for not teaching them better, boy!" Ms. Karen said as she hugged both Lil Dee and me as if we were her own family and not the worthless offspring of a drug whore. "And you'll get your share too Ms. Christy. You only get one chance to raise babies up the right way, you mess up too many girls and they might just come limping back home one day, bleeding and hurting," Ms. Karen said, pointing at Bobby's stained pants.

"We put her up there where she liked to sit," Carl said as he pointed towards the back wall of the shop and the cemetery it hid from our sight.

Bobby shook his head in a knowing way as he said," Yeah I kind of had a dream that you would have let her rest there Carl, and I thank you for it. I best be headed up to see her I guess."

"Well since you're gonna to be staying, you can either stay at your mother's cabin or you can pick the one you like," Ms. Karen said as she pointed to Bobby's wounded leg. That's starting to smell, you need to come back after you see your mother and let me clean you up some," she continued, as she looked over at Momma for help with convincing Bobby to let her help him. "You better come too — when you own an old tomcat, that likes to stay out fussing and fighting all night, it's best you learn how to be a doctor," Ms. Karen said as she reached out and rubbed Brother Carl's arm without realizing that she was doing so, as old people in love always do.

"I'll come back down Karen, y'all girls ain't gonna to start ganging up on me!" Bobby said as he moved far enough away from Ms. Karen to not get pinched and gave Momma a warning look. He then turned and motioned for Lucy to follow as we began our first trip up Cemetery Ridge to my first and only true home, leaving Carl laughing at the idea of us girls not being able to gang up on Bobby.

"Boy, you sure don't understand women!" Carl said as he laughed.

Cemetery Ridge was so steep in places that the graves had to be dug into the hillside at an angle so that the coffin rested flat allowing the honored to sleep in comfort. As we came to the top of the first step, I could see that the hill just stopped and turned into a broad flat area covered in tombstones and dogwood trees leading to another steep hill covered in tombstones like the one we had just climbed. Suddenly Lucy, with her babies in tow, stopped racing about and sniffing the ground and violently jumped into the tall grass covering the grave of an old Civil War veteran named Wilson, chasing a covey of quail out of the brush.

Lucy's puppies acted just like their mother, just as the young quail acted as their parents had taught them to do — somehow, I understood that there was a message in what I was witnessing, but the name Wilson on the headstone caught my eye and made me catch my breath. It had been three days now since Bobby had killed them. Percodan's family name was Wilson, Lucy's babies had followed her into the weeds just as the quail babies had followed their parents out of those same weeds, just like Lil Dee and I were following Bobby and Momma.

Would Lil Dee or myself follow the same road that Momma took to reach a place like Ruby's truck stop? Would our lives be poisoned by drugs? Why was Bobby so mean if this gentle mountain was his home? Did Jessica forgive me for not saving her from Bobby's wrath? Were they burying Percodan and the others today at the same time as I was walking in a graveyard? Would I have gone to their funerals if I were still at home in Kermit today? Why did I feel shame and guilt over my part in their deaths? Why did I secretly enjoy knowing that they got exactly what they deserved? Their brains splattered all over Jesus and his stupid friends. How could a man like Jesus allow a sweet baby like Lil Dee to be harmed as she had been? These were questions that raced through my mind and heart in the time it took a covey of quail to take flight and escape a family of beagles. Yet even today, after so many lost years, those questions remain either unanswered or simply unanswerable, nothing more than the ghosts of childish ideas left behind to haunt the mind of an old women as she remembers one of the best days of her youth.

The climb to the top of Cemetery Ridge had been hard on all of us now Bobby's leg was open and bleeding again. We were standing at the top of Cemetery Ridge, with its cabins, as Lil Dee and I became lost in the beautiful stained-glass windows of the church. The building was nothing to brag about, just your basic old country church, built to last, plain and not fancy at all, yet God (or was it life?) had added an immeasurable amount of beauty to the plain wooden structure.

"The old man who built the church had the fifty-three stained-glass butterflies, the large cross, and the sunburst around it on the rear wall made by a real stained-glass company and shipped here. That's why that wall of the church, the one facing east, looks like it belongs in one of those fancy churches in a big city when the morning sun hits it. All of the other butterflies on the other walls are homemade, that's why they're all different sizes. Hell, some folks even used old pop bottles for colored glass!" Bobby said, as we stood there staring at the odd little church which was nearly completely covered in glass butterflies.

"Why butterflies Bobby?" Momma asked. I was amazed to hear a child-like tone in the voice of a woman who I thought I knew so well.

"Carl's a better storyteller then I am, but from what I'm led to believe, the man who built the cemetery and church was a little Cajun-Frenchman who got stuck up here when the boat he was on sunk down in the river. Y'all see all the pieces of ribbons hanging in the trees? They came from him too, but they're Native American Indian, in meaning, whereas the butterfly represents the spirit, or maybe a ghost, to the French. So he put one butterfly window in per person buried under the church, that church is their tombstone really. We hang the ribbons every year. They're spirit ribbons — that's tobacco and herbs tied in a ball there on the end of the ribbon, as a gift to the spirit that the ribbon honors. You see, girls, when Natives smoke tobacco, they pray and the tobacco smoke then carries their prayers up to the young golden eagle, or spotted eagle, 'Wambli Gleska', who then carries our prayers up to the creator. Well, it's something like that, you'll have to ask Carl about it," Bobby said as he touched a small tin cross with the bloodstained toe of his boot. I instantly forgot about spirit ribbons and the Cajun-Frenchman as I realized that the rusting cross that held Bobby's attention was all that there was to mark his mother's grave, and that it seemed out of place in a graveyard full of cut-stone monuments, stained-glass windows, and colored ribbons filled with tobacco.

Momma seemed to sense the storm brewing in Bobby's heart, and I saw a desperation in her eyes when she heard him mumbling about Carl, poor man's crosses, and that he could not believe they had not given his mother anything more to mark her life than an old, reused tin cross meant only to be used until a real stone was cut. "Bobby, I don't think Carl meant to be disrespectful; headstones are expensive, don't be mad at him," I heard Momma say, her words spoken quickly, almost desperately, as in my mind I saw Bobby's hand wrapping into Carl's long hair as Bobby smashed his face into whatever was near, with Lil Dee giggling at the sight the old man's blood as she screamed, "I told you to stay away from my dogs old man!" and I instantly understood my mother's fear. Bobby had killed over a drugged-out woman and her kids as calmly as most men would eat an ice cream sundae. He had then danced a happy dance as he beat a doctor and his nurse to death over the poor doctor's attitude — so what would he do now, to the poor old couple who had disrespected his mother's grave? "Oh shit!" I thought as I strugled to find the words to save the beautiful old couple waiting for us down at the bottom of the hill.

"What's wrong with you two?" Bobby asked. "This tiny piece of shit is not Carl's fault. It's mine! Fuck me! Are you people that stupid? I am the one who is responsible for my mother's memorial. Those odd and poorly made butterflies on that church over there ain't Carl's doing, those were each made by someone who loved a person buried on this stupid ass hillside!" Bobby angrily stated as he pointed to the church with one hand and beat his bleeding leg with the other. Despite the pain and fresh blood each touch of his heavy fist cost him, I was happy that he was not angry with the beautiful man who had greeted us as if he had been waiting for us to come home our whole lives. No one is happy to see you arrive at a dope house — it's not you they care about, it's the dope you might have to share with them, or the ride you might provide to find some more dope. No one is ever happy to see the daughters of a sack-chasing whore which is what Lil Dee and I were considered to be.

Lil Dee began to laugh as she sat down on Bobby's mother's grave to play with her puppies. "You say funny stuff when you're mad Bobby, even when you're mad at yourself!" she giggled as she smiled confidently up at the man I was still unsure of. Bobby was like my mother — a time bomb. Yet Momma was on her best behavior, still trying to catch Bobby. At that point in my life, I hadn't thought about my mother's abusive ways with men, but I knew that she would not flip out on or begin to test Bobby until she was sure that he was hers to abuse. Yet I could not forget the joy Bobby took in beating the doctor's whore, as he called the poor woman he had beaten to death — after all, wasn't Momma a whore?

Mickey said that her own mother was a whore and that all women who trade their daughters, themselves, or allow anyone else to trade them are whores, even Mickey herself, and at times even me and Lil Dee — after all, the candy and soda pop we enjoyed in those stores was not really free was it? Momma had taught me to accept her abusing herself and us girls, to enjoy receiving sweet treats as payment for her body as easily as Lucy had taught her puppies the smell of quails. In my mind, Bobby could easily beat my mother or me if his moral compass allowed him to view being a whore as reason enough to kill a woman, yet, at the same time, I prayed to have Bobby as my father and protector.

"Jesus F-in Christ!" Bobby said, "The way I've been acting around y'all is crazy! Fuck me! Y'all must think I'm insane?" Bobby said with a questioning look in his eyes. "I'm not insane, I just know that I've screwed up my life so bad that I'm gonna die for it, so why not kill any asshole who deserves it? I don't have to be nice to the Percodans and doctors for pills anymore," Bobby said with a slight stutter as if he had lost the words that he wanted to speak.

"When are you going to stop being nice to us Bobby?" Lil Dee asked her hero. "You ain't even kissed Momma yet. Percodan said ain't nothing free! If you want free, then go stand in line at the welfare office with the coloreds and the white trash! " Lil Dee calmly stated as she used a small stick to play tug of war with her puppies.

"Bobby was raised right, young lady, and we don't say coloreds either," Ms. Karen said, scaring me at how easily I had given in to the peacefulness of the mountain cemetery and forgotten to watch the world around us for trouble. "Bobby's a good man!" Carl boldly stated. "And good men don't accept payment for doing the right things, ain't that right?" Carl asked as a playful quality returned to his voice at the end of his statement, reminding me of the way Bobby often spoke, using tones to express his meanings. This was odd to my ears, because the emotional tones that slipped out were not like a poker players tell but instead were a very controlled use of tones and I began to see that Carl too had once been an addict because only addicts and conmen understand the shepherding effects of voice tones.

"I'm not sure if you understand this Bobby, but the man you once were is dead — he died somewhere out there!" Ms. Karen said as she pointed down the hill, out past their house and towards a world that I was beginning to feel protected from as if the cemetery was a cocoon wrapping us in its warmth.

"I don't know what caused you to champion these two little girls, but you did, and now you have to see the job through. You cannot quit like you quit everything else when you see yourself reflected in a mirror or after going too long without a storm to blame your failings on," Ms. Karen said as she stared up at a cold-blooded monster as if she was looking at a child who had misbehaved.

"We failed you," Carl said as he pointed down at the grave my sister was playing on. "She ain't got a better headstone because I hate her for what she did to you and your sister, and besides it's your job to figure out the right amount of love to show her in death, not mine. So, Karen and me have decided that you're staying here until you bury the monster you were out there in the world and at last realize the type of man you were honestly meant to be!" Carl lovingly said as he reached an old hand out towards Bobby, causing Bobby to smile as he accepted the handshake without showing the same physical reserve I had seen in his body when Carl had hugged him earlier. It was as if Bobby had accepted the hug as a formality, yet genuinely wanted or needed the honest words and loving touch the old people were offering him.

"Come on, it's too cold this time of year for these babies to be playing in this old grave yard. Plus that leg's not gonna clean itself," Ms. Karen said as she took Momma's hand and escorted us to our cabin home.

Bobby swore that in his earliest memories the cabin had only had an outhouse toilet and no real bathroom, a memory that Carl confirmed.

"That's right — your mother cried and complained that not having a real bathroom was the reason she took you away from here the first time y'all left, after your daddy died. Sure is funny how folks will make up the silliest reasons for running away from what's good and right in search of what's bad. I'll never understand why a lie slips over the lips easier than the truth does," Carl said as he rubbed Lil Dee's hand and touched my shoulder as if to emphasize the lesson hidden in his words.

As Ms. Karen made Bobby take a shower, Momma sent me to drive the car up the back of Cemetery Ridge on the old church driveway and to park it beside the old shed where it still rests today, waiting to be discovered by a lying archaeologist sometime in the future. I doubt if the fool will understand how nice it was for Lil Dee and me to race the dogs down the hill to the car and then to laugh happily as I slowly guided the big Delta 88 home. A laughter that I had thought lost until Bobby killed Orville.

Chapter 18

Andy looked up at the noonday sun, angry with himself for believing that Sara would have given in to her desire, gotten high and decided to come out to the park to help him earn today's dope. They had a good thing going: he appeared to be just what he was, an addict but still in control of his addiction, while she looked like someone's little sister, cute and trustworthy, unlike the bottom feeders who seemed to hate themselves for using drugs, never cleaning themselves up, looking homeless, begging from one high to the next.

Andy knew that most of those types were not so much addicted to drugs as they were addict to self-loathing, as crazy as that sounded. Andy knew that if Sara aborted their baby, or if the child was born somehow damaged by her drug use, she would become a self-loathing addict, hating herself for getting high yet at the same time not valuing herself enough to stop using drugs. Addiction and the reasons people refused to get sober and stay clean were incredibly varied. Andy had long ago come to understand that most addicts were assholes — crying out for help, wanting people to see them and feel sorry for them. He knew that they didn't really want anyone to help them, but wanted the world to blame their addiction for who they were, how they lived, and not blame them personally or to see them as the worthless human that they honestly knew they were deep inside of their rotting hearts, a purposeless human who they themselves could not help but see when they looked into a mirror, and the same person that they knew they would once again become if they got clean, went straight, or did the 'Old Friend of Bill' deal. "Fuck that!" Andy thought. Playing rehab games was a surefire way to end up dead, overdosing, in search of pity.

Of all of the types of addicts out there in world, Sara was the worst type, even worse than the rich kids who ended up couch surfing through addiction. The rich kids could at least blame their need for attention on their hollow home life — sure they had everything that money could buy, but all they wanted was the comfort that loving parents can give. But cunts like Sara? They had it all — good loving parents with just enough money to take care of their children, but not enough money to allow their life options to create a distance between them and their offspring. Sara, he thought, deserved everything she got out of life. She was Andy's own mother — a child from a good loving home who for some reason could only find self-confidence through drug use, which of course had led to Andy's birth.

Good Catholic girls don't have abortions, but they do, like the many rumors about Mary Magdalene, sell ass like the whore all women truly are. Andy silently laughed to himself as he pictured Jesus pimping Mary out at a truck stop while wearing a slick pimp suit and hat. Yet, as funny as that image was, there was nothing funny about the fact that Jesus could accept Mary for whatever she really was, but Andy's good God-fearing grandparents could not accept Andy's mother back into the family fold after she had sold herself to men to support her high. "Fuck family!" Andy thought, "and their evil self-righteous."

Andy's father either turned his mother over to a pimp after he went to prison or abandoned Andy and his dear mother — the story changed depending on the amount of attention his mother thought she could obtain from her listener. But what never changed was the fact that sex is money. Andy was four years old the first time he could remember his mother dropping him off at the house of an old pervert. The man wasn't bad as far as 'pervs' went, he simply wanted to sneak around and see Andy's naked body. The dude was always buying Andy clothes so he could help Andy try them on, or helping him take a bath.

He never really touched Andy, and in fact it took Andy years to realize that the guy was just as sick as the other men that his mother would sell him to in the years to come. But those men were at least honest — it's one thing to know you're getting 'perved' on, but it's a whole other thing to get high one day and sit down and think about your childhood and it dawns on you that your one true childhood adult friend only bought you clothes so that he could see you naked! "How stupid could I have been not to see that sooner?" Andy thought to himself as he considered the situation that Sara was forcing him to face today.

Andy's hustle depended on the housewives and rich kids who honestly believed the fake ass gangster hype on TV and in rap music. The honest truth was that good dope boys understood that they would take a loss now and then; but they knew that while hurting or killing some dope fiend to make a point made good TV, it didn't work well in the real world. Sure, there were the stupid ass dealers who believed that life was like a rap video, but those guys did not last too long and were prison bound almost as fast as you met them. But housewives and rich kids didn't know this and would gladly pay Andy to go get their dope from the big black guy for them — better for the gangsta to kill Andy to gain some street credit than for him to kill them. But Sara was the key to this hustle's constant success.

Nashville was a great place to find lonely rich kids and bored rich housewives, so lots of lone drug users did what Andy did to stay high and having Sara's country ass to sit and wait with customers kept Andy busy. Without her today, he had only managed to round up two sales so far, and even after buying three papers for the price of the one that he would pass on to the mark, Andy knew that he could not afford to lose Sara. Sure, he could force her to come out with him, but she was bound to explain her condition to the people she was waiting with, and Andy would find himself being crucified by fake ass dope heads who felt that God had meant for them to meet Sara, that it was fate that they save themselves by saving Sara and her child from the evil world of addiction. Never mind the fact that Sara had willingly given Andy her arm to inject a shot of dope into. No, Andy thought, God and fated events often fail to concern themselves with the honest facts of mystical life changing events, and the truth was that anyone who rescued a pregnant dope whore would be raising that baby alone. Because until Sara learned to like herself, to see herself as worth something more than drugs, she was sure to continue getting high no matter how magical or fated she was to meet her hero while selling dope off Old Hickory Boulevard.

No, Sara was going to kill the kid and return to the game, and Andy would punish her this time until he found her replacement. Punish her for being a whore like his own mother, Andy thought to himself as finally some rich kids that he had dealt with before asked him if he could score a C-Notes worth of dope for them. Maybe God does care Andy laughed to himself as he took the kids' money and went in search of his favorite dope boy.

Chapter 19

Bobby would be down sick and mostly bed ridden for nearly a week. His leg was said to be the reason, but a part of my heart was sure that he was scared. Not of Carl and Ms. Karen, but of the man they expected him to be while here on Dogwood Mountain. Masks are very heavy things to wear every day, they tend to force their shape on to your face, and you begin to enjoy them and to believe in the persona that you feel that a person hidden behind such a mask should have. Like Mr. Bear seemed to be a big strong mean man at first sight but he was as gentle as a kitten. And I'm sure that Gay Tom did not act gay before he came out and told the world to call him Gay Tom. Nor do I believe that Mickey acted like a gangster pimp as a child. These were personas and not the people that they were deep inside.

But now Bobby was at home, with two beautiful people who knew him as a child. I'm sure that he was worried because although he was not everything that the mask he wore represented him to be, he also was not the child he had once been. That's why people say that you can never return home once you leave. And it's true — home is like this stupid mountain, it is solid, slowly weathered by time, seldom changing, while people are tender, soft, and constantly changing, growing inside. That's why Einstein was an idiot, all of that time travel crap is as bad as those grave robbing assholes because we can never go back in time to be the sweet angel child that our family remembers. And Bobby was a coldblooded monster today, no matter what Ms. Karen thought.

I was trying to look out the window that I told you about earlier, the one behind our TV, the one that overlooks our old car. When we first came to Dogwood Mountain, the cabin windows were beautiful. Bobby said that the sun had heated them up everyday for years and years as gravity constantly pulled the glass down. When I first saw them, each windowpane was very thin at its top, thick and wavy in its middle and fat and lumpy at its bottom where the window's frame forced the glass to pool, unable to sag any lower. I could not help but touch each window in wonder, my fingers feeling bumps that had taken lifetimes to form. Bobby got up from the couch and stood beside me touching the glass too.

"These are the same windows I would touch as a little boy — but they're not, they've changed, like I have. Someday, they will get so thin that they will break, and we will have to change them, Page," Bobby said, and I could tell that his heart was far away from the windows we were touching.

"They love you, Bobby. They know that you're like these glass panes, they know you've changed, just like I know that Lil Dee was changed when Orville hurt her, and then once again when you killed her monster. She's not the same, but at the same time I see glimpses of her in the way she laughs. That's all Ms. Karen is asking to see of you Bobby, just a little piece of the happy child that you once were. Mr. Bear would tell you to fake it til you make it! Bobby," I said trying to help him sort his heart out.

I wish that I could tell you that my motives were pure, clean of any of my own personal desires, but I'm an addicts kid. My first hero, my mother, always found a way to get what she wanted, and my second hero was a grownup little girl who pretended to be a butch dyke pimp, and I knew the sweet taste of candy earned by the abuse of my mother's womb. So I'd be lying if I told you that I didn't hope to convince Bobby to stay here on Dogwood Mountain where our world was clean, and at peace, because honestly, there was nothing that I wanted more than to stay here, hidden among the dogwoods and the tombstones.

"You're right Page, time changes us," a smiling Bobby said. "I just hope that I don't let y'all down." I couldn't help but scream in joy so Momma and Lil Dee would hear me and join in, happy that Bobby had decided to at least try to make Dogwood Mountain our home.

Now you can't forget that my mother was every bit as crazy as our hero Bobby, and Bobby had now been in our lives for ten days, sleeping alone either in a separate bed in motels, or on the couch here in the cabin that was becoming our home. We knew that Bobby's leg was not hurt that bad so even I was starting to wonder about him. I was shocked that Momma had not exploded in rage by now. And on this day, after Bobby seemed to accept that we were to stay here and make a home, I was sure that if he failed to take her to bed that Momma would burn the cabin down and then drive our car over every tombstone on this stupid hill on her way down to Ms. Karen's house where I was sure that she would at the very least flip Carl and Ms. Karen off as we left Dogwood Mountain and Bobby behind. But in typical Momma fashion, she didn't come straight out and ask him if they were a couple and if they would consummate their love that night. Instead, she went into the small living room and picked up Bobby's sheets and blankets, intending to put them away in the closet where they belonged.

Today, I cannot help but feel bad for my mother when I find myself laughing at the memory of the gift that Bobby handed her when she foolishly picked up those blankets. Momma's only worth was her body. Sometimes I believe that she is like me: a virgin. Although she had physically been with many men, I doubt if she had ever made love to a man at that time. So for a man to turn down the offer of her body, the only thing that men had ever asked her for, was a soul-crushing, heartbreaking event, and very confusing to the Three Musketeers'.

"What are you doing? Those blankets don't need to be washed yet," Bobby said upon seeing Momma picking up his bedding from the couch.

Momma shocked Lil Dee and me when she began to cry, asking Bobby if he didn't want her because she was a whore, or because she was a bad mother who allowed Orville to get away with hurting her daughters. I could not help but cry with her as I had never seen her in so much pain before.

Bobby began to laugh, a deep belly laugh at my mother's expense, and I was ready to hand Momma the matches and send Lil Dee out to start the car because Bobby was being an ass and deserved everything that Momma was sure to do to him if he continued to hurt her.

"Christy, listen to me. When I met you at Ruby's, I was sure that I would enjoy a night with you in Knoxville, but after everything at Percodan's, how can I ask you to give yourself to me? I would always wonder if you felt that you owe me, or that you only gave yourself to cover Orville, money, pills, or any of that shit. Those things have no value, they're trash. But you, you're worth something far more valuable than pills, money, and justice. So, I figured we could wait for the sex and silly stuff. Hell, maybe you won't even like me after we really get to know each other," Bobby said with a smile. "Honestly, I like my girl a little on the dirty side anyways!" he said with a laugh as he hugged Momma whose tears of pain had changed to tears of relief.

"Now Bobby, are you saying that if some guy came by to pick Momma up that you wouldn't care?" Lil Dee asked in an impish way, causing Bobby's face to change from joy to near rage and then back to joy and amusement in the blink of an eye.

"Dee, if that happens, I will feed him your puppies, raw! Because they didn't chase him off and you didn't bring me my gun so I could shoot him!" Bobby jokingly said, but Momma, Lil Dee and I had seen the rage flash through his eyes, assuring us that Bobby was as hooked on Momma as she was hooked on him. "It sure is funny how a mouth will say anything!" as Mickey used to say, "but the heart and eyes tend to tell the truth without us even knowing it!"

Now, every one of us at one time or another has had an 'oh shit!' moment or two in our lives. Maybe it was the first time you took your driving test down at the License Bureau. That's an 'oh shit' moment because you know how to drive and now you have to let your ball sack swing like Bobby would laugh and say. But at the same time, you have to be careful because not only could you hurt your balls if you hit something too hard, but chances are, the clown giving you the test is not a big fan of swinging balls sacks or people acting all big and confident.

So, you struggle to start the car, to change gears, maybe you run over a cone or two. You're nervous — part of you wants to tell the little drivers test man to sit down, strap in and shut up as in your mind you perform a flawless test like you're a race car driver in a movie. But in reality, you're scared to death, so you limp along, knocking over orange cones, making funny faces, feeling stupid, bumping into things. At the end of the test, you're left praying that the man will be nice enough to give you your license and not embarrass you by running away from your car screaming in fear, thanking Jesus to still be alive! Now that is and oh shit moment, and the day after Bobby agreed to stay with us, Momma was having herself one big oh shit moment.

You have to understand that most of Momma's relationships began only after a long night of booze, drugs and sex. Hell, half of the time, she was unsure of the guy's name for a day or so! And now Bobby had said that he wanted her, but not until they were sure of their feelings for each other. He had not challenged her to prove herself to him, nor cut off her dope supplies. He simply wanted to get to know her, and to not receive her body in exchange for treating us as humans. But the problem was that Momma didn't even know how to value herself, so like most people do when they face an emotionally overwhelming situation in life, she refused to accept the truth in Bobby's words. Instead preferring to believe that Bobby was lying and that he had no intention of sticking around long enough to get to know her as a person. After all, Bobby was not the type of man who could ever love a truck stop whore, Momma told herself.

Late that night I got up to walk the puppies who had developed the habit of licking my nose when I was asleep, and they needed some attention. I found Momma sleeping in a chair besides Bobby who was comfortably lying on the couch, snoring as if he had not a care in the world. I did everything within my power to keep from laughing at her when she jumped out of her chair, embarrassed to be found sleeping at her guard post as she had been.

"He's going to run off Page!" Momma whispered as she walked back to the bedroom I shared with Lil Dee and the dogs.

"No Momma, I believe him. Besides, he ain't lied to us yet," I told her, as she laid down to hold me as we talked.

"This is different Page. Men are funny about stuff like this, they never really tell you the truth. And besides, what else have I got to offer him?" Momma asked and I felt her tears wet my hair where her faced rested beside my head. The blunt way she had stated her estimations of her worth stole the words that I could have said to her from my heart, proving that I was still a child and not as smart as I needed to be for her that night. In the millions of times that I have relived that conversation over the years, my words were crisp, clean, educated, always reflecting my attitude at the moment. But all I could find to say that night when she needed me was, "Maddie, my puppy's name is Maddie, Momma." Now it's your turn, what are you gonna name your puppy Momma?" causing Momma to briefly giggle before sleep found us.

Bobby stared at a large black granite headstone, holding a white crayon in one hand as if it was a club, as he sat there with a blank look in his eyes. His facial muscles seemed to be resting, naturally, without any tension or shape, as if waiting on Bobby's emotions to tell them what configuration to form themselves into so they could become whatever mask Bobby's heart would need to wear to protect him from the memories thundering through his mind.

Lil Dee and I followed the puppies into the monuments shop in search of our missing hero. Momma was absolutely broken after following me to bed last night instead of listening to her instincts. I was afraid that if she had lost Bobby, as she now thought, that it was was my fault. Little did I know then that the simple morning walk I had taken down to the shop was the beginning of my life's work and only love. On that morning, there was no way that I could tell that I was standing at the very beginning of my life's work and joy. The way the puppies were dancing around the stool where Bobby sat, each of their tiny footsteps causing puffs of rock dust to form ghosts and then vanish just as quickly, gave no signs of what was to come.

"Tell your Momma that you found me. I have to make my mother a stone, and I don't know how to, so go tell her to relax, and to stop pissing her pants! Yesterday I told her that I ain't going nowhere, and I mean it! I ain't no liar!" Bobby said, moving his eyes up a fraction from where they had been when I first walked into the tiny shop. His face was now alive with tension as if he was angry at us for interrupting his thoughts. The look on his face reminded me that we were in a graveyard and that the man staring at me was a monster.

"Robert, those are little girls! Peeing, son, say peeing her pants, not pissing!" Ms. Karen's firm voice said from the doorway of the house. "And besides that, is that the way a gentleman says good morning?"

"I ain't no gentleman Karen, and that woman don't believe me, she don't trust me not to run off. She drives me crazy. I don't know if she really don't believe me or if she's one of those girls who's always wanting a man to prove his love or whatever. But I'm not the guy for that stuff, so maybe you should walk your old ass up the hill and talk to her about sleeping in a chair, worried because I won't sleep with her!" Bobby said, slightly turning his head towards the sound of Ms. Karen's voice. The angle of his forehead forced the shop's single lightbulb to cast a shadow across his face s deep and dark as the hole in his heart. A hole that I would learn had been left by his mother, just like the hole that my own mother would leave in my soul.

"Boy, you're not too big for me to get a switch and beat you!" Ms. Karen said as she stepped into the shop, anger etched deep into her face. We could hear Carl laughing as Lil Dee grinned, waiting on the showdown that would teach us to either respect Ms. Karen as Bobby did, or to ignore her. "I'm not your momma, she's the one you're mad at. She's the one that put them marks on your back and them stains on your soul. Don't get mad at me because God left you the task of paying honor to her. Why boy, you're sitting there crying that Christy might be one of them girls who don't like themselves. One of those girls who ain't got no self-worth so she needs to be assured that everything is alright. But you're doing the same damn thing! Acting like someone should help you love your Momma. Why are looking at these baby girls like they did something wrong by coming down here to see you? Now wipe that nasty look off your face and remember that you're teaching these baby girls how a man should treat them!" Ms. Karen smiled as she ordered Lil Dee into the house for breakfast and asked me to run and fetch Momma.

Bobby showed us that Ms. Karen had caught him red-handed trying to be mean about Momma when it was something inside his own heart that was eating at him.

"Yes Ms. Karen. I'm sorry girls, it's just that things between me and my mother are a lot more twisted up than I thought they were," Bobby said as he smiled at us. "Can't tell no lie on a tombstone, it's bad luck and all that. Ms. Karen's right, I got no right to be upset about it. Just find some way to warn your mother that I really just want to get to know her, to sort things out, and that I won't abandon her, Bobby said. He then looked back down at his mother's blank monument, as Ms. Karen mumbled that was better and I ran to assure Momma that Bobby had not run away. As I ran past Bobby's mother's tin cross, I thought about Bobby's scar covered back and wondered why he would even care to honor his mother.

Hating a woman like that would be common, and more than she deserved. But then I saw my own mother peeking out of the cabin door acting as if she were a teenaged virgin and I was the friend she had sent to see if the cute boy at school liked her or not. I couldn't help but feel both sick and happy at the same time — sick because I knew that she was a whore who cared more about drugs than her daughters, and happy that she trusted me to carry out such an honored mission. In the end, the happy little girl inside of me won control of my voice, and Momma and I danced like lovestruck twelve-year-olds in the tiny kitchen. We were laughing happily because he had promised in front of Ms. Karen not to abandon us, as if she were a Bible and Bobby an honest preacher and not an addicted killer on the run from himself well as the law. But these are the memories of a lonely old woman, and not those of the foolish little girl that I was that morning, a child who still believed in love as I walked back down Cemetery Ridge holding my mother's hand, easily forgetting the smell of my sister's pee on the cold vinyl seats of our car, and the sound of Bobby laughing as he killed.

Later that same day, I stood in the shop's doorway watching Bobby struggling to draw his mother stone. Lil Dee was outside in the yard, enjoying the sun with the dogs, and Momma was inside of the house learning from Ms. Karen how to be a proper woman. Each time I heard my mother's voice, it made me want to scream at her, to remind her of the day she raced out of the rehab center and failed to keep her promises to us, and about our life at Ruby's, a time when she was a reluctant whore, only selling herself to feed her high, never once doing so to feed her babies.

Yes, I know that selling herself for any reason is wrong, but she had chosen the path that we were on: she chose not to go to the police about Orville; she chose not to take us back home to the Bears were we would be safe. In choosing to take us with her to Ruby's, she was also choosing to love us as much as she loved her pills. But I learned that we were nowhere as important as drugs were to her, and I began to understand Mickey's mean attitude with her girls. It had bothered me, Mickey being abused by her own family and then abusing women who came to her for support, but Momma's lack of love for us taught me that while what Mickey was doing was not right, it was certainly understandable. Women always say that their kids are all that matter to them, that they would do anything for their children. Nothing hurts more than learning that your mother is a liar.

Bobby shocked me by tossing me a white crayon and then pointing down at a blank stone and telling me to draw, to copy everything that he was drawing for his mother. Carl, drinking homemade sumac berry wine, laughed at the shock and fear that Bobby's command had caused in me.

"Page, you ain't got nothing to fall back on other than drugs and Ruby's truck stop. Start drawing with me; it ain't much, but it will give you something to depend on rather than following your Momma down the road back to Ruby's when they kill me," Bobby coldly stated, reminding me of just how foolish I had been to get caught up in Momma's little girl games earlier that morning. I could not help but compare Bobby's wholehearted acceptance of his responsibility for his actions to Momma's failure to accept that she was every bit as responsible for Lil Dee's and my life as she was for her addiction.

"I can see it in your body girl!" Carl said as he pointed at me. "Every time your mother laughs with Ms. Karen you don't like it, and you don't trust yourself to keep quiet. That's why you're out here with us and not in there with that evil old Ms. Karen! Bobby will learn — the stupidest thing he could have done was to let my Karen get her claws into his girl. Ms. Karen will ruin her for sure!" Carl said and then he laughed at himself.

"I'll ruin you if you don't put that liquor away Carl!" Ms. Karen said from inside of the house and Carl instantly began to hide the bottle of wine, complaining that Karen could hear a mouse pissing on a cotton ball from a mile away. "Peeing Carl, not pissing! There's a lady present, now act like it damn it!"Ms. Karen screamed, causing Bobby to laugh at her.

And what in the hell are you laughing at Mr. Austin?" Ms. Karen asked from the kitchen door with Momma standing right behind her, unconsciously mimicking Ms. Karen's every move, as Lil Dee and our dog pack rushed in the shop to join in the family fun.

"Well Ms. Karen, for a lady as proper as we know you to be, it seems odd that you would say three dirty cuss words to stress the point that Carl should not even say one foul word in front of these children," Bobby said in his best imitation formal voice, before nearly falling off of his stool laughing at the look on Ms. Karen's face.

"This is a graveyard! Don't either one of you son-of-bitches forget that!" Ms. Karen screamed as she motioned for Lil Dee to come in the house and told me to do what Bobby said, to draw. "It will do you good," she said as her face got more and more red listening to Carl and Bobby laugh.

"Why is she so mad? I whispered to Bobby.

"People tend to get right in life, clean up, find God, stop drinking, and they present themselves as if they were so pure and clean that they could shit a bouquet of rose's thorns and all and not need to wipe afterwards," Carl said. "I guess I just reminded Ms. Karen of her own past." He laughed and continued: "No girl, there's only one way a person can get their butt hole big enough to shit rose thorns and not need a good wipe and a band-aid or two, and it ain't by being proper!" Carl grinned at Bobby as he offered him a drink of wine and they both began to laugh even harder than before, causing Ms. Karen to swear that she would shoot both of them if they didn't stop their shit, stop acting like little boys and remember they were grown men.

I spent the rest of the day following Bobby's hand and crayon as he drew a line that would turn into a rose or a cross. He once even drew angel wings on the stone before getting mad and, like with everything else he had drawn throughout the day. He was frowning, mumbling his displeasure with some part of the artwork and taking a cloth wet with Carl's wine and scrubbing his stone clean, forcing me to do the same thing. Seeing me struggling to understand, Bobby tried to explain to me and maybe to himself why he was unhappy with everything that he had drawn.

"Dead folks don't really care what's carved on the rock," Bobby said with a shrug of his shoulders as he pointed down to the clean stone. "Things like that only matter to us, the living, and only after we realize how easy it is to die. When I was in prison, guys would talk about death, scared of it, and would ask me to draw them some type of design that they could send home to their family. When someone died, sometimes an old lifer would die, I would draw for him. After living here on Dogwood Mountain as a child, I thought that I sort of understood how important saying goodbye is to a person's heart, but she's teaching me just how little I know about it," Bobby said as he again stared down at the blank stone as if hoping that it would tell him what to do. "I'm sorry I keep messing up Page," Bobby mumbled.

"You ain't hurt that girl none at all!" Carl said with a laugh. "Make her learn boy, make her practice."

"The old man is right for once in his life!" Bobby stated. "But that sure don't make this easier on me."

"I liked the one you drew with the roses Bobby. Not mine, the one I tried to draw looked stupid, I can't draw though. But yours was pretty Bobby," I said to him, hoping that he would explain more of his pain to me. I could see a great slow storm of emotions rolling deep inside of Bobby's eyes. It wasn't a violent thunderstorm, with the rage of lightning and the smashing of thunder, but I could still tell that it was raining something fierce in Bobby's heart.

"You can draw, Page, everyone can, it's our own personal language. We get embarrassed, afraid of the small mistakes that we think we made in our art, so we stop trying to draw, to speak with art. They say that humans are good at adaptation, adapting, learning new things, but that's a crock of shit. All we're really good at is avoiding the things that embarrass us or make us feel afraid!" Bobby firmly stated as he began to tap his mother's stone with his knuckles while his eyes burned a hole into my soul.

"Page, this bitch is here!" Bobby said, anger beginning to roar out of his heart, warning me, reminding me that thunderstorms grow into violent storms when two or more clouds crash into each other as they compete for the same place in the sky. I could see that Bobby's emotions were fighting for the same place in his heart and that violence, the rage of lightning was near. "This bitch don't deserve to rest here, she'll poison the soil. Someday, a bunch of folks will all get sick with cancer and it will have come from this single hate-filled woman's grave." Bobby slammed the crayon down against the stone, shattering it, as if to emphasize his words.

But I could tell that he was not acting, he was not putting on a show, but was speaking from his heart and hurting deeply.

"People don't ever think about it," Bobby said, "but, if science is right, and God is right too, then we get buried and rot, only to then return to the soil around us. Our atoms all mix together until one day they get absorbed by a plant, which then gets eaten by a bug, who feeds a bird or a deer. On and on until we become the food that a mother or father need, and will use to make both the egg and the seed that then will combine in the mother's womb to grow into a new person. We never think about who we are rotting in the ground beside, how an evil woman's grave will destroy a beautiful mountain like this." I could see a tear threaten to escape his eyes as Carl spoke up and I heard the creaking of the floor under Ms. Karen's feet as she quietly came to stand at the shop's door.

"The world handed your mother a heavy load to carry," Carl said. "It broke her down, don't let it break you too."

I'm about sick of hearing that, Carl. Everything that my mother did wrong, everyone blamed on my daddy's death, but that's bullshit!" Them folks I just killed, am I suppose to blame that on my daddy dying too? I mean it! Think about it, Carl. If she was messed up because she lost him, and then she messed me up in the head, then neither of us are responsible for anything. No Carl, she banked on her meanness being overlooked, her being able to return to this mountain, forgiven, because my daddy failed to make the trip up the mountain the foggy morning he crashed and died. And yes, maybe we can blame some of her pain on that, but sooner or later we have to look at our lives and then step up and be honest.

This bitch was just plain mean, and now I have to either tell the world that she wasn't worth the time and money for a headstone, or I have to lie and draw something beautiful for her so her grave shines like a Dogwood Mountain grave should shine. It ain't fair!" Bobby said, his tears silently falling on the black stone below. "Why can't I carve 'Evil, nasty, hateful bitch' on this rock and be done with it? What's wrong with being honest?" Bobby looked up at Ms. Karen, as if knowing that she would be the one angered by

187

his questions.

"You're a big boy," Ms. Karen said. "Ain't no one going to stop you from carving whatever you want on that rock, so I guess you have to ask yourself that question. Now, give Christy some money, I'm taking her and these girls uptown. Preacher will be here this weekend, and y'all need Sunday clothes," she stated as she told me to get my sister and meet her and Momma up at the car.

"I tricked the boy here into helping me make some stairs, Karen, so get us a couple of bottles of that stamp pad ink folks use to to stamp bills and such," Carl said as Ms. Karen rolled her eyes and shook her head, mumbling that Carl had best not be drinking too much while we were up town. "See!" Carl said to Bobby. "That's how its starts right there! Karen's meaner than a two-headed cottonmouth. She's gonna ruin that pretty Christy of yours, and the baby girls too. Hell, it won't be long and even the dogs won't pay you no attention!" His words caused everyone to laugh happily, like a real family does over something silly.

We drove down Cemetery Ridge with the smell of Bobby's blood soaked car seat reminding me that fantasy, the mind's peaceful way of dreaming of being something more, somewhere better, like being a member of a family, was a nice dream, but a dream that was unlikely to ever be realized for us after the mess that Bobby had made. Yet I couldn't stop myself from dreaming that Bobby had found us a long time before we ever met Percodan, before Lil Dee had been hurt, before I had come to understand that Momma loved her pills more than she loved us, her babies. I couldn't help but imagine that each person who saw us drive past that day and waved at Ms. Karen knew my name and that this was my home. A foolish dream yes, I know, but it was better than to have no dream at all.

Ms. Karen's idea of church clothes was a style that had come and gone long before the day that we went shopping with her — plain off-white dresses that nearly touched the floor with small bright white flowers embroidered on them here and there, white gloves, a hat and black shoes. Lil Dee and I began to pretend that we were high-class ladies at a tea party and I noticed that we both actually liked the nice clean new outfits. Seeing Momma step out of the dressing room, dressed as all three of us now were, took my breath away. She looked so beautiful standing there smiling in the mirror, looking at herself. It was more than the new dress or the fact that she now carried a bottle of Oxys with her and was not burdened with having to hunt for a means to get high anymore.

No, her look was something more, special even. It would take years for me to come to understand that Momma felt needed, she had a goal, a reason to live, to wake up happy every morning; she even enjoyed having Ms. Karen there to guide her and watch her grow into a woman who Bobby could love. Like our time in Huntington waiting to get Lil Dee back, Momma was free to destroy or to punish herself. She knew that she would never reach her goal if Ms. Karen did not approve of her, just as she had known that the judge would not return Lil Dee to us had she misbehaved. Her goal was as much as fantasy as my own, but maybe, just maybe, her dreams would come true. And so, without a word spoken between us, Lil Dee and I agreed to do all that we could to help her reach her goal — our was it really our goal too? Do mothers want a good man for the same reasons that abandoned daughters pray for a good father?

"Bobby ain't gonna wear no tie!" Lil Dee said with a hint of grin on her impish face when she saw that Ms. Karen was picking out new clothing for Bobby also.

"Ain't is not a word Lil Dee, and nor is gonna. You two young ladies need to learn to speak like ladies speak and not like hillbilly trash!" Ms. Karen firmly stated as she gave Momma a harsh look that told me that Ms. Karen was aware of the control she could easily exert over my mother. I couldn't help but hear Carl's warning again about Ms. Karen ruining Bobby's girl.

"Bobby needs a clean white shirt with long sleeves for church meetings, and the ties are for him to wear at his funeral once they kill him." Ms. Karen said in the cold hard way that the truth must often be spoken, causing Momma to gasp, and Lil Dee to make a whimpering sound much like one of her puppies would softly make. Both of these sounds angered me — Ms. Karen had no right to ask us to come to town with her, to act like a normal family would act, to show us how nice it felt to dress and look in all white, and then to poison our day, to destroy our hopes by being so honest.

"You old bitch! They won't kill Bobby! You're no better than them gossiping whores in Kermit, always talking about Momma, saying she died when she was little. You just don't want her to take your Bobby away!" I screamed at Ms. Karen, as she smacked me harder than I had ever been smacked before, teaching me that a quick punishment is often far better than a lingering lesson taught by silence.

"Those are your Sunday clothes! You want to call me names? That's fine, but respect yourself, and don't cuss or act like a whore when you're dressed like a lady on her way to church. Do you three hear me?" Ms. Karen asked, neither expecting nor waiting on us to reply. "Bobby is dead, he died years ago. The man he is now, like the woman your mother is today, is not the same person that either of them were meant to be. Maybe they can learn to live again, maybe they can find a safe place and teach you girls that life is not the pain and filth you know it to be. But that's just a maybe. Them folks the boy killed are most certainly dead, ain't no way to fix that!" Ms. Karen said as Lil Dee began to laugh.

"You said ain't Ms. Karen!" Lil Dee said as shock, anger, love, joy and amusement all raced through Ms. Karen's face and body, leaving her no choice but to laugh at herself as she hugged me and asked for my forgiveness. That is something that I am still unsure that she needed to ask me for, as part of my soul wanted, even needed, the love that her one slap offered me. That day, I could have chosen to live with anger in my heart towards Ms. Karen for smacking me. This would have caused me to question her, it could have even made me feel entitled to question everything she said or did for us from that day forward, allowing my hatefulness to spoil the love that she offered us, and stealing the very family I had spent my life praying for.

It is amazing how, when we dream of a better life, we never consider the roughness that has to accompany the glory that a family really is. Never forget that hate is a poison, it rots everything it touches. I had lived an almost undisciplined life, one without an adult to trust, but Ms. Karen was going to teach me that I could trust her, and the value that the gift of discipline can be to a broken child; not abuse, or bullying, but discipline, loving, concerned discipline.

Sara could tell from her bathtub nest that the time was nearing noon. She had managed to bathe and clean herself up; she had even foolishly believed that a hot bath would ease her body's aches and pains. The hot water only made her feel worse as she began to sweat, which caused her to flood the tub with cold water. Now, after several attempts at going from hot water to cold water, before realizing that much of her nausea was being caused by not eating for days, nor caring for the child she was carrying. Sara was again ready to give up, to get high and to find Andy so that she could at least get some money to eat something before she starved to death. "Fucking ghost or not, I have to eat, and I can't go outside like this," Sara mumbled to the child in her womb as she stood up from the tub and left the bathroom for the first time all day, fully intending to get high.

He stood staring at her with a smile on his face. "You're the young Bear?" Sara asked, laughing at how easily she had accepted the fact that the man she saw was a ghost. He had changed — where he had been bloody and wounded before, he was now clean, as if ready for a parade.

"It's funny how the brain works, Sara. You never once thought to sell or trade the drugs Andy left you for food. No, you just decided to get high, and were willing to use the child's health and need of food as a reason to do so. An excuse to give in to your own needs and desires. That's not love Sara, motherhood does not love like that!" Bear's ghost said as he pointed towards the phone. "Call Page, she needs you as much as you need her Sara." And then he was gone as if he had never been there at all. Without even trying to remember the phone number to the coffin shop, a number she had seldom had to call before, she dialed the phone, praying a silent prayer that her aunt would answer the phone and not another member of her family. On the third ring, Sara heard a gentle voice of a women who she had thought to be crazy until only hours ago. But now, the old woman's voice felt like the embrace of a long time friend.

"Aunt Page, it's me, Sara. Can I come home?" she softly asked, as her strength gave way and she began to cry, praying that she was not dreaming and that the beautiful old women on the other end of the phone was true. That she would honestly understand Sara and the life choices that she had made and not hold her foolish ways against her.

"Sara, this mountain is as much as your home as it is mine, you don't need to ask for permission, honey," the gentle old woman said. "But I think what you're trying to say is that you need some help finding your way back to us," Page softly said. "Just hold on a little longer Sara. I'm on my way down to help you now. Just hold on for that beautiful child growing inside of you, and for the beautiful children, it will reward you in the years to come. Hold on Sara, you're not alone, we're on our way honey," Sara heard Aunt Page say before the phone line went dead.

"Keep reading! a hard man who Sara instantly knew was her great grandfather Bobby Austin said in the voice of a man who seemed used to issuing demands and not asking people to do things. He smiled a loving smile at her as he handed her Page's notebook and then vanished, leaving Sara no choice but to sit down in the chair below the bloodstain and bullet hole and read until Aunt Page made it to Nashville to help her.

Chapter 20

We returned home to find both Bobby and Carl playing with Lucy and her puppies on Bobby's mother's grave, a woman who I was more unsure of how to feel about than any person I had known before. It was as if I could not love her if Bobby did not love her, and at the same time I had seen Bobby go crazy with my own eyes, why should Bobby's opinion about his mother matter to me? He was, after all, violent and insane.

In the years that came after those first weeks on Dogwood Mountain, I came to understand that I had no self-worth, no value to myself, so I based my love or need of Bobby on my mother's need of him. I had done this my whole life — self-worth came only after my mother's and sister's needs were met. Had I found a worth years before, perhaps I would have abandoned my mother to her own failings, taken Lil Dee away, never met Bobby Austin, never seen death up close. I would have never smelled baby's pee mixed with blood and the aroma of car seat vinyl, nor ever felt the pain of being unable to help my little sister.

Those were questions that I never thought to ask myself or to think of that day, standing on the grave of a woman that I didn't know, a woman that I had wanted to look like so that I could easily pretend to be her granddaughter, a woman that I would soon come to hate. That day though, Carl hugged Ms. Karen with one arm and reached up above her head to touch the bright spring green bud of a dogwood flower as he looked at me and said, "Won't be long now Page, God will teach you the beauty of the world. I doubt that you've seen much of the pretty parts of life, but this year, I promise that you will Page. Ain't that right Bobby?" Carl asked a smiling Bobby who could only grin and nod his head in agreement as Ms.

Karen began to lead Carl home and Momma began to act as if cooking dinner for her family was a normal daily event.

"You girls get cleaned up, dinner will be ready soon," Momma said from the doorway of our cabin and I instantly ran towards the house like a good child, only to almost hate myself for doing so.

I had to learn how to sleep — well, not really learn how to sleep, a person's body just sort of knows how to do that, but I had to learn how to wake up from sleeping. Before Dogwood Mountain, every part of our day was controlled by Momma's addiction and its needs. On the nights after a day when she was unable to get many pills, she slept poorly and would get up before the sunrise the next day. While on the days that she had been able to get as high as she could ever hope to get, she would sleep as if dead the next morning, leaving Lil Dee and I to take care of ourselves. But now things were different —- there was no fear of tomorrow so we could sleep as long as our dreams wanted us to sleep, awakening only to answer our own personal clocks.

Bobby's clock began before sun up everyday. He could move without making a noise; Momma said that this proved that he was Native American. When I told her that was a racist thing to say, this caused Bobby to laugh and say that there is nothing racist about the truth.

"Page, if you see a fat black man or woman cooking and selling barbeque on the side of the road, you just know that it's going to be good eating: you don't care that they may have dropped sweat on the food. But if you see a white guy selling the same barbeque, you tend to get out of your car looking for the black folks who you hope are really doing the cooking. Now that ain't racist at all, but it sounds like it is.

Turns out that both the white guy and the black guy might both be using the same recipe, but cooking good barbeque would get a man out of the fields into a better job back when personal talents were all that black folks owned. So we sort of instinctively know that a black man selling barbeque on the side of the road has put his pride, heart, and soul into his cooking, just like his daddy did, and you know that you can put your trust, your faith, into what you grew up being taught. So without question, you will stop to buy food from a black man on the side of the road and never worry at all if it's clean or safe, that's how you were taught.

Natives live in very close communities where everyone is family, so you are born just knowing instinctively to be respectful of others who are sleeping. So telling the truth ain't racist or wrong Page, some good things, and some bad things get passed down in families just by the children watching their parents. My grandpa learned to be gentle in the mornings and I suppose it rubbed off on me, "Bobby said, trying to teach me about something far more important than barbeque or silence. But I was a girl changing into a young woman, and I did not like to be spoken to as if I were a ignorant child. I could accept it from Carl and Ms. Karen, they were old and had not poisoned their position of authority in my heart like Momma had. It's hard to see someone as your leader when you know them to be weak, and untrustworthy, so like a child trying to assert my equal position with my mother in Bobby's eyes, I foolishly asked him if that meant that I would become a whore. I stopped myself from saying like Momma, but I saw that my words had hurt her, just as for some inexplicable reason I had hoped to do. But Bobby's words crushed me, striking me harder than Ms. Karen's painful slap.

"Page, you and Lil Dee are already whores," he calmly said. "You will do anything asked of you to get a person's love or attention. When I told you to let me teach you to draw, you didn't say 'No Bobby, I don't like to draw,' or 'I don't want to learn to draw'. No, you instantly began to warn me that your artwork would be bad because you didn't know how to draw. Pimps listen to the words a young girl says and how she says them. Honey, you were willing to trade yourself just to be near me that day. I told you then that you had to learn that there was more to life then Ruby's truck stop. I should have told you that there's a lot of ways to whore yourself out that don't include sex and that, sadly, all that watching your momma has taught you to do is whore. Maybe it's like being quiet, or cooking barbeque, and it's all that her family passed down to her, but y'all gotta see it for the abuse that it is and change it," Bobby said as Momma began to cry.

"Is that why you killed Orville?" Lil Dee asked. "Was that your way of whoring yourself out for Momma? Lil Dee's voice and eyes were hard and protective of Momma as she raced over to protect her.

"Yeah Lil Dee, violence is all I got worth giving away as a gift, so I guess you're right. I'm just as much of a whore as anyone in this room, but that ain't what I mean. I ain't trying to hurt your Momma, Page, or you. I'm just trying to tell you to get to know your heart, to see things as they really are so no one can pimp you out or use your heart against you. Folks always wonder how old men, perverts and creeps trick young girls into bed with them. Most often the kid learned it from their parents, their only value is in what they could do for someone. Orville needed to be killed, I chose to do that as a gift, not because you whispered sweet words in my ear and asked me to do it. No one pulled my strings. You three girls, your strings are hanging out for anyone to pull," Bobby firmly stated that day so long ago, but it would take years for me to fully realize the meaning of his words.

Today I remember those quiet mornings: Bobby gently waking me and us walking down Cemetery Ridge right before sunrise, springtime fog hanging heavy down at ground level around the tombstones as Bobby would point to a swirling pattern and playfully apologize to the ghost that we had scared. I suppose that's why I have never been afraid of Cemetery Ridge, nor of her ghost. Bobby made it a game, as if we were the ones who were interrupting the spirits, just one of those small lessons taught by a parent without thought or planning that come to mean so much as the years slowly pass by.

Carl would be there every morning waiting on us with fresh hot coffee. Ms. Karen without fail would call me into the kitchen for a breakfast of bacon and eggs and then she would make me put cream and sugar in my coffee, after explaining that I was still too young to drink black coffee. "Young ladies and children drink coffee with milk, Page black coffee is a grownup's drink. Stay a child as long as you can," she would smile and say as she gave me the gift of her undivided attention for a few minutes each day. This was her way of teaching me how wonderful it was to be loved and cared for, to be treated as if I were special. This is just one more thing that I know will be lost to time, something that the archaeologist and grave robber who find this hill will never understand or glean from the dust of my bones.

Bobby had decided to place sets of two and three stairs not only where they were needed on the steep climb up Cemetery Ridge, but also where they would force people to walk over by some of the older graves so those folks could get some visitors too. Bobby told me that the loneliest place that he had ever seen in his life was a prison graveyard. That most men were lonely just being in prison, but the ones who died there did so knowing that no one would ever love them enough to visit their grave or to place flowers in memory of them. He said that after growing up on Dogwood Mountain, where everything was done to honor and love each person buried there, that it was hard to understand how people could so easily forget their families and friends who came before them.

"A tree don't really shed its bark like a snake sheds its skin. No, Page, it just sort of builds a new layer on top of the older ones. People are suppose to be like that too," Bobby said to me one day. "You're suppose to tell the world about not only what Orville worthless ass did to your sister, but how it hurt you also, and about both the right and wrong things that you learned from the way that I dealt with him. That's why all the bad things in life keep repeating themselves over and over, Page. Folks don't want to talk about what happened before, they tend to act like things never went wrong before as if it's wrong to teach folks by pointing out our father's sins, or they act like Ms. Karen, pure as snow. But ain't none of us pure Page.

When you tell your story, tell all sides of it — Orville didn't just hurt Lil Dee, and my killing him was not a cut and dry thing.

Tell the world how you got to Percodan's house in the first place. Tell your story without blame, tell it as the fact that it is, good and bad, because to be honest with you, your momma is as guilty as Orville's worthless ass in what he did to you girls. At the same time she is as innocent and as blameless as you are. Stories are funny that way Page, make sure that you remember I told you that," Bobby said the day that he convinced Momma, Lil Dee, Ms. Karen and me to be angels for a few minutes.

Momma had chosen to put on a show for Bobby everyday at lunchtime. I call it a show, I'm sorry, I don't mean to sound rude or angry about how she acted, but at that time in my life I felt like I was on a seesaw in a school playground, going up and down, and then being stuck dead center in the middle. I could never decide whether to blindly forgive my mother, as Lil Dee had so easily done, or to openly challenge her, and attempt to do things better than she was capable of doing them. And then there was the fact that I liked stabbing her with the truth every now and then. It felt good to see the pain in her eyes each time that I slipped it into the conversation that she was a whore and that she didn't love us girls as we loved her. So, I simply stood on my seesaw rocking up and down until the day that reality knocked me off of it.

That day when Bobby and Carl began to lay out the long black stones they had chosen for their stairs, I was not shocked to see Momma carrying our lunch for us to eat and walking down Cemetery Ridge as if her knees had never gotten sore on those long nights chasing a high in Ruby's gravel parking lot. Bobby's emotions were high, and I kept my evil feelings about how Momma's knees got scarred up to myself.

"Karen, you and the girls get out of here, Bobby needs you!" Carl said from the shop doorway.

"And take them damn shoes off too!" I heard Bobby say as Ms. Karen began to scold him for cussing in front of a lady again, and Carl began to laugh and joke with Bobby over his choice of words and how Ms. Karen was not above washing Bobby's mouth out with soap as she had done when he had used bad language as a child. "She won't do that today, not after we tell them why we need them out here in their bare feet," Bobby said with a laugh as he smiled at Ms. Karen who was only pretending to be upset with him.

"I ain't quite figured out what to carve for my mother, but I know that I need some angels' footprints on these stones," Bobby said as he pointed down to the rows of stones laid out before us and Carl poured two full bottles of blue stamp pad ink that Ms. Karen had bought for him at the store the day that we went shopping.

Momma began to blush, and even Ms. Karen seemed to melt into a bashful young lady as Lil Dee looked at me giggling. She was still young enough to see herself as innocent and as clean as an angel — children have that way about them, we humans don't begin to blush until we know that we are guilty and unequal to God's angels. So after being hateful to my mother, unable to forgive her, I began to question my right to walk on those cold stones beside them. Lil Dee was perfect, clean and without sin; Ms. Karen and even my mother may have been truly innocent of their sins in life, after all, I knew more about how Mickey had ended up on the streets than I did about Momma or Ms. Karen.

In fact, the only thing I was certain of was that I took pleasure in doubting my mother and her attempts to grow and change and I began to dislike myself for it. "No Bobby!" I said. "Let them do it! I don't deserve to. I let Dee get hurt, and I've been being mean, I ain't no angel!"

Momma reached out her hands to me and said, "Not without you, Page," and I began to cry as our hands touched, praying that this time Momma would not forget to love us as she had so easily forgotten before. Forgiveness weighs nothing, yet you weigh a million pounds less the moment you forgive a loved one for hurting you. So it was with this lightness and a sense of peace that I began to dance with Momma, leaving our footprints behind as proof that we were angels even if it was only make-believe.

Now don't get all watery eyed over that story because what was a moment of love and understanding for me became Bobby and Lil Dee's first real clash of wills. Carl had poured his blue ink onto a thick piece of plastic; we were to first walk in the blue ink and then on the remainder of the plastic on our way to the rows of stones. Then Bobby said that we were to relax, and to play on the stones — we were not to try and make perfect footprints. Now this harder to do than you would think; it's like being told not to look at a camera — you can't seem to stop yourself from looking at it after that, or from making a complete fool of yourself trying not to get caught looking at it. But in time, as we began to relax and play, I lost track of where I was and just had fun.

Momma's still nameless puppy came bounding into the shop and went straight to the sheet of plastic, now covered in blue ink. He not only walked into the ink puddles, but then calmly lay down and rolled over as he began wrestling with the edge of the plastic sheet, all before either Bobby or Carl could rush over to save him from becoming a blue mess. For Momma, this was a gift from God, as it gave her the name of her puppy: Blue. We now had Lucy, Buttons, Bowser, Maddie and Blue, and the world just seemed right as we laughed together, pretending that we were angles dancing in a tombstone shop on the edge of a cemetery.

Lil Dee saw the added joy that Momma's puppy gave us by playing in the ink and decided to set Buttons down and to allow him to put his paw prints on the stones with us.

"No Lil Dee, no, there ain't no doggie angels, so no doggie paw prints!" Bobby said as he gently pushed Button away from the pool of ink. This was not something that Lil Dee expected to hear from Bobby, and he had pushed her dog away when he had allowed Momma's dog to play in the same ink, and now he had firmly stated that there are no dog angels. This all combined into a rage in my baby sister that I had never seen before, anger that Bobby failed to notice as he continued to jokingly explain why there were no doggie angles.

"What? No doggie angels?" Lil Dee asked confused.

"Nope! God didn't build a dog right to be an angel!" Bobby playfully said. "Now just think about it, Dee. You put a big old set of angel wings on Buttons and then how can he take a shit?"

Bobby said as Carl nearly choked on a mouthful of wine that he was drinking. Momma and I could only smile and giggle as Ms. Karen grinned ear to ear, rolling her eyes and shaking her head at Bobby's playful nature.

"Just think about it Dee, Buttons would be all hunched up trying to shit out a big old turd and a wind gust would come along and blow him over. The poor thing would never get to shit in peace!" Bobby said as we all began to laugh at the image Bobby's words had painted in our minds of Buttons hunched up trying to shit with big fluffy angel wings.

"Angels don't shit, Bobby!" Lil Dee said and I began to see a meanness in her body. She had stopped walking and making footprints and I could tell that she was mad and no longer the Lil Dee that we all loved. I had seen a small flash of this same anger when she had told Carl that she would shoot him if he hurt her dogs. Now Bobby, her hero, was telling her no and not allowing her dog to do as she wanted it to do and everyone was laughing at her. Lil Dee exploded, first screaming that angels don't shit and that Bobby was an asshole, and then she began to throw anything that she could reach at Bobby. Her actions reminded me of the way Bobby had beaten the doctor and his nurse. It was a sort of blind hate-filled rage that shocked Bobby into silence as Ms. Karen stepped over and grabbed Lil Dee, pulling her into a hug and telling Bobby to shut up, for us to stop it, to stop laughing. Only then did I see my lost baby sister return to Lil Dee's eyes as she instantly stopped screaming at Bobby and began to cry, as confused by her outburst as we all were.

I'm still not sure if silence itself is a heavy weight that keeps a person from speaking, or if it is just not knowing what to say that feels so heavy in your heart after you go through something as scary as watching an angel turn into a monster. But that day, not one of us, not even Ms. Karen, knew what to say as she carried Dee into the privacy of the house with Momma following closely behind, leaving Carl, Bobby and I in a state of shocked silence, wondering what had just happened. Please understand, this was not a spoiled baby's tantrum, this was pure rage, and I could see that Bobby may not have known the words to explain it to me, but he knew in his heart that his actions had caused this change in Lil Dee and it hurt him deeply.

Both the fear and hurt had replaced the joy and confidence that only moments earlier seemed to have owned what was going to be a perfect day. After all, it had to be perfect — even Ms. Karen had taken a child-like joy in leaving her footprints on stones to be carved into angels' steps. And up until the very moment that Lil Dee exploded and began to blindly throw things, Bobby had no reason to believe that his violence had harmed her, but now he knew different. I could see it in his actions and almost hear it in the silent way he would look at the door of the house as if praying for Ms. Karen to find a way to absolve him of his responsibility for my sister's rage. But this time there would be no absolutions. Bobby had performed in front of a broken mirror, and that mirror was my little sister, and she had reflected his rage flawlessly. It was now up to Bobby to save her again, not from a pervert or a greedy doctor, but from becoming the mirror image of the twisted soul that Bobby knew in his heart that he truly was. He could easily just let this pass by, maybe make a joke out of it, in a sense, reward her and myself too I suppose, reward the both of us for mimicking the killer that he was.

Although I had no real understanding of any of this that day, Carl and Bobby began to pick the stone stairs up from the ground and make small talk about how nice the stairs would look once carved and placed on Cemetery Ridge. In time I would come to see that Bobby's greatest gift to my family would not be the bullets that gave Lil Dee her voice back, but the simple fact that Bobby Austin needed no one to tell him that he was wrong to take pride in teaching a child to admire the monster that he was. I had seen men almost take the blame for their actions before, admitting that they were wrong 'But' — there was always a but, a way to deflect the blame. Yet Bobby knew that far more was at stake here than his pride. As the years have gone by, I myself have found many 'buts' that Bobby could have used to free him from his guilt — Orville, as Bobby had said, just flat out needed killed, but not at the price of a child's life. Bobby seemed to know that he was playing Dr. Frankenstein in this play, and Lil Dee could end up a monster, or a daughter, the choice was how he should deal with her in the future, and how to teach her not to admire him when he was wrong.

That night, we all ended up sitting in the shop, as Bobby and Carl began to carve our footprints and to teach me to carve along with them. In time, Carl began to tell us the story of how Dogwood Mountain came into existence. Only then did Bobby sit and gently take Lil Dee in his arms and say that he was sorry as she rested her head on his chest while Momma wiped tears from her eyes as Ms. Karen's smile told Bobby that she was proud of him.

"Men are far the dumbest people on earth!" Carl said. "Now that's about the shortest way to tell you the story of this here hill. But a long time ago, a little Cajun fellow got shipwrecked down on the river there," Carl said as he pointed to the river. "Girls, men want girls to love them and you might think it's kisses, money, stuff like that, but not rightly so; it's close, but close only counts in the game of horseshoes. No, men want to be a hero, and to have means of impressing a woman. For some, it is money, but that ain't enough really, that's why girls are always dreaming of knights rescuing them and stuff like that. Well men are just as silly, they want their girl to be impressed — a man has just got to have a dragon to slay or a mountain to climb, and it turns out that our Cajun boy had found himself a girl over in town to love, but there ain't been too many dragons around these parts for a long time. Now his girl, she was pure Tennessee gold, she didn't want nothing but for the Cajun boy to love her. Tennessee girls are just good that way!" Carl said as he winked at Ms. Karen who blushed and said, "Now Carl, you know I'm from Kentucky!" and we all laughed with them.

"Well, it turns out that some white folks had seen gold over in the Blackhills of South Dakota, and as there no war to fight, or dragons to slay, the Cajun boy decided to go get himself a fist or two full of gold from out that way. He promised to write his girl no matter what, and to tell her everything that he saw on his trip, and for the first year or so everything was good between them. He would write her and share his adventure, and she would write and moan and fuss like all women do, telling him to come home and well basically acting like Ms. Karen does when she sees me drinking and enjoying myself!" Carl stated, instantly moving out of the way of the gentle smack Ms. Karen playfully aimed at his side. "The girl just wanted him to come home, gold or not. Women are good about stuff like that — if they love you, then gold don't matter," Carl explained as Bobby continued to hug and apologize to Lil Dee.

"Well, back in those days, folks would dig a burial pit away from town so if a person died and they didn't understand why, or from a sickness that was going around the hills, then they had a safe place to put the dead folks so no one else got sick. Now this goes back in history to them plagues over in Europe a long time ago, but people here always thought that dying of a sickness like the flu was somehow evil, so they weren't very respectful of the dead bodies, and they often just dumped them in a pit, covered 'em up and tried to forget them as soon as they could." Carl paused to drink some wine from a jar that made its way from Carl to Bobby, to Momma, Ms. Karen, and even to me. Only Lil Dee was too young, and Ms. Karen made me promise to only sip wine when she was there with me.

"Now it turns out that the Cajun boy being a Frenchman helped him out in many ways as the Indians didn't like the white man at all, and the mountains were sacred to them, holy, like church is to us. Well, the French had been falling in love with them pretty Native girls for years by then, so our Cajun boy got to be considered family and he was always asking them to teach him about their ways so that he could then write home and tell his girl what he learned. Funny thing is, no one bothered to tell him that his girl had died of the flu that year and was buried up here on this mountain with fifty-two other souls. The Cajun boy just figured that his girl was mad at him and that she had stopped writing just to get under his skin, to make him come home.

"Finally, the Cajun boy wrote and told the town that he had found gold and that he was on his way home. Well, the town folks put an ad in the Saint Louis newspapers bragging that the local son had done well out west and was on his way home; they even arranged to be sent a message telling them when he made it to Saint Louis so they would know when to watch for his arrival." Carl paused for another sip of wine, and shook his old head as he said," Folks tend to be stupid when money is involved. They always mistake money, gold, for honor, honesty or good morals, but bad people have money too. When the Cajun arrived in town, they were about to have a big party for him, but all he wanted was to see his girl, to tell her about the house he was gonna build her." Carl pointed over to the house that he and Ms. Karen now lived in.

"Well, them folks just handed him all of his letters that had stacked up in the post office since his girl passed on and the Cajun boy went crazy, asking why didn't a single person write and tell him that she was gone. I'm told things would have been alright had them folks known exactly where they had placed her in the grave. That, and watching the Natives take loving care of their dead, just made the boy hate everyone in town. So, he bought this whole mountain and set about destroying the town." Carl laughed at the idea that the Cajun boy actions had saved the town instead of bringing it to ruin.

"First he tore out every tree up here and replaced them with dogwoods. Now girls, the mountains out west ain't like Tennessee, where the mountains get all white on top every winter with snow, so the Cajun just figured that once the dogwoods bloomed, then at least for a few days each year, this mountain would look snow covered. Then he built the cabins and the church and had the butterfly window put in, one butterfly for each person buried there under the church, and he began a lot of things that we still do every year at Easter time. For the Native, it's the beginning of the new year, first of spring and all," Carl said as he noticed that Lil Dee was asleep in Bobby's arms. "I guess all of the rest can wait until some other time, it's best that y'all get on up to bed now," Carl said as he hugged me goodnight. Then, as a family, Momma, Lil Dee, Bobby, me and the dogs made our way up Cemetery Ridge to our home and beds.

Sleep came easy that night and I dreamed that I was loved by a man like that Cajun boy who would stop at nothing to prove his love for me as we fought the world together. Yet no matter how many times my heart begged for my dreams to end in a happy way. They always changed from dreams of a good life into having to fight everyone in town alone, all of us united against the same monster with no friends to guide us. Today, I understand that after having to face so many hardships alone, after being abandoned so many times, that this part of my dreams represented how I wanted life to be, a true family that would stand together against all odds. Had the Bears really loved us, they would have come to Percodan's and saved us instead of leaving us to suffer. And then, just as we would stand united as a family against the evil townspeople, my dream would again change as the hard work of living a good life became too much, and Momma and Bobby gave up and got high again. The reality that a good life takes hard work and faith would set in and Momma would give up. She would then begin to force our world to explode as I had seen her do before over and over.

It would take years before I would come to understand that my dreams followed the same patterns as Momma's relationships with men: at first, she was full of hope, then she would worry the poor man, constantly forcing him to prove his love, starting over again and again only to then become desperate and unbearable when the relationship got to hard or involved more action from her than sex. Without meaning to, Momma's life had affected the way that I dream. I could never have a dream that ended in 'Happily ever after' because Momma never taught me that happily ever after was even possible.

The next morning, by the time I had eaten breakfast and enjoyed my private time with Ms. Karen, Bobby and Carl had already cleaned all of the extra blue footprints off of the stairs that

Bobby planned to set on Cemetery Ridge that morning. I carried a shovel up to where they were working and tried to help them dig a level place to set the stairs. I thought that the stairs would need a flat, level place to rest, but Carl explained the need to set each stone so that it was pitched higher at the back, near the mountain, in a way that would allow the rainwater to wash and clean the stones instead of pooling up and seeping in behind the stones, turning the ground to mud, then causing the stones to move or to wash away.

Today, I laugh at those same stairs each time I step on them, still so solid and firm, pitched so gently that no water can pool upon them or seep in behind them and ruin their foundations. I have to wonder how something so small and trivial can be so important. I wonder why no one ever taught Momma that same trick to use in her life. Momma only knew how to start building a future, no one ever showed her any tricks to use to make love stay. Surely there are simple tricks to building a good home around a solid love, something simple, some small preparation for the coming storms that all lives must endure.

We placed those first four stairs and walked back towards the shop, Carl telling us stories about the funerals of certain people whose graves we passed, their nicknames and sometimes how they earned that nickname. I couldn't help but to feel close to those souls as I smiled and laughed with Carl and Bobby over silly pieces of their lives, things that only matter to families. Then suddenly our day was interrupted by the sound of a car speeding up the road to the top of the Cemetery Ridge and I became scared. Bobby was almost certainly being searched for by the police by now; also in my heart, I felt that nobody but one of us had the right to drive up Cemetery Ridge anymore — this was our home. Then, just as I caught my first sight of the intruder's big car peeking out of the cloud of dust that had formed around it, Carl mumbled.

"God damn preacher!" His voice and eyes were both full of hate for the man driving the car. "Hell's gonna be full of them type of assholes!" Carl assured Bobby as Momma with Lil Dee and most of the dogs ran down Cemetery Ridge to stand with us as we faced this new uncertainty.

The preacher was older than the young girl who got out of the car to stand beside the man who Carl had already poisoned my opinion of. I don't mean a hillbilly smart younger woman married to an older man, where the woman is a few years younger and has picked a man with a good job. I could see that this girl was not much older than me and I felt at odds in my heart as to how to treat the young woman. I respected preachers and their wives, but this one was just a girl.

"We normally stay in the cabin you're in now son!" The preacher said as he stuck out his hand for Carl and Bobby to shake. "It's more like a home, makes it easier for me to focus on the sermons if you know what I mean?" he continued as if he expected us to move to one of the other cabins.

"Not this week preacher! It's my home! Best you remember that from now on, asshole!" Bobby said as he displayed a sly grin, and I thought about the doctor's office and shuddered. If Bobby baited this fool into a fight, he would win, of that I had no doubt, but we would lose — we would have to run away again, and my heart had fallen in love with the peace of our new life.

"Why preacher, I see you got married!" Ms. Karen said as she walked up and pinched Carl's side, warning him that she was not happy. She turned the preacher and his young bride away towards one of the open cabins, trying to assure him that she would help him make it just as homely and peaceful as Bobby's mother's cabin was. I felt a wave of relief wash over me as Lil Dee began to laugh and giggle as she wrestled with the dogs on the grave of a woman who had lived and died years before Carl had been born.

"Snakes! Fucking snakes!" was all Bobby said as he stared at the preacher's shiny car, sitting there reflecting the sun in a way that Momma's old paint could not do anymore.

"Where?" Momma asked as she looked down to search the ground around where Lil Dee was playing with the dogs. Her protective action was frightening to Lil Dee and appealing to me — frightening because there could be snakes near, and appealing because my mother was trying to protect her child from them.

"Not out here!" Carl said with a laugh as he rubbed Lil Dee's head.

"I thought you were a country girl?" Bobby playfully asked Momma as he gently hugged her. "Girls, can't you smell that? Old cucumbers, just starting to rot? That's the smell of copperheads! Motherfucker must have a trunk full of them!" Bobby said and I could see his anger starting to grow again.

"Why's he got snakes, Bobby?" Lil Dee asked. I heard fear in her voice as she pulled herself into Momma's side and watched the car as if the preacher's snakes would escape at any moment.

"He's a conman, honey. Had he showed up here with a normal wife, acting like a normal preacher, I would think that he was just a goodhearted Christian man who had been misled about them snakes all that stuff in the Bible," Bobby said.

As he paused, Momma spoke up. "The book of Mark? Is that what you mean Bobby?" she asked, and I was shocked to hear the name of even one book of the Bible — after all, if it hadn't been for churches giving us free food and picking Lil Dee and me up for Sunday school, I doubt I would have even known the names of Matthew, Mark, Luke or John.

"Dee," Bobby said, "The book of Mark is about the most plain of all the books in the whole Bible. It's my favorite, it ain't full of all kinds of funny words and stuff. If the gospels were flowers, Matthew is so pretty that it would be a rose; John would have to be an iris, the way it's written, and Luke maybe a carnation. But Mark would be nothing more than a dandelion, just a weed, not something you would pick a bunch of to give to someone you love," Bobby said as he touched my shoulder with his hand.

"Back when folks first came over to America to live, they saw the Natives dance with snakes and get bitten but not get sick and die, so the preachers remembered the book of Mark and how it says that a person could pick up snakes and not be hurt, and even heal themselves. But that ain't what Mark meant; what he meant was that if you just let go and trust, believe in God's love without any doubts, that your belief will heal you and that nothing can harm you. Had Jesus been alive today, he might have said guns, or car wrecks, but in his day, them snakes in the Middle East were the most dangerous things around, not like these toy snakes we got over here.

Hell, a copperhead won't even make you sick unless you're really old or just a baby, and a cottonmouth ain't much worse — it will cause an ugly scar, make you sick and all, but they ain't nothing compared to those nasty snakes over where Jesus was from. And most of the time, snakes just dry bite a person anyway — they won't even inject you with poison. That poison is used for food, for hunting, and they don't want to waste it, especially after the preacher tames them down some by handling them and milking their venom. Hell, it takes a lot to get them snakes mad after a couple of shows," Bobby explained as Carl nodded his head in agreement.

"It's a con game, really, nothing more, but it gets everyone excited at the church meetings, and excited people put more money into the offering plate!" Bobby said, and I could once again hear anger in the tone of his voice. "Ain't right to play with God. Hell, what Jesus said was pretty simple really — just love each other, it's kinda hard to judge each other if you love them. Look at how you'd judge me if you didn't know me as a person; love me less than you do and you would be scared of the things that I've done. Love is funny that way. Jesus said to just have love, faith and trust, and the Lord will heal you no matter what, or at least give you the strength to face things," Bobby said as he looked over at the church building.

"Why ain't Jesus healed you and Momma? Why do y'all have to eat so many pills?" Lil Dee asked. "Bobby gets mad a lot, but I know it's his way of hiding his hurt, and Momma, sometimes you just look so sad that I hope that you get high and be happy again. But if this Jesus can heal you, then why ain't he done it?" Lil Dee asked in a voice that at first had sounded confused, full of child-like wonder, but had changed into a voice full of doubt. The voice of a child who had once really needed Jesus, prayed for him to save her, and been abandoned by him. I have to admit that I was not really buying into the whole Jesus story either — a loving God would have cared enough to have awakened me that night so I could save my sister from Orville.

"God can't do anything until you choose to trust him Lil Dee, and even then, it's not Jesus who saves you, but your faith. Remember that it's your faith in God that heals you. Jesus could touch you ten times and it won't help unless you believe," Ms. Karen said as she walked up to join our family standing there staring at the preacher's car.

"Why in the world do you let that man preach here Ms. Karen?" Bobby asked in a soft voice. "You know he ain't no good at all — he ain't fit to marry or to bury me! I should just go ahead and kill him, be done with it, and save that child he calls his wife!" Bobby said as his anger began to boil.

"That man is all we got; good preaching is hard to find any more in a traveling preacher!" Ms. Karen replied. "Besides, you gave up any right to complain when you walked away and forgot about preaching!" We make do with the preachers we can get; don't you forget that" she stated firmly. "That man is standing behind a pulpit that you chose to abandon! That makes you just as responsible as I am for his being here."

There is a weight in the truth that ends foolish debates and, although I had no idea that Bobby had once wanted to become a preacher, Ms. Karen's words, heavy with honesty, ended Bobby's complaints about the preacher, snakes, young brides, and gospels written to honor a man who had refused to save my sister from being raped. A man who had refused to save Momma from her own pain, a man who had allowed me to see and face all that I have faced in my life. No, on that day as we turned away from that car full of snakes as a family and walked down the hill to the shop, I didn't know or like Jesus, nor the idea of him. I won't blow smoke up your ass now by telling you that Jesus rushed in wearing a cape and saved us, but seeds of hope were planted that day.

"Y'all girls ain't seen inside the church yet," Carl calmly said as I began to try and carve more footprints into the stones we planned to set on Monday. Bobby had drawn small feathers on the stones around some of the footprints. Ms. Karen had sworn to skin Bobby alive if he so much as thought about working tomorrow. "We only get a preacher to come through this way once a month, and you're gonna act like you were raised right!" Ms. Karen firmly said.

"Now Karen, after all that I've done in life, don't think that God will send me to hell for missing church tomorrow and working on the stairs," Bobby said with a tiny smile on his lips and playfulness in his eyes.

"You sure are going to hell, I won't lie about that, you earned it, but these babies got to be taught right. When you took them in or they took you in, you decided to teach them right, and by God, you will go to church, and you won't work tomorrow or else! Do you hear me!" Ms. Karen said as Carl laughed at the look on Bobby's face, and I realized that the church meant a lot to Ms. Karen and that Bobby would listen to her no matter what.

Chapter 21

The Sunday morning sun felt warm on my face that first day of church. Yes, we had been to church before, but never just for the sake of going to church. We had never bought clothes for church before, we had never planned to go to church before; church and dealings with God were never combined. God was someone we cussed at or prayed to when things were really bad, while church simply meant free food and handouts; we went only as a form of payment to the people who fed us. After the near theft of my sister, I saw all church communities as the same: pointless and evil. Yet there we were that day, standing under a crisp blue sky, dressed in our white Sunday dresses, complete with gloves and hats, surrounded by the many shades of springs greens; you know the color, a green that's almost yellow, so bright and fresh that it hurts your eyes.

This is another of those things in life that archaeologists will never understand, even though it is the root cause of so many of the tribal beliefs that those educated fools waste so much money and time trying to explain to me on TV every day. Spring is a force, it is energy, it is life. It's there just under last year's old grass, glowing fresh and bright, proof that we too are alive, proof that we are connected to something more than our own tiny lives. So, it's not hard to understand why ancient people would hold ceremonies celebrating having survived another year. On that Sunday all those years ago, I felt the energies of spring and honestly wanted to go to church with my family. I wanted this chance at a new and fresh life that a God or the perfect placement of our earth and sun was offering me.

Bobby was truly speechless when he saw us, his three girls

dressed and ready for church. Momma was so beautiful — not one single trace of Ruby's truck stop remained; she seemed to glow, just as fresh and new as the budding dogwood flowers growing in the trees above our heads. Bobby too had a glow about him, dressed as countrymen dressed for church in clean fresh pants and a bright white shirt, ironed stiff that same morning and buttoned up to the top. I felt alive as we were escorted by our pack of beagles across Cemetery Ridge to stand with Carl and Ms. Karen as one family, saying our hellos and being introduced to people, good people, who seemed to honestly want to know us. People whose questions were genuine and just not searching for our wrongdoings to judge us by.

Today as I write this, I'm tempted to go on explaining this to you, as if our lives had suddenly changed into a fairy tale. But they hadn't, and nor would they ever — the world had not changed at all, but instead, I had changed. The new people's good-natured questions were just as searching as those of the evil, judgmental, gossiping women in Kermit, or those of the good church going women of Huntington who had so easily sat in judgement of us at court that day as we prayed to get Lil Dee returned to us.

As I write this, I think about all of the times people acted as I had expected them to do simply because I expected them to act that way. How many times had I passed judgment on myself only to then blame others for the opinions of me that I assumed that they held? How many doorways and opportunities in our life had Momma and I slammed shut because she was a dope fiend whore and I her child, her stained broken child? How many children see their parents for who they really are and believe that they are somehow predestined to be nothing more than a dope fiend whore themselves? All because they foolishly believe that the world around them has already passed its judgment on them? Ms. Karen's loving need of church gave me the chance to walk up to the church doors dressed as if I belonged with those people who were standing in the spring sun, flooded in the bright green glow of new life without the stains of our past to shadow my opinions of my tomorrows. It's funny how we know when we are living wrong and then try to blame others for how we feel about it. How easy it is to see exactly what we want to see in the eyes of another person, creating bad feelings where none were before. We scream at them for judging us, yet it is our own shame we are screaming over.

The small church was breathtaking, a simple wooden building covered in handmade stained-glass butterflies, their odd shapes all jumbled together, placed wherever a hole could be cut. Yet nothing had prepared me for the beauty of seeing them from inside of the building's one room. The Cajun had built his church so that the back of the building faced the east and the morning sun, and it was this wall that held the large glass cross and sunburst that Carl had told us of, all surrounded by fifty-three large butterflies that appeared to be flying into the cross and its light. The butterfly represented the soul, Carl had said, and the effect of the wall, its beauty, made me want to have a stained-glass window of my own there with the others. The rest of the church was plain, wooden walls only, stained with a whitewash years before, its hardwood floors polished to shine by years of leather-bottomed Sunday shoes, simple flooring that matched the plain unstained pews, but what was most amazing was now the butterflies cast an ever-changing bath of colors, all caused by the sun as it danced within the clean walls of the country church.

"Ain't no two Sunday services the same, Page," Carl said. "The sun is always changing a little, and every time it changes, the colors seem to change, sometimes all at once, like when a storm is coming, and other times, it's so slow that you can hardly see it. But that's what I love about this room, it's like life, never exactly the same," Carl said with a grin as Ms. Karen pointed to a pew near the back of the church. This shocked me — I was sure that she would have a pew at the front.

"I only want to be the least in the Kingdom of Heaven," Ms. Karen said, reading my mind about the placement of our family's pew. "Someday, I hope you understand what I mean when I say least."

Bobby being Bobby quickly put on a mask to hide his heart

and began to be critical of the preacher almost immediately. "I should just go ahead and shoot this asshole right now, do the world a favor!" he mumbled, only to draw a slap on his still sore leg from Ms. Karen. I knew that Bobby always carried a small pistol in his pocket, and after Ms. Karen smacked his leg, I was sure that he would shoot her too if she touched his leg again.

"Shut your mouth, the man's all we got. Remember, you chose the path you're on, you set your own table! Now you have to sit down and eat your dinner at it! I won't have you disrespect God or yourself by acting like you are better than the sinner God sent to lead this service today!" Ms. Karen said.

"Would you go upfront and take that preacher's place?" Carl asked. "You know why you're here, ain't no point in making things worse."

"Don't mean I have to like what the man says!" Bobby said in his defense. "How are these baby girls here supposed to know how to spot a son-of-a-bitch if I don't tell them when I see one?" Bobby asked quickly, drawing another smack on the leg from Ms. Karen and a laugh from Carl.

"You know better than to cuss in church!" Ms. Karen said as Momma reached for Bobby's hand, sympathetic to his pain and afraid that he might get mad and walk away from what for her heart was a perfect day. It's funny how we humans all have fantasies about why we're doing something today and about how our tomorrows will be better because we did it. For Ms. Karen and Carl, they had fantasies that by helping Bobby they were making up for not saving him years before; Momma saw her day in church as proof that Ruby's truck stop was just a small part of her life and not her future. And for me? I was so foolishly caught up in my own make believe world, telling myself that the people at church thought that I was Bobby's daughter, and that I belonged there on that church pew with him, that I was more than the child of an addicted whore sitting beside a stone-cold killer who had no future of my own, that I failed to see that for Lil Dee this was not a fantasy. She listened to every word the preacher spoke and then compared them to Bobby's now whispered complaints and explanations, as Ms. Karen smiled happily at Bobby because he was now teaching Lil Dee instead of just bitching about the preacher.

There are lots of ways preaching, but traveling preacher tend to focus on services that make you want to repent for your sins, Bobby said. Next to pulling out snakes, the altar call was about the biggest con that a preacher could use to fill up his offering plate. So it was because of money that preachers focused only on getting people to come down and kneel before the altar and accept Jesus into their hearts.

"But just ask a preacher what to do next!" Bobby said with a laugh as he explained his opinions to us that day. "I ain't never seen a preacher who could tell a man how to live his life once he let Jesus into his heart."

"Go on boy," Ms. Karen said in response. "You're a big man, you can figure out what to do tomorrow if you live that long! Now get up and do the right thing, the babies need to see you do the right thing, so go up there and make peace with God."

Bobby nodded his head as he mumbled a simple "Yes Ms. Karen," then stood up and walked up to the alter to kneel before man to ask for God's love to fill his heart. When the preacher saw Bobby coming forward, he smiled happily at everyone as if it had been his words that had drawn the sinner out of his seat and back to the Lord, yet today, as I write, I know the truth and I am thankful to Ms. Karen for giving us that day.

Lil Dee saw Bobby kneeling before the altar, bathed in the sun's light and the ever-changing colors that danced on the floor, marking the holy spot for all to see, and she too stood up and went forward to kneel besides her hero, to accept Jesus. Momma stood to go forward too, and as she wiped the tears from her eyes, she reached out her hand to me and, like so many times before, I blindly took it and followed her. I wish I could tell you that I had told myself, "Well, Page, you've been to carnivals, bars, whorehouses and everywhere else with Momma, why not follow her to heaven?" But the truth is, I wanted God to redeem himself. He had failed to be there for me so many times before — he had left me crying with only the ghost of a dead soldier to keep me safe. But up here, on this tiny mountain surrounded by graves, drenched in the energy of spring, everything was right — new, clean and bright.

The killer and the whore who had brought me here were suddenly alive and not racing towards their death. They didn't start and end their days in pursuit of opiates and money, but instead by going to work. And now we were being guided to accept God into our hearts; he would protect us now, he would save us from the killings and the gore of Bobby's past, but above all, he would rescue me from the stained future that I would endure if I continued to trust my mother. That day, as I walked up to the altar, I wanted God's love, his forgiveness for my sins, his forgiveness for not giving myself to Orville and saving my sister. As crazy as it sounds, I often thought that if I had gone to Orville, he wouldn't have raped my sister, and that Momma would still have her business driving fiends in search of drugs; that I would never have seen her down on her knees in the truck stop, trading herself, kneeling before a fat man much like we were now kneeling down to accept God's love.

I was a sinner I told myself as Momma and I found our way to Bobby's and Dee's side to kneel down and pray. My failing to save my sister had gotten all of those people killed — Percodan and Jessica would still be alive, and Bobby would not be on the run for murdering them. These are the sins that I silently carried in my heart; the sins I prayed God would forgive me for. These are the burdens that I laid down that day in front of my new church family as we prayed to God to save us. Then the preacher's young wife began to pass large copperhead snakes around as we all sang and prayed, and even Lil Dee showed no fear of the evil snakes, taking one in her hands when it was offered.

It's funny how a person's want, their heart's desire, can trick them into believing anything. Bobby had explained to us that snake handling was a conman's trick, meant to fill the preacher's pockets, but I wanted our new life so badly that I convinced myself that God, the Lord Jesus, was protection against those tamed snakes. I prayed and danced, lost in the overwhelming power that surged through the tiny church that day, pulsing with each song that we sang. I felt new, reborn, and loved as we walked outside into the noonday sun, clean and forgiven of my past evil ways, now a member of a family.

Today I know that desire is the energy that fueled those feelings of rebirth and forgiveness our first day in church, and on many others since. My need, my desire for forgiveness and for a new life made me feel things in that tiny church that I am still afraid to dismiss or to call delusions. Commonsense says that I was caught up in my desires. Commonsense says that Bobby was right and that we had tricked ourselves into believing that God loved us. And my head knows that Bobby was right, but my heart doesn't have any commonsense, because no matter the many years I have wasted, rotting, broken and alone, our first Sunday church service remains magical to me, the only proof that I need to know that God exists, even if the bastard does not listen very well.

Reality is a cold and unloving truth. No matter how hard we try to avoid reality, it still gets us, knocks us down, kicks us in the face. For Bobby, reality was a shield to hide behind, protection against his own fantasies, his own desires. As we stood outside of the church saying goodbye to our new church family, wrapped in the magical feeling of being born again, Bobby smacked us all in the face with reality. He stood there smoking a cigarette like the lead actor in an old movie. Each puff of smoke exhaled on cue, each movement performed as if thought out and planned, then he reached into his pocket and took out a handful of money. Without even counting it, he reached over and stuffed the money down the dress and into the bra of the preacher's young wife, shocking us all into silence.

"That money is for you! Not him, stupid! Someday, you're gonna wake up and need to escape that piece of shit pervert you're married to, so save that money, then you ain't gotta beg him for money to buy yourself a bus ticket back home to your family," Bobby coldly stated, smacking us all in the face with the cold uncaring truth, and poisoning the day's magical feelings. In less than an instant, the mystical spell that God, desires, singing and our prayers had woven together was broken. The sun still shone brightly as it had before, the green of spring was still breathtaking, but Bobby's words had tainted the moment.

The preacher's wife looked child-like, as if she had been caught playing dress up and wasn't the wife of a powerful preacher at all. My white Sunday dress now seemed stained. My hat lay heavy on my head, and I began to smell old rotten cucumbers on my hands as Bobby looked at the girl and said, "There's a lot of ways to sell yourself, little girl! You're most likely not the type to sell yourself for money, not the kind of woman to just work a straight, honest business deal with a man for money, but you have no problem giving yourself to that man nightly after all your work, milking the venom from them snakes for your man. It makes you feel good to be his wife, to be a part of his act. It makes you feel good to trick people with them snakes. I understand how you feel, it's nice to be somebody, to stand out in the crowd. But you're a whore, trading your body and your future to that man just so you can feel important, just so you can stand out in a crowd of country women. But you're playing with folk's souls, girl. This ain't no truck stop, you're not getting down on your knees in gravel for money, this is a church!" Bobby said as Momma smiled in agreement, confusing me as to how I should feel about Bobby calling the girl a whore.

"It ain't God that you're playing with, he's used to idiots doing wrong in his name. It's these good folks here and at the churches who you rob with your tricks. You're hurting good folks who just want God's love. You're lucky that you're not my baby girl!" Bobby said as he nodded his head at Lil Dee and me. "If you were, your man would be one very dead preacher and you wouldn't be trading your body and soul to an old pervert for the price of being respected as a preacher's wife!" Bobby said as he turned away. After calling for the dogs to follow him, he took Lil Dee's hand, made a joke about Ms. Karen frying Sunday chicken for dinner and walked away, leaving Momma standing there holding the young woman's hands.

"He sounds mean, but above all he is truthful! Us women tend to sell ourselves for the craziest things. The show you put on ain't much different than them girls who dance at strip clubs, yet what they do is honest. Now save that money girl so you can go home one day!" Momma said as she kissed the girl's cheek and wiped her tears away. I felt proud of Momma as we turned away from the preacher's child bride and went to catch Bobby, Dee and the dogs before Bobby could eat all of the good pieces of chicken.

That Sunday evening, we began work carving angels' footprints with fallen feathers placed here and there on the hard black granite stairs that we planned to place tomorrow. I was happy; our evening gatherings were turning into a family routine, with Bobby teaching me about art, and Lil Dee playing with the dogs until she got too tired to run anymore. Carl would sit peacefully on a stone meant to mark a grave, drinking his sumac berry wine, telling us stories, hoping that Momma would keep Ms. Karen busy in the house and out of his hair until he was too drunk to notice or care about her complaints about his drinking. Home, like so many times before, I felt that I had found my home, but this time I had God's ear. There was no way that God would take my home away from me again, not now, not after I had given myself to him. I silently told my heart this as I asked Bobby why he hated the preacher and his wife so much that Ms. Karen had known not to ask the couple to come to Sunday dinner with us.

"My mother was crazy, Page," Bobby said. "But only part of her craziness was real or due to her mental health. The rest was caused by the way that she was raised and by my father and the way he taught her to live, to survive. People tend to forget that we often over or under react to normal things in life because of how we were raised, how we were taught to believe. Sixty years ago, folks would never go to church with black folks, now we marry them, love them and laugh about the past. We learned that what we were taught was wrong, so we changed, we grew. But add trauma to a person's foolish ideas and they will overreact every time they see a black person and never realize that it's the memory of the trauma that they're reacting to and not the color of a person's skin."

Bobby shook his head as he looked down at the stairs that we were carving and I could tell that I had asked a question that Bobby wanted to answer, yet he seemed to need to talk through his feelings about it. We had learned that Bobby was cut and dry, short and to the point when asked a question that he did not want to debate or answer. He could be very curt, as if warning you to mind your own business and leave him alone. When he answered your question with a joke, this meant that he had no idea what the answer to your question was, but tonight he had a willingness to discuss this topic, as if his soul, like my own, had felt the power of God's touch earlier today. I saw that Momma had made her way out to the shop to sit with us. She could hear in Bobby's voice what I had heard — that Bobby wanted to explain his heart.

"My back," Bobby spoke in a soft tone as he took his hands and rubbed the scars on his shoulder that he could reach. "These things are reminders of each time I missed quoting the Bible. My daddy had been a preacher, and my mother his young bride. He died one night after sneaking off with a woman from a small church like this one here. His death left my mother alone when she was still a child herself but with two babies of her own to care for, my sister and me." Bobby paused and I heard the floorboards creaking where Ms. Karen was standing in the doorway to the house, her cheeks wet with tears. Lil Dee had found her way onto our mother's lap, while Carl and the puppies waited for Bobby to finish speaking.

"My mother had nothing, she was nothing, she had no skills, no self-worth. Her greatest achievement and the only sense of self-worth she had was in her being the preacher's wife. This would not have been a bad thing had my father just died, but to die after being in the arms of another's woman, one from one of the small churches that my mother was supposed to be a spiritual mother of. Well, that made my mother a fool, a fool with nowhere else to go and no way to get there. Sometimes she would beat me to teach me to be the best traveling preacher ever so I could out-preach even my own father, and at other times her goal was revenge. She treated me like a fighting dog, and she wanted me to destroy." Bobby began to laugh as his eyes seemed to look inward, into his heart and memories.

"I wanted to be preacher, I really wanted to be like my father. I had no way to know that my mother was crazy or that the people we lived off as we moved from small church town to small church town felt sorry for us because of my father's death and for their failure to confront him for the way he had lived. Guilt, false respect, and some foolish idea about never speaking badly about the dead all combined and led to no one telling me the truth. So, I foolishly accepted anything my mother did to me. It was nothing compared to what Jesus endured, and a good son, according to the Bible, never questioned his parents." Bobby paused and began to laugh deeply, a scary laugh, the laugh of the insane, I thought as fear raced through my body. I remembered that he had laughed this same way as he had beaten the doctor's nurse, but that his laugh on that day had been accompanied by the snapping of bones and the woman's death.

"Now calm down," Bobby said as he looked over at me. I could see that the darkness had passed in his heart and he was wearing the face of a clown, the happy playful face that I had seen him wear when he was trying to deflect a question or avoid conflicts.

"So, you won't tell them all of it, Bobby? "Ms. Karen asked, still hidden and crying in her darkened corner.

"No point in clouding up the story with blame, Karen. Who my father was with is of no importance is it? My mother was crazy, my father traded his soul for the power he felt standing before a church full of people and misleading them. And I walked away from God because I felt that he had tricked me into accepting being abused, beaten, and destroyed by my mother and the men she would give herself to. A good God would not punish us for loving him, Karen. I did what the Bible taught us to do and all I got was beaten for it. Yet once I started hurting and killing people, I stopped being beaten. Funny how that worked out!" Bobby said with a laugh.

"No son," Carl said. "You're wrong about that. You replaced the beatings with drugs. Them pills you and Christy eat may not leave scars on your back like a switch does, but they rip and scar your soul just as much, and these two baby girls here. Their hearts are just as scar-covered as your back is boy."

"Bobby grinned at his old drunken friend; his grin told me that Bobby accepted the truth of the old man's words as Carl leaned forward to allow Lucy to drink from his jar of wine. Seeing this caused Lil Dee to laugh at the idea of one of her dogs getting drunk.

"Springs in the air," Carl said. "We ain't got a lot of time. Best we all get some sleep and start over tomorrow."

As we walked up Cemetery Ridge to our home, Bobby told us that for the Native Americans, spring was the beginning of the year, and because of this, it was traditional to decorate the cemetery not only for Easter Sunday each year, but also for the Native New Year. That night I went to sleep dreaming about a holiday that until earlier that Sunday had held very little value to me. The Easter Bunny, dyed eggs, candy, new clothes and Last Suppers tend to cost money and a person's attention, two things' addicts don't have much of after feeding their addiction.

Chapter 22

At lunchtime the next day, Momma came to eat with us. There were days when I would see her walking towards us, carrying a basket of food that she had taken the time to prepare by hand and I hated her for it! What gave her the right to step on the stone stairs that we had worked so hard to carve and install? What gave her the right to follow the path we were struggling to build from the base of the mountain all the way up to the doors of what I now considered was my church?

I could see a look in my mother's eyes that I knew too well — it was the same look she wore when she was pretending to be a person she wasn't, and not the look of honesty that she wore when we stole food from a store together. My heart could see that once again, Momma was not suffering to reach a dream. In the past, her sex, her body, was the small price she would pay to live out a dream. But now, with Bobby, there was no price being asked of her, and worse, every step we took was one step deeper into her fantasy.

She was learning to cook, to be a good salt of the earth woman, to pretend to be Ms. Karen. Even God had accepted her without a complaint — the church did not begin to groan and shake as she knelt down to pray; God failed to scream down and ask her to explain why she had allowed Lil Dee to get raped, abandoned us to sleep in a cold car, and then seemed to only mourn the loss of her job as a drug runner and not the innocence of her daughters. Once again, my mother was being rewarded without working for or earning those rewards. She had all the pills she could ever want, money, an old woman to teach her how to act, and now she even had God in her heart — all of this freely handed to her, without anyone asking her for even one small apology for the wrongs that she had allowed us to suffer.

I did not blame her for my not going to school, or for many other things that I had seen or endured in our time together. But she had left me alone in our car with my sister, broken, bleeding, unable to speak, and I had no way to help her. When people you don't know or love are hurt, it's instinctive to want to help them. When it's a family member, an innocent child as Lil Dee was, it's not only instinctive to want to help them, but it's also instinctive to wish to trade places with them, to suffer the pain for them. So you reach into your heart and try to end their hurting as fast as you can. Somehow you believe that by making them feel better you are not as guilty or as responsible for their pain, you feel vindicated by the act of making everything better for them. But Lil Dee had remained hollow-eyed and silent for weeks, and each word that she had failed to speak had felt like a knife stuck deep into my heart. So for me to watch our mother carry us a homemade lunch as if fixing us lunch was a reflexive action, as if her pure heart forced her to cook for us out of love each day, made me want to scream at her, to remind her of our hunger as we set outside of a motel room listening to her service men, praying that there might be enough money left over after they got high to order us a pizza.

As if reading my mind, Bobby touched my shoulder and said that, in time, I would have to face how I felt about my mother. This caused me to laugh because Bobby had refused to draw anything for his own mother's tombstone for over a week now, safely hiding from his own demons within the work of building the stairs in a graveyard.

"Don't be a shit head Page!" Bobby laughed. "I guess I ain't the best example of forgiveness for you to follow."

"Son of a bitch!" Carl said with a sense of child-like joy dancing in his voice and eyes. "Look, son, it's blind ass Nickels!" Carl laughed as he pointed down the mountain at a man walking towards us with a dog happily running around freely near him. I was confused because the man I saw walking towards us could not have been blind. He was using a walking stick not the red

red and white cane used to search the world before him, and the dog was not a guide dog at all but more of a playful companion. From a distance, the man looked as if he were homeless, possibly black, but definitely not blind. Lil Dee looked at me and I saw the confusion in her eyes over the approaching stranger.

"Come on!" Carl said, happy to see that his old friend had made his way back to Dogwood Mountain for another spring. We raced the puppies and Carl down the steep hill, laughing as a family.

The old man walking up the road towards our new home owned my sister's attention; she couldn't take her eyes off of him or his dog even though he was still a long way from us. I saw that her worry had infected not only Lucy but also the puppies; they all seemed to be standing guard, waiting on Lil Dee to react to this new threat. Today, we can easily see her response as post-traumatic stress. Lil Dee would forever worry, even fear new people who were not honest, or acting as they should be. Carl's words and praise of the old man had assured us that he was blind, but the normal gait of his walk and his confident step argued that he was not crippled at all, and for this reason, Lil Dee feared him even from a distance. I couldn't blame her — after all Orville had used kindness and holiday spirit to separate her from anyone who would stop him from taking her.

"Do you two young ladies stare at every blind old black man you see?" the man asked as he drew near the tombstone shop where Lil Dee and I now stood awaiting his arrival. The man's dog, a mutt, a mixture of shorthaired farm dogs, raced up to my side, seeking love and attention without concern over Lucy and her brood who were as intently focused on the blind man as Lil Dee was. I sensed that this old man had best be blind or Lil Dee, with the help of her dogs, might kill him before Bobby could run outside and stop her.

"You ain't blind, motherfucker!" Lil Dee said, her voice dripping in hate and anger, leaving both the man and his dog certain of my sister's feelings.

"Oh, so it's just old black men you stare at?" Nickels asked with a laugh that was meant to calm Lil Dee.

"Who are you laughing at?" Lil Dee screamed as she stepped forward in a defensive manner, causing the dogs to begin to bark a protective warning to the blind man. I saw confusion and concern in the man's face and grey eyes as Ms. Karen raced to pull Lil Dee to her side and hug her. She yelled not only at Lucy and the puppies, but at Nickels for playing a game that she had warned him against playing many times before. "Nickels, you damn fool! Playing around with folks that don't know you again. How many times have I told you that folks don't know how to act around you at first? You're acting like you ain't blind! One of these days, you're gonna ask some redneck if he likes starting at old black men and the fool's gonna kill you!" Ms. Karen said as I began to laugh at Nickels and Carl raced up and hugged him.

Bobby began laughing too while Momma was acting the part of a concerned mother. She placed one hand over her mouth as she stepped over to Lil Dee and Ms. Karen began to apologize to Nickels as if Lil Dee had never said motherfucker before and Momma had no idea how she learned such a dirty word. Her voice, tone, and actions made me want to vomit. I realized that I did not like this version of my mother, nor did I feel that she had any right to act as she was now acting. Jesus had moved into her heart only yesterday. Momma had been nothing more than a confused self-hating addict, little more than a friend of ours for years, not a mother and there was no way she had changed overnight.

"Well, Karen," Nickels smiled. "One thing's for sure — whatever some pissed-off redneck decides to do to me, I sure as hell won't see it coming!" This caused us all laugh again, even Lil Dee. The dogs also seemed to sense the tension leaving her and began to play with their new dog friend. Carl seemed to grow younger as he passed Nickels a jar of sumac berry wine and we all walked into the tombstone shop together as a family.

That night I learned more about God and the nature of his grace by listening to three old friends telling stories, catching up with each other as they sipped homemade wine, than I would ever learn by sitting on a church pew. Nickels seemed to be blessed by the touch of an angel, but he was quick to tell you not to think such foolishness. He had earned the nickname of Nickels because he carried a jar of old silver nickels with him wherever he went and would fashion them into the prettiest rings in the world.

I watched him sit down on a blank headstone, fart, and then joke with Carl by asking what name was meant to be carved on the stone, and if Carl thought that they would mind him farting on their monument. Bobby could not stop laughing at the two old men who seemed like playful young boys. Even Lil Dee could not help but laugh when Carl crept up behind Nickels and let out the loudest fart that I have ever heard, causing Nickels to suggest that Carl go see a doctor because he might have strained his butthole! Lil Dee's laughter was Nickels' chance to make peace with my sister.

As I said that old dusty tombstone shop held more of God's love and grace than any church could ever hope to. Today, as I sort my life's tiny worth out and stack it into piles of memories, I have to believe that when we go to church, we are so worried about not making a fool of ourselves that we stifle God's love. We act as if we were having tea with a queen or eating lunch with a president when we are supposed to be curling up in the arms of God, snuggling with him, relaxed, unashamed, as if he were a loving grandparent who tells us stories as he jokes about farts and our mischievous nature. As Ms. Karen and Momma rushed to cook God's favorite meal, and Carl tried to work up another really big fart, one so smelly that it would make a blind man's eye water, Nickels would teach me that anything is possible if you want it and believe it with all of your heart and soul. The problem is, we often live our lives following people like Momma and Bobby, so by the time we meet God, and feel his love, we are too broken to trust or love him.

Nickels must have sensed Lil Dee sneaking to look at him to see if he really was blind, much like I was. It was still hard to believe that a blind man could walk all the way from town out to Cemetery Ridge alone and unaided. The playful old blind man was laying out old misshapen spoons that he used as hammers and old nails with their points filed into tools that he used to bend and shape his old coins into rings shaped like roses, belt buckles, finely braided ropes, the leaves of any tree that you liked and many more pretty things. I saw Nickels pull a cone shaped piece of old iron from his backpack and place it on the table as the centerpiece of his small workshop, and I could not help but notice that his fingertips were stained silver in contrast to his dark brown skin.

"It's the wheel hub off of an old Ford, Page. Darn thing makes a perfect anvil," Nickels said, causing me to look over at Lil Dee to see if she could explain how a blind man knew that I was not only watching him, but that I wanted to learn about the many homemade tools he was laying out on the table around him. Bobby and Carl had been teaching me to carve and I was amazed by the many types of chisels, and how one chisels' point was the right point to use to make a certain type of cut or line and others were not.

You might think that any piece of steel hit with a heavy hammer would carve into rock, and it will, but it might also crack or even break the stone. Man has spent thousands of years learning how to shape the tips of different chisels to work in the most effective way possible, and then teaching someone else about chisel points: an ancient art passed on in a timeless unbroken line, and now passed to me. I cherished the idea that I was part of that line now, that I had roots. I was still the bastard child of a carnival man, the daughter of a cheap addicted whore, a willing Three Musketeer, a newly found Christian, but now I had roots that lead back to the beginning of time.

Lil Dee smiled as she leaned forward and quietly moved two of Nickels' nails from where he had placed them, all while watching the old man's face and grey eyes for any signs that he could see her as Carl laughed with Bobby over a joke told at Nickels' expense.

"I can see that either you have forgiveness in your heart for me Lil Dee, and that you also like to play tricks on folks, or you still don't believe that I'm blind!" Nickels said, again shocking both Lil Dee and me to the amusement of both Bobby and Carl who couldn't help but laugh at us.

"Give me your hand Lil Dee," Nickels said and I watched her

slowly reach out her hand after Bobby assured her with a look that Nickels was safe and meant her no harm. Nickels pulled her tiny ring finger and let out a nasty fart that stunk so bad that Lucy ran outside to get away from the smell. Bobby laughed as Carl playfully blamed Lil Dee for the loud noise and horrible smell.

"Now y'all leave the girl alone Carl. She can't help it if Karen's cooking causes a person to fart like a cow!" Nickels smiled as Lil Dee giggled in a way that only an innocent child can giggle. Then Nickels took a small ring made into the shape of a rose with leaves and thorns from his bag and slipped it onto Lil Dee's ring finger.

"I'm really sorry that I scared you Ms. Lil Dee, and I hope that you will forgive me!" Nickels said as Lil Dee leaned in to hug the old man without speaking one word. I could see that her eyes were full of genuine forgiveness; where fear had been only moments before, joy now shone, and I wished that I was still foolish enough to forgive people as easily as a child can.

I heard Momma laughing with Ms. Karen and I wanted to scream at her, to tell everyone that Lil Dee never would have screamed at Nickels, that she never would have doubted Carl's word when he said that Nickels was blind, had Momma not allowed Orville to rape her. If Momma had not placed Lil Dee in the position to be abused, then she would have only known a child's innocence. The innocence that makes fairy tales turn into wonderful dreams, an innocence that would cause a child to never doubt that a blind man can walk home from town by himself or that Jesus would suffer and die for her. Lil Dee's forgiveness of Nickels did not allow our mother the right to act as if she did not know the feel of random nameless men or the sting of a gravel parking lot on her knees. No, Momma had traded her body for the same pills, the same high that and caused Lil Dee to become the chimera that she was now, part innocent child, part evil monster capable of smiling as Bobby pulled the trigger on a gun pointed at another man's head, yet unable to sleep without her puppy Buttons in her arms.

"Someday you'll get your heart around the right words Page, the words you need to say, and the words your mother needs to hear you say," Bobby said as embarrassment raced through my heart from being caught thinking the things that I was.

"Don't worry, they're the same words that I was never strong enough to say to my own mother," he softly stated as he pointed over to his mother's still blank tombstone. "I have a feeling that those unspoken words are the reason why that rock over there is still clean!" Bobby said as if he was speaking to himself and no one else.

Carl cried out, "Amen, son, amen! You're learning!" as Ms. Karen called us in to eat dinner.

Later that night, Bobby told me to draw a small feather without his help on a stair behind a footprint that I was sure was my mother's. I was too afraid of messing up my drawing to even consider the vast contradiction between the hate I felt toward my mother's lifestyle and the act of carving her footprints into stone, complete with fallen feathers as if she were an angel. Bobby normally drew the feathers and I just carved what he told me to carve, simple lines scratched in stone.

Yet Bobby had a reason for asking me to draw and carve a feather by myself without his help, a reason that has granted me peace every day of my life since. It is truly odd how tiny, often foolish things can teach us the most about life.

"Page, if you'd messed up the drawing or carving on that pretty feather, done it wrong, made it ugly, or made it look like a chicken feather instead of an angel's, or worse, broken the stair by using the wrong chisel," Bobby said, looking down at my completed art, smiling, "would it have been my fault or yours?" he asked, as he rubbed his finger across the perfect feather I had worked so hard to make.

"Damn right it would have been your fault, Bobby," I said with a prideful laugh, trying to use humor as a protective shield. I was embarrassed to be as exposed as I was to the critical reviews of my family. "You know I can't draw or really even carve, so if I'd messed up, it would be your fault, Bobby, not mine! You're the stupid chicken head Bobby, not me! I just did what you told me to do!" I smiled as Lil Dee grinned at me, showing her support.

"Isn't that what you were doing the night Lil Dee got hurt or any other time your Momma told you to do something?" Bobby asked, and my heart shuddered at the memory of the night I had allowed my sister to be hurt. I felt guilt replace the feelings of pride that I had gained from carving a perfect angel's feather behind the footprint of my mother the whore.

"I felt guilty for years," Bobby said. "I did anything that my mother told me to do, never questioning any wrong or mean things that she did. I even apologized to her when she blamed me for her life being so messed up. I felt guilty every time she stole from or harmed people. That guilt grew out of the joy I felt while eating a good meal on the nights that my mother stole from people — we always went out and had a big meal, a meal that I enjoyed. The guilt was even worse when I would remember praying that she would buy me a Christmas present with the money she had stolen," Bobby said as he lowered his head in shame.

"Page, them folks were trying to help a poor family, that was my mother's story. She couldn't work, her husband had died, we needed help, and I prayed for toys and food!" Bobby said in anger as he pounded his fist on the stair that I had just carved.

"Now you calm down Bobby!" Ms. Karen said from inside the house where she and Momma sat talking after dinner that night.

"Mind your own business, Karen!" Carl said in a kind, soft tone that at the same time left no room for her to argue with him.

"For years, I felt guilty for stealing and lying to people. I felt guilty for not telling those goodhearted folks that she was lying and was just going to blow the money on drugs and fancy clothes and pointless things. But Page, I was no more guilty of stealing from those good people than you would be guilty of destroying this stair had you ruined that feather. I'm the adult, I'm the one responsible for this art, not you, Page. And you're not responsible for what happen to your sister, you're not guilty of any wrongs. You did what God said for you to do — you listened to and respected your mother, just like I did. Don't let the guilt you feel inside eat you alive kid; face it, sort it all out, forgive yourself before you begin to hate yourself the way I hate myself," Bobby finished. I saw tears pooling in his eyes, and I couldn't help but to break down crying as well as I reached out and hugged my sister.

As I slept that night, my mind was full of dreams about my life with Momma, but dreams are not like movies, they never seem to have an opening act or an ending. My dreams that night would jump from Mickey to Lil Bear's ghost and then to Bobby; sometimes all three of them would blend into one as they made excuses for my mother not being a woman like Ms. Karen. I didn't want to hear their lies; I wanted Momma to admit that she had cared more about going back to work for Percodan than she had cared about Lil Dee's or my pain.

The next morning, I woke up late, but for once I didn't forget my dreams, and I debated their meaning as I rushed to eat something on my way to work. I felt so bad about being late that I didn't notice that it was raining or that Cemetery Ridge was completely silent as I ran down to the tombstone shop in search of my family. As I entered the shop, I was shocked to hear Ms. Karen say that it was settled, and that Bobby and my mother would get married on Easter Sunday at the Easter celebration. Bobby's only concern was that Ms. Karen find someone to perform the wedding ceremony other than the ass clown with the underage wife. "I mean it," I heard Bobby say. "I'll kill that asshole if I see him again!" but no one in the room laughed.

This should have been a warning to me that I may have forgotten the world outside of Dogwood Mountain, but the world had not forgotten Bobby, and that Ms. Karen, Carl and Nickels knew that Bobby was a monster and was not playing or joking about killing the preacher. Children often run from reality, I know that now, but I paid this warning no attention. I was too caught up in hurting my mother. How dare she attempt to trick these people into believing that she was worth marrying!

"Bobby are you crazy?" I screamed. "My mother is a whore — worse, she never felt one ounce of pain when Orville raped Lil

Dee. Don't you see Bobby? She is the reason we were on the run from the police!" I shouted, and then turned and ran away from them. It hurt me to hurt my mother, but I could not believe that these people could accept her without some acknowledgment of her sins. So, I ran away to hide in our car where it sits today. I had found the strength to give voice to my growing anger, but not enough strength to stay and explain my heart to them.

Thankfully, it took hours for anyone to find me and even then, it was only after my breath fogged over the car windows and made my hiding place visible. Momma opened the door and sat down without asking and without showing any sign of anger towards me. My heart was hurting for her more than I was afraid of her being angry over the mean yet very truthful things I had said about her. I had never betrayed my mother before, neither in the times that she acted as a mother nor in the vast spans of our relationship when she acted more like a girlfriend or a Three Musketeer.

"I knew this was brewing Page. The way that you would look at me before we left Ruby's told me that something had changed between us. Honey, you need to tell me what's on your mind, even though I'm sure that I already know what it is," Momma said in a calm honest voice. It wasn't the tone she would use to manipulate a person, nor the tone she used when she wanted to argue and blame you for her failings, instead, this was a vocal sound that I was not prepared for. Over the weeks, I had been using my anger to build up the strength to allow me to be critical of her every action, and now she had stolen my ability to defend myself with anger. How could I speak to her as a child when I blamed her for the death of the faithful unquestioning child that I had once been? She had stolen all of my child-like wonders. Fairy tales were now simply lying, and Santa Claus is a fat pervert to be watched around Lil Dee.

It was her actions and not Bobby's violence that had destroyed my faith. Seeing Bobby kill was a joke compared to her betrayal. Each day at Ruby's, watching her mourn the loss of her job driving addicts to doctors' appointments, was a knife in my heart. Lil Dee being raped seemed like a burden to her as she went about grieving the loss of Percodan, never trying to help my sister, never trying to do anything to harm Percodan or her chance of being his faithful dog again. These things alone were painful to accept, yet for her to then openly sell her body to men only to feed her addiction without concern for our needs was something far too hurtful for me to ever want to find the words to explain. In the early days, when she serviced store owners, we her girls', were allowed to eat freely at the expense of the man she was servicing, it was a subject that was not open for debate. But before Bobby, we, her girls, were merely dogs, fed the scraps and leftovers after her addiction had eaten its fill.

"Page, I never had anything of my own before Percodan trusted me to drive for him, and I planned to start driving people for my own. When Lil Dee was raped on Christmas Eve, I thought Percodan had allowed your sister to be hurt as a way of punishing me for thinking of leaving him. You cannot understand how broken Lil Dee being raped left me. It was my fault because I know the nature of sick men. The 'It' that the women in Kermit gossiped about was my own rape, and they were right, Page — what my mother easily allowed to happen to me killed the girl that I was. Your father should have been my ride to a new life, a life that did not have rape as its defining event," Momma explained, and I began to feel sad for her. I started to see her more as I saw Lil Dee. But then anger raged through my heart again and reminded me that my mother survived by making people feel sorry for her. "It" had made her a victim, and being a victim is often a profitable role to play in life, if not in the terms of money, then in the gift of emotion. Being a victim allowed her to fail — or worse, to never try to be anything more.

"Momma, why didn't you at least look at Lil Dee's body after you got out of the hospital? I asked my mother, only to see rage burst bright in her eyes then smolder and die, all in the time it took for a raindrop to roll down the big car's front window.

Momma began to laugh a giggling type of laugh that made me

smile and laugh too. For years after our conversation, I relived that moment in my daydreams, finally saying the things that I wish that I had said, making speeches like a president, listing my mother's crimes, always asking my heart to explain to me why I felt the need to laugh along with my mother after asking her an honest and cutting question.

Time has taught me that when a child is raised as an equal, a co-conspirator in the parents' evils, there is a closeness, a bond that is far deeper than that of a mother and child. But deeper does not mean stronger. This is why so many mothers and daughters grow up to do drugs together, and to work at strip clubs and whorehouses together. Mother and daughter may gain a bond deep enough to laugh with each other without knowing why, or to feel the death of the other instinctively from miles away, but that bond is not worth the loss of a parent. Normal girls love their mothers as deeply as I loved Momma, but there is a line that normal mothers will not cross with their children — to do so would mean the loss of their authority, and a parent must be listened to, must be heard. That's how we were made.

In the caveman days, it was the parental bond that made the child run towards their parents' voice and away from trouble. Broken caveman children being raised by broken caveman parents were too busy laughing with their mothers at inappropriate times to understand that a saber-toothed tiger was hungry and nearby. I have sat in church over the years and watched many mothers and daughters grow apart as the child becomes an adult — and that's normal, the parent has to learn to see their child as an adult and the child has to learn to see their parent as an equal. Once this metamorphosis is complete, a friendship blooms and grows, a friendship far stronger and far more meaningful than any other. I must admit, I wish God had granted me the chance to know my mother first as a mother and then as my friend like a normal girl.

Momma and I walked away from our car that day holding hands in a heavy spring rain, happy to be together. Although neither of us said very much, I felt that a weight had been lifted from my soul.

I laughed as Momma bragged that she was able to get by on two Oxycodones now — when she had met Bobby, she needed eight Oxy 40's to get high for the day and four just to keep from getting sick.

"It's this hill, Page! It's you, Lil Dee and Bobby. It's church, Karen, Carl and Nickels. I feel needed and wanted Page. I have never felt wanted before. I never thought that I was worth wanting," Momma said with a laugh, and I understood exactly how she felt as we skipped like schoolgirls in the rain, happy to be together in the cemetery laughing about pills.

I would find myself the object of Nickels' attention the rest of that rain-soaked afternoon. No one said anything about my morning: the way Momma and I had laughed and almost danced in the rain was all that anyone needed to see to understand that we had to overcome our differences. But Nickels was not normal, he seemed to instinctively understand that I had merely placed a bandage on a very large and festering wound.

"I am blind Page because that drunken piece of shit Carl got me blown up!" Nickels said as he motioned over towards a sleeping Carl. Lucy had climbed up his body and was now sleeping on his chest, no doubt as drunk as Carl was, I thought as I grinned at Lil Dee. Bobby was stuck again, fighting with his heart to draw a memorial for his mother, drawing beautiful designs, one after another, until nearly complete, and then washing them off again, cussing God under his breath, thankful that Ms. Karen and Momma were inside the house pretending to be perfect salt of the earth women.

"No, that's not why I'm blind. I'm blind because I'm viewed as a worthless individual whose government tried to kill him when they drafted me and sent me over to kill Asians in Vietnam. Yeah, that's why I'm blind, Page, it's because I'm black! Yep, that's it. If I had not been born black then I would not have been sent over there and told to kill them Asian boys!" Nickels said. I became confused trying to follow this conversation as Lil Dee giggled and asked Nickels if he had drunk too much wine at lunch today.

"Lil Dee, I'm trying to figure out who is at fault for my being blind. I have spent all these years with no one to blame for my being crippled. It has to be because I'm black. No, that's not it! Carl is white and I got blown up when I ran back to carry him after he got shot in the left butt cheek one day. That's it," Nickels said with a joyous laugh dancing in his dead eyes as if he had solved a great mystery. "It's that drunk ass hillbilly's fault — he caused me to be crippled. Damn honkeys are always abusing us colored folks. Elvis stole our music, and Carl meant to get shot so I would get hurt when I ran back to save him! Damn honkeys!" Nickels said as he slapped the workbench he was sitting at with his open hand.

"Page?" Lil Dee said. "Nickels ain't making no sense! He's gotta be high or drunk!"

"No girls, I ain't drunk yet. I'm just trying to make a point," Nickels said. He was very aware that he owned all of our attention. "Y'all kids are as crippled as I am, even stupid ass Bobby over there and your mother," Nickels said as he nodded his head towards Bobby. "I know it's hard to see a big mean man like Bobby as a cripple. Hell, just the word cripple makes a person think of some poor carnival sideshow freak all twisted up and unable to walk on their own without falling down or wipe their own ass without help. Now, I don't mean handicapped, not some poor soul who walks a little funny and gets to park up at the front of the store's parking lot! No, y'all ain't handicapped. You're crippled, and it ain't worth spending time searching for someone to blame," Nickels said as he looked straight over at Bobby as if he could honestly see into his soul.

"Boy, how many times have you failed to draw that stone for your mother? Washed everything off, cussed and farted about, asking why you should draw for this evil bitch as you call your mother. And I have to agree with you, she was a truly nasty bitch, and she doesn't deserve a headstone at all! But boy, you're making about as much sense now as I do when I pretend to try to figure out why I'm blind or who to blame for my blindness. When you chose to accept these broken babies, you chose to teach them right from wrong. You're a parent now, and you can't afford to debate rights, wrongs, should have or should not have.

You got two children watching you now, you have to be responsible for them first and then worry about your broken heart. You know that you have to forgive your mother, and these babies need to see you forgive her because someday they will have to stand over a blank rock and search for the right words to carve on it for you. So, stop panhandling for sympathy and draw your mother something pretty. Forget what she did to you — hell, you already did forgive her, or you wouldn't be here, worrying about that stone while every police department in America searches for you!" Nickels roughly stated as he turned his dead eyes back to his small work area and the ring that he was braiding. Bobby's own eyes clouded over, and we heard a thunderstorm crack the sky above Cemetery Ridge as he slammed down the white crayon he was using on the black granite stone and walked out of the shop and into the raging rain.

"Go on boy, go on, them pills is what you need. Go on son, eat some. These babies need you to be a man, but ain't no sympathy to had in being a man. Boy you're about as useless as them crying ass people in the projects, always mad at someone, always blaming someone for their own faults!" Nickels screamed as I went to stand and run after our hero.

"Sit your ass down girl," Nickels said, the strength of his voice causing me to whimper like a dog afraid of its own shadow.

"Don't reward that fool boy for his playing the victim. By chasing after him, all worried and trying to comfort him, that is exactly what you would be doing. I'm not some big angry black man, mad at the world because I can't buy a Cadillac with food stamps, upset because my great granddaddy was a slave, so now I'm bullying a poor crippled white boy. I'm just an old blind man, nothing more, and that boy is a stone-cold killer. He could kill me without even meaning to do so, but he knows that I'm right this time, he knows that I'm speaking the truth. His mother broke him, put nasty scars on his back, his heart, and his soul. But the boy also knows that he chose to live his life like he is a victim. Always forcing himself to fail when his life was going good, always crying about his Momma every time he needed an excuse for fucking up his life. The boy could have stopped being a victim, he could have gotten some mental treatment. But girls, for those types of treatments to work, then Bobby, your own mother or anyone else has to accept the wrongs that they did and to apologize for them, try to make things right, not just to the person they wronged, but to their own soul. Girls listen to me, if you feel that you did something wrong, then you have violated your own moral code. That means you hurt the other person as well as yourself," Nickels stated as the anger left his voice, and the tone of a teacher flooded the small room.

"Bobby used violence on the world around him to hide personal moral sins. His heart hurt deeply every time he saw his mother misuse good people and their love of God. This for Bobby was far more painful than being beaten and abused by his parents — the scars on his back are tiny compared to how they hurt his soul." Nickels shook his head and sighed.

"They say on the radio that the boy went into a doctor's office and killed the folks in it?" Nickels asked, not waiting for an answer.

"Now Page, I bet you one of my prettiest rings that old Bobby swore that doctor was a piece of shit who deserved what Bobby did because he was selling pills and hurting people?" Nickels grinned as he said this, knowing by the way Lil Dee laughed at me that he had won the bet.

"Now that right there, just Bobby saying that, means that he knew in his heart that the doctor's way of life was morally wrong and that Bobby himself was wrong for all the times he searched for doctors like that to get pills from. That's the wrong of it, all of the hate Bobby unleashed on that doctor and his nurse was really Bobby just hating himself."

"Momma and Bobby are not eating as many pills as they used to!" Lil Dee said in Bobby's defense.

"Little one," Nickels said with sadness in his voice, "honey, them pills ain't your folks' problem. They could stop getting high altogether, but they would still be messed up. No girls, their problem is with the person they see in the mirror each morning. And those pills? They act like sunglasses, blocking out their eyes so no one can see into their broken souls. No, I'm sorry girls, these two need treatment for their minds as well as for their addiction."

"How did you really go blind Mr. Nickels?" I asked, hoping to pull Nickels' attention from Bobby and Momma's lives. They were broken, Nickels was right, but they were my family and I could not continue to talk about them behind their backs, it made me feel dirty.

"I told you, in Vietnam! I met old Carl at the Army induction center; we rode the same bus down to boot camp. The northern colored boys talked slick. The towns up that way must be really big because them northern white boys acted like they had never seen black folks. Not like down here where the world's so small that blacks and whites talk exactly alike." Nickels laughed and I swore that he sounded like an eighteen-year-old boy, drafted into war, yet, happy to do his part.

"Them Yankee boys is sneaky, mean and racist — both the blacks and whites!" Carl said as he woke up from his nap, causing Lucy to jump down to the ground as he searched for a fresh jar of wine.

"Turns out them boys don't like hillbillies at all, so Carl and me got stuck together, not that we minded. When we ended up in them jungles where it's so dark you can't tell the color of a man's skin, the way he talks is all that reminds you that you ain't the same. Only me and Carl, we were the same, hillbillies," Nickels said, trying to explain a bond that I had no way to understand.

"I got shot in the leg," Carl said, as Nickels laughed saying, "Ass, Carl! You got shot in the ass, now don't go lying about it! Remember in the hospital, you cried like a baby every time you had to fart because it hurt so much!" Nickels farted to emphasize the point of his story, as Lil Dee and I laughed deeply, as much from the story as from hearing Carl moan and carp about why God had not struck Nickels deaf and mute instead of just blind.

"Somebody had to go get the damn fool," Nickels stated, "but I was the only one who spoke hillbilly. Everyone else must have thought he was screaming about something else, but I knew he was calling for help. So I went to help my friend. Turns out, I got him up and moving and then he dragged me the rest of the way back to safety. We both sort of saved each other. But I got struck by a piece of metal in the side of the face and head." He touched a long scar that ran the length of his head and face but was so old that it was now the same dark color as the rest of him.

"Now you babies may not know about a man named Martin Luther King, famous people's stories tend to get twisted up after God calls them home. But old Martin Luther King, he gets all the glory for trying to bring folks together, and folks forget Vietnam. They forget that Vietnam put boys in the jungle alone with only each other to cling to. Girls, war and drug addiction are three things that prove to us that everyone is the same. Trust me, Vietnam did as much to help race relations in America as Reverend King did," Nickels said as Carl passed him a jar of wine. I noticed that neither man wiped the rim of the jar before taking a drink, nor did they make a funny face the way that Percodan would when he smoked a joint with a black man.

I remembered Jessica saving the old needles to be reused on the coloreds as she called them. Colored folks are stupid!" Percodan would say. "They think that just because a needle comes out of a little bag that it's brand new. They never consider the fact that Jessica has a whole stack of them needle pouches in the kitchen!" I remembered Percodan's hate-filled voice as I looked at Carl and Nickels and could only see an easy comfort that comes from love. I had to wonder if Percodan had gotten shot in his ass and was screaming for help and a black man like Nickels had risked his life to save him whether Percodan would have then saved his hero as Carl had done or would he have let him fall and die, never once feeling guilty about doing so? Would the men of their platoon had laughed as they called the black man a stupid colored for getting killed while saving Percodan?

Was racism a sign of weakness just as unconditional love is a sign of strength? Today I know that this question, like most of our life history, will be lost to time forgotten. When the pudgy bald men dig up my bones, the very idea of race will be forgotten. The archaeologists will assume that we were all one people — after all, we are all buried on this one hill together. It makes me sad to think that we are often not allowed to live our lives as one people now. Funny isn't it — they will call us cannibals in the future as they make insane claims about our life and time on earth, yet Carl's bones will rest with Nickels' bones and all of them may end up at the same museum, stuffed in the same drawer with Percodan's hateful bones. Just one more of our lifetime's biggest hurdles forgotten — race won't even matter when your bones are lost in a museum, so why does it matter now? Why are only drug addicts and war veterans safe from the ideas of race?

Bobby returned to the shop, dripping wet but seemingly happy, without anger or tension I was afraid of seeing him aim at Nickels.

"Shut up Nickels, you're right, you don't need to rub it in," Bobby said as he smiled at Nickels. "I'm obligated to teach these girls the right way to live. I have to forgive my own mother before my hurt and confusion teaches them to hate their own mother. So, I best get past it and draw her something pretty," he said with a laugh as Carl once again said, "Amen son, amen!"

That night as Ms. Karen curled up at the side of a drunken Carl, Lil Dee fell asleep embracing all of her dogs and Momma sat beside Bobby watching him draw. While they were talking and making silly eyes at each other, I asked Nickels how he learned to make rings out of old coins as he did, somehow weaving the copper and silver together in seemingly fewer layers, each color's beauty contrasting against the other.

"When I was a child like you and your sister, a drunken old hobo would come to town about twice a year. My family lived down by the train yards in Nashville, and that drunken old white hobo seemed to be the happiest man I ever met. Nothing seemed to bother him, he never got angry or lost his sense of humor," Nickels said, and I saw a light grow in his dead eyes that to this day, I believe was the same light that would have sparkled in his young eyes as he laughed with his drunken hobo friend.

"Well, you see, Page, first you lay a silver Buffalo nickel on a train track and then you put a cooper wheat penny about a foot in front of the nickel on the same track. Then you wait for a train to run them over and flatten them into thin pancake discs of pure metals. Then you pick those disc up and lay one on top of the other and fold them together into a disc as small as you can, all while racing over to the next train due to leave the yard. You let that train smash the two-metal disc into one, and after about thirty times of chasing the next train, you end up with a pancake disc like this one Page," Nickels said as he pulled a flat disc of layers of the two metals from his bag for me to see. "They would call that a Damascus steel pattern if it was a knife blade.

"Well, the old hobo hated to have to spend a day allowing the trains to smash coins into sheets of mixed copper and silver, so he got us local kids to do it. Now, if you always fold the coins the same, the colored lines will always run the same way, but you can fold it wrong and make a mess. The other boys would never pay attention to how they folded the disc together as they chased the next train — the coins belonged to a drunken hobo. But me? I was good at it, I could run while folding each thin disc, making them right and not into a puddle of color. So, the old hobo would pay the other kids a penny for every bad disc they made, and he'd pay me a nickel for every perfect disc I made. He could still make a ring out of the ugly mess of colors, but people paid better money for clean pretty rings. It was funny to me, watching the faces of the other boys who couldn't understand how I would make so much more money than them," Nickels said as he shook his head and laughed while saying one word over and over: Pride.

"After a few years, the old man taught me how to shape the metals into rings by using spoons as hammers and old nails as chisels and points, the same as I use today. He would sit there at night, drunk, with nothing more than a campfire to light his way as he told me stories about his life and made rings.

"When I came home from the war, I lived in a government housing project. They were first built as a place for any poor family to live until they got a better job and moved on to greener pastures. The idea came about in the 1940s. In those days, there were large active black middle-class neighborhoods that were just like white neighborhoods. Somehow, some things get lost when smart people try to make the world better instead of allowing nature to take its course. The funny thing about the people who were happy about the idea of government housing is that none of them realized that these housing projects were nothing more than new slave quarters, a way of making sure that we lived out back where we were out of the way and unable to be seen.

Any time you accept free money, well it ain't really free!" Nickels shook his head in disgust at this memory. "I needed help in those days, I could hardly use the bathroom on my own back then, that's how I qualified for housing and the other pacifiers that America was going out of its way to give out to shut black folks up and make it look like white folks all loved their black neighbors." Nickels laughed and a dark cloud drained the light from his eyes, and I knew in my heart that he didn't enjoy telling me this part of his story.

"One day I was drunk, laughing, passing time with some other fools who didn't have a job or anywhere important to be, and I heard my girlfriend talking to a friend on the phone about how I was a good fish to have caught because I got more money to live on from the Army than I would be getting if I was on regular government assistance like my friends were. She said that my being blind wasn't too bad, that the extra work taking care of me was worth it for the extra money.

"Her words woke me up, them simple words. I remembered the pride I had felt when I would only make perfect pieces of mixed metals for a man who was just a low-class drunken hobo, the same pride I felt in the hospital around other soldiers when

Carl would brag about me saving his life. It hurt my heart to hear my girlfriend reduce me to the level of something simply worth dealing with, just for the extra monthly money! I got up, took a shower, and stopped leaning on my being crippled as an excuse for the conditions of my life. I accepted that I was disabled because I first chose to honor the call to serve my country, and secondly because I chose to honor my heart by going back to help my friend. Once I accepted my responsibility for those two things and stopped blaming our government for going to war and drafting the poor sons first, I stopped leaning on my being black, abused, and crippled as an excuse for being drunk and high all day and for my miserable lifestyle.

"I had made rings in the dark with that drunken hobo, and I told myself that I could make them while being blind too. So, I walked west to the train tracks. I figured out after I tripped over the tracks that if I walked south down the middle of them same tracks, and counted the wooden rail ties as I went, that I would not get lost and I soon found myself at that same hobo camp where I first learned to make rings. In time, with the help of some of the drifters, I could make rings by myself, and that's when I stopped waiting on my monthly checks and, with some help at first, I started to travel around making rings and selling them like the old hobo who had taught me to make them had done himself for years. I felt pride again, but I soon, due to the nature of my homeless companions, I would find myself alone and in need of help at odd times in odd places. This was the opposite of pride and self-reliance, and it pissed me off, so I decided that it was better for me to walk by myself into walls, traffic, or off of a bridge and to die trying to live the life God gave me than for me to give up and wait on the next broken homeless fool to come by and take pity on me and lead me around by the hand. It didn't take too long after that for me to learn to see with my heart," Nickels said with a smile as he touched my chest with his finger right where my heart sat beating.

"Your heart will never lie to you Page, but you, your mom and your sister will have to sit down and sort your hearts out, clean out all of the pain, find a way to make peace with the hells of your past. If you don't, you will never be able to trust what your heart says. All that pain you carry around boils in your sleep, creeps into your dreams, makes it impossible to trust God, your friends, or the voice of your heart. Page, if I'd not decided that I made a choice to go to war instead of arguing about being drafted, and also that I chose to run back to help Carl, I would still be living like a crippled man, always angry that I couldn't see, never happy or proud, stuck alone without the sound of my heart to guide me, stuck in a government housing project depending on other to help me find my way to the bathroom," Nickels said as his blind eye seemed took into my own and once again, I was sure that he was was pretending to be unable to see.

"Get yourself some help honey, don't let all that you have seen scar your heart and soul like Bobby's back. Get help, if not for yourself then do it for your mother and sister, they're going to need you, honey," Nickels said as he slipped a beautiful rose shaped ring onto my finger; its colors seemed like sparks under the glow of the shop's bare lightbulbs. Or maybe it was knowing the love and pride that went into one simple ring that made it appear so much brighter that night so long ago.

"What about Bobby? I found myself asking, aware that he had failed to include Bobby in his list of people who would be needing help.

"That boy, he shot the bullets that will kill him a long time ago, before he ever met you girls," Nickels said with a tear in his eye. "Maybe he can duck them one more time, but sooner or later, well, let's hope. God knows, I don't want to see him die either," Nickels mumbled.

Chapter 23

The dawn sun did not simply rise the next morning, it exploded in bright glorious light. A light that radiated life from within every tree, leaf, flower and blade of grass, as well causing sharp shades of new green grass to glow, leaving no doubt that winter was over, and spring owned the season. Yesterday's rainy sky had felt nasty, full of grey and purple clouds accompanied by angry voices of thunder, but today the world was new, fresh, and clean, causing some birds to sing a happy greeting and others to scream out angry warnings when our work on the stairs brought us near their new nest and family homes. Lucy was teaching her babies the difference between the two songs. She would softly howl along with the birds' morning songs of greeting and then bark deeply as she tried to climb the trees to chase any birds that did not like us being nearby. Soon the birds were flying down from their treetop homes to peck Lucy's and her puppies' heads only to go racing off as the dogs snapped and bit the air where the bird had just been. This caused Carl to laugh as he told Lucy that maybe she shouldn't try to catch birds after a night of drinking wine and staying up so late.

Bobby worked like a man possessed that day. His leg was healed, and he looked larger and somehow stronger than before. I had noticed that he seemed to grow when he was angry; maybe it was some kind of trick, but he would stand up a little straighter, his chest would expand as he filled the area around him with his confidence and his intentions, leaving anyone watching no doubt of his presence. It had been this type of boldness that had inspired fear in Percodan and that the doctor had foolishly ignored. But today, Bobby's size and strength were not mere tricks of posture or body language but were pure strength of determination. He would carry each large heavy stair up Cemetery Ridge on his shoulders without help as Carl and dug out the moist ground.

"It takes less time this way Page," Bobby told me with a smile as we laid the sixth stair of the morning, already two more then we had placed on any day before. Bobby was sweating, smoking cigarettes and smiling without even one sign to show that he was an addict, a child victim, a failed adult or a stone-cold killer. No, Bobby looked like I had dreamed that a normal father would look, working as hard as he could to build a pathway through a graveyard so that no grave was cutoff, alone, unable to easily be visited. This was the kind heart of a father and not the rage of a broken addicted victim. I was proud to work just as hard as Bobby was on that day, praying to God that Nickels' harsh words yesterday had helped Bobby make peace with his mother, a peace that would allow us to be a normal family.

"We got a lot of carving to do on my Momma's headstone before Easter Sunday, Page!" Bobby smiled and said as Nickels got attacked by a protective father bird, leaving us no doubt that Nickels really was blind. He tried over and over to strike at the bird with a worn-out baseball hat, cussing at the sky as his swings of self-defense missed the birds by a mile. Often swinging in the wrong direction, hitting trees and tombstones instead, to the amusement of a laughing Carl. On that day, a normal life seemed to be close to Lil Dee and I as the dogwood bloomed on the branches above our heads.

"Got to start making spirit ribbons in the evenings, Lil Dee," Carl said, looking up at the torn remains of small, faded ribbons wrapped around last year's flower buds. "No more sitting around the shop playing with them puppies and drinking my good wine until you fall asleep young lady!" Carl sternly said to my sister.

"I ain't been drinking your good wine, Carl!" Lil Dee said, at first in shock, only to then smile as she realized that Carl was joking around with her.

"Yes you did, I saw you drinking out of the same dirty jar as Lucy and them ugly dogs were sipping out of!" Nickels said, his voice filled with conviction, like a witness in a courtroom, making Bobby laugh and stumble under the weight of a heavy stair.

"You ain't seen shit Nickels!" Lil Dee said in mock anger. "Hell, you're lucky you can wipe your own ass without Carl having to do it for you!" she laughed as she began to imitate Nickels trying to hit the birds. We all laughed until it hurt as much from her imitation of Nickels as from the look of confusion on his face as he demanded that Carl tell him what Lil Dee was doing that was so funny.

"Never mind, you old fool," Ms. Karen said as she and Momma came to tell us that lunch was ready.

"Lil Dee, ladies don't cuss, even when they're playing with old idiots like Nickels and Carl," Ms. Karen said as she winked at Lil Dee and put her arm around me smiling.

I couldn't help but notice that Momma seemed younger, cleaner, less burdened today. I was unsure if it was because of the spring air or because Bobby was alive and moving with purpose today. Before, he would move in a direction, but he was stumbling as if he didn't want to complete the task at hand, but now a sense of purpose poured from his soul like the sweat of his hard work poured out of his body. The only other times I could remember him being completely committed to the task at hand was walking into Percodan's house to kill Orville, and at the motel when he had left the door open so he could watch and protect us as we played. Even when he had attempted to get Momma to abandon him at the doctor's office it was halfhearted compared to his actions today. I liked seeing Bobby's energies mirrored in Momma's eyes, and I found it hard to believe that just yesterday I wanted the world to know every sin she had ever committed. Today, I could not bring myself to be mean to her — yesterday was in the past and our future looked normal.

"You take a handful of tobacco out of this can right here Lil Dee, then you make a ball about the size of your fist out of it, and then tie it to the end of these colored ribbons. You got to do ribbons in all the colors! This is religious stuff, so you can't be messing around!" Carl said. I could feel a frustration growing in his heart. Lil Dee was having fun at Carl's expense by asking "Why?" over and over, questioning everything that Carl told her to do and then smiling at me when I would act like I could not understand Carl either. I was learning to stipple shade a rose petal on Bobby's mother's headstone. Bobby had finally drawn a large rose with a ribbon in front of a wooden cross being cupped in angel wings. Momma and Ms. Karen were in the kitchen, cutting ribbons to be hung in the trees, and Nickels was making rings. My life was normal — I had my family around me and I had not thought about pills even once today. I was comfortable in our daily routine.

"Alright you little shits, I'll explain this to you one more time!" Carl said as I winked at Lil Dee, warning her not to play too much. The idea that these ribbons held a spiritual significance to the Natives made me want to act respectfully of them.

"Natives call America Turtle Island. It doesn't matter what tribe they're from, they all seem to agree on that name, and that the tobacco plant is sacred, holy, special. A lot of other things, they don't always believe exactly alike, but tobacco is about as holy as it gets, so they take these ribbons, each color is a color on what they call a medicine wheel," Carl said and then paused as if searching his heart for the right words.

"Now medicine to them Natives ain't the same as it is to us. It ain't like them pills white people take. To a Native, medicine is your spirit, your life force, and the wheel represents the cycle of life. Each color is placed at a certain point on the wheel as a reminder of where you are in life. But some tribes use different colors on their medicine wheels, and different pipes to smoke tobacco out of. Some tribes use corn husk, some use the red kalinite stones, and others make clay pipes. It doesn't matter, because all of them believe that when you smoke tobacco and pray that the tobacco's smoke carries your prayers up to Wambli Gleska, the spotted eagle or young golden eagle, then Wambli carries your prayers up to heaven, up to God. So, we tie tobacco in the end of these ribbons, then we hang them in trees to honor the memories of our people who have passed on, they love the smell of sacred tobacco. You should say a prayer every time you hang one of these ribbons in a tree. That old lost Cajun boy went to a small mountain out west called Bear Butte; he fell in love with the beauty of seeing thousands of spirit ribbons hanging from the trees, each one representing a prayer," Carl said as he tied a ball of tobacco in a yellow ribbon.

"Prayers ain't just words girls, sometimes you have to do some work too. Now when some fool tells you that these here ribbons are evil, you tell them that eating bread and pretending it's Jesus don't seem right either unless you know the story behind the act, and same goes for this Native stuff. It ain't wrong to say hello to your family that ain't here no more — in fact, I'll haunt both of you imps if you don't tie tobacco in a ribbon for me and hang it out there on a tree after I die!" Carl laughed as he said this but I knew in my heart that he meant every word and that he felt a real need to keep the traditions of Dogwood Mountain even if some Christians didn't completely understand.

"The birds steal the ribbons. If you go out into the deeper areas of the woods on this mountain, you'll see colored ribbons in every bird and squirrel nest around. Some of those prayer ribbons are as old as me. It sure is funny how something hung up in a tree, meant to honor dead folks, can at the same time protect little animals from the cold. That right there is proof to me that there is a God," Carl said, nearly mumbling as if his mind had wandered off into the woods, following a stolen spirit ribbon on its way to become a home for a new bird family.

"Girls, God has a bad habit of not being on hand when you think that you need him, yet just think about all the baby birds he keeps warm every year by wrapping their nest in scraps of stolen ribbons." Carl smiled as he tapped the worktable where Lil Dee sat, now intently working on making ribbons to hang for our new family.

"Grace, Carl!" Ms. Karen said from inside the house. "They call that proof of God's grace."

As I worked, placing dot after dot of shading on Bobby's mother's stone, working with my hero Bobby, I couldn't help but to search my memory for times that Ms. Karen would call God's grace, small things that would cause Carl to mumble in wonder if I told him about them. The husband and wife at the small restaurant who fed and cared for us that week after Christmas without pushing their own needs or opinions on us, they just showed us love. Mickey teaching me to laugh and joke until I could pee into a small bottle with a police officer watching my naked body. Even the judge buying me donuts was an act of God's grace.

Part of me wanted to include Bobby finding us in this list, but I couldn't equate the sound of Bobby's gun and Jessica's screams with something as gentle as a spirit ribbon blowing in the wind. Grace must be gentle and unexpected, not bold and punitive. Singing songs in church, out of key, and drenched in the light of so many stained-glass windows was grace, whereas dancing with pet snakes was a human act, nothing more. In the end, that night, as I worked on Bobby's mother's stone, I decided that God's grace is any act that lives on like the spirit ribbons do, first serving our selfish human desire, and then going on to fill one of God's needs without our permission or complaint.

Momma found her way over to Bobby's side to talk and play as they were now fond of doing. Bobby still would not sleep with her, and I was beginning to believe that something special would die in my mother if he suddenly decided to take her or use her in the way that she had allowed so many other men to thoughtlessly do in the past. Just a few words Momma had shared with me as we sat in our car were enough to ease my own hurting heart and I found myself growing more and more lost in the dream that Bobby and Momma were weaving. It was spring, soon the dogwoods would bloom, Easter would be here, Bobby and Momma would get married, and Lil Dee and I would never endure watching our mother service men for her need of pills, self-hate, or food again.

Also, Momma would cure Bobby's need to hurt and kill. She would be the rudder on his storm-tossed ship, as he would be the wind that filled her sails. That is honestly what they were — two ships, one purposefully racing headfirst into every storm it could find and the other drifting aimlessly, praying for the wind to push her forward. I know that it's foolish of me to write such silliness, yet God has recently taught me that being blind does not mean that a person cannot see. Hell, I was so caught up in our fresh new life that I completely forgot that God is the type of prick that would allow his own son to be served up as a sacrifice. As I have said before, God and I have a few things to talk about if he's brave enough to meet with me someday.

"I met a really nice college girl once when I lived up north," Bobby said as we worked together, placing stairs on the path of angels, although it was embarrassing for me to call it by that name knowing that my feet were used as a pattern for many of those angel feet. It's one thing to want to be an angel, but I had slept dreaming of Santa Claus and praying for Christmas presents while my sister was being raped by a man who I considered friend. I had eaten freely if not greedily as my mother degraded herself servicing store owners. I had not warned Jessica that Bobby was death. And I openly tried to hate my mother when she was broken in the same way that Lil Dee had been broken. No, I had no right to find joy in claiming my footprints to be those of an angel, yet these are the regrets of the old woman I am today as I struggle to complete this story. The truth is that on that day when Bobby began to tell us his story, I was still lost in the magic of our new life. I was still dancing while holding a large copperhead snake, safe from poison, wrapped in God's love, wanting to be a normal girl, and for once in my life, sure that I had finally become one.

"I always had the Bible and art; those two things were all my mother would let me own as a child," Bobby said as Momma and Lil Dee stopped placing spirit ribbons in the trees. Carl had said for us to hang them near the dogwood flower buds that were growing fat and soon to open; he swore that there was magic in the contrasting colors of red, black, yellow, and white, and the pale creamy color of the dogwood flowers. "Beauty is a magic, Page! Try your best to not to grow up and become ugly honey, it just ain't worth it!" Carl liked to tell me, but it took me years to figure out just what he meant, years to come to understand that ugliness is a heart condition that has little to do with a person's looks. I don't think that God ever allowed an ugly looking person to be born, yet, at the same time, I know that he does little to stop a person from growing and becoming ugly either.

"I had just come home from prison again," Bobby said. "I went to see an old friend of mine hoping that he would front me a couple of ounces of cocaine so that I could get on my feet, but when I got his house, I ran into another friend from prison. The guy was a pimp as well as an addict. I would party some, drink a little, but I had not become an addict at that time, so I felt that I was above the old, addicted pimp. I started making jokes about him, about his not only having worn out old hookers but a habit also. There was little the pimp could do to me, he was old, and he was a drug addict. My friend and I were drug dealers and not drug users. But the pimp said something that put me in my place," Bobby said with a frown.

"He told me that no matter what I thought about him that he was at least honest and that I was an idiot, a complete fool to be out risking being sent back to prison for dealing drugs when I was not an addict and I had other better options than dealing. I wanted to smack him around some, but he was a customer of the same guy I was asking for a handout from. I thought that the old man would get all racial with me, claiming that being a white boy gave me options that he would never have since he was black," Bobby said with a laugh. "If he brought up race then I could stomp his old ass, white boys were sick of hearing how they were better off than blacks or somehow responsible for the past racial sins of America. We had learned that apologizing for the past only made you look weak, so we would fight to earn our respect." Bobby laughed again as he shook his head still in awe of the events he remembered so well.

"The old pimp said that I had what the dope boys and drug addicts wanted: art. That he had watched me tattoo my way through prison, and that I was a damn fool to be risking my freedom messing with dope when I didn't even have a monkey on my back!" Bobby laughed even more as he knelt down to check if a stair was seated level.

"I couldn't get mad at him because I knew he was right, but I didn't have any money or the tools to open a tattoo shop. So that became my long-term plan, my reason for hustling drugs: I was saving up to open a business I told myself and my family.

"Then I met that college girl I mentioned a moment ago. She was spotless, clean, safe, the type of girl who you could have a family with," Bobby said and I could see ghosts dancing in his eyes and heart as he searched for words to continue his story.

I looked over at Momma and I could see that Bobby's opinion of this college girl was worrying for her — clean and safe were not things that Momma could ever be again. Sure she could put her past behind her, act the part of a Ms. Karen, and trick people — but mirrors simply cannot tell lies! Momma would forever see the woman she had once been in the eyes of the person she was pretending to be. I knew enough about A.A. and N.A. to know that she would need to make amends to the people she had harmed throughout her life if she could, and if they would allow her to. But I also knew that she would never forgive herself, she would never apologize to herself for all the pain she had caused herself to live through. Even back then on the day Bobby tried to explain his soul to us, I knew that my mother, like so many other victims of child abuse, would not admit to herself that the devastating effects of her abuse had destroyed her adult life and, by association, Lil Dee's and my own.

No, Momma would have no problem admitting that she was an addict and unable to manage her life and laying all of the blame for how we had been forced to live at the feet of her addiction. But she would never try to face the deep guilt and confusion that all child abuse victims feel when they finally realize that they are firstly the victims of a twisted home and are unable to interact with the world in a normal way because of it and then, secondly, that they are thieves, addicts, whores, killers, or some other type of broken soul. Nor could they admit admit that confusion governed their opinions of the world. The abused live as as outsiders, feeling different and alone, as drugs, bold talk and unbelievable stories offer short-term comfort and social acceptance, only to then crush them as truth proves them to be liars, or their bold talk turns hollow, and the monster that is addiction takes control of their souls and becomes their new abuser, one they have missed not having in their lives since they escaped their childhood abuser. It is a cycle that will never be broken until they face their internal confusion. No, my mother might fake it, find a way to stay dry and off drugs, but she would never face the monsters that stood between her and her finding true sobriety.

Guilt is a monster. You hate yourself for accepting the beatings and abuse that you were put through, and you feel that you allowed it to happen. You hate your abuser, but at the same time, you love them deeply and cannot understand why they hurt you. All the while, you live your life digging hole after hole, destroying any love that is offered to you and heaping more and more guilt into a pile that you can easily avoid facing by simply blaming your life on your addiction and never admitting that you are still a broken child, confused and hurting. It would be one thing for Momma to have been abused and to have sought help, learned to live as a victim of child abuse, and then to have started her adult life knowing that she was without guilt, without fault in the abuse that she had endured as a child, just as Lil Dee was blameless in her own rape and the death of so many. But guilt for Momma began to pile up with every mistake that she made in life as she tried to avoid being abused again — from my own birth all the way up to her driving Bobby over to kill for my sister's sake.

I wish that I could tell you that I recognized the ghost of Bobby's college girl and my mother's fear of her that day and that I sat Momma down and explained to her about guilt and her need to forgive herself as I have written it for you. I know that for Bobby, it is the things like child abuse, guilt and addiction that are the true reason he made me promise to write our family story down and that it's terribly important that you face the monsters that made drug use so appealing to you. But on that day, I was lost in Bobby's voice as Momma was, and saddened to see fear in her eyes over Bobby's opinion of this college girl.

"I ended up back in prison on a parole violation, just as the old pimp had said that I would, and once again I took care of myself by tattooing, only this time I had more than art, the Bible and my temper — I had my safe, clean college girl. She had chosen to stand with me, and I had promised to get out of prison this time and do things the right way, to try and live as a man she could be proud of. Somehow, she had not realized that I was extremely broken inside and unable to live as a normal person," Bobby said, and I felt fear boiling inside of me because of the sound of rage in Bobby's voice. If Bobby exploded today while telling his story, who would be hurt? Would he ever tell us about himself again? Momma was still too concerned with her appearance compared to Bobby's college girl to have heard the anger growing in his voice or to see his need for her strength to help him to continue to speak honestly with us. "You stupid truck stop whore!" I wanted to scream at her as Lil Dee walked over and took Bobby's large hand in her tiny one and smiled up at him the way only an innocent child can smile. I saw Bobby's pain melt away instead of turning into a destructive rage.

"Go on Bobby, tell us about her. Was she pretty? Did you love her? Was she nice? Was she as nice as Momma? What happen to her?" Lil Dee asked without waiting for Bobby to respond nor showing any concern for Momma's tender feelings. Nickels laughed as he sat down on a tombstone, amazed that Lil Dee had sensed that a storm was coming and had so easily changed its course.

Bobby could not help but smile down at Lil Dee. Somehow, she understood that there were emotions crashing into each other inside of his soul and that, given the chance to, he would gladly allow our mother's attitude to be his reason to rebury his memories.

"This ain't really about your Momma, it's more about me and the things that make me crazy," Bobby said. I could see from his body's posture that he was asking her for permission to continue his story. The man we saw before us now was not the bold unforgiving man who had gently carried my sister in his arms as he walked into hell with the confidence of an angel, nor was he a broken little boy either. Instead, Bobby seemed to know that what he had to say was so important that he must put it into words and speak it out loud no matter what, and that he needed Momma to control her own fears and allow him to speak without forcing him to shade his words so as to not cause her pain.

Ms. Karen went to Momma and hugged her. "The boy is asking you to let him talk to you. He's not telling you that you have to let him talk, he's not saying things like, "Bitch, you're gonna let me speak or else!" That hurt and confusion in your eyes, girl, it ain't fair! You need to learn Bobby's story, and he wants to tell it to you. It would be a shame to cheat yourself out of this chance just because you ain't some prissy clean-cut college girl!" she said, as we all laughed a little.

I had seen a change roll through my mother. When Bobby had first begun to talk, I saw a common jealousy blaze in her heart, then a fear that this girl was somehow more like Jesus' mother than Momma could ever be, and by the time Ms. Karen took her hand, Momma had shrunken inside of herself, resigned to defeat. There was no fight left in her eyes, no anger, as if she had been waiting for Bobby to snatch a rug out from under her, causing her to fall into a pit. After all, Bobby's college girl was the type of woman that a man could value enough to marry, but Momma had only valued herself at the low price of one single twenty milligrams of OxyContin, and Bobby gave those away by the handful. Even I knew that he would throw a single pill away if it got dirty, so how could he value Momma when she never valued herself?

"Conversations about your heart ain't easy to have!" Carl said as Nickels nodded his head in agreement. I saw that Lucy and her babies were playing tag. They were racing from the tombstones to the trees and from our cabin to the church, unburdened by the weight of our human emotions, just happy. I had to wonder if God had been drunk when he had made us complicated humans, and sober when he made dogs. Dogs do seem to be free of all the emotions that get in the way of our faith.

A smile came first from her eyes as Momma realized that Bobby's lack of assertiveness was because of his concern for her feelings. "Oh Bobby, tell me about it, I understand," she said as she reached to take his hand.

"It ain't really about her. She was just one more woman I tried to love, but I sabotaged myself." Bobby grinned at me as he spoke. "One day, I was walking to work. I didn't have a driver's license and my life was so good that I wouldn't risk driving without one. I had promised my girl and myself that I would not fuck up this time. Everything was good except for my fears of failing — they were always there, laughing at me, waiting on me to fall. There is bridge up there that cuts the city of Toledo in half. My shop was on the east side of town, so I had to walk across the Maumee River every morning to go to work. Well, after about a month of crossing that bridge, it dawned on me that everything was wrong.

I was headed due east, the sun was rising to the southeast, but the river was flowing north from my right to my left and not south as it should. The sun was reflecting off the wrong part of the waves. It was all backward, and worse, it had taken me a month to notice it. For fucked up people like us Christy, a month is a death sentence! Our souls depend on us seeing the next attack coming and knowing exactly where it is safe to run to. So, a backwards river is a bad thing. I had grown up where all the rivers ran south, no matter what — stone drunk, beaten half to death, blind, or whatever, I always knew that I could run until I hit a riverbank, jump in and it would float me home, no matter if I could swim or not. Yet had I run for the safety of that river, I would have been swimming against the current, trying to get home but never going anywhere because every time I would take a break, the current would drag me back to my problems. The whole thing is stupid I know," Bobby said in an attempt to avoid facing the rest of his story.

"No Bobby, it's not stupid at all! I always plan an escape route too!" Momma said with the understanding of a fellow abused child.

"When I got to my tattoo shop, I couldn't wait to tell my girl about the river. I never considered that what was abnormal to me was going to be perfectly normal to her. She laughed over my excited yet pointless realization that the river flowed north towards Lake Erie and not south towards my mother and the abusive home that I had fled from but silently knew that I was meant to return to. After all, they beat us into these abnormal beings, knowing that we can never survive in the normal world.

"Long story short, I hated being laughed at. I felt like I had pointed out that two plus two equals four, and not that I had missed something as important as the direction home. Don't get me wrong, my girl was right to laugh at me, she had no idea just how far out of my depth I was. I had not sat down and considered my life and how absolutely fucked up I was inside either. So, I laughed along with her, never realizing that I had seen my future reflected in the waves of the Maumee River that morning and that any attempt to live a normal life would mean swimming against the current," Bobby calmly said.

"In time I would force my world to fall apart, like a no-account worthless preacher. I had convinced a good woman to love me, I had found my good life, but I did not know how to live it. I suppose that's part of why I hate that piece of shit preacher who we knelt with girls. He knows what to say to get you to fall to your knees and accept Jesus, but he has no idea about how to live a good Christian life. He reminds me that I made that girl and her family promises that God allowed me to keep, but that I was too stupid to trust her to help me to learn to live in a normal word. Pride is a hard rock to climb!" Bobby said as Nickels farted on the headstones that he was sitting on, causing Carl to laugh so honestly that there was no way for us not to laugh along with him.

"I might have figured it all out and asked her to help me, but addiction was something that I had never faced before and didn't understand," Bobby said. "I had never drunk or gotten high every day before I found pain pills. Christy, I used to get prescriptions of pain pills and eat a couple for the pain then throw the rest away. But then I started eating them just to get high, and then I couldn't live without them. The worst thing was that those pills eroded all of the walls that I had built around my bad memories, so the times I tried to stop using them my mind was flooded with bad dreams and old fears." Bobby shook his head in shame. "The absolute worst memory would come up if I rode a rollercoaster. My girl loved them, and I could ride the old ones with the little bar that went across your waist, but the newer ones with the metal shoulder bars were hell on me."

Bobby stopped speaking and I could see that he was again searching for the words to express his pain. "My stepfather was a big man. I should have killed him, but I wanted a father. I wanted to be loved, so I accepted everything they did to me. After all, the Bible says honor thy father and mother. Jesus got beaten and crucified because his dad told him to allow it to happen, so I accepted everything they did. But one of his favorite punishments was to beat me until I balled up as small as I could make myself, and then he would put all of his weight on me until I couldn't breathe. Girls, before you die, your body fights for a few seconds as hard as it can, trying to breathe, trying to live, then your brain realizes that you're dead, and you give up just before you pass out. You just accept your death. This happened over and over until I stared to hope that this time that I wouldn't wake up. My stepfather and mom loved the look in my eyes as I would struggle and then give up and die," Bobby said and I saw tears race down his cheeks.

"That fucking roller-coaster would make me want to scream when they strapped me in. I could force myself to ride the thing with her once, maybe twice, and then I would get mean if she asked me to ride anymore. Crazy mean, but how was she to know what those shoulder straps did to me? I had no way to explain my childhood to myself much less to her. Worse, if I'd found the words to explain my memories, she would have then stopped asking me to ride rollercoasters with her, allowing my parents to steal the joy of those rides not only from me but from her also.

"That right there is the hardest part of having to tell your story. You don't want the person's advice, you don't want them to change or treat you differently, you just want them to understand that you're scared and that you love them enough to try and get better. But they feel insulted by your inability to trust them. So you both end up avoiding those painful memories instead of working through them, and you can't blame them for not knowing what to say or do, the shit's so messed up that no one could understand you. Girls, learn your stories before you get married, don't punish someone for loving you the way I punished my girl. She didn't deserve it and your lover won't either. Hell, that's why I'm talking to y'all now, so you know that I'm stone-cold crazy before you decide to love me," Bobby softly said.

"Bobby, the rivers all run south down here!" Momma said with a smile. "Somehow, we will be fine if we remember to try to talk about things, won't we?" she asked not only Bobby but all of us, and I prayed as deeply as I tried to assure my mother that we would be fine.

That Sunday there was no preacher at church, but still everyone gathered to sing and pray as plans were made for next week's Easter services and Bobby and Momma's wedding. Cemetery Ridge had to have all of the spirit ribbons hung before the dogwood flowers bloomed so that we could enjoy the flowers next to the colors of yellow, red, white, black, green and blue. Dogwood flowers are tender and will fall of the trees quickly and cover the ground. That's when Cemetery Ridge is at its prettiest. "It looks like snow," Carl said, as Nickels told him to tell me about the ghost.

"Are you scared of ghosts Page?" Carl asked and I thought about the young Bear protecting us, along with Jessica and the others as I laughed and said, "No, I'm more scared of you two choking me to death during one of your foolish farting contests!" and everyone laughed along with us.

"Well girly, Carl said, "once the flowers fall and cover the ground like snow, you just stand still and watch the ground. You'll see ghost walking all over this hill, sometimes playing with the spirit ribbons, or dancing to music, just enjoying Easter the same as us," he said, as if hoping that I would doubt him, but those long cold nights after Christmas had taught me more about God, ghosts and unexplained things than the church ever would.

"Just you wait, Page!" Carl laughed. "You'll see!"

Over the next few days, our lives were full of activities that I felt sure in my heart were normal family activities. Nickels spent his time making rings to sell to the boys who would come to the dance that was always held the Saturday night before Easter Sunday morning.

"All the boys in town are gonna want to buy a ring and dance with you girls. That's the price of a dance you hear me?" Nickels said, teasing us as Lil Dee and Carl made thousands of spirit ribbons and Carl explained how to tie them in the trees in such a way that the birds could easily steal them. All the while, Bobby was spending as much time teaching me about art as he could, carving more stairs and working on his mother's headstone. My favorite time was at night after we had eaten together as a family. Momma would find her way to Bobby's side, then Bobby would tell us about his attempts at living a normal life and we would compare our own emotional experiences with his. One night I asked him how he had gotten all of the money and pills that he had in his gym bag.

"The way that you worded that question tells me something about you Page," Bobby said. "Both your mother and I would have asked first about the pills and then about the money. Addiction can really mess up your brain Page, cause you to forget what's important. A person knows that money can fix almost any problem and that pills can easily become money, but an addict sees pills as the most important part of their life and money is simply more pills," Bobby stated with a shrug of his shoulders as he looked at Momma for her support. We were stipple shading the sky around the winged cross on his mother's stone one tiny dot at a time.

"When I got out of prison the last time, I had long ago burned my bridges with my college girl and lost any desire to have a good life. That's what happens after you fail enough times — you just quit trying, accept the fact that you're a fuck up, and tell yourself that you might as well be the best fuck up that you can be!" Bobby said while laughing and shaking his head in disgust at himself. "I knew a guy who needed someone to rob pharmacies. The guy's brother was a salesman for a medical company, and he had some extra bottles of OxyContin, all brand new. His problem was that every pharmacy wanted to buy extra pills from him. Pills that there was no paperwork on, pills that they could sell to addicts themselves. But my friend's brother only had twenty-five extra bottles of pills. Somehow, he had started collecting them before Oxycodone got popular, and his bosses either forgot he had them or didn't care. Well, the scam was that he would sell them to the pharmacy and then I would come in and take them back. They liked me doing it because I didn't accept no for an answer. I knew the pharmacy had the extra pills and I didn't mind twisting a finger or two off to make the pharmacist give them up!" Bobby's glowing eyes and laughter reminded me of the joy he had taken in hurting the nurse.

"My mom had been an addict for years, pain pills mostly. She, my little sister and my stepfather had all died using opiates. If you take them too long, they weaken your heart and you have such a high amount of the shit in your system, well trying to get off of them can kill you. So, I blamed the pills, the doctors and the pharmacies for my family's deaths even though I knew that they all killed themselves more or less. That's the funny thing about killing people — folks try to blame anyone other than the victim themselves. Think about it," Bobby said. "If you die while climbing a mountain, it ain't the mountain's fault, it's yours! But this tombstone right here is the reason we try to blame anything other than the truth!" Bobby said and I saw that hurt was rolling like a thunderstorm in his black eyes.

"Page, when I die, promise me that you will put the word asshole somewhere on my tombstone and not a bunch of lies. I think people would live more carefully if their sins were sure to be carved in stone for all the world to see!" Bobby said while looking deep into my eyes, leaving me no choice but to agree to his demand.

"In the end even though I was strung out on pills myself, I got to kill the pharmacists after punishing them for the sins of my mother's addiction. Worse, I would open brand-new bottles of pills thus making them unable to be sold again to the next pharmacy. Funny how a pharmacy will not buy open pills off of the street, but they will sell pills on the side without any remorse at all. In the end, after a conversation with some bullets, it was decided that we would close our little business and that I would take everything and go out on my own," Bobby said. laughing at himself and causing Ms. Karen to react.

"Why Robert Austin, you pathetic excuse for a man! How dare you act as if you are somehow above the preacher who comes to serve us. Only a worthless soul would joke about selfishly killing his friends. The whole town knows what you did to help these girls, and that's the only reason you're safely hidden on this mountain. Most of the men around here like to think that they would act as you did to get rid of a child rapist. But you're no better than a child rapist yourself. In fact, you're worse — you steal people's lives, and there's no chance for them to grow or change, no chance to ask for forgiveness for their sins.

"You kill and use drugs because you're not man enough to face your childhood, to put your soul in order. I believe that you look forward to blaming all of the lives that you have stolen on your childhood! Why else would you joke about the way you killed those men? The way you stole from your friends? How dare you teach these babies to find humor in selfishness!" Ms. Karen said as she took my hand and forced us to come into the house with her while saying that Bobby was not safe for anyone to be near or to lean from until he sorted out his heart out and could be honest with himself about his evil ways.

Ms. Karen's anger was nowhere near as telling as Carl's and Nickels' complete silence. Seldom did they not find humor in any conversation they heard. Momma seemed confused as to what to do. Should she leave Bobby's side or stay with him? I could see the confusion in her eyes as Ms. Karen screamed at her.

"You worthless piece of trash! How dare you sit there beside that man? Your place is here with your children, walking in front of

267

them, guiding and protecting them! Not sitting there praying that this fool loves you! Why would you want a man who would allow you to take his side over that of your children. That is exactly why your life is so messed up. You're worried more about what some stupid man thinks of you than you care about these two souls that you gave life to! Don't you understand? You gave them life; they are pieces of you! Now get in here, you girls will have to stay in here with us from now on. Bobby, if you really care about these babies or their mother, then you need to learn to be honest about your life and stop joking about the sick things that you have done." Ms. Karen continued to scream as Momma jumped up and ran to our side, leaving Carl and Nickels in their silence, and Bobby staring down at Lucy until she too abandoned him to follow Lil Dee and her own babies into the house.

Ms. Karen was not finished with Momma, but I was happy to hear her saying things to her that Mickey had wanted to say years before. They were the very words that I had been struggling to say to her since Christmas.

"Girl, these babies lived inside of you, you felt their life, you felt your babies growing, forming, that is a miracle that no man can ever feel or begin to understand. These are your children, not your little sisters. The greatest sin for any woman is to place a man before her offspring. When you agreed to give birth to them, you made a contract with the world that you would do whatever you had to do to raise and protect your babies. To put them before anything else, no matter who raped you as child, no matter what drugs you decided you liked, and to put them above any man who came into your life!

"Christy, when a woman raises her children, she is giving them to the world. When she lives as if she does not care about them, when she lives wrong and teaches her children to live wrong, then what kind of gift is she giving to the rest of us? I know that you were a prostitute, and it bothers you, but you're a fool. Men were made to live hard and die early, hunting animals with sticks and stones. Women were born to care for the children. Prostitution did not start because of horny men's needs, it started the first time a mother realized that the father of her children had died while out hunting and that she had no way to feed her children. Do you think that a horny caveman would give up meat that he faced death to earn to a crying widow? Hell no! They wanted sex for it, so the mother couldn't grieve for her lost man, she had children to care for first.

"So, she cleaned herself up and slept with the next best hunter that she could find. There is an honor in her doing that for her children, but what did you trade yourself for? It is instinctive for women to trade themselves to save their children. An instinct as old as mankind, but a broken, petty, whore like you would gladly give your children to monsters just to have a man act like he loves you. When you let any man speak like a fool or try to teach your babies something that you know is wrong, then you are trading your children to that man. Don't allow someone to make jokes about killing in front of your babies ever again!

"Do you hear me? Bobby cannot love you, nor you love him, until you each learn to love yourselves and realize that these children's futures are all that really matters anymore. Bobby joking about nasty things that he's done is no way for him to be honest, and you sitting there besides him, laughing at every cute thing he says, is not protecting your children. Now grow up, forgive yourself for the things that you have done, and honor your obligations to these children! Be their mother, their guardian, first, and that fool's boy's girlfriend second. If you are too broken or too fucking stupid to do that, then give these girls to me so that I can try to undo some of the damage that they have lived through," Ms. Karen said as she reached out to take my mother's hand.

Sitting here today, I'm able to enjoy the clarity that sixty-odd years bring when I think of the major events in my past. I can see that Ms. Karen was as big of a fool as both Bobby and my mother were because she accepted my mother's apology, her hollow words, and her pointless attempts at mimicking Ms. Karen. Momma was an addict, she would go out of her way to please anyone, all the while working towards her own private goals. Why Ms. Karen did not see this then I don't know.

That night, holding Lil Dee and smothered in dogs, dreaming of our future, I awoke to find my mother sitting at the foot of our bed crying. "What's wrong Momma?" I asked in a slight whisper, afraid to wake Lil Dee. "Me!" One simple word, me, was all Momma could manage to say before she told me not to worry and to go back to sleep as she left our room. Today, once again sheltered by sixty-odd years of time, I think I understand what my mother meant when she said "Me" that night. It's easy to fix others. It was easy for me to see the real Mickey, and it was easy for Ms. Karen to see the real Bobby, and to chew him out over his acting the fool, proving that pointing out the splinter in your neighbor's eye and explaining to them how to get it out is easy, but fixing yourself? Why, that's almost impossible. Me, you, or whoever — we cannot fix ourselves; we need others to help and admitting that you are your own worst enemy is the start to learning to live as a human once again.

I wish that I could tell you about Bobby's night alone without us, but I don't think that even Momma was daring enough to challenge Ms. Karen's commandments. I awoke with the sunrise, prepared for Ms. Karen to refuse to allow me to work with Bobby anymore. I could not see Bobby easily accepting Ms. Karen's hard words, but I was wrong. I made my way to the kitchen table for breakfast and was amazed to see Bobby already sitting there, laughing with Ms. Karen.

"She was right, Page, what she said to me yesterday," Bobby said, answering my unspoken question. "I'm trying to get my head right, to care for you girls and your mother, as well as these ugly dogs," he continued with a laugh as he bent down to scratch Lucy, playfully calling her a traitor but happy to be loved by her again.

"Our stories are too important to joke and laugh about, Page. Ms. Karen even thinks that I need to explore the reason why I show sadness when I talk about some things and then I try to use humor when I speak about other things. In my heart, I know that I violated my friendship with my partners, so I tried to avoid talking about it yesterday. I didn't want you girls to find out that I am capable of betraying my friends." Bobby mumbled an apology, but I didn't hear him because I was too busy thinking about the times that I had worried about or been afraid of how Bobby might react when he was mad about something. Before that moment, I had never considered that Bobby might harm us — we were his friends, but so were the men that Bobby had killed and stolen from. Bobby was all we had so I quickly hugged him, and Ms. Karen was thankful that Bobby had found a way to make peace with me.

We spent that day laying the last of the stairs. Bobby had managed to build four distinct paths that all converged at the front of the church where he laid more carved stones with their footprints all leading to a point and forming a flat level area to stand on.

"A place without a current, Page, a place to stand in peace when the world gets too heavy, that's what this hill is to me. I'm able to be me when I'm here," Bobby said as if he had just realized this himself.

Momma seemed lost in Bobby's words, so much so that again I forgot what Ms. Karen had pointed out the night before — Bobby was a wanted man and that our time on Dogwood Mountain was a gift to us and could end at any time. But neither Lil Dee or I wanted to think about the truth. For us, Bobby would marry Momma, and he would overcome the problems we faced outside of Dogwood Mountain, leaving us to grow up like normal children with a father and a mother, and with Ms. Karen, Carl and Nickels to act as the grandparents that our life of addiction had so easily stolen from us.

In spite of Bobby's apology to Ms. Karen, she would not allow us girls or Momma to return to sleeping in our cabin with Bobby as we had been doing.

"Three more days and y'all will be married — you can wait that long," she said with a laugh as she went on to explain that it was not Bobby who she was concerned with this time, but instead it was Momma. This caused Momma to blush like a schoolgirl as she attempted to assure Ms. Karen of her chastity, causing Ms. Karen to laugh. I had to laugh too as I realized that Momma could hardly wait to get married to Bobby and to complete her metamorphic change from addicted truck stop whore to married Christian wife and mother. Today, it was easy to understand that we fool ourselves into believing the craziest things, but back on that day, waiting for Easter, watching the dogwood flowers begin to open, I was depending on Momma to change from the ugly duckling into the gracious swan. Because I was not an individual, a person in my own right, my ego was tied so closely to my mother that if she changed, then I would change too. I felt sad for Momma but at the same time found humor in Ms. Karen's distrust of her. "Three more days," we all said as we laughed together, causing Carl to make jokes about taking her car keys away so she could not kidnap Bobby and elope.

"That's fine with me!" Bobby said as he pointed to his mother's nearly completed headstone. "Page and I can finish this up tonight and we can set it up tomorrow morning and be ready to start our new life with one less piece of history to weigh us down."

"Then what will we do?" Lil Dee asked with typical child-like innocence, but no one heard her, well no one attempted to answer her. We had come to a point where our fantasy would soon be tested by reality, and no one was willing to answer her at that time because to do so would risk one of us realizing that we could never be normal and that Bobby's past was not the only ghost haunting his and my mother's chance at a future.

Chapter 24

The day had started off slowly, forcing Andy to consider how foolish he had been to allow Sara to return to Tennessee where she had grown up. Now that she was here, near her family, she had options, people to cling to besides Andy. Girls like Sara needed someone to cling to, a reason to live beside themselves because they had no self-worth, just a desperate need to be wanted, to be loved. It shone like a light in their gestures and sad faces, calling out to pimps and users like Andy: "Come love me or at least pretend to love me! Please! I'll do anything you want!"

"Sara, you bitch! You tricked me into bringing you home! Hell, I bet the whore's been pregnant for months and it's too fucking late to abort the thing!" Andy said aloud without concern for who might hear him. A small part of Andy knew he was wrong to blame Sara for this, for what he was sure was going to be the death of their relationship. But he would never blame himself — he had chosen this lifestyle, he loved it, needed it even, knowing that to survive in this twisted world meant using and taking advantage of suckers like Sara every day.

"No one cared when I was being used! No one ever tried to save me!" he said with a laugh as he thought about the complex nature of an addict's life and the many ways there were to thrive in your addiction as you killed yourself at the same time.

Andy was not a pimp. The truth was that Andy hated pimps — it had been pimps that his mother had submitted to. Pimps to whom she had gladly sold herself, the same pimps she had allowed to sell Andy too. Andy shook his head while gritting his teeth as memories of his childhood hells began to melt his high away. In prison, guys joked that sex with other men "only made you gay if you liked it." Guys were always quick to say that they weren't gay only to be tricked, back into a verbal corner by old shower sharks and butt bandits who would quickly ask them how could they know for sure that they weren't gay if they'd never tried it?

Anger and violence were the proper response in prison when asked such a stupid question, yet Andy had seen quite a few heterosexual men flunk this test. It was this lack of violence that concerned the butt bandits, because in prison, just like children who were forced to have sex with perverts or like Sara turning tricks to get high, no one cared if you enjoyed the sex or just endured it. In fact, you had more control of the guy if he didn't enjoy the acts that he performed and knowing that violence was not the man's first instinct, you had no reason to fear him since the coward would do anything to keep his acts a secret.

Andy had hated every sexual act that he had endured as a child. But he loved his mother. "All kids love their mothers, so it was normal to do things to please your mother!" Andy mumbled in defense of the foolish child he had once been, as guilt began to stalk his heart. "Only a fool would have allowed them to do those things to you! A fool or a homosexual! A queer boy!" Andy again spoke out loud, knowing that he was neither a fool nor gay, no matter how looking back at his childhood made him feel. Just thinking about his childhood felt to him like trying to figure out complex math problems — it made his head hurt and caused his mind to go blank. Worse still for Andy was his conflict of emotions over his taking joy in making his mother smile at the same time as hating her for selling him to perverts.

Thinking about how he could hate it and enjoy pleasing his mother at the same time was like looking into a broken kaleidoscope. No matter what a person thinks, a kaleidoscope is simply repeated patterns, shapes and colors, nothing is random at all. Only once broken does your eye focus on the repeated patterns and you come to understand the illusion. "Why didn't you pick up the phone? Call the police? Why didn't you run away?" Andy asked himself aloud, knowing that these questions were the chains that bound him to his addiction. These were the questions that normal people asked you when you were foolish enough to tell them about your childhood.

Andy had fallen in love once. He had gotten clean, stopped using all drugs, he had even gotten a normal job. But desperate to find help in sorting his soul or trying to warn the poor girl that the monsters in his past were real unlike the monsters living under her childhood bed or in her closet. Andy had opened up to his lover, hoping that she could help him put his feelings in order, fix the broken kaleidoscope that was his heart. But logic and love cannot occupy the same space at the same time and Andy's girl had applied logic by asking why he had not called the police, asked for help. "It's not too late," she had said. "We can go hunt the perverts down, you know where some of them live," she had said. "You know where your mother is. We can go to the police and punished them!" she had screamed with a sound of vengeance in her voice.

"No!" Andy had said. "I didn't tell you about all of this to get you to help me punish these people. I told you so that you could help me to forget," he had cried in response, without realizing that he was pushing her away, acting illogically. Soon, he heard that she had told his secrets to her girlfriends and family. Some of them felt that he was really warning her that he was gay, twisted inside, unsure of his desires, and that by not seeking to punish those who had abused him, he was as much as admitting that he had liked it. Would he then do it to children himself? Andy's normal life went from one of love to one of guilt and self-doubt. It was then that Andy sought out heroin once again. He did not simply fall off the wagon, he leaped off without calling for the driver to stop its forward momentum.

Andy's mother refused to accept that she was an addict. She used drugs because of her ever-changing medical needs she claimed, and she sold herself because she was a businesswoman, not to please her pimps or because of the high cost of her addiction. A pimp was just a piece of the life she lived. Andy had sworn to himself that he would never lie to himself about why he got high, or about the fact that he was addicted. And other than when scamming a new college girl into buying him a day's worth of heroin, Andy had kept his promise.

"Sara was meant only to be temporary!" Andy mumbled. "Like how many others?" he asked himself. Normally his relationships lasted no more than six weeks before the girl's family saw what was happening and raced in to save their darling little angel. If the girl had wanted her parents' attention, she had it now because bank accounts and credit cards don't lie. Daddy might be slow to accept the fact that his precious daughter likes to get high and fuck wild-eyed boys, but he has no trouble rushing in to save the day when the bank calls about bounced checks!

There had never been anyone rushing in to save Andy. Maybe that was why he enjoyed 'catching the dog' as the college girl game was called. The fact that catching dogs was a pimps' term taught to Andy by a pimp didn't bother him. Although he hated everything about pimps, Pennywise, his mother's long-time man had sworn that the day would come when he would find himself and accept that he was a pimp, and that women were dogs, willing to do anything to be loved, even selling their own children.

The dogcatcher game had a short lifespan — it was meant to be used by young pimps to build a stable of girls. "You let your girls live together and all of them whores will start to get their periods at the same time each month. Hell, all of them fucking you and only you can cause them to start to bleed around the same time, so a pimp always needs fresh pussy to fill in during the bloody times," Pennywise had calmly stated once when he was explaining to Andy the mystery of getting women to sell their bodies. Andy thought that because he didn't use the dogcatcher game to trap and then turnout wallflower-type girls, but used it just to get a free high, that he was not acting like a pimp but, in fact, was doing the girl a favor, teaching her that love is nothing like storybooks.

Yet regardless of the reason for Andy's use of this tool, it was a tool, and it came with an expiry date. At a certain age, the pimp stopped looking like a poor young man struggling to make his way in the world and changed into a pervert in a young girl's eyes. Years of drug use may have helped Andy drink in underage in bars, but it was not helping him now — he would not be returning to any college parties. If he tried to pick up another stupid bitch like Sara at a college party now, the girls would scream that he was a freak, a pervert. Playing the dogcatcher game depended on the girl being lonely and hoping to be loved by a man who was a little dangerous but not the type of pervert who wanted to tie them up in the basement or hurt them, and Andy now looked more worn and dangerous than ever before.

Thinking about looking dangerous caused Andy to laugh out loud as he looked across the city park where he and Sara plied their daily trade. The idea of danger and violence had fed his habitats for more than eighteen months now, allowing Andy to stay high. He only had to send Sara out to turn tricks in emergencies or when some perv offered him way more money than she was worth. It was all an illusion, a magic show. Perverts see a sweet young girl and dream of saving her. Old fat ass men see worn-out whores and believe they're helping by turning a twenty dollar quickly. The Saras of this world smile as they sell themselves to please their man, a man who they think loves them more than he loves his addiction. Drug dealers go out of their way to appear dangerous, hoping that it will be enough to keep someone from robbing them. Addicted housewives and spoiled kids fool themselves into trusting guys like Andy to act as a go-between when they buy a shot of dope — first they say that they're scared of the big dangerous dope boys and then they tell themselves that they are not addicted because they never really buy any dope but instead, they hook Sara and Andy up with a free high.

It's all just an illusion. Andy would steal the kids and housewives' money in a heartbeat if desperation set in. A violent dope boy is just a Hollywood concept, as guns, violence, and dope sales equal more time in prison once you're caught by a caring police officer. Sure, there are the crazy guys who act like they're in a rap video, carrying guns, acting the fool, but they don't last long before they do something stupid, trying to look cool, or one of the dope heads calls the cops on them. It's all an illusion, and Sara was the only reason it had been working so well. She was country, homely and trusting, and people would wait with her as Andy went to get dope. She made friends with everyone.

But now the illusion, the magic show was over. Andy was doing alright today without Sara; she had befriended enough suckers for Andy to survive for a few days. But addiction is like the ocean, always washing up on the beach in waves. You have money to get high on today and dry sand, but no cash tomorrow. So, men like Andy were always in need of fresh drug users — they depended on the housewife growing from a twenty dollar a day snort to a fifty dollar a day habit and then teaching her friends about the joys of snorting heroin and explaining how she herself had learned how to touch heaven. With the kids who got high, the credit cards they used would always lead back to mommy and daddy along with a stay in rehab. For Andy to stay high every day, he needed as many fresh drug users per day as old ones.

This was just one of the lessons Andy had learned from his first trip to prison. He had been young and stupid then; he had an apartment in those days and not a Sara. He would allow the dope fiends to stay at his apartment while he went out to get dope for them, and before long there was always someone getting high at Andy's place. Life was good until some fool drug dealer cut his dope wrong and twelve addicts died in one day. The first thing Andy lost was most of his clients and friends, as fear of dying led many of them to tell their parents and to seek help. Death has a way of scaring the hell out of the people who are pretending to be addicts — out of fear, they tell on their friends, and everyone involved.

Three days after the mass deaths, Andy found himself broke, withdrawing and being searched for by the police as three of the twelve dead addicts had been known to get high at Andy's place. Once in prison, a sober Andy thought about how he had ended up as he was and how to make sure it never happened again. First, never stay in one place for too long. Second, never depend on one crowd to stay high off of. It had been withdrawal that had gotten Andy caught, and he only fell into withdrawal because of the rich kids all abandoning him and blaming him for their friends' deaths. Although not one person had died in Andy's apartment, his was the only name they had known, and his was the only name the rich kid's very concerned parents were now screaming.

Things like that could not happen again Andy told himself as he shook off the memory of past mistakes and began to plan for the coming change. He would need time to hustle up enough cash to buy a large enough amount of dope to start dealing himself while staying high at the same time. If Sara aborted or lost the thing, then nothing would need to change, but he could not have a fat pregnant Sara standing in the park talking to dope heads as he went to get dope for them. The cops would not allow it, the dealers would not accept it, and Andy's customers would be turned off by the reality of the lifestyle that is heroin addiction. So, he had no other choice — he would give Sara the day to come to her senses, abort her trick baby and start getting high again or he would break her as he had watched pimps break and punish his mother when she had misbehaved.

He had often felt sorry for his mother and the whores he had called his aunts, as he watched them suffer. But Sara was teaching him what Pennywise had meant when he had told Andy, "It takes a hell of a man to beat and abuse a woman, but it takes an even bigger bitch to deserve it! Just make sure your whore deserves it! Trust me, they will hate you if you just beat on them for the fun of it, or to look like a big man, but they'll love you for beating them if they deserve it! Andy laughed out loud again as a kid of about fifteen walked up asking for Sara and hoping to spend one hundred dollars. "Bitch deserves it!" Andy thought to himself as he set about convincing the kid that Sara was at home sick and that Andy would not rip him off.

Chapter 25

God has to be either a genius or he really is up there hanging out with his friends playing joke on all of us! The many varied interpretations of the Bible prove that I'm right — it's as if there is a combination lock on God's goal for us and we have to break his code. Ms. Karen swore that there was a proper way for good Christian women to drink or have a good time, but she could wear a white Sunday dress all day while working on an oil well and dress would only get whiter! Well, that's what the ladies from town liked to laugh and say, not behind Ms. Karen's back but in a joking way so as not to hurt her feelings. Folk have a way of getting hurt and upset when they hear other folks making jokes about the odd things that we all tend to say or do. Seems to me that there's nothing wrong with being honest, or having a little fun, yet it's hard to learn to laugh at ourselves or how other folks see us in relationship to the world around them. Maybe if God was not so busy farting around up there with his friends, he could take a moment or two and give us the eleventh commandment: "Thou Shalt Laugh at Thyself!" Because we are silly and fun to be around when we're not sticking our noses into other folks' business or passing out judgment like we know exactly what God is thinking.

It was the Thursday before Good Friday and women from town were coming out to Cemetery Ridge to help us decorate. Ms. Karen would thank them for coming out, hand them some ribbons and tobacco or candles in jars and send them on their way to work only to then mumble her complaints behind their backs, claiming that they just couldn't wait to get a jar of Carl's wine to sip on or their reasons for being here were not pure. "She's not here to serve the Lord!" She just wants a reason to drink wine or gossip about the good women who've not come out here to help yet!"

"Now Karen, it seems to me that Jesus' momma got him to brew up a nice fresh batch of wine once at a wedding. Why do you suppose she had to do that?" Nickels asked, causing Ms. Karen's eyes to shine with anger.

"It's not the same thing Nickels!" Karen quickly replied.

"Seems to me that it is Karen. Had you been there at that wedding, things would have been boring as hell!" Nickels said with a laugh.

"Nickels, you know as well as I do that since neither of us was there at that wedding that neither of us knows the moral of that story!" Karen said in her defense.

"No Karen, that ain't quite true. I think that God put that story in the good book for just this reason, so folks could argue the morality of Mary versus the morals of know-it-all folks like you! Now, Karen, I know that your daddy was a mean drunk, and that you ain't always been pure as the snow, and that alone is a big part of the cross you carry. We all have our own ways of punishing ourselves, carrying a cross, struggling just like Jesus did. I wonder if Jesus judged all of the folks who did not reach out to help him that day as he struggled bleeding under the weight of his cross on his way to his death the same way you judge these women each year when they come out here to help us at Easter time?" Nickels calmly asked, leaving Ms. Karen standing there silent.

"Page, you need to go help them glue candles to the headstones," Ms. Karen said. Her tone left me in no doubt that she was embarrassed by the honesty of Nickels' words. Her embarrassment spoke louder than anything that I had heard her say, but it taught me that we all say and do things around our friends and family that we would never do in front of strangers. For Momma, it was getting high with Lil Dee and me watching her, for Ms. Karen it was judging others by her own moral code and then saying mean things about that person. Just one of the many lessons I learned about life that beautiful Easter weekend so long ago. Just one more piece of my life not carved into stone stairs waiting some retarded fat man with a PhD in archaeology to find. Why are all the best life lessons, the really important things, so easy to forget?

"You gotta put four candles on each stone, Page," Nickels said to me as we walked up Cemetery Ridge leaving Ms. Karen alone.

"All the stones face east towards the morning sun. You put the yellow candle on the far left, then red, next white, and then the black candle on the far right of the stone. It's important because that's how them Natives put them in a medicine circle. The tree sap not only smells good, that's why we use it to seal coffins up too, but mostly we use it to glue the jars to the tombstones because it's a natural glue, so like us it washes away with time," Nickels grinned.

"Ain't this stuff religious?" I asked Nickels. "Why does Ms. Karen get upset about the women drinking a little wine, and that's in the Bible, but she doesn't seem to care about all of the Native religious stuff we do?"

"Because she never got beaten on by no Indians! She ain't afraid of the Native things, yet she is afraid of what she's had men do to her after a night of drinking, and even worse, she's embarrassed over what she herself has done after a night of drinking. Watch her, she will start drinking a little wine before long, pretending to fit in, but she won't let herself get good and drunk like they must have done at that wedding when old Jesus helped out!" Nickels said with a laugh, and for a moment I dreamed about how fun it would have been to drink Jesus's wine with him at that wedding. Of course, no one knew who he was at that time, so I bet that wedding was fun — someone's cousin probably got sick, while another said silly things.

"Page," Nickels said, allowing his voice to draw me back home to Dogwood Mountain. "Honey, your momma, Lil Dee and you yourself are going to do things like Ms. Karen does, you might even try to use God as an excuse. And you girls will go on for years telling yourself that you will never harm your children in the ways that you were hurt. You will even set up great big walls around your hearts to defend against the ghost of your own monsters. Karen is so afraid of her past that she forgets that you are her future and that you will mimic her every step. Karen wasn't wrong to say what she did, but she was wrong to forget why she was saying it. That poor woman from town, like yourself, would have no idea where Karen's criticism was coming from had she heard Karen. No way for her to know that Karen was really mumbling about her own fears, trying to warn the woman and you, Page, about drinking," Nickels said as he put his hand on my shoulder causing me to look up at him and again, I saw the sight in his dead eyes.

"Page, don't expect your children, husband or friends to understand what you're afraid of if you never tell them the truth. Don't hide your childhood or your fears, share them, speak of them often so others can learn from your pain, so you can learn from it also, but most importantly so that your heart's pain does not begin to rot and fester as Bobby's did. Jesus' momma drank wine and had a good time at that wedding, proud that her son could save the day, but Karen would have you think that it's wrong to drink or enjoy a wedding at all just because the pains she's suffered in her life."

Nickels' words that day were a gift, a gift that I buried deep. I avoided them, like I have avoided everything else in my past, too embarrassed to share my knowledge. How audacious I must be to talk about archaeologists as if they're evil! It's just hard to be honest about your childhood when you don't want anyone to know that you ever had one at all.

Carl's yelling drew the attention of everyone on Cemetery Ridge, causing some men who had gathered by the church to roast a big hog to rush over to help Bobby. Somehow, he had lifted his mother's heavy tombstone and was carrying it up Cemetery Ridge by himself.

"I don't need no help! Leave me alone!" I'm fine," Bobby said as he began to breath hard, staggering, trying to climb the steep hillside. I saw that the bullet hole in his leg had started to bleed again, and I remember getting mad at the the doctor for not stitching it up for us. "Had the fool fixed it for Bobby, then it wouldn't be bleeding today, and you wouldn't be a dead asshole!" I heard a smiling, happy voice in my heart say. It was my voice, yet

Ms. Karen's tone, but then the memory of the pretty nurse's moans reminded me that Bobby had taken joy in smashing her face into the desk, and my confused heart embarrassingly began to cheer for Bobby to complete his quest to reach his mother's grave unaided. I easily could have continued to fault the doctor for the way Bobby staggered up the hill, but I knew that I was wrong to do so. The bullet that had torn my hero's leg had been fired from Percodan's gun, but it had been searching for Bobby for years, long before Percodan pulled the trigger.

We are television people, and we want our heroes to stand framed in perfect light as they gallantly overcome their burdens, never a hair out of place, yet the reality is nothing like that! Bobby nearly failed many times; it was becoming embarrassing to watch him fight the stone's weight and the steep pitch of the hill. I began to wish that he would ask for help seeing Bobby look so unheroic was becoming painful. Then he looked at me, and I know that he saw the shame and embarrassment dancing in my heart. I was not afraid that he would fail but that he looked like a fool, and heroes should never look so human.

"Shorty! This fucking stone ain't shit!" Bobby said as Momma and Lil Dee rushed over to stand beside me. "I got this!" he said as he found new strength and began to stumble less.

Then he was there, standing on his mother's grave, grinning as he gently lowered the heavy stone, placing it with care where it stands today, as if it weighed nothing. I thought by the way he had said "I got this!" that Bobby would now begin acting a part, swaggering, letting his nuts swing as he loved to say, but instead he fell down on his knees with tears in his eyes and started crying.

"Forgiveness," he gasped as he tried to speak. "I know that I hurt her deeply leaving her up here for so long without a stone. I had to carry it by myself, to let her see that, no matter what has happened between us, I love her."

Bobby's words and actions left me deeply confused. I had come to realize that he would carve his mother a stone as much to shut Ms. Karen up as to honor his mother. He was a southern man, with a southern sense of pride and honor. Lots of men do things out of honor and duty, but to see Bobby's tears confused me.

"That bitch doesn't deserve your forgiveness!" I heard my heart scream as the pretty nurse's moans echoed again through my soul. I could accept Bobby pretending to forgive his mother for pride's sake, yet seeing his tears, knowing that he really had let go of his anger and hurt for the very woman who destroyed him, hurt him so badly that he could take joy from crushing a woman's face, confused me. Bobby was a monster, simple as that, and his mother deserved no headstone or grave at all as far as I was concerned.

Then I saw Momma, standing there, trapped in a halo of spring sun with a backdrop of fresh green in the trees and bright flashes of reds, yellows, white, and black spirit ribbons moving in contrast to her stillness. Momma was alive, her eyes were clear of the haze of opiates. She, like Bobby, had just slowly stopped eating pills. There had been no fight, no sickness and no words spoken of a planned goal, if it had been a goal at all. But somehow, they had both walked away from their poisonous false god and were now here together crying for a dead woman. Lil Dee hugged me, and I saw in her eyes the answer to the mystery unfolding before me.

Bobby's mother was dead, and she could not feel the gift of Bobby's forgiveness, but Bobby and me felt it deeply. Each day as he struggled to sort out his heart to forgive his mother, he ate fewer and fewer Oxys — he didn't need to hide inside of their peacefully embrace anymore, and this made the Oxys' evil siren song less appealing to him. Momma's time in A.A and N.A. had pointed her towards this same metric, yet no one had ever just sat her down and said, "You hate yourself and your way of life, and because you can't get past this pain in your soul, you will forever need pills or drink to keep your memories at bay. You're simply running from a monster and into the arms of a demon." No one ever told Gay Tom to come out the closet and accept himself for who he was, or to stop being the person he thought he needed to be to please his family. Had someone done that, how many years of addiction and suffering could they have saved Tom from? Or how many lives could have been saved from Bobby's rage and self-hate?

I was watching as Bobby's forgiveness of his mother was freeing him of his need to hide within an opium fog. The man kneeling down at his mother's grave crying would be the type of man who could easily laugh at himself now. Forgiveness was not a gift to be enjoyed by the forgiven, but instead it was a gift enjoyed by the forgiver.

"I'm proud of you son," I heard Ms. Karen say as Bobby rose from the ground to draw us all into an embrace. Today, I find myself stopping at Bobby's mother's grave just to run my fingers over the beautifully carved headstone, five roses surrounding a winged cross with a sun setting behind it as the word Momma floats on a ribbon. Nothing else, no explanation about who she was or even a hint of Bobby's pain. But it's there, my fingers can feel his hurting — rough and hate-filled in the earliest lines he carved, and then a peace begins to show as Bobby began to forgive her, only sometimes to be interrupted as he must have been struggling with a bad memory. But he always overcame his venom and the peaceful smoothness of his love returned to flow through his artwork.

"Boy, I thought for sure that you were just gonna carve something simple to shut old Karen up, but this?" Carl said with a smile as he pointed to Bobby's artwork. "This is the prettiest stone that I have ever seen! Hell, I think I'll change my name to Momma so I can rest under it!" Carl said and we all laughed along with him.

"It was the girls here that caused me to do so well on it," Bobby said. "It was something about them watching me and knowing that they would someday have to do the same for their mother or me that caused me to see that my mother was sick and unable to understand what she was doing to me. She didn't hate me, she hated what her sickened mind told her I was or would become. Her hatred of me has been the hardest thing for me to accept, but it turns out she didn't hate me at all," Bobby said as Ms. Karen rubbed his arm and smiled, proud of herself as well as Bobby. I saw Nickels lean down and pull the tin poor man's cross from the ground and I couldn't help but whisper in Lil Dee's ear that I was still sure that the old fool was pretending to be blind and that pissed off rednecks was going to be the least of his troubles if it turned out that he was playing a joke on us! Lil Dee giggled in agreement as the dogs rushed to our side to take part in our family gathering.

There was very little good about that Good Friday! Well, I don't mean that literally but, for me personally, it was a day filled with silly embarrassing moments. Momma and Bobby spent the afternoon and evening before in the tombstone shop, laughing and talking after we finished placing Bobby's mother's headstone and, like most emotional conflicts at that time in my life, I failed to come to terms with my heart over Bobby's forgiveness of his mother. I'm sure that the potential of losing Bobby as a father if I questioned his desire to forgive her played a large part in my willingness to forget my own reservations about his mother.

The men from the town were working in shifts, watching the hog spin slowly around as they sipped wine and told lies. Every so often, Lil Dee and I would first hear the men laughing hard and loudly and then hear Karen mumbling that Carl must have made a complete ass of himself to get everyone to laugh at him so hard. I began to feel sad for her as she was clearly lonely and missing Carl's company. She had not been herself since her earlier conversation with Nickels. We seem to understand that there are monsters living under our own beds. Pieces of our past that are just too painful to face, but we never consider the pain we inflict on others when we force them to face their own demons as Nickels had forced Karen to do. I have to wonder how many husbands and wives have fought to the death of their love over silly things, never once realizing that their buried monsters were honestly at fault. Nickels was able to gently mention Karen's past and her father — a husband would not soon be forgiven if he betrayed his wife's trust in that way.

Lil Dee and I were supposed to be sleeping but it was hard to sleep and to eavesdrop on Bobby and Momma's conversation at the same time, especially with the men's laughter drifting down Cemetery Ridge as thick as the heavenly smell of fresh barbeque. In time though, Lil Dee drifted off to sleep in my arms and I had time to think about the events of the day. I still found it hard to forgive Bobby's mother. Lil Dee could accept without question anything Bobby or Momma said because she still owned the innocence of a child, where my faith in adults had long ago been deeply bruised if not shattered.

Suddenly a thought struck me like a bolt of lightning. I only knew Bobby's side of the story and had measured his mother by his actions, never considering that Bobby's life between leaving his mother's home and today had helped to make him the man that I had seen him turn into. Prison time with men like Percodan and a million other holes that Bobby had dug for himself between leaving home and today had all shaped him. Had Bobby been a monster as a child at home, Ms. Karen would surely not love him the way she did, nor would anyone in his mother's house have beaten him until his back was as scarred as Bobby's was now. Although Bobby's mother had done things that had sent him down the road to being a killer, Bobby was the one who had thrived in and enjoyed that type of life.

I had to wonder what type of man Bobby would have grown to be if he had gotten mental help, true and real mental help. How many people would have lived longer lives? Where exactly would Momma, Lil Dee and I be sleeping tonight if Bobby had got mental help? And the problem was that Bobby had never gotten any mental help, he was broken inside like we were, Good Friday, Momma, Lil Dee and I were to be fitted for our wedding dresses so that Bobby and Momma could be married on Saturday. So, I forgot about asking Bobby if he had ever tried to get any mental help — and besides, I wanted the life that having Bobby as my father offered, even if he was a monster.

Karen awakened us with the smells of breakfast the next morning, and we ate, laughing, as the women from the town began to arrive for what was to be a girls' day of sewing dresses, telling stories about wedding nights, sipping wine and relaxing. I swear I heard Mickey's ghost giggling at me when the ladies began to debate my small budding breast. My being a girl had seldom really mattered before and had only been the focus of attention when Momma's friend had attempted to get me to accept that I would be a whore, or when we lived up in Huntington and I had to give urine samples with all of the other women. Other than that, it was only mentioned to gain a sympathetic response, 'Poor little girl' and things like that. I was not ready to be thrust upon a table then touched, advised, and measured by a bunch of women who I honestly didn't know.

Momma was, of course, the focus of most of the attention. Women love weddings and dances, and soon everyone was telling stories about wedding nights, or first kisses at dances. That fact that Momma had been a hooker did not stop the women from sharing wedding night stories, many embellished to draw laughter. Lil Dee was trapped in a protective bubble of innocence and left out of most of the jokes or stories — it was just not polite to talk of such things in front of a young girl, so code words were used near Lil Dee's tender ears. My budding breast seemed to scream to every woman in the house that I was not only old enough, but that I was in need of advice on every subject from catching a boy's attention to being polite to boys I didn't really like as this was a small town and this Easter's toad just might be next year's prince.

Karen brought me a jar of iced sumac berry wine and made me promise to never drink it quickly or after it had begun to make me feel lightheaded. "That's a surefire way to lose control around the boys, Page! God didn't mean to, but he made love almost irresistible, it can make you feel higher than all the wine or pills in the world, and a young lady has to be careful since wine does not tend to make girls act smart!" Karen said as the women from the town began to laugh, telling me stories about boys, dances, wine, and love. One woman who looked to be over a hundred years old gave me an old hatpin to stick in the boys' legs if they got too frisky, teach them some manners. She claimed that the hatpin had been given to her at her first dance after she began to bud as a young woman. This caused Karen to laugh wholeheartedly as she joked with the poor old lady that the hatpin had been used to pin the boys in place so she could have her way with them and not to teach them to behave at all! This brought howls of laughter and even more stories meant to teach me the ways of boys and dances.

I doubt people have changed all that much since Jesus cooked up fresh wine at that wedding — people are people, then as now. Soon it was decided by the older women that my breast would be placed on display, with a stitch here and tuck there. For some reason it was the boys' opinions that mattered and not my own. I once again heard Mickey giggling in my heart and I silently swore to never wear the dress these crazy women were making for me and Mickey just giggled even louder.

Not long after lunch, Lil Dee and I were released from our captivity. I had finally started to enjoy the sour taste of the iced wine, but Lil Dee was still young for wine or for dresses that accented her womanly body. Ms. Karen must have thought that, after I was accepted and treated so well by the ladies from town, I would choose to stay in the house with them, laughing and joking about boys. But I was still embarrassed over their concern for my breast and, besides, all that I had learned from them was that all men are still boys and that sometimes a boy might be the one in need of a hatpin to keep a girl in line. I had no intention of ever being close enough to find out if I would need the hatpin to teach the boys! I raced Lil Dee out of the house in search of Bobby and our dogs.

Carl had all of the dogs, even Buttons, doing tricks for small pieces of pork but, to my surprise, Lil Dee was not happy with either Carl or Buttons over their behavior. Buttons was supposed to love only Lil Dee, and his love of fresh pork and Carl brought out facial expressions in Lil Dee that reminded me of Momma when she felt hurt or betrayed by her man. When Momma's face twisted up in a certain way, it normally meant jail or trouble for the man until Momma got to feeling better. I began to wonder if Lil Dee would be mean to Buttons like Momma would have been mean to her man, but then Lil Dee smiled as she began to reward Buttons for doing tricks for her while ignoring Carl.

"Buttons, don't hunt Carl!" Dee said in an ice-cold voice. "You can teach the other dogs to hunt, Carl, but not Buttons!" Dee firmly stated as the men standing around laughing with Carl began to laugh at him being put in his place by a little girl.

"Why not shorty?" Carl asked in his defense. "Seems to me that you'd have better luck stopping a fish from swimming than stopping a beagle from hunting," he wisely stated as he stood up straight and took on the attitude of a schoolteacher. "Some things just are Lil Dee, and beagle dogs are hunting dogs."

Anger was boiling in my sister's eyes, and I was sure that she was going to explode if Carl continued to bother her over Buttons. Carl liked to be the center of attention and Lil Dee had stolen his show for the moment. I began to look for Bobby, hoping he would be close enough to stop Lil Dee if she decided to deal with Carl as she felt that Bobby would. But then I saw her face change, in the blink of an eye, and her anger seemed to evaporate, and she just smiled as she explained that she had no problem with Buttons hunting, but that neither she nor Buttons would go against Ms. Karen who had already told Carl that he was not allowed to hunt again after he shot his last dog. Her words drew more laughter from the men at Carl's expense. Even I could not help but to laugh along with everyone, never once realizing how deeply afraid I had been that Lil Dee would someday take joy in violence as her hero Bobby had taught her to do.

It's foolish of me, I know. Lil Dee was so young, and although she had smiled at Orville as he died, and giggled as Bobby hurt the doctor, there were no signs that she would resort to violence when she was too angry or frustrated to think clearly. But babies do first learn to walk by watching their family walking. Horses must be able to run within moments of being born; it is instincts that drive their need to stand up, to nurse, and then to run. Deer at least have the luxury of a few days rest and hiding from their predators before they are forced to run. But humans? We spend months crawling before we try to walk. We learn by watching our family, and Lil Dee watched her hero attack without fear or anger, and she had enjoyed it.

It is thoughts like these that made keeping my promise to write our family's story down easy to forget. How do tell a story and express joy, need, love, desire, hope, and fear all at the same time? How do you tell the world that your future depends on a man who kills others for little or no reason at all? Commonsense screams for you to run away from him, but we were happy to be racing towards him and his fate. Our life up until meeting Bobby had been so hellish as to make my sister's emulation of her hero acceptable — anything better than the silent world that Bobby had rescued us from.

Nickels was walking up and down all four pathways that Bobby had worked so hard to place. He told me that he loved how all of the stairs ended in front of the church and that there was something important to this for Bobby, as if Bobby was trying to tell us something about his heart or an unspoken fear. Something that even Bobby himself did not realize.

I can understand why Bobby made four trails that passed by every grave on the hill. First was the Native idea of the four directions and how they form a circle. Then there is the idea of folks' graves being lonely, unloved, forgotten, as the generations pass on, leaving no one to either love or remember you. This is a common fear we all share as we grow old. Yet these four paths were more than Bobby's way of making sure that his grave was never forgotten.

"Page, Bobby has been alone his entire life," Nickels calmly stated. "That's why he gets violent, it's his way of scaring people away before they can hurt him. Well, that's why he was that way when he was young. But like most learned skills people develop, Bobby turned violence into a life tool, and before long violence was such a part of his ego that he used it to both scare people away and to draw them near him. You see Page, Bobby never wanted to be alone, he just didn't want to be hurt again. Bobby needs you girls; he needs to be your hero just as you need him to be a hero. The problem is that Bobby knows all too well that he has no idea how to be normal, or how to live a normal life with you girls.

I'm praying that he ended his walkways here in front of the church as a silent reminder to himself that once you girls are safe and don't need him to be mean that he can learn to trust God instead of self-destructing as he has done so many time before," Nickels said, causing me to see the four paths in a new light: we were not just random footprints carved in stone pretending to be angels. No, we were Bobby's angels sent to lead him home no matter which pathway he chose. I remember standing in front of the church with Nickels that day, his blind eyes allowing me the privacy to relax without fear of seeing my face or judging my reaction to his message from the look in my eyes.

Spring was here, there was beauty in the many shades of green, the explosion of dogwood flowers, and the bright spirit ribbons contrasting against the blue sky, and Nickels had just told me that we were saving Bobby's life at the same time as he was giving us a chance to live. No one likes to be a burden, and stepchildren learn that it is easy to become a burden, not only to your new parent but also to your birth parent. They are the ones getting married, starting a new life, and the child often feels like a ball and chain until they grow old enough to head off to college and adulthood. But Bobby needed us, and if Nickels was right, we would all gain a new life, leaving no one in debt to the other since we all needed each other, simple as that. By this time tomorrow, we would be one complete family — with four pasts but only one future.

Good Friday came to a close as even more families from town began to arrive. As night fell, Carl helped Lil Dee and me to light the candles we had placed on the headstones. He swore that if we sat still and watched the ground around the graves in the soft light, we would be able to see the grass move on its own as if someone was there walking or dancing and that the fresh fallen dogwood flowers would move, proving to our hearts what our minds did not understand.

Carl swore that no one really dies, and that Cemetery Ridge would prove him right. I wanted to tell him about Lil Bear, and that the idea of ghost being here on Dogwood Mountain was perfectly acceptable to me. I wanted Dogwood Mountain to be special, like nowhere else in the world, but the idea of seeing Mickey, the Detroit drug dealer, or anyone from Percodan's house scared me. How could I apologize to Mickey for not convincing Momma to stay in Huntington where I could have helped Mickey the night they tossed her like a bag of trash out into an alley to die? How could I apologize to the man from Detroit for not stopping him from going out into the woods with Percodan? And Percodan would torture me for not saving him and Jessica.

Percodan had no problem reminding a person of all of the nice things he had done for them when he felt that they betrayed him — and bringing Bobby to his house in search of retribution for the loss of Lil Dee's voice would be unforgivable in Percodan's eyes. These fears kept me from grasping at the magic that Carl swore I could find in the sweet light of the candles if I watched carefully. It would even go on to cause me to steal this same magic from the other girls my age, leaving me both temporarily proud of myself for being smart, but at the same time, I have punished myself for years over my theft of their innocence and for being so mean.

The girls who were my age were too old to be treated like children, so they were allowed to come out to Cemetery Ridge on Friday night as well as Saturday. With Sunday being Easter, and folks having jobs, and responsibilities, it was understood that few people could spend all weekend relaxing, drinking wine, and telling jokes, so the girls my age and some a little older were expected to come out and finish decorating the mountain. Yet by evening on Good Friday there was nothing left to be decorated. This simple social rule was draped in church morals, as no young men were allowed anywhere near Cemetery Ridge on Good Friday night. The men cooking the hog were married to the women who had spent the day down at Ms. Karen's house, drinking and playing like the children we, all still are, deep down inside.

Today, I know that this social rule was meant to allow bond to grow between the young women, as it would soon be up to us to take care not only of the Easter Sunday preparations, but also of the funeral services of the older women who were sure to be called home before us. Good Friday night was a reward, a chance to laugh, play and to drink watered-down wine as we walked the candlelit cemetery in search of fallen flowers that move on their own, or grass that showed footprints. None of us were afraid of ghost. We were too old for to be childishly afraid of things like a ghost, but at the same time, we were still children, able to enjoy the idea of walking up Cemetery Ridge searching for spirits of those who had loved this mountain before us, giggling as we talked about boys and our chance to dance with this boy or that boy tomorrow night.

For once, I felt as if I belonged. I have had friends at school before, but other than when Lil Dee was born, I had never felt like I belonged to or was accepted by a group of girls my age — between Momma's reputation and my butch girl Mickey mask, I never really tired to fit in. Yet here, it felt heavenly, being treated like an old friend, and being judged not as my mother's daughter but as myself. I was being warned about which boys understood how to use deodorant and mouthwash and those who had yet to see a social need for them.

"My mom says that since boys don't get the blood, they ain't got no way of knowing that they're changing and growing up like us girls do," one girl said. Another girl laughed, saying that some boy named Tommy sure acted like he didn't know that he was a man now! And all the girls laughed as they joked about this Tommy being half Mississippi leg hound and warned me not to kiss him or to sneak off with him because he was a handful.

It felt good to belong and I filed away Tommy's name, laughing to myself and deciding instantly that I would stab him in the leg with my hatpin as soon as we started to dance tomorrow night, drawing the line right there and then, telling him that I was not interested in kissing any boy, especially one in need of deodorant and mouthwash!

Soon the girls took me into the church so I could watch the

ghost dance. We had all been drinking what was supposedly watered-down wine, but it was being watered-down by girls not much older than us who would quickly wink as they handed over a jar of wine and then assure Ms. Karen that it was safe for girls of our age to drink. No one got so drunk as to embarrass themselves or to poison this tradition, but we did get to feeling good, in my case feeling good enough to be blatantly cruel. No, I'm sorry, that's not true — I was more than cruel that night in the small church. I was downright mean.

Our church being clean, white and plain inside, it could not help but glow in the colors reflected through the large glass butterflies. Candlelight is so soft that we consider it romantic because it strikes our eyes in an odd way as opposed to normal light from a lamp, so in a sense we are trained to feel silly in a room filled with candlelight. Throw in young girls, wine, ghosts, and giggling, and anything is possible. That night, the chapel was ablaze with soft colors. The candlelight that reached the room through the butterfly stained-glass window cast soft, beautiful colors onto the floor, pews, walls and even onto us slightly drunk, playful young women, all willing to see what we were hoping to see. Once our eyes had adjusted, we could see the shadows of tree limbs and tombstones, all seeming to move in the flickering light, and small beams of color dancing on the floor and walls across the bolder colors. For a moment, I held my breath, awed by the beauty of their tender movements.

A girl called Jenny said, "My daddy told me that the old Cajun man who built the church said that these lights are the spirits of his Indian friends who died ghost dancing at a place called Wounded Knee. Seems that the soldiers shot them all dead at Christmas one year for ghost dancing, so they stop here every Easter to let their old friend know that they love and miss him."

There was a magic to what I was seeing but I was still unhappy with Lil Bear's ghost for not waking me up the night my sister was raped. I was sick of being considered stupid by kids at school because I was always behind in my work, and above all, I was drunk, surrounded by children pretending to be seeing Indians' ghost dancing in a white man's church.

"They ain't no damn ghosts, are you girls stupid? That story about that Cajun fella is just that, a story! Them lights ain't ghosts at all. Look at that wall full of homemade butterflies — they're made from trash, small pieces of broken bottles, so the candlelight moves in an arc as it passes through the curved pieces of a bottle on that wall. It's all bullshit, not ghosts at all. Besides, Carl said that the homemade butterflies were put in long after that Cajun man died!" I proudly stated as if I were a teacher tired of my stupid pupils' silliness. I had seen and taken part in things that these girls would never understand. I knew what good men, like their darling fathers, did at places like Ruby's when no one was around who knew their names. I had been punished for missing school by prissy ass girls like these new friends of mine. And the wine helped me to say what needed to be said, to warn them off, to show them that I was not a child.

"It doesn't hurt to believe!" a girl named Tammy said as we began to pair off in silent sets of sisters, and I began to hate myself for saying anything about the dancing lights at all. And to be honest, I still don't understand why I needed to ruin the fantasy these girls were sharing with me. I still don't understand why it felt good to sound so smart, when only moments later I began to hurt as I prayed for God to show me how to breathe magic back into the tiny room. And above all, I still don't understand why, at my age today, I still feel pride in myself for being smart enough to see the real cause of the dancing ghosts, while at the same time, I am still ashamed of myself for being so mean and uncaring on that night so many years ago.

I suppose that this event will be forgotten unless I carve it in stone for the archaeologists to find in a million years. Even though it would be a lot more fun to carve a recipe book in stone about the proper way to cook and serve a sacrificed virgin! Then when some want-to-be Indiana Jones smart-ass with a PhD in grave robbing finds the remains of our church and its windows, and finds me in my coffin, with my arms crossed and hands on my chest, both middle fingers extended and all the others folded down, flipping them off for waking me up, he will also find my recipe book for cooking virgins, then the college types will finally have proof that we practiced cannibalism! In fact, after I'm done writing this story for you, that's exactly what I'm going to do! Carve a stone recipe book, complete with a wine list and suggestions for what color wine to serve depending on the virgin's hair color, along with seasoning tips and ideas on how to tenderize your virgin daughters before you sacrifice them to an uncaring and distant God.

Then maybe in a million years, after the foolish archaeologists leave my mountain home, Native girls will walk this hill at night telling the story of how our generation, my generation, used silence to sacrifice its daughters to be eaten like cheap snacks at a party. Our silence being as deadly as a temple priest's stone knives. How we caused our daughters to become whores at a truck stop, addicts trading their wombs for a high. Women willing to be beaten in the name of love, or worse, how we left our babies in the hands of perverts, to be molded into broken vessels of motherhood that sexualized young girls grow up to become.

Then those future Native girls will scream out loudly, promising both themselves and our ghosts that they will never sacrifice their daughters again. After all, my lifetime of silence is the equivalent of my allowing a virgin sacrifice. Bobby did not make me promise to tell his life story, but instead to tell our life story. He was not afraid that he would rot away in his grave with both his good deeds and sins forgotten to time. No, my father wanted me to give the world our story as a way to save girls like Momma, Lil Dee, and me from the monsters who dress up like humans, eating the hearts, egos, self-esteem, and souls of the women who were broken as children, like Momma, Lil Dee, and me were.

I have been a fool, hiding away in this worthless graveyard, praying that my silence would keep people from judging me. From seeing me as the daughter of a drug addicted whore. All the while failing to realize that Momma was never just a drug addicted whore, she had once been a little girl like Lil Dee, praying for a loving father, naive and innocent, just like the tender girls that I stole the magic from my first Good Friday night on Dogwood Mountain. If Bobby had been a stone-cold monster when he was a child, then my mother was never a piece of shit in her childhood either. We grow up to become worthless, soulless, addicted pieces of trash, untrustworthy and rotten, but we are not born that way. No God would be so hateful as to force us to be broken vessels. It is our stories that will end the pointless sacrifice of so many children, once shared with children we are blessed to have, stopping fools like me from needing to destroy the innocence of other girls who only wanted to be my friends.

Chapter 26

We are all odd little creatures who like to hold on to our most painful memories. Memories that we would be better off forgetting. Like my memories of Orville, Percodan, and Mickey, I filed the memory of Good Friday night away, placing it in my toolbox of life experiences to serve me at a later time. But unlike a nonadjustable wrench or a specially designed chisel made to be used only to perform a certain job. These bad memories are more like pilers — I could take them out of my toolbox, remember each one in detail, relive each moment of it, and then apply it to that day of my life as I wanted to. Sometimes, I might want to feel smart or powerful, other times I might need to feel the sharp pain of regret to punish myself.

We all have memories like these — maybe we cheated on a lover or bullied someone weaker than us; we hate ourselves for our betrayals yet, at the same time, we enjoy knowing that we were strong enough to be mean. It is these types of memories, the pliers in out toolbox, that destroy most people, and their attempts to get sober. You see, pliers are a 'bastard tool' — they're only meant to be used in an emergency. If they're constantly used, they wear the square edges of the bolts away and, if reused on the same bolt too often, that bolt becomes rounded off, unable to be either tightened up or removed. And when we try to clamp two things together or hold them in place, the teeth of the pliers leave scars, ruining the shine.

When we try to get sober, we see the teeth marks of the pliers on important parts of our souls, reminding us first of our failure and second of our inability to properly repair the damage. Embarrassed, feeling like a mother whose child has dirty underclothes on in an emergency, we know that we need to throw the pliers out and repair any bolts that we've used them on so we can attempt to fix our hearts with the proper tools, but we like our pliers! We like to pull them out and apply them to any loose bolt we see — besides, a pair of pliers is so much easier to carry around with you than a big old heavy toolbox full of the right tools for dealing with life's loose bolts. And so, I filed my memory of Good Friday night's meanness at the church away.

Lil Dee and I were kidnapped again by Ms. Karen. She had Momma hidden in the house, being cared for by the women from town, as the men took turns sneaking around trying to catch a glimpse of the bride in her dress. Even Bobby joined in the fun, trying to come into Ms. Karen's house first for breakfast and then claiming that the water was broken in our cabin, saying in a sad pleading voice that he couldn't get married without first taking a shower. Ms. Karen told him he could take a bath in the creek as she gently hit him with her broom and chased him back up the hill away from the house. "It's bad luck to see the bride!" she said. "I'll beat you within an inch of your life if you don't stop pestering me!" It was all done in good fun — the men from town loved to hear their wives laugh and squeal as the game was played.

Momma glowed; she had not shone as she was shining now since the day she came to take me home from foster care. She was sober, clean of the opiates that had owned her soul, but I was too young still, too caught up in the magic of her wedding day, to stop laughing and playing 'Hide the bride' with the women from town to tell Momma that she was not the same woman today that she was only weeks before. I was too stupid, I suppose. I could have given my mother a new tool for her toolbox, just by showing her who she was today as opposed to the truck stop whore she had been, depressed and waiting to be called back to work by a man who was better off dead. Yet, like so many important times in life, I didn't recognize the importance of that moment until years later when I needed to feel the nasty sting of regret that dissecting memories can bring us.

Ms. Karen made all of us younger women and girls promise to stay clean as she released us from our captivity. The women from town were going to dress in soft white dresses with gentle embroidery, but favorite part of our almost community outfits was what Bobby called our halos. The women from town had stayed up most of the night braiding thin strands of spirit ribbons and small limbs from the dogwood trees into crowns for all of us to wear, each with several dogwood flower buds on them. It felt magical wearing them and hearing the men gasp when they saw their daughters dressed more like angels than girls on their way to a wedding. One man cried as he hugged his daughter and no one, not even Carl, made a joke at the man's expense. I could see in each man's eyes the true worth of womanhood. Unlike the sick, abusive stares of debasement and perversion we had endured from the men at Ruby's truck stop, there was nothing but love and respect in these men's tender eyes.

"Bobby?" Son, as beautiful as those two babies of yours are, you probably need to keep one or two of them pistols of yours handed — the boys are gonna be chasing both of them and I'm too old to run them off!" Carl said with a smile as the other girls, and I walked up to stand near the barbeque pit and picnic tables. Bobby just stared in silent awe as Nickels swore that Lil Dee was not his Lil Dee at all but some other little girl. His claims brought protest from Lil Dee — she even told Nickels to smell her, afraid that the perfume she was wearing was the reason Nickels did not recognize her. When she was near panic, Nickels reached out his hand to feel her head, then yelled loudly, "It is you!" I can feel your horns!" Then he laughed as Lil Dee's face first flashed with anger and then joy as she hugged our blind friend, happy that he had been teasing about not recognizing her.

I'm not sure if Lil Dee realized what she was doing or what she was going to cause when she sat down and took her shoes and socks off. At the time, I thought that, like me, she felt odd, dressed up so nice and she was afraid that she would ruin her pretty new shoes. We seldom if ever owned new clothes and had never had a pair of shoes meant only to be worn to church. A pair of church shoes cost the same amount of money as a twenty-milligram OxyContin, and Momma needed to eat two of those just to keep from being sick before Bobby found us and brought us home to Dogwood Mountain. Soon though, all of the girls, myself included, were barefoot, as Lil Dee mumbled about not wanting to make Ms. Karen upset by getting our shoes dirty. It made sense to us girls as the wedding was not due to start until noon, and we could be playful. Besides, it was spring, and the grass felt good on our feet.

Bobby had been called away from the group of men cooking to talk with Deacon Miles. The good deacon was going to perform the wedding today as long as Bobby answered some questions correctly. I knew that Miles Thompson was a county judge and that he had known and loved Bobby his entire life. Bobby also said that Deacon Miles was the real reason that we were safe up here on Cemetery Ridge, he would warn us if the outside world found out where we were. In my heart, I felt sure that the good deacon could protect us forever, and in his own way he did. I just had no way to understand that forever is a different amount of time for each one of us.

"Son, you gotta keep your word! You're a man now, you gotta do what's right for your family," I heard him say, then I saw Bobby smile as he hugged his old friend before they walked back over to where we were all gathered listening to Carl and the men from town debating the proper recipe for brewing up a good stinky fart. Men are silly that way, they tend to take pride in any competitions they can dream up, from lawn care to farts. They all have their own technical way of doing things — just get them to brag and you'll be surprised at what they will say, and Carl loved to brag.

Nickels called me over to show me a whole bag of five-dollar rings that he had made, telling me that a boy named Sammy had told all of the other boys not to waste their time or money buying a nice ring for me because he was staking his claim to me!" That means every boy in town will be buying you one of my best rings so that you won't think that they're cheap or afraid of this Sammy fella!" Nickels said with a laugh. "I knew you girls would be a gold mine! I just knew it!" he said as he smacked his knee and laughed loudly, happy about his good fortune.

I was not exactly sure how I felt about Nickels' joy over his pending ring sales at my expense, and I told him that he had best make the money last because there would be no more next year as I planned on stabbing every boy who asked me to dance. "It might be custom for them to give me a ring, and custom for me to dance with them, but it's not custom for me to make sure they enjoy their dance! I will be using my new hatpin to fix your moneymaking venture if you don't stop laughing right now!" I said to him. I was embarrassed enough without hearing his plans on how to spend the money, and for the first time since getting dressed up, I remembered the women from town and their conversations about my bubbling womanhood and I began to fear that somehow my blind friend could see my chest too.

My thoughts about stabbing the boys with my hatpin were interrupted by the sound of music. The men from the band had decided that their limbs and joints were sufficiently lubricated with Carl's favorite oil, pink sumac berry wine, to begin to play for us, warming up as Carl liked to say for tonight.

"Now you young ladies know the real reason why we make the boys buy y'all a ring, and why every boy has to dance at least one dance with each girl?" Carl asked the crowd of us girls as we played with Lucy and her pups, fighting the men cooking the hog for the pups' attention and not doing so well.

"So that lazy ass Nickels doesn't have to get a real job and stop pretending he can't see!" a man from town said as everyone, even Nickels, laughed along with him.

"Now we all know that old Nickels has been bullshitting us for years — if anyone thinks he can't really see, just drop a dollar bill on the ground and see how fast he picks it up!" Carl said, continuing the fun at Nickels' expense.

"Carl now, you're always too busy saying something stupid, or thinking up something stupid to say, to hear what's going on around you! Maybe if you just stopped farting and were quiet, you'd hear things happening too!" Nickels said with a grin.

"Folding money, paper money, don't make no damn noise when it hit the ground, least not enough noise for you to know if it's a one-dollar bill or a five, and the serial number of the damn thing!" Carl said, causing more laughter, and then he raised his hands for everyone to be quiet.

"Now girls, Nickels pockets ain't really why we have them boys get you angels a ring. We do it because the boys have to work hard and save the money to buy all them rings, and then they get a chance to talk with and share time with each of you. God made a million types of angels — some have a heart of gold while others have a heart of stone. All the same, some men need a hardhearted angel to guide them — why just look at me, Ms. Karen is meaner than a rattlesnake with a toothache! But I'm just stupid enough to need a woman that mean," Carl said as the crowd laughed and made small jokes about him and Karen.

"We want our sons to know that they have to earn the right to chase you girls, and that starts by being respectful to all women. Why, there ain't a boy from these hills that don't open doors for y'all girls, and they all speak respectfully to you ladies. Now I know that it cost each boy about twenty dollars to pay for all those rings each year. If a boy fails to earn enough money, old Nickels helps them out, but the boy has to set his ego aside and ask for help. He knows that he's having money trouble, but he wants to be respected by you girls; he knows that you're watching and that any boy who misses this dance either doesn't care about girls yet or he is just lazy and prideful. What I'm trying to say," Carl said as he stumbled with his thoughts, "what I mean is that you young women are the future, you're the only gold that men can find in these hills. That's what the stories about that old Cajun are meant to teach us, that's why he spent every piece of gold he found out west building this church and cemetery — he was trying to tell his girl that she was gold of higher quality than any gold he ever found." Carl spoke in a soft tone that I had only heard him use to convey deeper messages to Bobby.

"Ladies," Deacon Miles said, taking over from Carl, "there is a lid that fits every jar. We make the boys get to know all of you, so they understand that you're all angels. But don't y'all be in no hurry to accept a boy that don't fit. When y'all grow up and wander away from these hills, remember that real men will respect you, they won't call you bad names, or abuse you. Now I know that you're smart enough to know that your parents get into arguments, say mean and hurtful things, and you kids will too, that's the nature of finding a lid that fits. But don't just pick a man because you're afraid that no one else will love you. Now, let's get the band playing us some music and stop all this teaching and explaining. It's my day off Carl!" the deacon said as he slapped Carl's back and laughed.

"Y'all forgot the most important reason why we make the boys pay for a dance with a ring," Nickels said as he stood up, grinning. "Because the ghost that will be watching all the dancing on this hill tonight ain't got no money so they ain't got no rings!" he said with a sly grin, trying to leave the impression that the ghost would be trying to dance with us girls tonight. I began to see that the idea of the ghost was being placed into the girls' minds as a means of warning them that people were watching and to act like young ladies as any ghost on Dogwood Mountain was related to them in some way and no one would want to be rude to their great-great grandfather or mother, or worse to get caught sneaking off with a boy. It's probably hard to concentrate on kissing when you think that the ghost of your grandma is watching you! But these silly foolish traditions were like the music that was being played that day by a rusty band practicing for the night to come — you heard its melody until it drifted off, lost in the woods around us to be absorbed and forgotten like I had hoped that our past had been.

As I grew up, I stopped the dances, and the lessons that were meant to grow in each young heart raised on Dogwood Mountain. I sit here harping on about silly archaeologists plaguing my TV when I have purposefully destroyed the gentle traditions of my own people while doing my best to leave no trace of myself behind.

It was pain that made abandon our wonderful family traditions, and now it is a deeper pain that has shown me how wrong I have been to steal them from the many angels who were born here and cast out to face an increasingly hate-filled world without the lesson those simple traditions would have taught them.

The dogs raced about, playing fetch for gifts of juicy pork fat. A million gentle conversations were being spoken, and laughter and joy filled the air causing the music to build a soft backdrop to what should have been the best day of my life. I was at home in a cemetery, waiting on the noonday sun to shine down and bless the wedding of my mother and father — but a storm was blowing in and threatening to ruin all that we had prayed for.

Lil Dee seemed to hear it first. I saw her face and eyes change from child-like amazement and joy to eyes filled with fear and concern. Only then did I hear the throated rumble of the car racing up the road from town to Cemetery Ridge. Bobby heard the car too, and turned to see who it was, and how many police cars were coming for him, his hand instantly reaching for the pistol that I had not seen him carrying for days now. Somehow, like his need of pain pills, Bobby had just forgotten the need for his gun, but I was now wishing that he hadn't, as fear and confusion shaded the eyes of my hero, now standing alone and unsure.

"It's that damn fool preacher!" Carl said and I instantly saw relief flood through both Bobby and Lil Dee, leaving me happy that I didn't need to decide if I should run and get Bobby his favorite gun or stand back and allow the police to take him away before he could marry Momma and complete our family.

The preacher's car slid to an angry stop causing a cloud of dust and dirt to stain the dogwood flowers around us. This caused the men cooking the hog to complain that the dust would ruin the barbeque. Bobby, like Lucy and her puppies, needed to hear no words of anger from the preacher to know that he meant trouble. I saw all of them readying themselves to attack the foolish man.

The fool preacher stepped out of the dust, almost swaggering proudly in a superior way as if he had caught his children smoking a cigarette out back behind the shed. I had forgotten that some men automatically presume that their wife must submit to them after marriage and that often preachers believe that they are somehow smarter than or superior to those they serve. I knew enough about Bobby to see that he was going to enjoy killing this fool and I found myself slowly drifting into my place among the now growing dogs.

Instincts are what has kept mankind alive. Had the preacher not been so drunk that day, he might have sensed our animal-like movement to encircle him; he might have smelled our wolf-like musk as Carl, Lil Dee, Bobby, myself and the dogs took our places, ready to attack once Bobby leaped on his prey. This time, unlike the doctor's office, I would gladly, without a thought, help to destroy the threat that the preacher represented to our family.

"Why, isn't this just grand!" the preacher stated, trying to build his voice to sound evangelical. "I knew that this drunken fool Carl would be helping this lowlife murderer here," he said as he pointed to Bobby and then looked around at the town folks as if he was ashamed of them. "But I never thought that you all would be here in support of a worthless murdering coward like Bobby Austin here," the drunken preacher continued, and I swear I saw doubt, fear, and shame race through many of the town's folks' faces. It was then that I swore off religion as it was man's idea of religion and not God himself that caused these good men, our friends who had gathered in support of us, to now question themselves. The preacher was nothing more than a drunken liar who both used and fed off of good people's needs of church and community.

"Watch what you say preacher!" Nickels said in almost a playful tone. "These folks ain't done nothing wrong yet, but even if they were wrong, you're not in any position to judge them," he continued, only to be cut off mid-sentence.

"Why, the mighty blind hobo speaks! The great black prophet of Dogwood Mountain! Nickels, white folks are tired of having to bow down to you poor black souls, we're sick of being called a racist if we're not nice to black folks. I'd be careful of what I said if I was you!" the preacher smugly said as he looked to the townsmen for support of his claims. He knew that he was right in what he was saying, and that many white families had blacks married into them and were perfectly happy about it, yet at the same time, whites were constantly being accused of being hateful to blacks when they weren't. These were the types of private conversations that a traveling preacher would hear after church on Sundays, allowing him to tailor his sermon to fit each community's attitude. I am sure that the preacher had sermons written for the most hate-filled community, as well as for the most loving and accepting of communities as most were in those days. But Nickels being the lone black man here, and a hobo, had caused the preacher to guess wrong about Nickels' place in our families.

Bobby began to giggle like a schoolboy, stunning the preacher who could now see that his comments and name-calling were deeply misguided and without support on Cemetery Ridge. I saw Carl grab a large cooking fork and begin to step towards the preacher, his eyes dark with anger as the dogs' growling seemed to grow lower, almost nightmarish in tone. Suddenly, I was no longer standing still but, without thought or plan, found myself leaping towards the fool preacher with a large heavy rock in my hands.

Nickels screamed as he grabbed me with both hands, knocking the rock away as he did so. Frustrated that I had been stopped, I screamed a hate-filled rant at the now shocked and scared preacher as Bobby gasped and said "No!" His voice sounded almost sad compared to Lil Dee's impish laughter and Lucy's devilish growls.

"No Page! You can't face the world like this, trust me this ain't the way honey," Nickels said as he held me in a bear hug struggling to contain me. He was begging me to calm down, but I had stayed calm when Momma had traded herself to store owners for candy. I had stayed calm when the SWAT team kicked our door in, pretending to care as they stole my family from me. I had stayed calm after being stripped naked in front of every dope fiend whore in West Virginia. I had stayed calm as Percodan openly laughed about killing a man over drugs.

I had refused to abandon my mother and to take Lil Dee to get the love and help that I knew the Bears had to give us after Orville destroyed my baby sister's soul. I was done being calm, and this maggot of a man pretending to be a preacher was standing here threatening my family and our chance at being normal. "Fuck you, Nickels!" I screamed. "Let me go! I'll cave his fucking face in! Let me go!" I continued to scream as Carl began to laugh while telling Lucy and the pups to behave. I could hear Ms. Karen scream "No!" as Carl turned and punched the preacher in the mouth as hard as he could, knocking the man to the ground.

"That's for saying trash like that on my mountain," Carl said as he pulled his leg back and kicked the downed preacher. Only then did the men from town race forward to stop him.

Seeing Ms. Karen's face, and Momma crying, seemingly broken compared to this morning at breakfast, I stopped struggling in Nickels' arms and began to cry. Only then did I notice that Bobby had walked away from us and was sitting between the candles on his mother's headstone with an almost child-like look of confusion masking the adult features of the monster I had expected him to be only moments before. It is amazing how we humans will act as we believe those around us will act. I had believed that Bobby would have destroyed the preacher, so I took my place ready to take my part in the man's death only to then be embarrassed by reality.

Ms. Karen represented order to me, and order is not such a bad thing when your world is spinning out of control. So, I was glad to hear her order the men to help the preacher as she told me to act like a lady and for us girls to all straighten up and get ready for the wedding as it was near enough to noon. Then she began to laugh, telling the whole crowd stories of the prior fights she had seen at weddings and funerals over the years, her voice tenderly guiding everyone back from the edge of insanity.

I saw Bobby look down the hill at us. He seemed hawk-like, sitting on his mother's headstone, watching from above. His eyes settled on Momma, who looked beautiful and without a flaw. Her past lost, the weight of its sins forgotten, and again I believed that the world could be made right if we could just become a family.

Lil Dee, Lucy, and Bobby all seemed to hear them first. I had begun to apologize to Nickels when his face changed, and he raised his hand to stop me. His body language showing fear, confusion and betrayal all at once, causing me to look over at the preacher to see what evil he was up to, yet taking comfort in knowing that Ms. Karen was here to keep things in order. Then I heard Deacon Miles say, "No Bobby, no!" as Bobby leaped from his headstone seat, pushing it over and knocking it down as he fell to his knees, digging in the fresh loose soil, then standing up straight and proud with his favorite pistol firmly in his hand and the old, dedicated look of confidence in his eyes. Over the past few weeks, Bobby had seldom looked confident, he had seemed to be just as human and unsure as we all were. But the look in Bobby's eyes now was the same look that had told Percodan that Orville was going to die. It was the same look that the stupid doctor had misread, and my only question was why? Who was Bobby readying himself to face down?

Again, I felt Nickels' arms come in close around me, only now he embraced Lil Dee too. His body soft and caring as he tried to force us to turn away from watching, covering our eyes with his now crying chest. All of this was happening in the time it took for Ms. Karen to grab Momma, and for Deacon Miles to cry out "No Bobby!" and then look towards the woods behind us as he waved his hands, screaming, "Stop!"

All at once, Bobby was enveloped in pink light as his body shook once and then fell straight down into a heap, like a puppet whose strings had all broken at once. Only then did the sound reach me, only then, amidst its echoes, did I turn and see them coming out of the woods. Probing carefully at first, afraid that Bobby could still hurt them, their evil red dots dancing on the fallen body of my father as they had danced in our motel room the morning they took Momma and Lil Dee away from me. Suddenly, the world was an eruption of sound and movements as fathers and mothers grabbed their baby girls, pulling them to the ground and covering them with their own bodies in case the fight was not over. I saw Momma drop to her knees as Ms. Karen held her, and I screamed out in pain, as if shot myself. I watched the SWAT team members pour over Cemetery Ridge as Lucy and her pups rushed to offer the only resistance to be offered, their feeble growls and charges marking the death of my family.

Deacon Miles was screaming over and over, "The boy was going to turn himself in after the wedding!" as the SWAT team leader yelled about Bobby's gun. Carl exploded again and started attacking the preacher; this time, several men were helping him, feeling that the preacher had put all of the women in danger, and the police had to rush over to break them up. It was then that I noticed that the preacher's young wife was not with him, and I knew that he had purposely brought my dreams to their end not for a Christian goal or reason, but to serve his own selfish desires for revenge and prestige, and again I had to wonder why God would allow so many to be misled in his name.

Years later, I asked this same question of Lil Dee, and she said something about wide is the way, but narrow is the gate, and preachers like this were part of the width of that roadway. "No, Dee!" I said, "Jesus was talking about money, riches, and stuff."

"Money is only important to us! There's lots of stuff that ain't gold or money that people hoard, Page," Lil Dee said. "Lots of things they put their faith in beside love — look at you, you put your faith in Bobby, and you ain't lived a day since we buried him!"

There are some questions best left unasked, and for me this was one of them.

Chapter 27

The sun had set outside of Sara's motel room marking the end to her second day without using heroin. She still felt sick, as if she had the flu, yet she had managed to nap for short periods of time throughout the day. Her leg muscles screaming in protest the whole time, moving on their own, waking her, as her body begged for heroin, food, and sleep all at the same time. Every nerve in her body ached in pain.

The control of pain in the human body, the ghost of Lil Bear told her in a dream, was a matter of tolerance and understanding, much like heroin and opium addiction. Without drugs, the body's nerves constantly feel the weight of the body, the force of its movement, so our nerves build up tolerance to it, the nerves only screaming in protest when something out of the ordinary happens to the body. Opium works to numb every nerve in the body as the heart rate is lowered and this causes the feeling of sinking into a bed of sweet cotton candy. A bliss-filled fall, which allows your brain to give in to the urge to turn from its fears, concerns and worries as dreams take form, like flowers blooming, and then they die as your body frees its nerve signals, feeling weightless and seeming to float like a balloon in a peaceful sky. This, Sara knew was the 'Siren Song of the Needle' constantly calling heroin addicts to embrace the needle. Even though each shot needed to be larger than the last one, even though death was the end outcome of loving a syringe. A song that was unexplainable to a nonaddict and at the same time irresistible to those addicted to opiates.

Yet Sara also knew that the longer she used opiates, the more tender her nerves would become, and that there was a direct link between the amount of heroin she needed to get high and the amount of time it would take for her nerves to stop registering life's normal rhythms, living, moving, and breathing as pain. She hoped that the child growing inside of her could hear or feel her thoughts, knowing that she had only gained the strength to stop using after she had accepted that the child growing in her womb was a life far more important than her own. By explaining their shared pain, a pain, that she was sure her baby was experiencing right now along with her, she hoped to ease its pain, or even help her baby to forgive her for their addiction.

Sara shook her head in shame as she closed her eyes, afraid that she might see herself reflected in the room's mirror, evil and worthless. Only an evil human being would beat, rape, or hurt a child as Lil Dee, Page, and her own unborn child had been hurt. For Sara, acceptance of this fact meant that she was no better than Orville. He had taken his pleasure from Lil Dee without regard for the pain or damage that his sick needs were going to cause Lil Dee or her family, and Sara had gotten high, putting off getting sober as long as she could without any concern for the selfish pain that her continued drug use was causing her child.

Prior to the moment when her heart told her, as all mothers' hearts do, that she was pregnant, Sara had been free to abuse herself in any way that she chose. But once she became an expectant parent, every shot of dope, every missed meal, even missing sleep, was a risk to her child, a child that she was solely responsible for. Andy wanted to use her feelings of guilt about risking the child's health as a reason for her to abort it. Yet even before Sara began to read Aunt Page's words, she knew that her growing child was a source of strength. A reason to live, a reason more powerful than her love of Andy and her addiction combined. But sometimes, it was hard to remember this. Sara laughed at her thoughts, knowing that weakness was lurking, waiting on Andy to come home and aid it in its goal of getting Sara to take the shot that would lead to her choosing heroin over motherhood.

"I called Aunt Page!" Sara said as she touched her small paunch, as if warning her child that she was not strong enough to face Andy on her own. A tear began to grow in her heart and eyes as the child's soul reminded her that she was Bobby Austin's offspring and that there was strength in that. "No, my little one!" Sara mumbled. "Page was strong! Bobby was like us, broken. And we are not blood relations of Page!" Then she felt her child laughing at her. "What's blood got to do with anything?" was the last thing Sara felt her child say as Andy, without warning, opened the door and stepped into the room, ending Sara's private thoughts and conversations, forcing her face Andy alone. "Where are you Aunt Page?" Sara mumbled as she saw hell burning in Andy's eyes.

Andy had a successful day in spite of Sara abandoning him. She was so trustworthy that most of their normal customers still trusted Andy without her being there today, but teens, wives, and closet heroin users were dependent on credit cards, bank accounts, and a weak code of silence. All three of these things meant that at any moment, their hidden lifestyle could be found out, ending in intervention by loving families. Not only eroding Andy's customer base, but also exposing him to vengeful parents who would blame him for the addiction that was destroying their perfect home. Andy understood that kids, housewives, and closet addicts paid extra because they were not really addicts at all; they would in time become dope fiends, living off the land, but they were still early in their addiction and, as soon as mommy, daddy, or a spouse asked them who gave them the drugs, they would point Andy out so fast that his head would spin. Thus, Andy never stayed in the same area of a town, city, or state for very long. Without Sara's innocent face, this Chapter in Andy's life had to change, and starting over without Sara was not an option.

For Andy, every life change, each failed game in pursuit of his addiction put him one step closer to fulfilling Pennywise's twisted prediction that Andy was a pimp at heart who would someday use, abuse, and profit from women and their primal need to be loved just like Pennywise himself did. Now Andy stood in their cheap motel room staring at Sara as hate boiled in his heart. Her refusal to get high today or to come out to the park to be with him was a betrayal more hurtful than his own mother's desperate need to please Pennywise by allowing him to pimp Andy out to perverts. Even worse, what Andy thought to himself, was that Sara wanted to control him pimp him out as his mother had done, to use love to bind him. Sara knows what she's doing to you, he told himself as he drew his fist back and punched her in the face, knocking her from the bed. If she was going to betray him, he would force her to pay a high price for the pleasure of doing so, Andy told himself as he pounced on Sara, remembering to avoid hitting her in the stomach for now.

"At first, just punish her! Just smack the whore around to start with!" Pennywise had preached. "As you beat her, explain to the bitch exactly why she deserves your anger, make her accept that she deserves it. Don't knock the bitch out, a sleeping cunt can't hear you!" Andy heard the memory of his mother's pimp say. "Keep the bitch awake, so she searches for a way to make things up to you. Trust me, the bitch will enter into negotiations quickly once you make her bleed some." Andy heard his mentor whisper as he continued to beat Sara. But she didn't try to negotiate with him as he had seen his own mother do when being punished by her pimps — and as all of Pennywise's girls had also done. Breaking down and accepting not only that they were wrong, but that Pennywise was beating them out of love for them and not sheer meanness.

But Sara simply rolled into a ball on the floor, crying and asking her child to forgive her for what was happening to them. Again, she was betraying Andy for the trash growing inside of her — "How dare she love a trick's baby more than she loves me!" Andy's black soul screamed, causing him to give in to his rage and act in an un-pimp like manner" he heard Pennywise say as Andy drew his leg back and began to stomp the life out of both Sara and the child that she loved more than she loved him.

A sharp stabbing pain caused Andy to freeze, he saw an old woman laughing as she pushed him away from Sara with one strong hand before stabbing him in the side again with what Andy was sure was a butcher's knife. She was laughing the whole time, her arm lashing out again and again, repeatedly stabbing Andy in his side and face as she began to preach to Andy the same way Pennywise had told him to preach while punishing a whore.

"If you ever touch her again, I'll kill you!" the evil old woman gently said as if she was explaining to a child about touching a hot stove or about playing with matches. Her words and tender tone were far more fearsome than anything Andy had ever heard before and left no doubt in his mind that she would keep her word and kill him if he didn't escape the room somehow.

"Now go away boy! You're not welcome here. Next time, I'll use my daddy's gun on you and not a stupid hatpin. Now go, before I change my mind! the old woman said as Andy saw her pull a large black pistol from the pocket of her faded sweater. "You won't be the first asshole this old gun has sent to meet God! Now get boy, get!" the woman said, causing Andy to jump over the bed and stumble into the hallway. The old woman giggled like a schoolgirl as Andy continued stumbling in fear and confusion. "She only stabbed me with a long pin, but it felt like a knife! I'm bleeding inside!" Andy told himself as he crashed into the wall, leaving a large blood smear, before regaining his balance and escaping from the building through a door marked exit. His anger, pride, and curiosity all forgotten at the sight of the pistol and the death that the old woman's voice implied.

Andy had learned a long time ago that pride and addiction cannot exist in a dope fiend's heart at the same time. "Fuck Sara and the kid — let the old bitch raise the kid. I got a pocket full of dope, I can't afford to have to deal with the cops." Andy's addicted brain screamed as he began to search for a safe place to get high and clean up without having to worry about the cops. Then he saw a woman driving by in a minivan with a child's safety seat still strapped in the back seat — one of the wives that he had gotten dope for several times over the past few days. She was looking for a friend awfully late at night, Andy thought as he waved for her to stop, and she smiled back at him. Andy saw that his future was just a shot of dope away, and that this whore had no problem with getting high instead of being a mother. Pennywise had been right when he had said that a good pimp never has to force a whore to be a whore! "Them bitches can't wait to volunteer, you just gotta give them a reason to do it!" Andy smiled to himself, knowing that once he got this new bitch high she would follow him anywhere.

Sara could not stop herself from laughing along as Aunt Page helped her get to her feet. She hurt deeply from withdrawal, from Andy's savage attack and with the embarrassment of having to be rescued by an old woman who Sara had done her best to avoid while growing up. To now have this same old woman not only reaching out to help Sara clean her bloody, bruised body, but also being kind enough to allow laughter to take the place of words was more than Sara thought she deserved. She felt herself begin to cry, not from pain, but for every day that she had missed sharing with the gentle old woman who now was filling a tub of bathwater and softly chattering about how her daddy had been right, it did feel good to beat fools up every now and then. "I should have tried this years ago!" Page happily said as she continued to laugh while trying to explain to Sara how silly Andy had looked trying to get away from her.

"Shouldn't you lock the door, Aunt Page?" Sara heard herself say as Page began to help her undress and to climb into the bathtub.

"The doors are fine, girl, "Page said sternly. "I'm sorry to be the one to tell you, but you don't mean that much to that boy, if you did, he would have at least tried to argue with me. Beating on each other is harder to explain. Folks with capital letters behind their name say that ain't love neither, but I saw Momma smack more than one man that she loved. It ain't right I know, but folks don't always do what's right. But that boy wasn't upset over you dancing with another fellow at the bar, and those weren't confused or hurting inside smacks that he was throwing at you — that was hate, plain hate, and he never even thought about stopping in the hallway. Sooner you come to terms with it, the less it will hurt, girl. That boy never loved you nor anyone else," Page said as her eyes searched Sara's face to see how well she was taking her hard words.

Age had taught Page that love causes more violence than anything else in the world and that Sara could just easily get mad at Page for telling her the truth, then run off after the fool boy, trying to prove to herself that Page was wrong and that he did love her. "No one likes to be used Sara. I know that you think that if he loves you then you weren't being used, because love is a pair of hearts fighting to reach the same goals, but what you've been living ain't love," Page said, lowering her head to hide her own growing pool of tears which caused Sara to begin to cry anew as Page leaned into the tub to hug her, allowing silence to ease both of their pain.

Later, Sara layed on the bed, amazed at the prospect of going home in the morning, while Page sat in the same chair that Sara had sat in her first night without using heroin. "Why did they kill Bobby, Page?" Sara heard herself asking, almost certain that it was her unborn child who had forced her to ask such an uncaring question.

Page smiled at her, a truly loving smile that told Sara that Page was not hurt or upset by her question. "Now just how far did you get in reading that damn book girl?" Page asked, both embarrassed at having someone read something that she wrote, yet happy to see that Sara had honestly spent time reading her words while fighting with her withdrawals.

"Bobby just died," Sara said she looked sadly at the floor. "Although I'm really unsure how my grandpa, Lil Bobby, you brother, came to be if Bobby and Christy never were together."

Page couldn't stop herself from laughing as she explained. "Momma got pregnant the traditional way, girl! She and Bobby snuck off together just as soon as Ms. Karen started watching them, acting like a mother trying to keep them apart. Nothing makes folks want each other more than to know they're not supposed to be together. But trust me, we were all shocked when they let Momma out of jail, and everyone found out that she was pregnant. Ms. Karen acted like she knew what Bobby and Momma were doing, but no one did.

"Years later, I remembered Bobby talking about how, when he was a child, people snuck off to the garage to smoke dope or get high, and how they didn't brag about who they were sleeping with in front of little children. It dawned on me that Bobby had said all of that to me in front of Carl and Nickels because he was hunting, trying to find out if either of the two old fools knew what he and Momma were up to when no one was watching," Page said with laughter in her eyes.

"Bobby had buried some pistols and OxyContin under his mother's headstone as a way of marking a change in his heart, proving to himself that he could live without all of the ghosts of his past — his mother, guns, drugs, and his self-hate had destroyed every step Bobby had ever taken in life. I have to think that he felt that burying all of them together had some symbolism, but of course, I never got to ask him about it," Page spoke as if she was no longer in the room with Sara, her voice growing younger and more child-like.

"The police weren't going to risk allowing Bobby to escape into the woods around Cemetery Ridge. He grew up in those woods and they just felt it was safer for them to fight him out in the open once they saw him get that gun," Page's voice seemed to fade as she began to remember that painful day. "The truth is Sara; Bobby was a very scared little boy. You can reason with a grown man, but Bobby was a boy who learned to be violent first and to ask questions later. I've spent my whole life trying to explain this line of reasoning to myself, to not hate the police for killing him, for not waiting to see what Bobby would do before they shot him. But Bobby had pretty much left them no reason to doubt that he would fight and that someone would get hurt besides Bobby.

"Sara, blame is a terrible burden on a heart. Once you get to placing blame on others, you tend to only blame others and not yourself or the truth," Page gently said as she looked deep into Sara's eyes. "The truth is, Bobby fired the shot that killed him long before we ever met him, it just took a while to find his heart and bring him down. Oh sure, it was the police that shot him that day, but it had been Bobby's way of life and his repeated failures at getting the mental help that he needed that led to that day. And girl, if you go back to using drugs, then it will be your own fault, no matter how you die, and every pain or trouble that baby of yours faces will be your fault too. When you get home, no matter how embarrassing it is, you have to get help, not just for your drug use, but for your heart. If you don't, you won't only be killing yourself, but the child too," Page said through her tears, causing Sara to promise to do as Page had said.

"Momma came home after three weeks in jail. The police had recovered all of those pills and some guns, everyone knew about Lil Dee and what Orville had done so it was just easier to let Momma go and forget we ever existed. Nickels called Momma's story a force multiplier — he said that in the Army, a big machine gun was a force multiplier, because it needed only one man to operate but it took a lot of work to overcome," Page said as she looked to see if Sara understood her. "Nickels said that it was like a black guy and a white guy getting into an argument about money or something and the white guy kills the black guy. Now if he uses a gun, it's just a simple argument gone wrong, but if the white guy were to hang the black guy, then the story becomes more important than the reasoning behind the argument. For Momma, Lil Dee being raped by Orville was all that folks would need to hear in order to let her go, just like all folks would need to hear is that a white man hung a black man. Seems it was easier to forget about us than to risk folks seeing Bobby as a hero and questioning why they needed to shoot him. So, Bobby's crimes listed kidnapping us and, on some days, it feels like he did because I certainly have never been free," Page almost mumbled as she spoke, scaring Sara and causing her to wonder what Page meant by her words.

"Momma came home and walked the path between Bobby's grave and the church all day, rain or shine, back and forth, talking to Bobby. Ms. Karen was worried about her, but Momma was sober, clean of all drugs, so for Lil Dee and me it was heavenly. Lil Dee would go to school, and I would practice craving all day. At night we would play games like families do, Momma would even cook for us; she acted normal aside from pacing back and forth in a cemetery all day. Soon though, Lil Bobby was born, and he put a life force in Momma that I had never seen before. She stopped pacing back and forth and began to take Lil Bobby to visit his father each day on their way down to see Ms. Karen and Carl. We went to church even. Lil Dee had decided that she would become a preacher and of course this made Ms. Karen happy. Carl seemed sure that I would grow up and take care of Cemetery Ridge, so when Ms. Karen bragged about Lil Dee, Carl could not help but brag about me," Page said and her eyes began to almost glow as she remembered the good days that Lil Bobby had brought them.

"Time and dates really are a terrible thing, Sara. Soon it was spring, and we were readying Cemetery Ridge for Easter. Momma swore that she didn't mind, and that this was Lil Bobby's home so he should grow up enjoying the traditions of his father. With the way Easter moves each year, it wasn't like we would be partying on the anniversary of Bobby's death. We hadn't continued with the dance the year before — with Bobby and the police and all, it hadn't seemed right to anyone. So, we had to have a dance that next year," Page said, looking up, as if expecting Sara to agree with her, to tell her that she had not been wrong to want to have a dance the Easter after Bobby's death.

"I woke up early the Saturday morning before Easter Sunday. Maybe I heard her?" Page questioned. "Or maybe I just knew that something was wrong. But when I got up to look, Lil Bobby was asleep, happy in his bed with Lil Dee snoring like a piglet just a few feet away," she said as she giggled at the memory of her sister snoring. "Everything was right Sara, I promise you," Page cried out, desperation filling her voice and face causing Sara to lean forward to comfort her aunt.

"Momma often got up and went to visit Bobby early before breakfast, and it being that Saturday, I never thought that anything was wrong, even when I saw her dancing in front of our car. Well, I thought it was her, the glass in those windows only allowed you to see the outlines and colors, but what other woman would be dressed all in white dancing in front of our car on that Saturday morning?" Page asked herself as much as Sara. "She stopped dancing and I swear that she looked right at me through those horrible windows and smiled. It was a smile that said I love you and forgive me at the same time," Page said as she gave in and began to truly cry as she had not done before.

"I have no memory of the sound of the gunshot that killed Bobby, even though I saw him die, but Momma's death is different. At first, there was a flash of orange that seemed to throw Momma backward towards the car as the sound of the gunshot reached my ears. And then, before I could even scream the word 'No!' those horrible old windowpanes began to shatter and break, just as Bobby had promised me that they would," Page softly said as Sara broke down too, crying in pain, sorry that she had burdened this beautiful old woman by becoming a drug addict and forcing her to remember her past.

"It's funny how those windows survived all those years, never cracking or breaking, it was almost like they knew that I couldn't see Momma well enough through them to understand what she was doing. I just stood there like fool, watching her dance, happy that she was at peace with our life," Page plainly stated. Her tears were all but gone and her voice had changed into one void of emotion and very matter of fact, shocking Sara at the speed of the change in the old woman yet at the same time reminding her that her mother swore that Page was crazy as a loon, and now Sara could see why her mother felt that way.

"Carl and Nickels found beauty in the way that Momma had fallen. The dogwood flowers had been blowing all over. The mountain looked like it was covered in snow, and the trees were alive with movement and color from all of the spirit ribbons. Sara, a body does strange things when it gets shot by a gun. Nickels said that the bullet pushes the air in front of it into and then through the body and, as the bullet comes out the other side, it creates a fine mist of blood. He said that was why the sunlight around Bobby turned pink for an instant before he fell to the ground, and that was also why all the dew-covered flower petals on the ground around Momma were stained pink. She lay there on a pink bed of flowers smiling," Page said with a grin. "The nasty selfish bitch was smiling, as if she knew that I would take care of both Lil Dee and Lil Bobby. We were never enough for Momma to love, she always had to have a man, or a habit. But us, her kids, we just didn't matter, did we?" Page asked leaving Sara speechless.

"Needless to say, we never attempted to have Easter dance again. That's something you will have to bring back Sara. Something you can give folk to enjoy again," Page said as she smiled and patted Sara's hand. "It will be fun I promise."

"I spent four years not only blaming but hating Bobby for Momma leaving us. I refused to make him a headstone. In my heart, I felt that he called Momma to follow him or that he meant to make the police kill him. I thought that had he kept his word and just gone to jail, then Momma would have clung to him. She would have stayed with him, going to prison to see him as Lil Bobby grew up. But I was wrong to blame him, or anyone else for that matter. It took Nickels to set my heart straight. He came home one year as he normally did. Just showed up one day, but this time he was sick, said that it was cancer and that he couldn't be fixed even if he wanted to be. All he wanted was for me to carve the name Nickels on his stone and to bury him across from Bobby, Momma, and Bobby's mother so that he could keep an eye on Bobby if he got silly or anything. Carl was beside himself, hurting something awful. I felt sure that he would die the same day that Nickels decided to leave us. Sara, you cannot imagine just how mad Nickels got at me when he saw that I had marked Bobby's grave with that same tin cross that had hurt him so badly when he saw it on his mother's grave," Page said as she laughed an almost evil laugh.

"Fuck Bobby Austin!" I told Nickels when he questioned why I could still not bring myself to honor his grave. 'He stole my mother from us, he made them kill him! Bobby is lucky I don't dig him up and toss his bones to the dogs!' I boldly told Nickels as if I were the queen of Dogwood Mountain," Page said as she shook her head in dismay at her memories.

"Why you selfish little bitch!" Nickels said as he tore into me without concern for my feelings or tears," Page said.

"Girl the only reason you're not getting high, turning tricks and arguing with your mother over pills is that Bobby gave you a home. The only reason Bobby is dead is that he came home. That boy didn't kill your mother — she killed herself because the pills were calling her name every day after she gave birth to Lil Bobby. Carl and me used to watch her come out and sit in the car and eat the pills that they had stashed away. She killed herself so you wouldn't follow her off this mountain and back to the truck stop that y'all came from.

"Now girl, don't you dare think about making me no stone until you learn that blaming folks doesn't make it true. That boy loved you enough to try to teach you something more than how to sell drugs or turn tricks. The least you can do is be honest and make him a headstone!" Nickels said. And he was right, even Lil Dee had seen Momma taking pills from the car. Turns out that I was the only one too blind to see. Still hoping for a normal life, I suppose," Page said.

"Nickels died two weeks after I completed Bobby's stone. He loved it and couldn't stop laughing at how Bobby had asked me to write the word asshole on his stone and I had kept my word and done so. We lost Ms. Karen when Lil Dee was first back from college. She went down to New Orleans to learn to be a preacher, so Ms. Karen got to see our church have a real preacher before she passed on. Carl was broken after losing both Nickels and Ms. Karen, even Lucy had long since gone on to whatever is next. But Carl hung on until your grandfather Lil Bobby graduated college and got married and then he slipped off to be with our family," Page said as she walked over and got into bed to hold Sara.

"I suppose that I could have gone off and found a man, started a family myself. Lil Dee swore that she was married to Christ and that I need not worry about her, but the truth is that I was worried about Momma's and Bobby's monsters. They were dead, Lil Bobby was normal, and no one was still alive who knew who Lil Dee and I really were. If I had gotten married then I would have had to remember everything I wanted to hide from," Page said and the sound of shame tinted her voice.

"I'm sorry Aunt Page," Sara said as she began to cry once again for causing her aunt to have to write out a story that she had fought so hard to forget.

"Sara, there ain't no reason for you to be sorry. Now try to sleep girl, morning will be here soon," Page said as Sara found comfort in being held in her aunt's arms and easily fell asleep.

Chapter 28

The sun felt like it was burning Sara's eyes after spending three days inside of the motel. Page gave her a few dollars to buy something to eat at a small store across from the park where Sara was sure Andy was working to get high. Part of her hoped to see him, the other hoped that he had come to his senses, and that he would see her at the store. That he would try to go home with her to start a new life, or at least come tell her goodbye and that he did love her. He could easily say that he needed to know if it was alright to go to the motel room. After all, they still had two days left on the week's rent, Sara thought to herself as she walked out of the store and looked over at the park.

"That boy ain't coming to see you girl," Page said as her eyes looked right into Sara's soul, causing her to shiver. "He said his goodbyes last night! Maybe you were crying too hard to hear the words, but that was a goodbye child," Page coldly stated. "You can't give in to your fear of loneliness child! That boy was trying to kill you and the child! That wasn't a slap shared between two frustrated lovers. That was hate, the same hate I saw in Bobby's eyes when he killed that doctor."

"I know Aunt Page," Sara began. "But I feel like a fool. I can't help but think that it would be nice if he cared enough to come and say goodbye," she said and giggled from her embarrassment.

"That's love girl, hope; that's your heart trying to give you an excuse to see him, excuses to stay here where you don't have to face your family and the things that you have done," Page said as they started walking towards downtown Nashville and the Greyhound bus that would take them home. "If that boy came over here right now, if he offered you any reason at all, you would stay here with him even after last night. You need to ask yourself if the death of your child is worth not having to face your family. Because you know that boy is poison, but what you don't know is that your folks love you and they just want you to come home," Page said and then grew silent as searching for the words to express her heart.

"Sara, I refused to live any type of life, hoping that the mental illnesses and pains that destroyed Bobby and Momma would die once we forgot them, once no was left alive to talk of them or to remember them," Page said as she took Sara's arm for support. "I was wrong Sara, wrong to hide our story. Bobby had been right, there is nothing to be embarrassed about. Tell your story girl so others can learn from it. You did nothing wrong if you use your mistakes to teach others. Holding that knowledge back, hiding it from the world, that's not only wrong but it's a sin really, it's selfish. Who cares what people think about you? Look at me Sara, Page said. "I wanted people to believe that I was normal. That I was more than the daughter of a carnival man and a drug addict. It cost me a lifetime of loneliness and nearly the baby you're carrying," she said as tears began to wash down her cheeks.

"I thought that Lil Dee had found God and was safe. She never spoke of her youth, so I never did either. You heard her preach, she seemed to love the Lord and the church more than anything. But think of the strength that her story could have been to so many other girls like herself if she had shared it? But instead, like me, she chose to run from our past, to pretend to be normal, and she died alone, Sara. Very alone," Page said in a mumbling voice, confusing Sara because she had been at home when Aunt Dee had passed on and she had been given a big funeral.

"The day she died, Sara, they called me to come to the emergency room, and when I got there, the doctor came out to tell me that she was gone. Her heart had finally stopped beating after being broken for so long. Then the doctor handed me this gun," Page said as she pulled the black pistol from her sweater pocket. "This is the same pistol that Bobby carried and died with. The same nasty tool that Momma used to blow a hole through her heart. Lil

Dee had a pocket sewn into every pair of underwear she owned. She told the world that Jesus could save them, heal them. I thought that she had allowed him to heal her own broken soul, but no, she carried this nasty thing every day of her life, as we hid our past, afraid to confront it or to learn from it. Sara, feel this side of it," Page ordered as they stopped on a bridge over the Cumberland River. Sara could feel that the handle was polished smooth on one side yet rough on the other.

"My baby sister's body, her pubic area wore the roughness away as it polished the pistol where it rested against her body. That took years to accomplish. She may have wanted to trust Jesus, but she had faith that this pistol would be there to protect her when Jesus was busy as he always seems to be," Page said as she tossed the pistol into the river.

"Girl, neither you nor your baby will have a pistol to hide behind. That damn thing has done nothing but take from this family. No, you and that child will have words to protect you. You'll share your story so you and others can learn and grow from it. Girl, there is nothing more important to our staying clean of drugs than your accepting every nasty thing that you did and learning from it as you teach other girls what you know. Don't let your embarrassment steal your happiness away like I let it steal mine!" Page pleaded, and Sara decided right then that she would never hide from her past. She just hoped that her story could save some other girl from the same pains, or at least show other girls like her that they are not alone. Page was right — the pistol killed threats, yet words freed you as you learned to live with the person you are.

The bus rumbled north towards home, causing Sara to feel tired. She was not over her withdrawals yet, her body still hurt without a reason to and the flu-like feelings seemed to come in waves now. But she could tell that her child was alive and happy. It seemed to enjoy Aunt Page's voice Sara thought as she took Page's hand and placed it on her mother's paunch.

"If it's a girl, I'm going to name her Lil Page," Sara said with a smile. She saw joy race through her aunt's eyes before she complained that to name a child that would ruin the poor thing. Suddenly they both began to laugh and joke like two old friends. The last thing Sara remembered asking Page was how she really felt about TV archaeologists, and Page going off into an in-depth reason why she should have put Bobby's pistol to good use on a few of them before she had thrown it in the river! Silently laughing in her heart, Sara went to sleep to the sweet sound of Page complaining.

Chapter 29

The squeaking sound of the bus's brakes tried to wake Sara, but her mind told her to stay asleep as Aunt Page would wake her when they made it home. Yet the bus driver would not stop calling her, over and over, forcing Sara awake.

"Where's Aunt Page?" Sara asked her baby as much as the bus driver who just looked at her in confusion as he told her that she was home, that they were in Dogwood, Tennessee, and to be careful not to fall stepping down off of the bus. Confused and still half asleep, Sara picked up the notebook that Aunt Page had cared enough to send her. She then stood up, apologized to the driver and stepped down onto the streets of her hometown. Far too embarrassed to be excited about being home, Sara felt sure that the people here knew every nasty detail of her life and addiction.

She pulled Aunt Page's old sweater tightly around her, hoping by doing so it would somehow hide her from the prying eyes of old friends and family until she found Aunt Page. As Sara became more awake, she noticed that she was alone, and the town was extremely quiet. It was then she turned to look towards Cemetery Ridge and saw what had to be every car and person in town standing together for what Sara was sure was the funeral of someone important. She heard herself say to her child, "Aunt Page must have gone on ahead to get us a ride," as she began walking the mile home hoping that doing so would show Aunt Page that she was strong enough to weather the coming storms.

Halfway home, Sara began to hear her family singing on the hillside before her, and she remembered Nickels making this same walk, blind and alone. As her body threatened to collapse in revolt, she mumbled Nickels' name and was sure that she saw him walking just in front of her, laughing and joking with both Carl and Lil Bear. They smelled of gunpowder and war. Sara saw that they were no longer old or blind, but instead young and playful as they must have been in Vietnam. Then she saw Bobby running towards her with a pack of playful beagles bounding at his side, happy that Sara was home. She was sure that she heard Bobby say, "I got you, honey, you're home," then she fell into his arms and passed out.

Sara saw her mother and father standing next to her bed, besides her grandfather, Lil Bobby. They were all crying sad tears over how she looked, worn down and beaten, and also crying tears of joy that their baby had found her way home.

"Aunt Page, where's Aunt Page, Papa?" Sara heard herself ask her grandfather.

"Honey, you got home just a little too late. My sister Page passed in her sleep three nights ago honey. That's why no one was there to give you a ride home", Lil Bobby said.

"Papa, Aunt Page wrote to me, sent me the book I was carrying. She rode the bus home with me Papa, I have her old sweater! Papa!" Sara cried, afraid to face life alone without the old woman to guide her.

"Sara, love can do all kinds of strange things, and I'm sure that if anyone could do as you say Page did, it would be Page who did it. I believe you honey, and I'm just glad that she found you!"

Epilogue

Sara heard the school bus struggling to climb Cemetery Ridge and smiled, knowing that Lil Page would soon be home. Lil Page was not like Sara had been at her age. She was strong and assertive, often in minor trouble at school or on the bus. Sara didn't mind it though, her child had been born healthy without any signs of the addiction that she had been conceived into. Sara had kept her word to Aunt Page. She had lived in recovery for the first years of Lil Page's life, as she had learned to carve headstones and to care for Cemetery Ridge.

Now seven years clean, Easter was due to arrive and, for the first time in years, they would decorate the church and cemetery as they had done years before. Sara would soon marry a wonderful man who understood and supported her need to help others in their recovery. Life was better than she could have hoped for she thought, as her daughter walked into the shop where Sara had just completed Aunt Page's monument. Sitting down heavily, as if angry, Sara saw that a storm was brewing in Lil Page's heart.

"Okay kiddo, what's got you so upset?"

"That damn Jimmy Wilson won't stop bugging me at school or on the bus ride home Momma," Lil Page said, anger dripping from her words.

"Don't say damn Page, and how many times have I told you, Jimmy likes you, he isn't trying to be mean," Sara said as she began to laugh, knowing her daughter, but unable to stop herself from laughing all the same.

"You won't be laughing when I punch him Momma! I promise, I'm gonna knock him out like Papa showed me how to do!" Lil Page exclaimed as she stood up and punched at shadows like her grandfather had tried to teach her.

"Now Page, I told you what to do, just give him a kiss," Sara said in a serious tone as Lil Page began to yell, "No! Never ever will I do that Momma, you're crazy!" They both laughed in joy, as they walked out of the shop. For once things in their lives were good, and they were able to live a normal life.

Acknowledgments

The truth is that a finished book is always a collaborative effort drawing on the insight and wisdom of a variety of people. I would like to take the time to thank my family, along with everyone who has supported and encouraged me through my journey to become a published author. I would like to give a special thank you to the following for their help in making and promoting this book.

Tracy and Anne Bottomly - UK, Vicky and Mary Smith, Robert Engelbach, Phiona Watkins - UK, The Ursuline Sister's of Youngstown, Cecilia Conley and Eddie of Designed Conviction, Marsell Morris and all of my colleagues at Blowboi Entertainment.

About The Author

E.O. Smith is an incarcerated author whose natural gift of storytelling has allowed him to build a loyal following of readers throughout the world. His next novel "Nothing Matters and What If It Did," will be released soon. As he continues to grow as a writer more novels will surely follow.

Lightning Source UK Ltd.
Milton Keynes UK
UKHW010629060223
416537UK00001B/125